A Man Favored in His Eyes

CYNTHIA D. RAGLAND

A Man Favored in His Eyes

TATE PUBLISHING
AND ENTERPRISES, LLC

Published by Tate Publishing & Enterprises, LLC
127 E. Trade Center Terrace | Mustang, Oklahoma 73064 USA
1.888.361.9473 | www.tatepublishing.com

Tate Publishing is committed to excellence in the publishing industry. The company reflects the philosophy established by the founders, based on Psalm 68:11,
"The Lord gave the word and great was the company of those who published it."

Book design copyright © 2015 by Tate Publishing, LLC. All rights reserved.
Cover design by Junriel Boquecosa
Interior design by Honeylette Pino

Published in the United States of America

ISBN: 978-1-68097-971-8
1. Fiction / War & Military
2. Fiction / African American / Christian
15.03.30

I thank and praise God for His divine inspiration and dedicate this book to Him and to all who believed in me and encouraged me in this endeavor.
God bless you all!

1

Esdell Brown had just finished scrambling a half dozen eggs. He moved the skillet to the backburner as he paused for a second trying to remember in which cabinet the dishes were stored. Just yesterday, he, his son, his daughter and her son had moved into a house he had purchased from his stepfather. His daughter, Karlena, had arranged the kitchen, so Esdell was unsure where everything was placed. He found the plates and the rest of the dishes just above the sink in his lemon yellow kitchen. He set out enough dishes for his family then scooped the eggs onto a plate and set it on the table. He walked from the kitchen to the living room and yelled up the stairs.

"C'mon kids, breakfast! Y'all come on before the eggs get cold!" Returning to the kitchen, he poured himself a cup of coffee and fixed himself a plate. Karlena soon entered the kitchen with her son, Micah, on her hip.

"Mornin', Daddy!" she said as she put Micah in his high chair. She gave her father a kiss, grabbed a mug, and then went directly to the coffeepot. "Boy, I sure need this coffee! I hope it keeps me awake in church this morning."

"Sunday morning came a little quick, huh? What's the matter, baby girl? Didn't you sleep well?"

"Not really. Micah was pretty restless last night, and I had to keep getting up to see about him."

"That's understandable. Last night was our first night here and the first time Micah had his own room to sleep in. That was a big step for you, wasn't it, li'l buddy?" He gently rubbed the top of his grandson's head.

Esdell and his children, until the day before, had lived with his mother and stepfather, Grace and Isaiah Willis. His mother had taken care of his children while he and his wife served in the military. Both had been stationed in Iraq, but his wife had been killed there by a suicide bomber. Esdell served until his discharge and then returned to his mother's house. The house he had previously owned with his wife had been sold and all of their possessions had been in storage. Now all of their things had been moved into their new place. Last night had been the first night that he slept in the bed he once shared with his wife. It had been a rough night for him as well, but he would never divulge that to his children. He had lain on her side of the bed gently stroking the sheets and then found himself crying. Esdell's wife had been gone for over four years, but the pain of her death seemed unrelenting. He loved her deeply, and it was only by his hope and faith in God that he was able to cope with his loss. He knew he had to hold himself together for the sake of his children and his grandchild. It did not matter that his "kids" were twenty years old; they were still his babies, and he had vowed to make a home for them for how ever long they wanted to stay with him.

"Good morning, Dad, Karlena. Hey! Wut up, dude? Gemme five!" Esdell's son, and Karlena's twin brother, Kareem, entered the kitchen and requested the hand greeting from his nephew who immediately slapped his uncle's hand. "That's my dude! You sure got it smelling good in here, Dad. We got any OJ?"

"Yeah, son. It's here on the table. Sit down and let's bless the food." After everyone was seated, the family joined hands and Esdell began to pray. "Heavenly Father, we thank you for this day. We give thanks for this home that you have blessed us with and pray that you will be ever present here. Now, Lord God, we thank you for this food and ask that you bless it and every person that shall eat. May it nourish our bodies so that we may better serve you—"

"Dad," Karlena interrupted, "may we add the children's prayer to teach Micah about blessing the food?"

"Sure, Karlena! I think that's a great idea! Listen, Micah! Altogether now!"

In unison they prayed. "God is great, God is good, and we thank Him for our food, Amen!"

Esdell pinched Micah's cheek. "Good job, Micah! Here, Kareem, let me pour you a glass of juice. How'd *you* sleep last night?"

"Man, I slept like a rock!" Kareem said before he took a sip of juice. "It sure felt good sleeping in my own room! I'm about to smash this breakfast, get dressed, go to church, and get my praise on! Karlena, pass me the eggs, please."

"Here ya go, Kareem." Karlena turned to her son. "Mick Mick, you gonna eat some eggs and toast for Mommy?" She spooned a small amount of eggs into Micah's mouth who eagerly chewed them up and grunted for more.

"Wow! Look at Gramps, li'l buddy, eat. He eats more like a five-year-old instead of somebody who's barely one!" Esdell beamed as he witnessed his grandson's hearty appetite. He loved to watch his daughter interact with her son. "Kareem, I'm glad you had a good night sleep. I'd hate to see you fall asleep in the pulpit."

Kareem chuckled. "That would be a trip, wouldn't it? I can see Grandma staring daggers at me from the choir stand now!"

"Yeah, and I can see Uncle Sammy and Aunt Christine laughing at you too!" said Karlena. Esdell's entire family was members of the Road to Damascus Baptist Church. Earlier in the year, Kareem had accepted his call to preach the Gospel of Jesus Christ and had become one of the church's associate ministers.

"Oh, Lord! Please don't give my brother and sister nothin' to talk about! Y'all know neither one of them got a lick of sense!" They all shared a brief laugh. "Y'all eat up. I want to get the kitchen cleaned up and get to church on time."

"I got the kitchen, Dad," Kareem volunteered.

Karlena looked at him in shock. "What? You gonna wash the dishes? God is good!"

"Yeah, I'll do it this time but don't expect me to do it all the time. Besides, by the time you get Micah dressed and do something with that mess under that do-rag that you call hair, we'd get to church just in time for the benediction!"

"Hey, I'll be ready on time. I don't have to compete for the bathroom since I have my *own* bathroom now. Uh-huh! Don't hate!" Karlena boasted.

"Yeah, and I'm still salty about you getting the master bedroom!" Esdell jumped in to stop the argument.

"She's the only woman in the house, and she needs her privacy. Plus, she has Micah. It made perfect sense for her to get that room."

"You're right, Dad. I'm just kidding!" Kareem ate a fork full of eggs. "The eggs are good, Dad! You da best at breakfast. I guess you'll be the one doing all the cooking. Promise me you'll do *all* the cookin'! Don't let Karlena cook!"

"Whatever, Kareem! You know I can cook. I learned from Grandma, the best cook in the family!"

"Well, you must have flunked half your classes!"

The argument was on, and Esdell just let it go knowing that's what brothers and sisters do. He smiled to himself as he watched his beautiful, brown-skinned children bicker back and forth. Micah, with a piece of toast in his hand and unconcerned, looked on too. After a few minutes, he interrupted.

"*Okay*, y'all, that's enough. We can all come to some sort of agreement on who's responsible for what chores. We're all adults here."

"Well, Dad, Karlena is the only woman in the house, and a woman's work is never done!"

Karlena darted her eyes at her brother. "Kareem, don't even go there! Don't try that antiquated 'woman's work' mess to try to get out of your share of housework!"

"She's right, Kareem. It's all work. Work that any of us can do or learn to do. We have to pull together so things run smoothly. All of us work and go to school, and Karlena has Micah to take care of."

All three of the Browns were college students. Esdell and Karlena were classmates at Indianapolis City College. Karlena had originally been accepted to Tennessee State but had become pregnant in her senior year of high school. Even though her family was willing to take the baby to let her go to school, she decided that it was her responsibility and felt it best that she attend college locally to get her nursing degree. Esdell had always planned to study graphic design and had enlisted in the army to get help with his college expenses. After his discharge, he, too, decided to go to City College. Kareem previously attended Clark College in Atlanta Georgia, but after accepting his calling, he came back to Indianapolis to attend seminary school.

"Its gonna be a joint effort," Esdell continued. "Let's just roll with it for now and see how things work out, starting with Kareem bustin' suds after breakfast!"

"Yeah, you jump on *that*, Kareem!" Karlena snapped her fingers. And the argument was on again.

Esdell finished eating and put his plate in the sink. "Y'all finish your breakfast *and* your debate now. I'm gonna go take my shower."

They acknowledged their father's instruction but continued to argue as they ate.

Esdell walked through the house. It still smelled of fresh paint and new carpet. The two-story home, which was just around the corner from his mother's house where he grew up, was in an older neighborhood on the east side of Indianapolis. All the family had worked together to remodel it. There were still boxes to be unpacked and pictures to be hung. He stepped out onto the front porch and enjoyed the sunshine and cool breeze of a spring morning. It was late May. The scent of peonies and freshly cut grass filled the air. The neighborhood was old, but the neighbors still took pride in their homes, so their properties were well-kept. He walked out on to his porch and saw the newly ordered Sunday paper lying on the curb. He walked out to retrieve it, waving at a neighbor down the street.

"Good morning!" he yelled. His greeting was returned. He walked back into the house and went to his bedroom. He sat on the bed and attempted to look at the ads in the paper. Esdell sighed heavily.

"Thank you, Lord! Thank you!" He found himself again on his wife's side of the bed, stroking the sheets. He whispered her name. "Kenya. Kenya, just look at us, babe! We've got our own home again. Oh, God, I miss you so much!" Esdell began to pray. "I need you, Lord. I need you! Please touch me with your healing hand to remove this pain I feel. I've grieved too long now! I know you said in your word, 'To be absent from the body, is to be present with the Lord,' but God, I miss her body. I still miss the touch of her hand and the sound of her voice. I miss her smile and her spirit. I know that she's present with you, and I rejoice, but I still miss her.' He sighed again. "Help me be the godly head of this house that you have blessed us with and help me to be an earthly image of you. I praise and thank you, Lord God, for all that you've done and all that you will do in all our lives. I count it all done. Oh, and, Lord, give Kenya a hug from me! I know she's watchin' us! Amen!" He rose and went down the hall toward the bathroom to take his shower. Karlena, with Micah, was ascending the stairs on her way to her room. She noticed the look on her father's face.

"Are you okay, Daddy? What's the matter?"

"I'm good! I just had a little talk with Jesus as your grandma would sing. It's all good! Kareem washin' the dishes?"

"Yes, sir."

"Okay, good. You go on and get ready." He paused. "I'll tell you what, you go get ready and I'll take Micah and get him washed up and dressed. Come get him when you're done, then I'll get ready myself! All my things are pressed and laid out. It'll only take me about twenty minutes to shower and shave."

"Thanks, Daddy!" Karlena answered. She could tell that her dad, for whatever reason, was a little down and knew that a little time with his grandson could cheer him up. She passed the baby to him. "Mick Mick, you be a good boy for Gramps. Okay? I'll bring you Micah's clothes and get ready as fast as I can."

"I'll come with you to get his outfit." Esdell and Karlena entered her bedroom. Esdell looked around. "Hey, you're 'bout done with your room, I see. It's nice in here!"

"I like it." Karlena gave Esdell Micah's clothes. "Me and Grandma picked out the comforter and curtains when me and Kareem first moved in with her. The colors reminded me of Mama."

"Yellows and oranges! Your mother loved those colors. It's why I let you pick out that yellow paint for the kitchen. C'mon, man, let's go get ready for church." Esdell quickly left Karlena's room before she could notice the tears forming in his eyes. His face further confessed the longing for his wife—his Kenya.

He went into the hallway bathroom and ran a sink full of tepid water. He closed the lid on the toilet and sat on it. Carefully he removed Micah's pajamas and diaper. He wet a washcloth and began gently washing Micah's face. Micah didn't like it much and started to fuss.

"Whoa now! Who's a big man? Who's Gramp's big li'l man?" Esdell bounced Micah on his knees and spontaneously sang a little ditty for him. "Who's the biggest li'l man? Who's the best in all the land? It's Micah! It's Micah! Who's as cute as he can be? Just because he looks like me! It's Micah! It's Micah! Big finish now! It's Miiiicaaahhhhh!"

Micah burst into laughter. The song was so silly that Esdell had to laugh at himself. But just as quickly as he laughed, he again pooled with tears. He hugged his grandbaby so he couldn't see his face. "You see him, Kenya? I wish I could see him with you. He's incredible, *our* grandson!"

Esdell gathered himself before Micah could notice. He continued to bathe him, again singing his newly composed song. "Who's the biggest li'l man?" He paused in thought for a second. "I might wanna work on that last verse though. Watcha think, li'l buddy?" He sniffed. "It's Miiiicaaahhh!"

A little over an hour passed when everyone met in the living room to leave for church. Kareem and Karlena looked as though they were standing for inspection.

"Y'all look nice. Let's get a move on," Esdell commented. Once in the car, Esdell drove toward the church. Gospel music played on the radio. Everyone seemed to be enjoying the sunny morning. It was an uneventful ride to church.

"It's a shame," Esdell said.

"What, Dad?" Asked Kareem from the back seat.

"No traffic! If this were a weekday, it would be bumper to bumper this time of morning. It should be that way now with people on their way to church."

Kareem agreed. "Yeah, Dad. People need to know they have to give God his due! One day, 'Every knee shall bow and every tongue shall confess!'"

"Amen, Reverend Son!"

They pulled into the church parking lot. Esdell drove up and down the aisles looking for a place to park.

"Well, at least our folks make it to church." Karlena said, noting that there were no parking spaces near the entrance.

Esdell drove back to the front of the church. "I'll drop y'all off at the door, then I'll find a spot."

Kareem, Karlena, and Micah went into the church. They greeted their fellow members as they made their way through the foyer. Everyone wanted to play with Micah because little babies were always popular in this loving church. They pinched and kissed his cheeks. Micah, being a happy baby, smiled at everyone who talked to him. Then suddenly he pointed and began to coo.

"Oh, you see Gran gran!" Karlena said. Gran gran was the name that was given to Micah's great-grandma, Grace, who was approaching them. "Hi, Grandma. Micah spotted you way over there!"

Grandma Grace held her hands out to take Micah who practically leaped into her arms.

"Hey, sweetie pie. How you doing today?" Grace covered Micah's face with kisses. "Mornin' y'all."

"Mornin', Grandma!" Karlena and Kareem responded in unison.

"Karlena, how'd li'l man man do last night in his own room? Did you miss Gran gran last night?"

"Oh, Grandma, he was so fussy! It was hard to get him quiet. Neither one of us got much sleep," Karlena answered.

"Well, that's understandable. He's used to sleeping in a room with you. It may take a while. I know y'all just moved out yesterday, but I miss y'all already. The house seems so empty, even with Isaiah and Sammy

Junior there. I also missed y'all in Sunday school this morning. Couldn't make it?"

"We were all so tired. Dad let me and Kareem sleep in."

"He parkin' the car?"

"Yes, ma'am," Kareem answered. "Oh, I gotta make it to Pastor's office for prayer. See you after church," he said, leaving the foyer.

"I need to get in the choir stand myself. Karlena, y'all coming over for dinner, right?" Grace asked giving Micah back to his mother.

"I guess so. C'mon, Micah. Sang purty, Grandma," she kidded.

Just as Grace was leaving her husband, Isaiah was coming toward them. "Hi, Karlena," he said. "Let's go, Grace, devotion is about to start. We got just enough time to get our robes on." He turned again toward Karlena to give Micah a little rub on his head. "Hi there, baby boy. How's Poppy's baby boy? Did he do okay sleeping in his room last night, Karlena?"

"It's a work in process, Pops! I'm gonna go sit down. See y'all after service." Karlena entered the sanctuary and spotted her aunt Christine with her daughters, Celeste and LeAnn. She went to the pew where they were and sat down. "Hey, everybody. Good morning!" They all echoed her greeting, and then Celeste, the oldest, reach for Micah.

"C'mere, baby cousin! Come see Celeste."

Karlena passed Micah over her and then asked, "Aunt Christine, where's Uncle Sammy?"

Christine pressed her lips together in discontent. "He called at the last minute this morning to tell me I had to drive myself today. That boy knows I look for him to pick us up for church every Sunday. Usually, if he wants me to drive, he'll call the night before or at least early enough to give me time to get ready! We barely got here on time for Sunday school."

"We didn't make it to Sunday school because we slept in. We were so tired from moving and all."

"Mommy, Uncle Sammy worked really hard helping Uncle Esdell and them move. He's probably tired too and that's why he couldn't pick us up!" LeAnn defended. She was crazy about her uncle Sammy! Christine did not want to discourage her twelve-year-old by talking about her uncle. It was hard for her to bite her tongue because back and forth insults and tacky jokes were commonplace between Christine, Esdell, and Sammy.

"Whatever you say, LeAnn," Christine relented.

"What's up, ladies?" Esdell had eased into the pew behind them. His sister and nieces gave him a little wave because the deacons had gathered at the front of the church and were starting devotion. "Whew, just made it! Where's Sammy, Chris?"

"I don't know!" Christine whined.

Celeste rolled her eyes. "Uncle Esdell, please don't ask! Mom is mad at Uncle Sammy and she's been raggin' on him all morning because he didn't pick us up! Asking her about him will only keep her complaining!"

"Did anybody ask you anything, little girl? You'd better remember who you're talking to!" Christine scolded. Like many mothers of a teenager, Christine's relationship with her fourteen-year-old daughter, Celeste, was often contentious. "Let's just enjoy the service!"

The deacons read scripture, prayed, and sang an old hymn, and the congregation joined in. The choir began to sing. Esdell looked into the choir stand where he saw his mother singing with all her might from the alto section with his stepfather standing next to her with the tenors. Esdell loved watching his mother praising the Lord in song. Then his eyes shifted to his son sitting in the pulpit. He was still getting used to his son being a preacher. Unbelievable! He sent up a silent prayer thanking God that his whole family could praise the Lord together. It was something that he did not take for granted knowing his kids could be anywhere else on a Sunday morning, but they were there with him. An hour and a half had passed and service came to an end. Kareem gave the benediction.

"'Now unto him that is able to keep you from falling, and to present you faultless before the presence of his glory with exceeding joy. To the only wise God our Savior, be glory and majesty, dominion and power, both now and ever. Amen.' Have a blessed day, everyone. See you Wednesday at Bible study!"

Everyone slowly proceeded to the church foyer, greeting one another along the way. As they left the sanctuary, Celeste spotted her uncle Sammy who was with his girlfriend, Danielle, who was also Christine's best friend.

"Run, Uncle Sammy! Run!" she said laughing. "Mom's gonna get you!"

Sammy, nicknamed Junya, pretended to be afraid. "Oh no! I'm doomed! Please don't hurt me, Missy Chrissie. Please don't hurt me!"

He gently grabbed Danielle and put her in front of him. "Don't let her hurt me, Danielle. Save me!"

"Sammy, you so crazy! Let me go!" Danielle chuckled.

"Yeah, let her go, Junya. It's gonna take more than Danielle to save you! Why you wait to the last minute to call me this morning?"

"My bad, Chris! I made some last-minute plans for me and my baby here. After I had breakfast this morning, I went out and sat on the front porch to look at the paper. Man! It was beautiful this morning!" Sammy reflected. "Blue sky, sunshine, cool breezes. Just beautiful! It made me think of Danielle. So I called her and made plans for us to spend the afternoon together, starting right after church." Danielle smiled. "I thought we'd go to restaurant downtown and then hit up some Naptown spots. After we eat, we goin' down on The Canal to ride the paddle boats and walk around for a while. Then maybe we'll go on The Circle for ice cream. Then after that…well, we'll just see!" He put his arm around Danielle's waist and then pressed his forehead against hers. She blushed, but when she saw the scowl on Christine's face, she felt the need to defend herself.

"Now, Chris, he called me at the last minute too, so don't be blaming me for Sammy not picking you up!"

Sammy frowned. "Wow, Danielle! Way to throw your boo under the bus! Maybe I'll just change my plans again!"

"You're better off under the bus, because otherwise, I would probably run over you in my car!" Christine taunted.

"Y'all really need to calm down out here! What y'all arguing about now?" Esdell was approaching the group. "Sounds like you need a referee." It wouldn't be the first or the last time he would have to assume this role.

"Yeah, Christine, you is in the house of the Lawd! 'Remember the Sabbath day and keep it holy! Right, Esdell?" Sammy mocked.

"Negro, please! You got nerve quoting the Bible to me! Junya, you just one scripture away from being a heathen!" Christine snapped.

"Heathen, you callin' me a heathen!"

"Shh! C'mon, y'all, let's head on over to Mama's!" Esdell started to herd them toward the door.

"Yes! Quiet down and head on out, Now!" Grace was nonchalantly passing by with Isaiah. She made her statement without breaking stride or even looking at them. "See you at home!"

The arguing stopped immediately. Everyone obediently started toward the parking lot, responding quickly to their mother's instruction. Even as adults, they still all snapped to when she spoke.

* * *

One by one, the family's cars pulled into the driveway at Grace's house. Everyone entered the house anticipating what was on the menu. Big Sunday dinners were a constant. Grace went to her bedroom to quickly change clothes to get dinner on the table. Everyone entered the house and assembled in the living room. Esdell hung his suit jacket on the coat rack and sat on the couch.

"Good service today. Pastor Edwards gave a good sermon. Choir was on fire today, Pops! I liked that new song y'all sang," Esdell said.

"Glad you liked it, Esdell, but it was a little bit too jazzy for my taste," Isaiah admitted. "I guess I'm getting a little old for the choir. The young people in the choir love that fast, contemporary Gospel music!"

"Well, Pops, the age difference is one of the things I love about our choir! Older and younger people all singing together. It uplifts the whole church. What's that old song? 'When all of God's people get together, what a time!'" Esdell sang but couldn't remember all the words.

"That song must be real old, Dad. I don't think I know that one," Kareem said. "But that one y'all sang today was on point."

"Well, glad y'all got into it, but ain't nothin' wrong with a little 'Pass Me Not, Oh Gentle Savior.' The old one…not the jazzy new one!" Isaiah smirked. "Now, I'm gonna go get out this suit!"

"Dinner will be ready in less than an hour," Grace said, passing through the living room on her way to the kitchen. "I got a big chuck roast in the slow cooker that should be just about ready. I got collards and cabbage in the fridge to warm up. I just need to do some potatoes, a few more sides, and some bread."

"We're on our way, Mama. C'mon, girls, let's go wash up," Christine said to her daughters, pointing toward the bathroom.

"I really need to change Micah, and from the smell of him, he's gonna need a whole new outfit and not just a diaper," Karlena said, pinching her nose. "I think there may be an outfit or two of his still in the laundry room."

"Hey, y'all, since we're just around the corner, let's go home and change and come back," Esdell suggested.

"Man, that sounds and feels weird!" The reality of the so recent move from his grandma's house suddenly hit Kareem and a bit of sadness briefly filled the room. "Okay, let's go. I'll drive."

"That's a good idea. Go change, then come back." Grace paused. "I want y'all to know that you are welcome and *expected* here every Sunday for dinner!"

"Okay, Mama, thank you. We'll be right back!" Esdell proclaimed.

Esdell and his kids left and returned quickly. Karlena assumed her spot in the kitchen to help complete the preparation of the meal. Her cousins, Celeste and LeAnn, set the table, and everyone took their place at the dining room table. They all joined hands and Isaiah prayed.

"Thank you, Lord, for this food we are about to receive. Please bless this food and the hands that prepared it. In Jesus's name. Amen!" Then Esdell and his children, keeping with their new tradition, recited in unison.

"God is great, God is good, and we thank him for our food. Amen!"

"Aw, that's sweet!" Grace declared. "Y'all doing that for Micah! That's so sweet!"

Serving bowls were passed around the table, and everyone filled their plates. They discussed the worship service and replayed Esdell's family's big move that had just occurred the day before. It was another great meal filled with good food and good conversation. The type of thing that keeps families bonded.

"Good as always, Grace," Isaiah said, rubbing his belly. "You keep feeding me like this, I can be the whale act at Sea World!"

"Thank you, baby! And I'm supposed to feed you good!" Grace kissed his forehead as she cleared his plate.

"Grace, honey, I'll clear the table and wash the dishes," Isaiah offered. "You sit and rest your feet."

Esdell looked at his son. "See, Kareem. That's just what we were talking about this morning. If everyone pitches in, things get done! Mama needs a break too."

Karlena gave her brother a victorious smirk.

"Yeah, Mama, it was a really good meal, and there was a lot more to go around without Junya being here eatin' up everything," Christine remarked. "That boy eats way too much! Big o' bum!"

"Don't talk about Sammy Junior when he ain't here to defend himself! Besides, we got something more important to talk about!" Esdell averted.

"What's that? You just takin' Junya's side like you always do!"

"The more important issue, Miss Chris, is that it seems to me that next Sunday is someone's one year anniversary!" Esdell fixed his gaze at Grace and Isaiah. "One whole year, and y'all still together!" he joked.

"It *is* next week!" Christine squealed. "Boy, that year went fast! What y'all gonna do?"

"Yeah, Grandma. What?" LeAnn asked with excitement. "We should have a party for you and Poppy!"

"Grandma's baby is so thoughtful. Look at you! We haven't really thought about it, have we, Isaiah? We've been so busy getting Isaiah's old house ready for y'all to move in to."

"And that's why I was thinking we'd have a big barbeque next Sunday at my house. It will be a perfect way to thank y'all for all you've done for us, and we can break in my new grill!"

"That's too much to do in a week, Esdell. You'll be way too busy unpacking and getting your house together, but thanks for the thought," Grace protested.

"We can pull it off, can't we, everybody? Me and the kids are out of school for the summer, so we got time. Whatever we don't get unpacked, we can hide in the basement. We'll have family and invite a few friends. It'll be fun! We gonna do it! The grill master has spoken!" Esdell insisted.

"Yeah right. Grill master? Whatever! I'm down," Christine said. "Sounds good to me! Esdell's house is proof of what we can do if we do things together. Done deal!" One by one, everyone sided with Esdell.

"Great idea, Daddy! You know me and Kareem are in!" Grace saw there was no need to argue. There would be a big anniversary barbeque bash at Esdell's house next Sunday.

2

Monday morning, Esdell drove his delivery truck through a strip mall talking on his cell phone to Sammy.

"Hey, man, I'm glad you and Danielle had a good time yesterday. Christine finally got over being mad at you by the time we finished dinner. Anyway, we need to get planning on the barbeque, so why don't you come over tonight after dinner. Call Christine and see if she can make it. I need to go, so I'll talk to you later. I'm tryna find this florist place. Later, bruh!" Esdell ended the call so he could concentrate on finding the location of his delivery.

"Hmmm, the address is 9101. Oh, here we go right here. 'While They Yet Live Flowers.' Ha, that's a clever name!" Esdell jumped out of his truck and entered the front door of the flower shop. There was no one at the counter or in the store. "Hello! Delivery!" he yelled.

"Deliveries in the rear! Drive around to the back, and I'll meet you back there!" a woman hollered from what appeared to be the storage room.

"Yes, ma'am!" Esdell returned to his truck and circled the mall to the rear. He saw a woman standing at the back door of the shop. He carefully backed into a parking space and quickly scanned over his delivery orders before exiting his truck. "Good mornin', ma'am!" he greeted. "I have five boxes of vases here, can you sign for them?"

"Yes, I can, but don't call me ma'am, it makes me feel old!" she joked. She looked up at Esdell's six-foot-three-inch body and thoroughly liked what she saw. "Follow me, I'll show you where to put them."

"Sorry, the invoice says 'Delivery only' to this location. I don't unload here, I just deliver. Is there someone else here to unload, ma'am?"

"Not right now, and didn't I just tell you not to call me ma'am?"

"Yeah, you did! Sorry…miss!"

"My name is Hope. Just call me Hope. My guy should be back in a few minutes. You thirsty? You can come in the shop, and I can give you a bottle of water. Got plenty of water in a flower shop, ya know!" she kidded.

"No thanks! I'll go over my paperwork and wait a few minutes in the truck. If he's not back soon, you'll have to reschedule this delivery."

"Oh no! We need those vases today! I'll unload them myself, if I have to. They can't be that heavy, and its only five boxes."

"Let's just give him a minute and maybe he'll be back. If not…well, sorry! I'll be in the truck."

"Why would the order say delivery only anyway? That doesn't make sense!"

"It was the owner's decision. The delivery is cheaper if the driver doesn't unload." Esdell had only been working as a truck driver for the past year and a half. He hated to seem ungentlemanly, but he had to follow the instructions on the invoice. "Sorry that I can't unload for you, but I will wait for a little bit, Miss Hope."

"And now it's Miss Hope! I guess that beats calling me ma'am! Well, like I said, I'll unload them if I have to, but you wouldn't let me unload those boxes all by myself, would you, E. Brown?" Hope had read Esdell's name embroidered on his uniform and was flirtatiously pointing to it, touching his chest.

Esdell had not paid much attention to Hope and had really made no eye contact with her. All he had noticed, as he looked down at his orders, was the pair of bright, white, Nike athletic shoes and ankle socks she was wearing, but when she touched him, he took a closer look at her. There stood a buxom, dark-skinned woman with her dark brown eyes and dark brown hair that was pulled back in a ponytail. Her face was pretty, and her smile was beautiful. She had on large gold hoop earrings and was wearing a khaki, denim skirt that stopped just above her knees, a white polo shirt, and a red apron to protect her outfit. He gently pushed her hand away.

"Let's just see if he shows up, okay?"

"*Okay*, E. Brown. What's the *E* stand for? Edward? Eugene? Earl?"

"None of the above!" Esdell said. He was clearly dismissing her advances as he walked to the driver's side of his truck.

"My middle name starts with *E*. We have something in common!" she relayed as she followed him, but Esdell ignored her and kept walking. "Humph! The *E* must stand for evil!" Hope proclaimed putting her hands on her hips.

"What's up, Hope?" By this time, Hope's coworker was quickly walking through the back door toward them.

"I'm glad you're back. I need you to unload this truck, since ole Evil here can't do it!"

"I got it, Hope!" answered the coworker. Esdell rolled his eyes at Hope and proceeded to the back of his truck to lift the door so the truck could be unloaded.

"Hello, sir, it's these five boxes right here. You need to sign for them. The young lady there never got 'round to it."

The man unloaded the boxes, sitting them on the ground and then signed the invoice. He began carrying boxes into the shop one by one.

Esdell turned to Hope. "Well, thank you, Miss Ma'am!" he said sarcastically. "You have a nice day! Bye!"

"Bye, Evil Brown! You have a nice day too!" Hope gave Esdell a big, fake smile and reentered the shop.

Esdell found the gesture amusing and smiled back her. "She's trippin' just a little!" he said to her coworker who had returned to get another box.

"Who, Hope? She's really good people. The owner made her assistant manager after only being here about six months. She's a hard worker! It looks like she has the hots for you though! Did you get her phone number?"

"Who...what? Naw, man! Not interested! She reminds me of my sister! Uh, you have a nice day too!" Esdell got back in the truck and mapped out the route to his next delivery. He had plenty of stops to make, so it was back to business. *Get her phone number?* The thought had not even crossed his mind. Esdell could only shake his head as he drove off.

* * *

The rest of the day went quickly. Esdell had finished his work for the day and was now on the bus headed home. He looked out the window and signaled the bus driver they were approaching his stop. He got off the bus and started the short walk to his house. Esdell walked slowly up the street and noticed his driveway was empty, which made it apparent that the twins were not home yet. Esdell let Karlena drive his car, since she had to go back and forth to his mother's house who babysat Micah while Karlena worked. Kareem was driving his grandpa Sammy's car. It had just been sitting in his grandmother's garage since his death. Esdell climbed the steps to his front porch and checked the mailbox, but there was no mail. He unlocked the door to enter his house, and his focus immediately went to the boxes yet to be unpacked. He plopped down on his beige, leather couch, took off his hat, and propped his feet up on the maple wood coffee table. He was trying to figure out whether or not he felt like doing any unpacking that evening. He looked around the freshly painted off-white living room, liking the way that the furniture was arranged. The drapes perfectly matched the walls. Two gold, brown, and beige accent chairs sat under the front picture window with an end table between them. Dark brown and maroon pillows were lying on the couch. After looking around, he decided to start dinner instead of unpacking. Entering the kitchen, he washed his hands in the kitchen sink. He opened the refrigerator and then the freezer. He had no idea what to fix.

"Daddy, you here?" Karlena was calling from the front room.

"Yeah, baby girl, I'm in the kitchen!" Esdell heard Micah crying so he went into the living room. "Hey, boy, what's the matter?"

"He didn't want to leave Grandma. He's been crying since we left her house. Would you take him, Daddy? I gotta get something out of the car."

"Sure! C'mere, li'l buddy!" Micah immediately stopped crying and reached for his grandfather. Karlena passed him over and went to the car. She quickly returned with a large casserole dish covered with aluminum foil in her hands, and a plastic grocery bag hanging from her wrist. "What's that?" Esdell asked. "Don't tell me. Mama!"

"Yup! Grandma sent us dinner!" Karlena said, carrying the meal into the kitchen. Esdell and Micah folowed behind her. "It's baked spaghetti. She sent some salad mix and garlic bread too!" Karlena set the dish on the countertop and peeled back the aluminum foil. "It's still warm and it smells so good! I'ma put it in the oven and set it on low heat, until we're ready to eat."

"That woman is something else! She can't be cooking dinner for us every day!"

"Grandma said she has to get used to cooking for just three people. She fixed too much food, so she decided to send us some. I'm glad about it too! I wasn't sure what I would fix if I had to cook today."

"Yeah, that's what I was tryna do when you came in, figure out what to cook. We really need to come up with a plan. It looks like cooking dinner will be between you and me."

"Well, we don't need to worry about it today thanks to Grandma!" Karlena happily stated reaching to take Micah from her dad. "Let's go get ready to eat, Mick Mick! I'm gonna change clothes and wash up."

"Micah can hang out with me while you do that. When you're done, I'll take a shower and maybe Kareem will be home from work by then so we can eat together. Your aunt and uncle are supposed to come over so we can plan the cookout for Mama and Pops."

"Yeah, we do need to jump on that. We only have a few days," Karlena agreed. "Be a good boy, Micah. Mommy will be right back."

"C'mon, buddy, let's go look in some boxes." Esdell walked with Micah into the living room just behind Karlena. "Who's the biggest li'l man? Who's the best in all the land? It's Micah! It's Micah!"

Karlena stopped just as she started to climb the stairs. "What's that you're singing, Daddy?"

"A little song just between me and Micah. Ain't that right, li'l buddy?"

Karlena shrugged her shoulders and continued up the stairs. Esdell went to an unmarked box that sat in a corner. "Hmm, mystery box! Let's see what's in here!" He continued to hold Micah while he pushed the box toward the couch with his foot. They sat on the couch, and he began to sort through the box. "Let's see. School papers, *Jet* magazines, a coffee cup full of pens…hmm, this must be our stuff that was just around Mama's house. Looky, Micah, your Colts football! Say ball, ball."

"Ba, ba, ba, baaaa!" Micah jabbered.

"Close enough! Here ya go, man!" Esdell gave Micah his baby-sized football and continued to search through the box. He thought the box was full of mostly junk until he pulled out a photo album that lay at the bottom. He stopped breathing, closed his eyes, and pressed his lips firmly together. It was a family photo album that Kenya had put together. He held the album in his hand, almost shaking. "Aw, man!" he uttered. He had not seen this book in a long time and was not sure if he was ready to look at it. Holding Micah securely on his lap, he exhaled and slowly opened it. The first photo was a five-by-seven-inch picture of him and Kenya in their army fatigues, standing in front of a jeep. His arm was around her shoulder. They were both broadly smiling as Kenya held up her left hand to show off an engagement ring. It was the picture taken of them just after he had proposed to her. "Wow!"

"Ba, ba, ba!" Micah cooed, slapping the album. It brought Esdell back from what may have become a tearful, faraway place.

"Micah, look, it's your grandma, Kenya. Isn't she pretty? Your mama looks just like her!" Esdell pointed out. He took a deep breath and started through the album page by page, explaining each picture to his grandson. There were snapshots of their wedding, pictures of each of them as they served overseas, pictures of them with the twins, and pictures of family vacations and holidays. What had started out as a potentially sad event turned into a beautiful moment of sharing memories and the chance to introduce Micah to his grandmother.

"Hey, fellas, what's going on?"

Esdell had become so engrossed in the photo album that he did not hear Kareem come in the front door.

"Hi, son! I was just showing Micah some pictures of us and his grandmother.

"Wow, Dad!"

"I know! That's the same thing I said!"

Kareem sat down next to his father and nephew. "Where did you find this?" he asked. "I've been looking for this album for months and months."

"It was at the bottom of this box."

"That's a box that Grandma packed. I saw her picking up random stuff around the house and putting it here. I bet she had it all along!"

"Maybe she thought it was too much for you kids to handle, too painful. I thought it would be for me too when I first found it, but its not. It's strangely comforting"—Esdell paused—"and a *little* painful."

Kareem looked at the album. "Mom was fine, wasn't she?"

"She sure was!" They continued to look through the album reminiscing about the good times they had as a family. It wasn't long before they were joined by Karlena.

"What y'all looking at?" She peered over her dad's shoulder and immediately recognized the photo album. "Oh, wow!"

"I know, right?" Kareem said.

"Sit down, Karlena. I'ma shower now." Esdell passed Micah over to her. "I'll be done shortly. Don't let the food burn up. Enjoy y'all."

As Esdell undressed and began to shower, his mind played back what he had seen in the scrapbook. A flood of memories overtook him—good and bad. He could not stop his mind from replaying all the years he had shared with Kenya. He smelled the spaghetti baking, he heard the phone ring twice, and Micah crying again, but none of this stopped the thoughts going through his mind. He finished his shower, dried off, and put on a pair of sweat pants and a T-shirt. He sat on the side of his bed.

"Thank you, Lord. I needed that! I needed to remember the good times with my Kenya. It's not good for me to be so sad everytime I think about her. You let Mama hold that album just long enough. What a wise woman. You are an awesome God! Yeah, yeah, just what I needed." He put on his house shoes and bounded down the stairs.

"Let's eat!" he said, clapping his hands going into the kitchen.

"Let's do it!" Kareem stood to follow his dad with Karlena and Micah close behind. "Hmm, smells like lasagna."

"Close," said Karlena. "Grandma sent over some baked spaghetti. Kareem, take Micah, and I'll get some plates down."

Kareem put Micah in his high chair and then went to get forks and napkins.

"There's salad mix too, Kareem. Would you wash it and get the dressing out? I'll put the garlic bread in the oven."

"No problem, sis!"

"I'll get the spaghetti out," Esdell said, reaching for the pot holders. With everyone working together, dinner was quickly on the table. They blessed the food and began to fill their plates to eat. "Who was that on the phone?"

"Oh yeah, Daddy, it was Uncle Sammy. He said him and Aunt Christine will be over here about eight to plan the cook out," Karlena answered. "Then Joseph called and offered to come help me unpack. My boyfriend is so sweet, isn't he?"

"He aw'ite." Kareem laughed.

"Yeah, he is!" Esdell really liked Karlena's boyfriend, Joseph. He had come into her life shortly after Micah was born. Karlena had been taking their relationship slowly. Micah's father was what Karlena called a checkbook daddy, barely seeing his own son and rarely sending a support check. Karlena was very cautious about whom she allowed to be around Micah.

"I want y'all to hang around too. I'd appreciate your input on the party plans. So…ah, how y'all feeling after looking at the album?" Esdell cautiously asked. His question was met with a moment of silence, but then Kareem began to speak.

"Well, Dad, I have mixed feelings about it. Like I said, I had looked for it before, but I couldn't find it, and I do think Grandma hid it from me. I was so angry when Mom got killed. I was mad at her, at you, and even mad at God. Grandma must've known that looking at the book when I was mad like that would've been...well, not a good thing."

"So you were mad. What did you do with all that anger, son?" Esdell had never talked to his children about the chain of events after the death and burial of their mother. He had to return to Iraq only two weeks after Kenya's funeral. During that time, he had to turn over most of his affairs to his mother to handle, including the raising of his twins. He felt that he had abandoned them, and the guilt he felt was sometimes overwhelming. Esdell was going to take advantage of this opportunity to finally find out how his children felt during those times.

"Well, Dad," Kareem continued, "let's just say I wasn't a very nice person!"

"That's an understatement if I ever heard one! Dad, Kareem was just hateful! He picked fights with everyone in the family, especially Aunt Christine. Kareem, you remember that day y'all almost started fighting in my bedroom?"

"Karlena, you know I remember that," he replied.

"What happened?" Esdell inquired.

"It seemed like everyone was getting on my nerves, and Aunt Christine just seemed to be the worse. But thank God for Grandma. We talked about how I was feeling, and she just told me to turn it over to God. I did, and He worked it out!"

"My mama is some special woman. Kids, I'm sorry I wasn't here for you then, but you were with the best person for you, your grandma. She taught me to pray over things, but sometimes we just don't feel like prayer changes anything. But trust me, they do. Just keep prayin' kids, keep your communication open between you and the Lord. Talk to Him through your prayers and let him talk to you through his word, the Bible." Esdell sighed. "Look at me trying to school Reverend Son. You are called a man of God. You got a direct line to Him!"

"Dad, why do you feel like you have to apologize to us about anything?" Kareem questioned. "You did what you had to do. And don't ever think that I can't take advice from you. You are my earthly father, and an image of my Heavenly Father. Yeah, I missed not having you here, but I prayed for you, God protected you, and you're back here with us. We can't get back the time you were gone, but I'm grateful.

So, so grateful that you are here now. We can't go back, so let's just move forward!"

"You're something else, boy!" Esdell rubbed Kareem's head. "You're right! But I still need to know…" He turned to face Karlena. "How 'bout you, baby girl? How did you feel after your mama died, and I had to leave so soon?"

"Kareem was trying to be all macho and didn't talk much, but it was different for me. I had Grandma and Aunt Christine. I would talk to them about how I felt all the time. Then Granny gave me Mom's Bible, and she had highlighted a lot of scriptures that always helped me. I was *okay*, Dad, all things considered. Kareem is right though, you have *nothing* to be sorry for. We understand that you left because you had to, not because you wanted to. But there is one thing."

"What's that?" Esdell asked.

"We were so young when Mama died, and sometimes it's hard for me to remember things about her, and that makes me feel so guilty. I mean, she was my mom. I should remember everything!"

Kareem shifted in his chair. "I thought I was the only one, sis," he said. "I feel ya, and it does make you feel bad."

"Let me tell you something, kids. Even though your mom is gone, she will never be forgotten. You may forget a few tangible things about her, but that spirit of hers will never be forgotten, and you know why? Because she's here!" Esdell clenched his fist to the center of his chest. "She's in our hearts and will live there forever! For whatever reason, God took her from us, and someday, we'll understand why. We have to ask Him for understanding. What're we suppose to learn from this, Lord? These trials come to make us strong! Believe that!" Though Esdell was talking to his children, he found that his own words were helping him heal too. "If y'all ever want to know anything about your mother or if you just want to talk about her, come talk to me. Okay?" The twins nodded their heads. "Well, enough of that! How was work today, y'all?" Esdell filled his mouth with a forkful of salad, relinquishing the conversation to whoever wanted to speak first.

"It was work!" Karlena said. "We're having a sale this week, and everybody and their mama is looking for gladiator sandals." Karlena worked at a popular shoe store that was located in a shopping mall a few miles from the house. "Shoe Carnival was poppin'! We got some really cute stuff in for summer. I really earned my $1.50 an hour!" she joked.

"I'm glad that we're out of school for summer break because I don't know if I'd have the energy to make it to class if I had one!"

"How many pairs of sandals did *you* buy?" Kareem asked.

"Not one pair! I was tempted though. If I shopped like I want to, I'd be bringing home bags full of shoes instead of a paycheck! I did see some cute sandals for Micah that I might buy when I get paid Friday. How 'bout you, Kareem? You make any money today?"

"No! Man, I have got to find another job. Selling vacuum cleaners is not for me."

"Kareem, really though! Who do you know that can afford an $800 sweeper? As much as Grandma loves you and wants to support you, she couldn't even buy one!"

"Girl, I needed a job and that's all I could find! But I'm looking for something else. I've got applications in all over Nap. I am *not* a salesman!"

"Work is hard to find these days. Just hang in there, son, you'll find something else."

"Well, since we're on the subject," Kareem cautiously said. "I really am thinking about quitting. It's straight commission, and I'm not selling anything! I'm not even earning enough to put gas in the car to make sales calls. Dad, I'm just going in the hole!"

Esdell sat for a moment, thinking about what Kareem had just said. "When's the last time you sold anything?"

"I sold two about two weeks ago, and I had made enough to keep me going 'til now. In a few days, I'll be broke. Dad, I wanted to take a class this summer at the Bible college, but I can't afford it! If I don't make some money, I may have to drop out of seminary altogether."

"Uh, no you won't! All you had to do is ask me. I can pay for your summer class! I'm not tryna hear about you quittin' anything, much less school!"

"I appreciate that, Dad, but I'll work it out on my own." A feeling of pride rose in Esdell.

"Your mama left money, and I'm trustee over it 'til you're both twenty-one. It's your money. I haven't touched it. It's yours. Look, y'all. I am here for both of you! I bought this house so we could have our own home again. I'm your dad, and I'm supposed to take care of you. Even though y'all are grown, you're still my kids. It'd be different if you were just lying around and just bummin' off me, but both of you are working, going to school, and trying to better yourselves. As long as you're doing that, I'll do everything I can to help you, with God's help and your mama's."

"Dad, I *am* about to be twenty-one years old," Kareem asserted. "I should be in my own place by now."

"I kinda feel the same way, Daddy," Karlena agreed.

"You guys make me so proud to hear you say that, but y'all ain't gotta go nowhere until you graduate school. I don't expect you be here forever, but you don't have to leave now. That's all!" The twins looked at each other and smiled. "Kareem, I'll give you a check to pay for your summer class, but you hold on to that job until you find something else. You're a better salesman than you think. Its already worked out, dude!"

"Okay, Dad! But I'll pay you back for the class, okay?"

"Nope! I told you, it's worked out. Its your money! Now, eat your spaghetti!"

"Whoa! The Daddy has spoken!" Karlena said. "Shut up and eat up! So, Daddy, how was *your* day?"

"It was busy. I had a lot of deliveries. I'm glad it was cool today. It made getting' in and out of that truck a lot easier. I like being out in the spring weather. I'm just a little tired. Kareem, you think you might wanna drive a truck? If you get a CDL, maybe I can put in a word for you. I don't really have any clout on the job, but I'll see what I can do."

"If it's a steady check, I am game! I'm driving all over the city anyway trying to sell those stupid vacuum cleaners. Do you think they'll hire me, Dad?"

"The only thing that can beat a failure is a try! I'll talk to my boss tomorrow. It might not help, but it won't hurt. I'll ask him if we need anymore drivers. If so, I'll give you the driver's manual so you can study to take the certified driver's license test."

"Thanks, Dad, but I'll keep looking for something else, while I try to sell those overpriced vacuum cleaners. So, do you like driving that truck?"

"It's not too bad!" Esdell confessed. "I don't mind the driving, and I sometimes I don't even have to unload the delivery. I had delivery like that today, and it made this lady a little mad!" He gave a fleeting thought to Hope but continued on with the dinnertime conversation.

The family discussed what they liked and disliked about their jobs. They flipped back and forth from that to the family photo album. It was now important to Esdell that they would always have dinner together as a family. He had missed so much time with his children already, and he wanted to take advantage of every minute. In the beginning, he wasn't sure that uprooting his children from his mother's house was a good idea, but he could see now that he had made the right decision.

"Hey, where's everybody at?" a voice yelled from the living room.

"That's Junya! In here, Junya!" Esdell yelled back looking at his watch. "We've just been talkin' and talkin'! It's eight o'clock already!"

"What's up, y'all?" Sammy said as he entered the kitchen.

"Man, you bustin' all up in here like you the police. You lucky I didn't bust a cap in you! You ever hear of knocking?" Esdell chuckled as he gave his brother a knuckle punch.

"No need to knock when you leave your door unlocked. You forget you live in the hood? What's up niece and nephews? Hey, Big Mike, come see Unc!" Sammy took Micah from his high chair, lifted him above his head, and blew a big raspberry on his stomach. "Look at that big o' belly! You been grubbin', ain't cha?" Micah burst into laughter and wildly waved his hands. "That baked spaghetti Mama made was da bomb, wasn't it? It's a good thing she sent y'all some or we'd be eating it for the rest of the week. She fixed so much!"

"Yeah, Uncle Sammy, that's what I was telling Daddy. Grandma said she has to learn to cook for just three people now since we've moved. C'mon, Micah, it's past your bedtime! I didn't realize it was so late. We're gonna take a bath then it's sleepy pie time for you!" Karlena took the baby from Sammy. "Say night-night, Micah. Dad, I'll be back down after Micah goes to sleep, okay?"

"All right. Nighty-night, li'l buddy! Sleep tight!" Esdell stood to kiss Micah good-night. Sammy and Kareem joined in, wishing him a good night's sleep. Then Esdell turned to Sammy. "Did you get a hold of Christine? Is she coming over?"

"Yeah, I just talked to her. She's on her way," Sammy answered.

"Kareem, let's get this table cleaned off. We can all talk in here."

"Okay Dad, but I think it should be Karlena's turn to wash dishes."

"It's not many. We'll knock 'em out real quick." Esdell tossed a dish towel to Kareem. "I'll wash, you dry!"

In no time at all, the kitchen was clean and ready for the family meeting. Just as they were finishing up, the doorbell rang.

"That's probably Aunt Christine now. I'll get it!" Kareem said. He left and returned immediately with Christine following behind him.

"Hey, fellas!" Christine greeted. "How's everybody?"

"What up, Chris?" Sammy said.

"I'm good, Christine," Esdell answered. "Glad you could make it on such short notice. Where're your girls?"

"They've been with Marcus since they got out of school. I'll pick them up when we're done here." Marcus was Christine's ex-husband. They had divorced a few years ago. Things between them had been volatile and there had even been the threat of a custody battle. Recently, however, things between them had greatly improved. They had even been on a date. Christine's daughters were both hopeful that their parents would reconcile and remarry.

"What's going on with you guys? Are you getting back together?" Sammy asked with an inquisitive look in his eye. "What happened after your date? Y'all do anything fun?" Sammy gave his sister a playful push.

"Why you all up in my business, Junya?" Christine laughed, "Seriously though, I don't know what we're doing. I'm just going with the flow and see where we end up. And no, we did not do anything fun after our date. Dang it!" The sexual inference was obvious.

"Uh, young nephew here! Too much info, Aunt Christine. TMI!" Everyone in the room enjoyed a lighthearted laugh at Christine's expense, when actually they were all glad that things were amicable between her and Marcus. Christine was too. She could not put her finger on exactly where their relationship failed, but deep down, she thought their divorce was the result of two hotheaded people not willing to compromise. With this realization in mind, Christine was open to giving their relationship another try.

"Oh, sorry about that, little Reem Reem! Woo, woo, woo!" She pinched Kareem's cheek. "But you know exactly where Auntie Chrissie is coming from! Okay, y'all, let's get this party planning started! I got my notebook here. Where's Karlena?"

"She's putting Micah to bed. She'll be down once he goes to sleep. Gramp's li'l buddy was full and sleepy. Sit down, Chris. You want something to eat or drink?"

"No thanks, Esdell," Christine answered as she took a seat at the kitchen table. "It looks pretty good in here. Yeah, the kitchen looks really nice."

"Karlena was determined to get the kitchen, her room, and Micah's room completely finished before the weekend was over. She got it done too! My baby girl can really get things done when she puts her mind to it. Okay, the first thing I want to talk about is the day of the party. I know I said Sunday, but I think Saturday would be better."

"I thought about that too. I don't think Mama was really in favor of a 'party' on the Sabbath day!" Sammy added.

"That's what I was thinking! Saturday would be better," Esdell declared. "I figure if we get started around one o'clock, we can be done by six, and that would give us time to get rested and get to church on Sunday!"

"Saturday at one o'clock sounds good. I started a list of who to invite," Christine said, flipping the page in her notebook. "Since time is short, I can e-mail or call the invitees from work."

"I'm sure you can with that cushy office job of yours! Do you really do any work? I bet you just surf the net and talk on the phone all day!" Sammy accused.

"Don't hate, Sammy! You couldn't do my job because it takes brain power. Something you don't have much of! You just keep your little mind on making those air-conditioning and furnace parts and don't worry about what I do at the bank!"

"I know I make more money than you do! How 'bout that!"

An argument was brewing, but Esdell jumped in. "Hey! Hey! Hey! Don't bring that mess in here! Y'all cut it out! We don't have time for this."

"Aw, Dad, it was just getting good!" Kareem laughed, egging on the argument.

"Kareem, they argue good enough on their own without you cosignin' on the side! We need to get this thing planned tonight, and like I said, we ain't got time for no mess! Christine, who do you have on your list?"

Christine rolled her eyes at Sammy and then directed her attention to the guest list. "The obvious, of course, would be their closest friends, and all of us. The problem is who we would invite from church. We can't invite the whole church! How many people did you want to plan for, Esdell?"

"We've got plenty of room in the backyard, so as long as it doesn't rain, space isn't a problem. We can borrow some tables and chairs from church, but I don't know? Thirty, forty people?"

"That's plenty, Dad! We can invite the choir since Grandma and Pops are both members. We should invite Pastor Edwards, of course. That'll cover the church members," Kareem suggested.

"Good thinkin', son. I was gonna invite Pastor over anyway to bless our house."

They all agreed to Kareem's idea for the guest list. They continued to plan the events of the day. The menu would include the usual barbeque fare: chicken, ribs, burgers, and hot dogs. Potato salad, corn on the cob, baked beans, chips, macaroni and cheese, pop, and fruit salad would be the side dishes. Karlena had returned to the kitchen to help plan the party. She said she would take care of a few decorations, order the decorated anniversary cake, and help her aunt Christine with the side dishes. Esdell and Sammy agreed to purchase all the meat and drinks, and they would tag team the grilling. Since Kareem was running low on funds, he could commit only to buying the bread and would buy some paper products from the dollar store. Between the party planning, Esdell talked about the scrapbook he had found. He showed it to Sammy and Christine who found it bittersweet, but it did not deter the party planning.

"That's about it, but what about music?" Sammy asked.

"I'll bring out my CD player," Karlena offered. "It'll play CDs, and anything on an iPod."

"I got this friend at work who wants to be a DJ. He's been talking about it for months, and I bet he'd come over here if I asked him to," Sammy suggested. "He'd probably do it for free just to get his feet wet!"

"Will there be enough room for him, with all the tables and chairs and guest and stuff?" Karlena asked.

"Like Esdell said, your backyard is huge! Besides, he doesn't have that much equipment. Mainly he just wants to get started somewhere. We'd be his first gig!"

"A DJ would be a nice touch. You think he has a variety of music? There'll be quite a range of ages," Christine inserted.

"I'll call him right now and asked him. I'll be right back." Sammy took out his cell phone and went into the living room to make the call. The rest of the family finalized the remaining party plans. Esdell thought it would be fun to have a spades or bid whist tournament. He had become almost an expert card player from serving in the military. They laughed at all of the trash talking that would more than likely take place among anyone who would participate and agreed it would add big fun to the party.

"It's a done deal!" Sammy said as he returned to the kitchen. "My boy, Dameon, is chompin' at the bit to come. He said he would do it just for the exposure and the experience, but I'll break him off a li'l somethin', somethin'. He says he has whatever kind of music we want. We won't have to worry with music at all!"

"All right then. Well, I think that's it, y'all! I'm gonna take Thursday and Friday off as vacation days so I can shop and get the house ready," Esdell proposed.

"I'll help, Dad. I don't have any calls scheduled this week so far," Kareem said.

"I put in to have Saturday off, and they let me have it, and I'll be working around the house when I get off work through the week," Karlena volunteered. Everyone else noted their individual assignments and then the meeting was done.

"Great, y'all! Just great! We gonna have a good time. No one deserves this more that Mama and Pops. God bless 'em!" Esdell voiced with excitement.

3

Five o'clock Wednesday morning, the sound of Esdell's buzzing alarm clock startled him awake. He hit the snooze, and after a few seconds, he sent up a silent prayer thanking God for a good night's sleep, free from vexing dreams, and for allowing him to awaken. He was not due at work until eight o'clock, so he continued to lie in the bed planning his strategy for the day. Before he knew it, his clock was buzzing again. How quickly those ten minutes went by. He turned off the clock, sat up on the side of the bed, sliding his feet into his house shoes. Yawning and stretching, he stood up and went into the bathroom. After relieving himself, he washed up in the sink. Esdell had taken his shower the night before, so this way, the bathroom would be free for Kareem. He returned to his bedroom to dress for work. His mind was racing with a mental to-do list. First thing though, he went downstairs to the kitchen to make some coffee. He wasn't sure what the twin's work schedule was for the day, so he made just enough coffee for himself. He fixed himself a bowl of cereal and sat down to enjoy his light breakfast. The house was quiet. Esdell took this time to meditate and talk to the Lord. He was always mindful of what God had done in his life. He had learned not to take anything for granted and to always acknowledge God's gift of grace and mercy. His mind would often return to those awful images of war, and he fought vehemently to suppress those memories. Then there was, as always, those moments that he thought of his Kenya. He thought of the photo album he had found. Esdell took a deep breath and made up his mind not to mourn today. He thought of the scripture Psalms 118:24, "This is the day which the Lord hath made; we will rejoice and be glad in it."

"Yes, rejoice and be glad, Esdell!" he spoke aloud. He finished his breakfast. The house was still quiet. He went back upstairs to brush his teeth. It was now time to leave, but first, he peeked into the rooms of his children. All was well. So again, he thanked the Lord.

Esdell exited his house, locking the dead bolt lock behind him. He walked to the sidewalk, picked up the morning paper, and then started toward the bus stop. He only had to wait a few minutes before the bus came.

"Good morning!" Esdell greeted the driver as he boarded the bus.

"Mornin'!" the bus driver said, returning the salutation. "This is the third morning in a row you've been on my route. Are you gonna be a regular?"

"Yeah, I am. I just moved down the block not too long ago. My name's Esdell Brown."

"My name's Don. It's good to meet you. Sit on down, Esdell, and we'll be on our way!" Esdell took a seat a few rows back and began to read the newspaper. He scanned the paper looking for sales that might benefit the anniversary party. Suddenly, he saw an ad for While They Yet Live Flowers.

"Ain't *that* a trip?!" He laughed, remembering his encounter with Hope at the shop.

"What's a trip? You talking to me?" Don asked.

"Huh? Oh, did I say that out loud? It's nothin', just an amusing ad in the paper," Esdell answered and got on with his reading. He looked up as the bus slowed, obeying the warning sign being waved by a construction worker. He thought how, as a truck driver, the frequent road construction in Indianapolis was so irritating to him, and thought that Don must have felt the same way.

"Man, they keep these streets torn up, don't they?"

"You got that right!" Don agreed. "It's just the beginning of the construction season and now these roads will be like this all summer long. Seems like they never get finished!"

"Yeah, no sooner than they get one street done, they're tearing up somewhere else. I'ma truck driver on a tight schedule, and the detours drive me nuts! East Washington Street has been a wreck for two years."

"Has it only been two years? It seems a lot longer." Don then stopped talking so that he could concentrate and maneuver the twelve-ton bus through the construction zone. "Well," he continued, "I guess it does show where some of our tax dollars go! Where do you work?"

"I work at Moore's Warehousing and Delivery Service."

"I hear that's a good place to work."

"It's not bad. Not bad at all. I like it just fine." Esdell returned to reading his paper.

Twenty minutes later, the bus was approaching Esdell's job. He rang the buzzer to signal his stop. Esdell walked to the door as Don slowed to a stop at the corner.

"You have a good day now, Esdell. I'll be looking for you in the morning! Nice meeting you."

"Thanks, man, you too, but actually, after today, I'm off the rest of the week. You have a good weekend, and I'll see ya Monday morning, God willin'."

Esdell descended the steps of the bus and started the two-block walk to his job. Upon entering the warehouse, he noticed a sign over the time clock that a meeting was being held in the employee lounge at eight o'clock. It was only 7:30 a.m., but after clocking in, he proceeded to the break room anyway. When he walked in, he was met by a coworker named Gary.

"Hey, Esdell, what you think this meeting is about?" Gary's blue eyes were almost glazed over with the look of fear.

"Good morning, Gary! How you doin'?"

"This isn't good, Esdell. I just saw the owner, Mr. Moore, go into Hank's office! I'm telling you, something's up!"

"Man, you need to calm down! Let me get you some coffee. We'll just have to wait and see what's up. Did you talk to Hank when you came in?" Hank was the warehouse manager. The company that Esdell worked for was a small family owned business, and as cliché as it sounded, the warehouse was like a work family because it was so small. Everyone got along well, and they all worked as a team to make sure that things ran smoothly. The employee benefits left a little to be desired, but what the company lacked in benefits was made up by the concern and fairness that the Moore family had always shown their employees. Besides that, the job paid well.

"Esdell, man, Mr. Moore's had Hank pinned up in that office since way earlier this morning. Moore never comes down here! And they're calling us into a meeting the same time we're supposed to go out on our runs. Not good!" Gary pushed his sun-bleached blonde hair from his eyes and sighed heavily.

"Sit down, Gary. What can I get you? You want some coffee or a pop or a Prozac or something?" Esdell joked.

"I don't want nothin', and this ain't the time to try and be funny!" Gary sat at a table, and Esdell sat next to him, putting his hand on his shoulder.

"Don't get yourself all worked up, Gary. What ever's going on, worrying ain't gonna help or change it. Relax!"

"I can't! I'm gonna go outside and take a smoke before this meeting. I'll be right back!"

"Smokin' ain't gonna help either!" Esdell said loudly as Gary rushed to the side door exit. Esdell stayed seated at the table and watched as the other workers filed into the lounge one by one. Other coworkers joined Esdell at his table, and all of them wondered what the meeting could be about. Each table murmured with speculation. Gary returned to the table, but all the seats were taken. He grabbed a chair from another table and forced a place next to Esdell. Gary's body tensed up as he saw Mr. Moore and Hank enter the break room.

"Here they come! Oh my god!" Gary nervously said.

"God is who you need to call on. Whatever this is, good or bad, He's the one who's in control. If you're a prayin' man, Gary, send one up now!"

Gary's face went blank, so Esdell quietly put his hand on top of his and simply said, "Calm and touch now in the name of Jesus!" He then quickly removed his hand and gave Gary an encouraging smile. Gary sighed and licked his lips.

"Good morning, everybody." Hank, a bald and rather short man, had positioned himself so he could be seen and heard. "I thank you for coming on such short notice. Is everybody here?" Everyone looked around the room an agreed that all the employees were present. "I know you're all wondering why you were called here, so, at this time, I'm going to just turn it over to our owner, Mr. Moore."

"Good morning to everyone. It's good to see you all." Mr. Moore rubbed his hand over his mouth and briefly grabbed his lips. "As Hank said, I'm sure you want to know why I'm here and why I called this meeting. In Friday's edition of the paper *Indianapolis Business Weekly*, there will be an article announcing the possible sale of Moore's Warehousing and Delivery. This is not a rumor, it is true. We are in negotiations. This information was leaked by someone in our head office. The final decision has not yet been made, but I wanted you to hear this from me first and to give you all the opportunity to ask questions. I didn't want you to be caught off guard." Mr. Moore, tall and portly, stood astride with his arms crossed in front of a snack machine waiting for responses and questions from his employees. The murmuring began again.

"Why? I wanna know why you would wanna sell the company!" Gary's panicked voice rang out. This was the obvious question and was echoed by most everyone. Mr. Moore directed his eyes toward Gary.

"My family started this company over fifty years ago. We've survived recessions, and all the ups and downs of the American economy. Times are hard again, and money is tighter than ever. We are evaluating our current bottom line and, frankly, it's not looking good."

"Who's lookin' to buy us and what's gonna happen to our jobs?" a voice clamored from the back of the room.

"I'm not at liberty to divulge the prospective buyer. The Moore's family's profit margin and your jobs are both being considered in our negotiations."

"You're considering your profit more than our jobs, I'll bet!" the same voice yelled. Mr. Moore's deliberate stance changed to one of apprehension. Esdell sat quietly but looked around as the room began to erupt with anger and accusing questions. He saw a look of angst coming over Mr. Moore's face.

"Hold up, everybody!" Esdell rose to his feet. "I think you're all jumping to conclusions. Didn't you hear Mr. Moore say that the final decision hasn't been made yet? Mr. Moore took the time to come down here to prepare us for an article with info that was leaked. He didn't have to do that! Now I know I've only been here a couple years, but I think we need to hear him out!"

"Man, sit your butt down!" The angry voice that had been speaking from the back of the room stepped forward. There stood a menacing man whose eyes were blazing with furor. "You haven't been here long enough to even open your mouth! We all know that in this economy, the rich are trying to stay rich! They don't give a damn about us poor people!" The jeers were escalating.

"The fact that I only been here a couple of years don't have nothin' to do with what I know to be true! This is a small company, but it pays better than some of the big companies in the city. How many of you have gone one year without a raise?" Esdell paused for a response; there was none. "Some of you may have got a raise when you didn't even deserve one! I know a lot of people who haven't gotten a raise in years, just to hold on to a job. Not us! *Okay*, I haven't been here long, but I can tell you that the Moore family has always considered the welfare of their employees. If you would calm down and think, y'all know I'm right about it!" Esdell paused again. The room calmed as his coworkers muttered in agreement. "Go ahead, Mr. Moore."

"Thank you, sir." Mr. Moore looked at Esdell and nodded his head. He did not know Esdell, but he was thankful to him for his quelling effort.

"Ladies and gentlemen, I have four children, three boys and a girl, and they're pushing me to retire. They are all college educated and are working at their own careers. They are living their own lives and don't want this company to be a part of it. They think in this economy, this place is a money pit. So, this is why we are looking to sell. The decision will be made within the week. You'll know when I know. I have nothing more to say. You all be careful on your routes today." Mr. Moore looked at Esdell once more and quickly left the lounge. Hank stepped up.

"Thank you, Mr. Moore. I don't have any more to add, so you guys go on to dispatch to get your orders for the day and do me a favor, would ya? Please keep the snake talk down to a minimum!" Hank warned before returning to his office.

Esdell looked at the angry man expecting a confrontation, but the man just stared momentarily at him and then stormed from the break room toward dispatch.

"You all right, Gary?" Esdell asked.

"No, I'm not all right! We're losing our jobs! I just know it! Man, I can't lose this job! It took me too long to find it. I got a felony on my record! I already know how hard it's gonna be for me to find another job!" Gary was borderline hysterical.

"You don't know none of that for sure. Just hold on and see what happens. Like I said, worrying won't change or help anything."

"Esdell, man, you should be just as worried as me! You just bought that house. You ain't even been in it a week. How you gonna pay for it now!"

"You're gettin' all worked up. Calm down. Take a deep breath."

"Stop tellin' me to calm down! I'm freakin' out here! How are you so calm anyhow? You're 'bout to lose your job and your house!"

"You wanna know how I can stay so calm? Because I know I am not in charge of anything. God is!"

Gary rolled his eyes. "Yeah, right! How you know that?"

"I'm here. I've been in a war that threatened my life every day. God kept me, protected me. He kept me safe and brought me back home to my family. I had nothin' to do with that. I didn't do it on my own."

"What about your wife?" Gary scoffed. "He didn't protect her!"

Esdell was annoyed by this question, but continued, "My wife's in a better place than we are. She's with God. Now I need to lean on God to strengthen me and show me what I'm suppose to learn from him taking her. I read my Bible and pray and I'm able to go on. Come go with me, Gary." Esdell gently tugged at Gary's elbow, leading him to the locker room that was just across from the employee lounge. They went to Esdell's locker, and after he unlocked it, he took out a small book. "See this little book? It's a devotional book that shows you where in the Bible to find a scripture that applies to just about anything you're going through. You look up your problem, and this book gives you a scripture. But you have to have an open heart and an open mind to receive what this book has to give."

Gary shook his head in confusion. Esdell went on to explain that all of the answers to the questions of life could be found in the Bible. He paraphrased Ecclesiastes 1:9: "What has been will be again, what has been done will be done again; there is nothing new under the sun." He explained that Gary's anxiety was real, but problems and trials have plagued man since the beginning of time, yet time continued with the grace and mercy of God. Esdell told Gary what Christ had done in his life and how he had faith that God would continue to keep him just like He had done in the past. Gary listened intently.

"I want you to have this book. I really believe it'll help you, man."

"It won't help me, because you said I need a Bible, and I don't have one." Gary looked at the floor. "I ain't never had one."

"Now you do!" Along with the little devotional book, Esdell gave Gary a Bible. He took out a pen and wrote his cell phone number in the back of the devotional. "Take these and read them together. If you have any questions, just call me, and I'll do my best to help you. C'mon, we'd better get on to dispatch so we can get on our routes."

Gary finally took that deep breath, and it was obvious that he was, at best, a little less upset.

"Thanks, man. I'll…" Gary did not finish his sentence. He took the books and walked away. Esdell prayed for Gary, asking that the Lord would give him understanding and peace. He also prayed that the words he had spoken to him had helped.

Esdell received his orders from dispatch and conducted his day as normal. His mind periodically returned to the meeting that had just taken place. He gave thought as to what he would do if he did, in fact, lose his job, but immediately sent up a prayer, turning all of his concerns over to the Lord. He decided that he would keep the possibility of unemployment to himself. There was no need to worry the twins.

* * *

After making all the deliveries assigned to him, Esdell returned to the warehouse, parked his truck, and clocked out. He was happy to be ending his workweek on a Wednesday. Plans for his mother's anniversary party began to flood his thoughts, almost completely blotting out the concern that was brought on by the early morning meeting at work. He got on the bus that safely returned him to his home. As he approached the house, he saw his car parked in the drive-way. Karlena was already there. He removed a few pieces of forwarded mail from the mailbox, he unlocked door and entered. The smell of chicken frying greeted him.

"Karlena, I'm home!" Esdell went into the kitchen. "You're frying chicken! It smells really good, baby girl!"

"Hey, Daddy! Thanks! I got home a little early so I started dinner." Esdell turned to say hello to Micah who was sitting in his high chair.

"Hey, li'l buddy!" he said, lifting the baby out. "Were you a good boy for Gran gran today? Huh?" Esdell kissed Micah on the cheek and put him back in the high chair. "How was your day, sweetheart?"

"Not bad! We were kinda slow today, so they let me off early. Do you want cornbread or biscuits with dinner?"

"Wow, if you're lettin' me choose between homemade cornbread or biscuits, I choose cornbread."

"Ha-ha-ha, Daddy! You got jokes." Karlena went to the pantry and took out a box of Jiffy cornbread mix. "Yeah, it'll be homemade all right, but just because I'm making it at home!" she smirked.

"Okay! Okay!" Esdell chuckled. "You need any help in here?"

"Nope, I got it covered. Go take your shower. Kareem should be home shortly. I can't wait to hear *his* jokes about my cooking tonight! If he has anything smart to say, I'll tell him to eat that leftover baked spaghetti!"

"What else is on the menu?"

"Mashed potatoes and corn. There's also some salad mix left from last night, and I think we should eat it before it wilts."

"Sounds real good. You got any plans tonight?"

"Joseph was coming over later, but he changed his mind. Why?"

"I'm gonna try to finish unpacking and get the living and dining rooms together tonight. We need to get crackin' on the house to get it ready for the party. Have you seen Joseph at all this week?"

"Not yet, but I think he's taking me to lunch tomorrow. Oh, and by the way, I bought a plant to put on that table in front of the window. It has a burgundy color in the leaves so it picks up on the maroon color in the chairs and the pillows."

"That's nice!" Esdell was pleased to see the pride that Karlena was taking in their new home. "Well, I think I'll go on and get started now while you finish supper."

Grabbing his toolbox from under the kitchen sink, he went into the living room. He looked at the way the furniture was arranged, and overall, he was happy with it. As you entered the house, there was an aisleway that separated the staircase and the dining room from the living room. The back of the couch and the end tables defined the separation of the rooms. The entertainment center that held the television and some pictures was directly across from the couch. He went to a large cardboard box that held two framed pictures of dark red poppies and some smaller pictures.

These will look nice hanging over the accent chairs in front of the picture window, he thought. *Karlena's right, that plant will look good on that table.* He measured carefully so the pictures would hang even on the wall. He hammered picture hangers into the wall and hung the pictures.

"Karlena, come in here a sec!" Karlena came just to the doorway of the kitchen to look into the living room because she did not want to get too far away from Micah. Esdell asked her, "How does it look?"

"Nice, Dad, really, really nice! Dinner's about done. You ready to eat?"

"I am but let me call Kareem and see how close he is to being home." No sooner than Esdell finished his sentence, the house phone rang.

"Hello?" he answered and listened to the voice on the other end. "Okay, son, I was just about to call you to see where you were. We'll see you when you get home. Be careful. Bye! Well, that was your brother, he has a late sales call, and he won't be home for about another hour. It's you, me, and li'l buddy for dinner tonight. Let's eat." He washed his hands in the kitchen sink. He and Karlena prayed over their meals and began to eat.

"I tried to make gravy, Daddy, but I haven't quite mastered it yet." Karlena passed the bowl of gravy over to Esdell. "How was your day?"

"It was okay. There's a real nice guy that drives my bus. He's real friendly. Happy people first thing in the mornin' is kinda rare. It's a nice way to start the day. Let me try this gravy of yours."

Esdell spooned the gravy over his potatoes. He was purposely trying to divert the conversation from his workday. He put a forkful of potatoes and gravy in his mouth. He rolled the food over his tongue and swallowed. He looked at Karlena and shrugged his soldiers. "Uh, the gravy's not too bad." Karlena took a bite.

"No, it's not *too* bad, it's *really* bad! I started to call Grandma to ask for help, but I thought I could make it on my own. Oh well, back to the drawing board!"

"Gravy's kinda hard, but the chicken's good. You a fine cook, girl. The more you do it, the better you'll be."

"Spoken like a loving dad, but I know my brother won't be so kind. I'll pour this mess out before he gets a chance to taste it." They chuckled in agreement. They discussed some events in the local news and went on to discuss their plans for working on the house.

"I'm off the rest of the week, so whatever we don't get done tonight, I'll finish tomorrow or Friday. I'll need the car, Karlena, I've got a lot of shoppin' to do."

"That's fine. I can ride the bus or hitch a ride with Kareem."

"I was gonna keep Micah tomorrow, but I'ma take him to Mama's, and I'll keep him on Friday," Esdell said.

"Oh, great! I was gonna ask you about that. Grandma wants to go shopping for a new outfit for Saturday. If you keep Micah on Friday, she can go then. I can't wait for this party. We're gonna have a good time! What're you buying the happy couple for their anniversary?"

Esdell raised his eyebrows and his face went blank. "Girl, I ain't even thought about that! That's a good question. I guess I figured the barbeque would be enough."

"Well, you know Grandma's not looking for anything else, but I had an idea. You know, traditionally, the gift for the first anniversary is paper, right?"

"Uh, if you say so!" Esdell replied in ignorance.

"Well, I was thinking the three of us could give them a night out package, gift certificates for dinner out, a movie or a play or something. Whatcha think?"

"Good idea, Karlena! They really don't do much. Maybe we could send them to a bed and breakfast or I can go online later to see if Beef and Boards Dinner Theater has anything coming up that they'd like to see. I like it! You're brilliant, girl!"

Karlena smiled broadly. "Again, spoken like a loving dad."

They finished their meal. Esdell fixed a plate for Kareem and put it in the microwave for him. Karlena washed the dishes and cleaned up the kitchen. Together they unpacked boxes, hung pictures, and arranged furniture. Micah was allowed to crawl around on the floor as two pair of watchful eyes made sure he was safe. It was not long before it was his bedtime.

"Time for bed, Micah!" Karlena announced picking him up. She took him upstairs as Esdell carried on with working on the rooms. More time passed, and Karlena returned to help.

"Daddy, where should we hang this wall clock?"

Esdell turned, and looking at the clock, he realized the time. "It's almost ten o'clock! Kareem should be home by now. Wonder where he is." Esdell thought for a second. "Give me the clock. I'll hang it on the wall over there." Esdell hammered a picture hanger into the wall and hung the clock. He again wondered why his son was not home.

Hedge of protection, Lord! he prayed in his head.

"Daddy, I am going to run the sweeper and then we are done! Yay, us!" Karlena smiled, giving Esdell a thumbs up. He returned the gesture.

The sound of a key unlocking the front door ended their little celebration. Kareem entered the house. He looked at his father and his sister.

"Hi, y'all," Kareem muttered.

"Hey, I was wondering where you were. How did your sales call go?" Esdell asked.

"It was a waste of time, gas, and positive energy!"

"I'm sorry, Kareem. There's a plate for you in the microwave. I fried chicken. You'll feel better after you eat. Uh-oh, I just left myself open for an insult on my cooking!"

"No insults. I'm not hungry. I'm going to bed! Good night!" Before Esdell or Karlena could say a word, Kareem had run up the stairs, taking two steps at a time.

"There's more bothering him than a bad sales call. Daddy, maybe me or you should go talk to him," Karlena suggested.

"No, baby girl, I know that look he had in his eyes. You're right though, something's weighing heavy on his mind, and as a man, he's trying to work it out himself. Whatever it is, it's between him and God. He'll talk about it when he's ready. Let's just leave him alone. Pray for him but just leave him alone, for now, anyway." Esdell put his arm around Karlena's shoulder and held her firmly to reassure her.

4

Friday, 7:30 a.m., Esdell sat in the recliner in his bedroom reading his Bible. He had been up for one and a half hour, and he felt relaxed and refreshed. Sleeping until 7:00 a.m. was considered sleeping in to him since he was normally up at 5:00 a.m. He was reading in the book of Psalms because it always encouraged and uplifted him. He read the full division of Psalms 61, which reads:

> Hear my cry, O God; listen to my prayer. From the ends of the earth I call to you, I call as my heart grows faint; lead me to the rock that is higher than I. For you have been my refuge, a strong tower against the foe. I long to dwell in your tent forever and take refuge in the shelter of your wings. For you, God, have heard my vows; you have given me the heritage of those who fear your name. Increase the days of the king's life, his years for many generations. May he be enthroned in God's presence forever; appoint your love and faithfulness to protect him. Then I will ever sing in praise of your name and fulfill my vows day after day.

He closed his Bible and began to meditate on what he had read and then closed his eyes and began to pray. He thanked the Lord for His many blessings and being a refuge. He asked for forgiveness for any and all sins he had committed and asked that God would direct his path throughout the day. He praised the Lord for all He had been in his life. Esdell prayed for his family and his coworkers. He prayed God would keep his hedge of protection around everyone.

"Finally, Lord, I'm asking special coverage for Kareem. You know what he's going through, and I pray that you give him direction and peace. I give hallelujah praise and thanks for your son, Jesus, and it is in his name, I pray. Amen!" Esdell had talked only briefly to Kareem on Thursday because his son had remained withdrawn all that day. He had left the house with just a mere good-bye to his dad and had not spoken at all to his sister. When he returned home, he complained about his lack of sales and went straight to his room. Esdell had heard the muffled sound of prayer coming from Kareem's room and prayed along with him. He was sticking to the decision he had made to leave him alone, trusting that Kareem would come to him if he needed him. But above all, he trusted that God would work it out for him.

Esdell had busied himself on Thursday working in the yard. He had cut the grass, raked, cleaned his deck, and arranged the patio furniture on it. He and Sammy had gotten chairs and tables from the church, and they had set them up as well. Sammy had given Esdell his share of money to pay for the meat so Esdell had done the grocery shopping. His plans for the day were to marinate the ribs and chicken and season and prepare the hamburger patties. He moved to his desk to make out a shopping list because he still needed to shop for some aluminum pans, barbeque utensils, pop, and other items.

"Daddy, are you awake?" Karlena asked as she tapped on his bedroom door.

"Yes, come in."

"Good morning, Daddy. I'm about to head out. It's about time for my bus. Micah's still sleeping, but he'll probably wake up in the next twenty, thirty minutes. I laid out his clothes. When you go out today, can you pick up something for me?"

"Uh-huh, in fact, I was just writing a shopping list. What do you need?"

Karlena entered the bedroom and stood by her dad at his desk.

"Aunt Christine and Grandma would kill me, but I'm going to cheat on the potato salad. If you can pick some up from a deli somewhere, I'll doctor it up for the barbeque tomorrow. I just won't have enough time to make it from scratch."

"Sure, and don't worry, baby girl, your secret will be safe with me!"

"Thanks, Daddy! I've packed the diaper bag already." Karlena kissed Esdell on the forehead. "Okay. I'm out! Oh, Kareem's still sleeping too. I don't know if he's got any calls today or not, but he's usually up by now. Oh, I better go before I miss my bus. Bye, Dad!"

"See ya later! Have a good day and be careful." *Hedge of protection, Lord.* Esdell prayed again and then rose to check on Kareem, but first he looked in on Micah. He was still sleeping. Then he went to Kareem's bedroom door and tapped on it.

"Yeah?" Kareem's muffled voice responded. Esdell peeped through the door to find his son lying on his back in bed with his arms folded behind his head, staring into space.

"Mornin'. You okay?"

"Yeah," Kareem answered as he sat up and put his feet on the floor.

"You goin' to work today. Got any sales calls?"

"Not that I know of. When I get to the office, maybe they'll have something for me. I'ma get up in a minute, in just a minute."

"Okay. You want some breakfast?"

Kareem did not answer. Esdell looked at him and frowned. He asked himself if now was the time to ask Kareem what was going on with him and he decided not to.

"Is that a yes or a no on breakfast?"

"Dad, I need to talk to you. Something happened Wednesday night!"

"What happened?" Esdell was uneasy. "What is it, son?"

Kareem took a deep breath.

"Karlena's gone, right?"

"Yeah, she just left."

The room went silent. Esdell waited patiently for Kareem to speak.

"Wednesday night, after I left my last sales call, I was getting in my car and these dudes I used to hang with recognized me and came over to talk to me." Kareem paused again. "Remember the other night when we were talking about how things were with me and Karlena after Mama died and we moved in with Grandma?"

"Of course."

"Well, I didn't tell you everything. Dad, I was so messed up, more than I let anybody know. I was runnin' the streets, and this gang was after me to join, and I almost did. Ma was dead and you were in Iraq and I just knew, at any minute, they'd be at the house telling us that you were dead too. So, I was down with it, I was gonna join. I was about to be initiated, but I backed out."

"What changed your mind?" Esdell asked calmly.

"You came home, and I knew it was by the grace of God. I couldn't become a part of a gang that's against everything God stands for, and against everything I'd ever been taught. I was scared though, I didn't know what they were gonna do to me for backing out!" Kareem sighed deeply. "Well, I took one good gut punch. It bent me over and I threw up. They all spit on me, a couple of them kicked me. They said I was too much of a punk to be in their gang, and it was over. They let me go."

"So what happened the other night when they saw you?"

"They started in on me again. The leader, Big G, said he heard I was a preacher now, but he knew all about me, and he wanted to know if I had really changed. He said there was an initiation coming up, and I could still join them. Then said the best part of the initiation was there with him. There was this girl with him. He told her, 'Go, do yo' thang!' She pushed up on me hard, Dad, kissin' and rubbin' me all over! Before I knew it, we were in the backseat of my car, and she was all over me, and they all stood outside my car just watching. I was about to do her, but a voice in my head was screamin' 'STOP! STOP!' I just got out of the car. Big G screamed at me, 'You still a punk!' They all laughed. The girl looked at me and laughed too. She said, 'Yeah, he ain't nothin' but a punk if he can pass up all this body!' Then they all left. I fixed my clothes and came home."

"You did the right thing, son. I'm proud of you!" Esdell was relieved with the end of Kareem's story, but sensed there was more. "So what's troublin' you?"

"Dad, I'm supposed to be a man of God! I shouldn't have let it go that far! I was on fire! I wanted that girl so bad it actually hurt! What kind of man of God am I that my body could betray me so fast?! And now, I can't stop thinking about it! That woman! They said I hadn't changed, and maybe I haven't!"

Esdell could see the torture in Kareem's face. He thought and prayed quickly before he spoke. He recalled the scripture he had read just moments before.

"Kareem, God called a man. You are a man first! A man 'born in sin and shaped in iniquity.' You didn't stop being a man. Once you accepted your calling, son, the devil was mad! He knew you're a warrior for God, someone that would fight to save souls by preaching and teaching the Gospel. He gonna work harder on you than anybody! You are not exempt! I was just reading in Psalms where we should call out to the Lord to be our refuge and to shelter us under His wing from our enemies. Now, you're not only a man, but you're a *young* man and sexual desires die hard and…well, I don't have to tell you!"

"I feel so weak! Would a truly called man of God have gotten in the backseat of that car? I should've been able to speak a word to them that would've made them think about what they were doing. Was I really called, or did I just make that up in my mind?"

"Kareem, I have no idea what it feels like to be called by God to preach. I ain't no preacher, but I can say don't doubt in your head what you know in your heart to be true! This whole incident is a testimony in the makin'. You were in a situation that might of turned to something that you might've regretted the rest of your life. That voice in your head that told you to stop was the Holy Spirit that lies so deep in you that you *did* stop! Not many men could've done that. You got a message across then without sayin' a word! What made you feel God called you to His ministry in the first place?"

"I…" was all that Kareem could say.

"Well, let's just go back."

Esdell recounted the events that lead up to Kareem's calling. It was Christmas time, and Kareem was home on winter break from Clark Atlanta College. He was ready to enjoy the holiday with his family when his roommate suddenly called him from Atlanta. His roommate had gone to his home for winter break as well but had returned to campus because of a heated argument with his mother. Harsh words were exchanged and his mother had thrown him out and told him never to come back. Kareem's roommate was an emotionally troubled young man, and the thought of losing his home and the love of his mother had driven him to the point of threatening suicide. He called Kareem to tell him of his intent. Without hesitation, Kareem left home and took a bus back to Atlanta to help his roommate. When he got there, he had prayed with his roommate and read scripture. He witnessed to him about how his belief in Christ had given him the strength to bare the death of his mother and had kept his father safe. With God in front of him, Kareem's words had saved his roommate's life, and now, Esdell could add that it was that same Spirit that kept Kareem from joining that gang—the same gang who taunted him earlier in the week. Once again, Father, Son, and Holy Spirit had kept Kareem from harm and had ordered his steps. Then on New Year's eve, at the watch night service at the Road to Damascus Baptist Church, Kareem proclaimed his call to preach the Gospel of Jesus Christ.

"Son, I don't know what God spoke to your heart that night. I only know that I had never been prouder of you! Just ask God for forgiveness and guidance. I know if you continue to pray and stay in your Bible, you'll remember what He said to you. Like I said, don't doubt what you know to be true! In spite of what them hoods said to you, you've changed. You have been changed by the grace of God! You hear me, boy?"

"I hear you, Dad." Kareem looked at Esdell and then with great force, threw himself into his arms. "My dad! Woo! Thank you, Lord, for my daddy!" he said loudly. It was a hallelujah shout that awakened Micah. Esdell returned the firm hug but then released his son.

"There goes Micah, I better go get him. You okay?"

"I'm better! Go 'head. Thanks, Dad! I love you!"

"Oh yeah! Back at cha! And, son, just when I thought I couldn't be more proud of you, I am!"

Esdell left Kareem's room to see about Micah. He walked into the nursery to see Micah standing, holding on to the side of his crib crying.

"Good morning!" He lifted him from the crib and spun him around. "It's Micah, it's Micah!" he sang. "How ya doin', li'l buddy? You and me gonna hang out today. How 'bout that? Would you like that?" He bounced Micah up and down until he stopped crying. "Let's go see Uncle Kareem." Esdell returned to Kareem's room and stopped just outside the door. "Hey, Micah wants to say good morning!"

Kareem was still setting on the side of his bed. He looked up to see his nephew. "Hey there!" he said with a forced smile.

"Okay, son?" Esdell asked.

"I'm gettin' there," Kareem answered. "I'm gonna shower now and then go on in to work to see if they scheduled any sales calls for me today."

"You hungry?"

"Yes, but I'll have to grab something on the way in. I'm already late." He stood up and went to his closet, and then turning to look at his father, he said, "I'm okay, Dad. Go take care of li'l man. Thanks again."

Esdell nodded his head and left the room feeling grateful for the bond between him and his son. Just a little of the time that had been lost while he was away in the service had been made up, and he thanked Jesus for it.

It was now time to start his day with Micah. After he and Micah were both dressed, they ate a light breakfast of cereal and bananas. Kareem came in while they were eating to say good-bye. Once they were done with breakfast, Esdell grabbed the diaper bag, and they were off for a day of shopping.

With Micah securely in his car seat in the back, Esdell drove to the ticket office of the local theater called the Murat. He had read online that a Gospel comedy play was coming to town next month and thought that would make a good anniversary gift for his parents. After buying a pair of tickets, he proceeded to their favorite soul food restaurant called Down Home Chews to buy them a gift certificate for dinner. He sang to Micah songs from the old school radio station he was listening to, and it seemed that Micah was singing along. They made a stop at the drug store to buy an anniversary card for the happy couple and then went to a fast-food restaurant so they could eat lunch and Esdell could change Micah's diaper. Esdell then drove to the Gordon Food Service that was close to his house to buy the items on his list for the barbeque. He put Micah in the grocery cart and started though the store aisle by aisle. He rarely shopped at this store, so he had difficulty finding what he needed. Finally, he had found everything on his list, including a large container of the potato salad that Karlena had requested. They were on their way to the checkout line when he heard a woman's voice.

"I'm open over here on register five, E. Brown!"

Esdell couldn't believe his eyes; it was Hope from the flower shop. He smiled slightly, shook his head, and went to register five.

"Well, hello, Miss Hope. I'm surprise to see you here. Matta fact, why are you here?" he asked as he loaded his items on the conveyor belt.

"I work here part-time when I'm off from the flower shop." She began to ring his order. "What you got goin' on? Looks like you're having a party! Hmm, my invitation musta got lost in the mail."

"Must have!" Esdell chuckled. "I'm having a barbeque for my mother and her husband. They're celebrating their one-year anniversary."

Hope looked at him curiously.

"What's that look for?"

"You don't strike me as the party-giving type! That's really nice. And who is this cutie pie with you? Hey there, Suga Wuga!" Hope said to Micah who responded by smiling and kicking his feet.

"This is my grandson, Micah. Say hi, Micah."

"Na, na, na, na!" Micah babbled.

"Oh, he's so cute! Grandson, huh? So, Micah, you're rollin' with Grandpa today! Where's Grandma, Grandpa's wife?" she asked continuing to scan Esdell's purchase. He looked at her and smirked.

"If that's your not so clever way of tryna find out if I'm single, I am. My wife is deceased."

"Oh, I'm so sorry!" Hope said shamefully. "Uh, do you have anymore grandchildren?"

"Nope, he's the only one! This is my li'l buddy!" he said proudly. "And whatcha mean I don't look like the party-giving type, anyway?" Esdell said to lighten the mood.

"You seem so serious! You don't seem like much of a partier. Well, Micah sure is a handsome little guy. Just like his grandpa!"

"Miss Hope, you are somethin' else! You sure don't bite your tongue, do ya?"

"No fun in that! Do you like biters?" Hope flirted.

"Whoa, now! Watch out! Uh, what do I owe you?" Esdell smiled broadly, almost blushing.

"Your total is $57.63! So when's this party?"

"It's tomorrow!" he said, taking out his wallet to pay.

"Is anybody helping you with this shindig?" Hope gave him the required change and finished sacking his order.

"It's a family affair! My brother and sister, and my kids. All of us are pitchin' in."

"I'll bet your brother is just as handsome as you and your grandson."

"Sammy? He sure would think so!"

Hope gave Esdell another strange look.

"There's that look, again! What's *that* about?"

"Oh, nothing. Well, here you go! I wish you luck with your barbeque. Thank you, very much, E. Brown. Come again and bring this pretty boy with you!"

"Thank you, Miss Hope."

"Hope, just call me Hope!"

"Okay, Hope," Esdell accommodated her request. "Say 'bye-bye', Micah! Say 'bye-bye'!"

"Bye, Micah! Bye, E. Brown! Hey, what's your first name? Fo' real though!"

"Esdell."

"That's different. Well, see ya 'round, Esdell. Take care of your grandpa, Micah."

"See ya!" Esdell pushed his cart through line and out the front door as Hope watched him all the way out. He smiled to himself all the way to his car as he thought of how Hope flirted with him. He put Micah in his car seat and loaded his groceries into the trunk. He looked up and saw Hope standing in the store window waving at them. He waved back and got in the car.

"Boy, she was a trip, wasn't she, Micah? Cute, but a real trip!" Suddenly, his cell phone rang. "Oh, it's Mommy!" he said, looking at the caller ID. "Hey, baby girl!"

"Hi, Daddy, where y'all at?" Karlena asked.

"We're just leaving GFS. What's up?"

"Can you come get me from work? I need to make a stop, and it would save me from having to come home to get the car and go back out."

"No problem. We'll be there in about fifteen minutes. Bye! We gonna go get your mama. Say mama. Maaama!"

"Mama!" Micah yelled.

"Yeah! Good boy! What a good boy you are!"

In just a few minutes, they were pulling into to mall and making their way to Karlena's job. He spotted her standing outside of the shoe store and pulled up to the curb. Karlena open the back door to speak to Micah first.

"Hi, Mick Mick! How's mommy's baby boy?"

"Mama!" Micah blurted.

Karlena gasped. "Did you hear that, Daddy? He said mama! Oh, my big boy!" She covered Micah's face with kisses in delight. She closed the back door and got in the front seat next to her dad. "Do you believe that? He said mama!"

"Li'l buddy's a smart one, all right. Where to, Karlena?"

"I need to go to pick up the cake and get a few decorations."

Esdell drove to the bakery and then by a dollar store so Karlena could buy decorations and pick up some helium balloon bouquets she had ordered. When those errands were done, they headed home. Karlena talked about her day on the job and said she was glad to be off for the weekend. Working retail did not often afford that luxury. Esdell then shared how he and Micah had spent their day. They had accomplished so much but still had much to do to get ready for the party.

They arrived home, and Kareem was already there. Esdell blew the horn, signaling him to come out and help with the packages. He immediately came out and carried most everything inside. Karlena carried a sleeping Micah into the house.

"Wow, y'all been busy! Li'l dude is knocked out! Give him to me, and I'll go lay him down," Kareem said taking him from Karlena.

"Thanks. You feeling better, Kareem?"

"Yeah, sis, I feel a lot better!" he said looking at Esdell.

"Good, I'm glad. Well, I need to jump in this kitchen!"

"You ain't cookin' again, is ya, gal?" Kareem joked.

"Yeah, you're feeling better. You're back to your ignorant self!"

"Okay, kids, don't start! Go on and put your nephew in the bed!" Esdell chuckled. He was glad to see that Kareem was getting back to normal after a rough couple of days. "I'm ordering pizza so no one's gotta cook."

"Okay. I bought the paper plates and buns and stuff today. It's all in there on the counter," Kareem said as he left to lay Micah down for his nap.

"C'mon, Karlena, both of us have things to do in the kitchen, so let's get to it!"

5

Everyone was up early Saturday morning to get ready for the big party. The house was in good order. Esdell and the twins finished what little cleaning needed to be done. He and Kareem had set up a few tables and chairs in their basement to be prepared in the advent of rain. Karlena had hung a Happy Anniversary banner on the railing of the deck and placed the helium balloon bouquets in strategic spots on the deck and in the yard. She had covered all the tables with plastic tablecloths and secured them with tape to keep them from blowing off in the wind. The center pieces were simply colorful citronella votive candles that would help ward off the mosquitoes. The barbeque grill was in place and filled with charcoal just waiting to be lit. Kareem had used his computer skills to make a sign that welcomed their guest and to also direct them to the backyard. Esdell was hanging the sign on the front door when Sammy, Christine, and her daughters drove up.

"What's goin' on, bruh?" Sammy asked exiting the car.

"Hey, y'all! Good mornin'!" Esdell said.

"All right, all right! It's 'bout to be on and poppin'! Where you want me to put this cooler?" Sammy said as he went to open his trunk.

"Take it 'round back and sit it in one of the corners of the deck. Let's get the pop on ice."

"We almost didn't have any ice!" Christine said when she got out. "Brainiac, here, forgot the ice! I had to make him stop to get some after he picked us up. There's ice already in the cooler, and there's another bag of ice in the backseat. C'mon girls, get out! One of you take that ice and put it in the freezer and the other one take the mac and cheese and put it in the kitchen. Then see if Karlena needs some help." Her daughters complied after a quick hello to their Uncle Esdell.

"Not much left to do. Me and the kids been humpin'!" Esdell went to the trunk to see what there was for him to carry in. "These bake beans, Chris?" he asked, removing them from the trunk. "They smell good!"

"Smell 'em now, cause we know how they gonna smell later! Beans, beans, the musical fruit…" Sammy sang.

"And how old are you, Junya? Take the cooler 'round back, boy!" Christine barked, pointing to the backyard.

"Yeah, it's on and poppin', all right!" Esdell repeated, watching Sammy stick out his tongue at their sister while heading toward the backyard. "Take these beans, Chris, and I'll get these bags. Girl, looks like you got a week's worth of groceries here."

"I wanna make sure we got enough for everybody! I bought some tiki torches to add to the decorations. And by the way, they're your house warming gift too!"

"Coo'!" Esdell said. He took the bags from the trunk and followed Christine into the house. Once inside, she saw Karlena and her girls sitting at the dining room table, which was covered with napkins, forks, spoons, and knives."

"Hey, Karlena. How you doing?" Christine asked.

"Hi, fine, Aunt Christine. How're you?"

"Good. Whatcha got goin' on here?"

"Celeste and LeAnn are helping me roll the cutlery in the napkins and putting them in a basket. I figured it would keep the serving line moving, plus it's more sanitary than having them sitting out in the open.

"Your college tuition well at work! Go 'head, nurse Karlena!" Christine encouraged. "Where's the baby?"

Karlena pointed down at the table. Christine sat the beans on the table and then bent over to look under it. There sat Micah quietly with his pacifier in his mouth, and his little Colts football in his hands.

"What're you doin' under there, Micah? You being a good boy?" Micah crawled out to see his great auntie. Christine picked him up.

"Micah, you are wrong for that!" Celeste complained. "He wouldn't come out to see us, Mom."

"Well, your mama just got it like that!" Christine boasted.

"Let me hold him, Mommy!" LeAnn asked. Christine passed the baby over.

"Be careful, LeAnn," Christine warned. "I need to bake that mac and cheese. Is there anything in the oven?"

"Yeah, I'm parboiling the ribs and chicken to get them ready for the grill," Esdell answered. "I'll take 'em out they're probably ready." He went into the kitchen with the bags of groceries.

Christine turned to Karlena. "How'd the potato salad turn out?"

Karlena's eyes bulged out slightly because she had not made the salad from scratch. She had taken the potato salad that Esdell had purchased from Gordon Food Service and added more onions and some chopped sweet pickles. She had also added a little bit of white vinegar and sugar. Now she was going to find out if it was good enough to pass her auntie's taste test.

"It's in the fridge, Aunt Christine. Taste it and let me know what you think."

Christine nodded and went into the kitchen, taking the baked beans with her.

LeAnn stood Micah on the floor in front of her and then, holding his hands, she walked him into the living room.

"When's he gonna start walking, Karlena?" she asked.

"I don't think it'll be too much longer. He's pulling up, and he'll walk around as long as he can hold on to something. You keep him entertained while your sister and I finish with the napkins. Oh! Take these balloons, LeAnn, and blow up a few so I can tie them on the tree out front. That way our company can find the house. You can give one to Mick Mick to play with."

"Potato salad's good!" Christine yelled from the kitchen. Karlena smiled knowingly. LeAnn took the balloons and sat in the living floor with Micah close by.

The whole family was busy putting the final touches on the party. Esdell had lit the charcoal in the grill and was ready to start cooking the meat. Karlena and Christine finished preparing the side dishes. They let Celeste and LeAnn prepare the hamburger patties, teaching them how to season the meat and make the burgers even. Micah was put in his playpen to keep him safe and from underfoot. Before they knew it, it was noon. Kareem was hanging the balloons around the maple tree in the front yard when a white minivan pulled up.

"Hey, man, is this the Brown's residence?" a man yelled from the driver's side.

"Yes it is!" Kareem answered.

"I'm Sammy's friend, Dameon, the DJ!"

"Okay! Hold tight and I'll go get him." Kareem went through the house and out the back door and announced Dameon's arrival to Sammy who ran around the side of the house to greet his friend. Dameon had parked and was getting out of his van.

"What's goin' on, Big D? Did you have any trouble finding the house?"

"Not a bit, Sammy, thanks again for this opportunity. I really appreciate it!"

"Ain't no thang, man. Let me drive around back. You can park in the alley and you won't have to carry your equipment so far."

"All right!" Dameon said, tossing Sammy his keys. Sammy drove around to the backyard and backed the van close to where Dameon would set up. They got out and began to unload the van.

"We got a table set up for you over here. There's a heavy-duty extension cord for you to plug into," Sammy instructed. "You need me to help?"

"I got it from here, Sam, thanks. My cousin is coming later to help me. I hope that's all right."

"That's fine. Hey, let me introduce you to my brother." Esdell was walking out with a roaster full of ribs. "Esdell, come meeet the DJ!" Esdell placed the roaster on the side of the grill and went to the DJ's table.

"Esdell, this is Dameon, my boy from work and our DJ for the day. Dameon, this is my much older brother, Esdell," Sammy clowned. "Much, much older brother!"

"Whatever, Junya!" Esdell said, extending his hand to shake. "Good to meet you, man. Thanks for helping us out today. Need any help? Can I get you a pop?"

"No thanks. My cousin will be here soon to help out. Uh, is there anything in particular you want to hear this afternoon?" Dameon asked.

"Old school. Lots of old school," Sammy said, snapping his fingers and dancing around. "Ma and Pops would probably like stuff from the sixties."

"And some Gospel too!" Esdell added.

"Okay, I gotcha! I got plenty of both. Got the sixties, the seventies, and on up to now covered. Okay, let me go ahead and set up. Good to finally meet you, Esdell. Sam talks about you a lot at work."

"I'd like to be a fly on the wall when those conversations are hap'nin! Let me get this meat on the grill."

"It's all good, bruh. Well, I'ma go pick up the guests of honor so they don't have to drive, plus that'll be one less car in the drive," Sammy volunteered.

Esdell returned to put the ribs on the grill, Sammy left to go pick up his mother and stepfather, and Dameon continued to set up his equipment. Karlena, Christine, Celeste, and LeAnn set up the food table and were confident that everyone would enjoy everything on the menu. It was quite a battle trying to keep Kareem from stealing a taste.

Shortly, Sammy returned with Grace and Isaiah, and he escorted them around to the backyard.

"Oh my goodness!" Grace exclaimed. "Everything looks so nice! Y'all have really outdone yourselves! This is too much!"

Karlena rushed to meet her grandmother. "Hi, Grandma and Pops! Happy anniversary!" She gave them both a big hug and kiss.

"Thank you, Karlena. Y'all have done a great job back here!" Isaiah agreed. "Hey there, Christine! Hi girls!"

"Hi, Poppy!" LeAnn ran and wrapped her arms around Isaiah's waist, nearly knocking him over.

"Hi, sweet pea!" Isaiah said, giving her a big hug.

"Grandma, you look really pretty!" Celeste commented as she walked over.

"Why thank you!" Grace said, turning around. "My outfit was part of my anniversary present from my dear hubby!" Grace was sporting a long, white broomstick skirt and a turquoise and white peasant blouse.

"Hi, Mama! You are lookin' foxy fine!" Christine complemented. "Y'all come on up on the deck. We got a special table set aside just for you!"

"Where's my baby boy?" Grace asked.

"Micah's taking a little catnap. I'll go get him in a little while," Karlena answered.

"C'mon, Grandma and Poppy, let's go sit down!" LeAnn insisted, and they complied.

It was not long before the guest started to arrive. The backyard was soon filled with family and friends including Sammy's girlfriend, Danielle, and her parents. Music was playing and the smell of barbeque filled the air. Grace and Isaiah were all smiles as they courteously welcomed their guest. The gift table filled up as everyone showed their love and appreciation for the happy couple. Grace went to the grill to talk to Esdell.

"Baby, this is so nice! I can't thank you enough. Good company, good food, and you even got a DJ!"

"You are most welcome, my dear mama. You deserve this and so much more! Can I get you anything?" Esdell asked.

"No, but I would love to hear some Temptations. Would you ask the DJ for me?"

"Yes, ma'am! Sammy!" Esdell yelled. "Come watch these burgers!"

As Esdell approached the DJ's table, he saw a woman standing there with her back to him talking to Dameon. Her wavy hair hung just above her shoulders. She was wearing a bright fuchsia, sleeveless sundress with metallic gold gladiator sandals. Esdell thought these colors looked especially nice against her dark brown skin. He did not recognize her, but she seemed oddly familiar.

This must be Dameon's cousin, he thought. "Excuse me, ma'am."

"There you go with that ma'am stuff again!" the woman said turning around. Once again, it was Hope! She stood there with the biggest smile on her face holding a vase of red and yellow tulips.

"I don't believe this! What're you doin' here?" Esdell could not believe his eyes. "You stalkin' me, girl?"

"Well, hello to you too, Mr. Esdell Brown. I believe you've met my cousin, Dameon. I'm not stalking you. I'm here helping him out with his first gig. Oh, these tulips are for your mother."

"Man, this is just too wild, and you brought flowers for my mother? How'd you know?" Esdell was perplexed.

"Well," Hope began, "when you were in the store the other day, you said you were giving a barbeque for your mother who had only been married for a year. Then you said your brother Sammy was helping you. Cuz here had asked me to help him with this gig his coworker Sammy was giving, and he had told me all that stuff. So, I just put it all together."

"So that's why you kept giving me those strange looks. Wow, this is a trip! So Dameon's your cousin?"

"Uh-huh!" Hope looked at Dameon who had on headphones and was bopping to the music. "I stopped by the flower shop before I came over here to pick up these tulips. I thought your mother would like them. Why don't you take me over and introduce me and I'll give 'em to her."

"Well, Mama's in the mood for some Tempts. Would you have your cousin play something?"

"Of course. That's what we're here for!" Hope tapped Dameon on his shoulder to get his attention. "Got a request for some Temptations. How 'bout 'Just My Imagination'?" She gave Esdell a look, hoping the hint would be obvious.

"Hold on for a sec, Hope. I'll be right back." Esdell ignored Hope's ploy, leaving for a moment, and returning with Grace and Isaiah. "Mama,

Pops, I want you to meet Sammy's friend from work, Dameon, the DJ, and his assistant slash cousin, Hope. This is Isaiah and Grace Willis, the folks celebrating one year of wedded bliss."

"Good to meet ya! Y'all doin' a fine, fine job," Isaiah said, shaking Dameon's hand.

"You really are!" Grace agreed "Thank y'all so much!"

Hope and Dameon returned the greetings and thanked them for their compliment, but Hope was a little irritated with the way that Esdell had introduced them. It was clear to her that he did not want his mother to think that they were any kind of way friends. She started to protest but decided not to make a scene. After all, she was there to help her cousin and did not want to ruin his reputation at his first job as a DJ.

"Mrs. Willis, these tulips are for you. Happy anniversary," she simply said.

"Thank you, Hope! These are gorgeous! You didn't have ta do this!" Grace and Isaiah continued to chat with Hope and Dameon. Esdell excused himself to return to the grill. After the last of the meat was done cooking, he went back to the DJ table and asked for the microphone. Hope handed it to him without looking at him. She signaled Dameon to fade out the music.

"Attention, everyone!" The crowd quieted and directed their attention to Esdell.

"We want to thank everybody for comin' out today to help celebrate the first anniversary of Mr. and Mrs. Willis." Applause resonated. Esdell signaled for his brother, sister, and children to join him. "Our family is what it is because of these two people. They've been a blessing and an inspiration to us all. Mama, Pops, we want you to know how much we love you, and you can see by all the people that are here, that they love you too. As for me, personally, I can't thank you enough for what you've done for me, and I can't thank God enough. Do y'all have anything you wanna say?"

Grace looked at Isaiah and he nodded his head. She took the microphone from Esdell and held it for a moment, composing herself before she spoke, holding back tears. She cleared her throat.

"I just got so much to say. I don't know where to start. I thank my family for this lovely party, and I thank y'all all for coming to share today with us." Grace looked up at Isaiah. "After Sammy died, I settled in expectin' to live the life of a widow. I wasn't lookin' for love, but God saw fit to bless me with something I didn't even ask for. I love you, Isaiah. I thank the Lord for joining us together to live out our golden years." She gave the mic to Isaiah as she began to tear up again.

"I thank y'all for everything. I thank God too, because if it wasn't for him, I'd still be an old bachelor. He blessed me with the best woman in the world. I love you back, Gracie."

"Woo, woo, woo! It's gettin' kinda thick up in here!" Christine inserted, making everyone chuckle.

"I know that's right!" Sammy Junior agreed.

Esdell took the mic from Isaiah.

"Okay! I know y'all ready to eat, so I'ma ask my son, Reverend Brown, to bless the food. After that, y'all line up at the food tables and get down like ya live! But these two go first! Reverend Brown, would you lead us in prayer, please?" he said, handing the mic to Kareem.

"Let us bow. Heavenly Father, we come, as always, humble before you and thankful to you. We thank you for the blessing of family and friends. We thank you for this couple that you have blessed with a year of happy marriage and pray that you will continue to bless them with many more happy, healthy years together. Now, Lord God, we give thanks for this food that has been prepared for us and ask that you bless it. May it nourish our bodies so we can better serve you! It is in the name of Jesus that we pray. Amen!" Kareem ended his prayer with everyone echoing his amen.

The music resumed. Esdell escorted Grace and Isaiah to the food tables and the guest lined up behind them. He noticed that Hope was glaring at him, so he went over to talk to her.

"You givin' me one of them looks again. Now what?"

"Can we walk around front?"

"Sure! Lead the way."

Esdell followed Hope as she walked around the side of the house heading toward the front yard. He could not help but wonder what was going through Hope's mind. Hope stopped at the corner of the house. She turned around and looked up at Esdell.

"I wasn't gonna say anything, but I just have to let you know that I resent the way you introduced me to your mama!"

"Huh?" Esdell asked.

"The DJ's assistant? Really? What's the matter? You don't want your family to get the wrong idea about us?"

"Us? What us?! I just met you this week!"

"I've been tryna figure out if you're blind or just stupid!" she exclaimed.

"Excuse me?" Esdell retorted. "What you talkin' 'bout!"

"I've been all but throwing myself at you and you just keep playin' me off! I couldn't tell if you were blind to the fact that I'm diggin' on you or if you were just too stupid to get with it!"

"Hope, I'm not blind, I'm not stupid. I knew what you were doin', and I did play you off. I'm in a place now where I'm just not lookin' for a relationship. I didn't want to lead you on. Plus, you just a little too aggressive for me."

"Aggressive? It was just a little innocent flirting. Esdell, I like...I liked you! That's all. And that 'not lookin' for a relationship' line is just an excuse."

"Look, Hope, I'ma tell you this, then I'm goin' back to the party. I'm in a rough spot right now. My head's messed up, and I'm praying and depending on God to help me. Remember I told you my wife was dead?"

"Yes."

"Both me and my wife were in the service, and she got killed in the war. I'm still tryna deal with that! Now I'm devoting everything I got into helping my kids get where they tryna go. My focus is on my kids! I don't have room for much else. Hope, don't get me wrong; I got joy, praise the Lord! But I'm still lookin' to find peace."

Hope shamefully hung her head. "I'm sorry, Esdell. I guess I'm a little messed up myself. I got issues. I know I do. I got a son that's in and out of trouble all the time and his daddy's nowhere to be found. My parents are out of the country most of the time. I don't have nobody, and I'm lonely! There's something that drew me to you. I *am* lookin' for a relationship, but I guess I need to look somewhere else. I'm sorry!"

Hope rushed back to the DJ table. Esdell watched her as she trotted away. He walked slowly to the backyard, deeply sighing.

"Touch us both, Lord, in the name of Jesus!" he whispered. He gathered himself and put a smile on his face to hide the sadness he felt for himself and especially for Hope. Sammy and his girlfriend, Danielle, met him as he approached the food table.

"What's up, bruh? I saw ya now! D's cousin's lookin' good. You feelin' that?" he said, nudging Esdell's arm.

"Sammy, you know you're dippin'!" Danielle said. "Are you feelin' her though?"

"Yeah, y'all, I am, but not like you think! Man, let me get over to this food table."

Esdell fixed his plate and sat with his family to eat. His continued to replay the conversation he had with Hope in his mind. He found himself looking at her from time to time just to check on her. He was touched by their encounter and knew that he would continue to pray that she, too, would find peace. He could tell she was still a little upset, so he took Micah over to her, hoping he could cheer her up.

"Micah wanted to say hi. You remember Miss Hope don't cha, li'l buddy?" Esdell said, taking Micah's hand and waving it.

"Hi there, handsome! How you doin'?" Hope smiled as she rubbed Micah's cheek.

"Did you and Dameon get something to eat? Can I fix you a plate?"

"D's gonna take a break here in a minute, and he'll fix us something. Thanks though."

"Hope, I'm sorry. I—"

Hope interrupted him. "You don't have to apologize. I'm coo'. But not as cool as Micah, with his fine self!"

Karlena was watching the exchange between her dad and Hope and walked over to where they were.

"Hey, Daddy, who's this?" Karlena inquired.

"Oh, hey, baby. Hope, this is my daughter, Karlena Brown. Karlena meet Hope...uh...uh," he stuttered, realizing he did not know her last name.

"Hi, I'm Hope Shah. Nice to meet you."

"Shah? I don't think I've ever heard that name before," Karlena commented.

"It's African," Hope responded.

"How y'all know each other?" Karlena asked.

"This is so tripped out!" Esdell started, sounding almost embarrassed. "First, I had a delivery at the flower shop where she works. Then I ran into her again at GFS, 'cause she works there part time. Then she shows up here because she's working with the DJ, Dameon. She's his cousin!"

"Wow, how many jobs does one person need?" Karlena said. "You're a busy woman."

"Yes, I am! Got things to do! Cute sandals, by the way!" Hope raised her dress slightly to reveal that she and Karlena were wearing the same shoes.

Karlena looked at Hope's feet. "You've got good taste. Especially if you're interested in my daddy!" she asserted slyly.

"Yeah, right, well, I'd better get back to work. I need to give Dameon a break. Nice to meet you, Karlena." Hope walked next to Dameon and took off his headphones. "I got it, D. Go get us some food! Just bring me a burger and some baked beans and a orange pop." Hope put the headphones on her ears, purposely redirecting her attention to the music.

"C'mon, Micah, let's go see Gran gran." It was clear to Esdell that Hope was uncomfortable talking to him now, so he left her at the DJ's table and went to sit with his mother. As he approached her, the song "I Wish" by Stevie Wonder started to play. This was a favorite of both Esdell and his mom. He gave Micah to Karlena.

"C'mon, Mama, let's dance!"

Grace protested, but he pulled her to the center of the deck and started to two-step with her. She smiled and followed his lead.

"Aw, shoot, that's what I'm talkin' 'bout! Let's dance, girl!" Sammy said, taking Danielle by the hands. Soon the rest of the family joined them. Isaiah danced with Karlena, and Christine danced with Kareem. The guest applauded as they watched the family dance around. A few more couples added themselves to the fun. After that, the party was in full swing. The family and guests mingled around. Some danced, some were playing cards, and others just visited. After a while, Grace and Isaiah opened their gifts, reading each card and thanking each person.

"My boy D and his cuz are cookin' ain't they, Big E?" Sammy exclaimed.

"They are!" Esdell agreed. "But look at Ma. I think she's 'bout partied out!"

"Yeah, they do look tired"

"I think its time to wrap this thing up, fellas!" Christine said, approaching her brothers.

"Yeah, we were just sayin' that. I'ma take Ma and Pops home now." Sammy went to ask the couple if they were ready to go and they were. He looked over at the DJ table, signaling Dameon to cut the music. He gave a loud whistle to get everyone's attention.

"Ma and Pops got somethin' to say. Go ahead y'all!"

"Thank everyone for coming. Y'all have really blessed us today. Y'all young folks keep on partying and us old folks is going home!" Isaiah said.

"Thank you all! This has been a wonderful day, and we've enjoyed every minute. Good night!" Grace said.

Grace and Isaiah said their good-byes as they went to Sammy's car. The guest waved to them as they drove down the street. Their departure pretty much ended the party, and it wasn't long until only the family and a few friends remained. They all dug in to clean the backyard. While they were loading up the trash bags and carrying things in the house, Hope and Dameon were packing up his equipment. Hope kept her head down. She did not want to even look at Esdell, but Esdell was looking at her. He had thought to go speak to her again, but decided against it. There really wasn't anything left to say. He had made his point clear about not wanting a relationship, but he still felt badly as he thought he had hurt Hope's feelings. She left without saying good-bye. Apparently, she had nothing to say either.

Sammy returned just as Dameon was loading his van.

"Great job, man, really great job! Thanks so much. Here's a little somethin' for you." Sammy gave Dameon an envelope, and in it was one hundred dollars.

"Thanks, Sam, but I told you I wasn't gonna charge you nothin'." Dameon tried to give the money back, but Sammy protested.

"Keep it. You earned it. Go get you some business cards made up 'cause you are now a professional DJ!" Sammy proclaimed. After a short conversation, Dameon left.

The backyard had been cleared and all the table and chairs had been stacked, ready to be returned to the church. The rest of the guest had left. Only Danielle remained to help the family. Everyone was in the house packing up the leftover food and cleaning up the kitchen.

"Now *that* was a party!" Sammy said.

"Sure was, babe," Danielle agreed.

"I had so much fun, Uncle Sammy. Grandma and Poppy were so happy!" LeAnn added.

"Yeah, everything turned out pretty well, but I got one question," Christine remarked looking at Esdell. "Who was li'l miss hotty in the hot pink dress?"

"She was really cute, Daddy," Karlena said.

"Friend of yours?" Christine questioned.

"No, she was the DJ's cousin, and just someone I met earlier this week."

"I was busy with the party, but I could tell something was going on. Confession is good for the soul, Esdell! What's up?" Christine interrogated.

Esdell rolled his eyes slightly. "Nothin'! Not a thing," he said. *But she is someone I'll be praying for tonight*, Esdell thought to himself.

6

A new normal was developing at Esdell's still new home. Everyone went back to work, and Kareem had started his summerclass at the bible college. Esdell and his coworkers were still waiting to hear on the selling of the company and the status of their jobs. A lot of the workers had already started looking for new jobs, expecting the worse. Esdell, however, had turned all of his concerns over to God. He knew that his worrying would not change a thing and had full faith that, one way or another, the Lord would take care of him. He spent a lot of time trying to encourage his coworkers, especially Gary. The past few days, they had been talking in the employee break room about what Gary had been reading in the devotional book, and the Bible that Esdell had given him. Though Gary had often heard others talk about Christ, he had never developed a personal relationship with Him. He had many questions that Esdell answered as best he could. Esdell had invited Gary to come to Bible study with him, but he declined the offer.

Esdell had also been thinking about Hope, concerned about how she was dealing with their little confrontation. He knew that even though she appeared to be a strong-willed woman on the outside, she could still be hurting on the inside. He remembered she had told him that her son was often in trouble, and that she had no one and was lonely, and he sympathized with her. Hope and Gary were names that he had added to his prayer list.

Esdell had just finished his daily route and was returning to the warehouse. He parked his truck and checked in with dispatch, turning in his invoices and other paperwork. As he was going to the locker room, he saw Gary.

"Gary! What's up, man?"

"Not much. What's up with you?"

"SSDD, same stuff, different day!" Esdell answered. "I had eleven runs today, how 'bout you?"

"I only had five, but I had to unload at all of them. I'm tired. Grateful, but tired!"

Esdell's attention focused on the word *grateful* that Gary had used.

"Yeah, Gary, we gotta lot to be grateful for, don't we?"

"I'm startin' to get that," Gary admitted. "Thanks for the books and spending so much time with me, but I still got a lot of questions. We never went to church when I was coming up. This religion stuff is real!"

"Jesus is real, Gary. We can't do nothin' without Him. The only way to heaven is through him!"

"Esdell, you got some time? Can we go somewhere and talk?" Gary asked.

Esdell thought for a moment. "Sure! I need to check the bus schedule though. Where you wanna go?"

"We can walk over to the Sports Café. I can take you home."

"Fine! I need to call my kids and let them know I'll be late."

Esdell called Kareem and Karlena letting them know that he would be home later than usual.

Esdell and Gary walked down the street to the Sports Café, which was a place that was frequented by Esdell's coworkers. They would meet there to view different sports events and to just hang out. They entered the restaurant and seated themselves in a booth with a window that looked out on the busy city street. Esdell saw that Gary was carrying the Bible he had given him.

"Hi, guys! What can I get cha?" a waitress asked.

"I'll have a beer," Gary answered. "Get whatever you want, Esdell. It's on me."

"Okay, thanks! I'd love some of that raspberry lemon-aid y'all so famous for!"

"Okay, gents, I'll be right back with those."

Gary looked down at the table. "Guess I shouldn't of ordered a beer, huh? Not the religious thing to do."

"No sin in drinkin' a beer, Gary. Drinkin' a beer every now and then ain't gonna doom you to hell," Esdell reassured.

"See, I always thought you religious guys thought drinkin' was a sin. That's why I wanted to talk to you, so you can help me understand what's right and what's wrong!"

Esdell smiled slightly. "I don't always know that myself, Gary. I'm no judge over the rights and wrongs of other people. It ain't my place. As far as drinking; the key is moderation."

"I heard the first miracle of Jesus was turning water into wine. Is that true?"

"Yup, and the apostle Paul said drink a little wine to settle your stomach."

"Really?" Gary was surprised by this information. "So it's okay to drink?"

"Like I said, in moderation. But if it's a problem for you or if it causes a problem for another person if you do drink, you shouldn't!"

"This Bible stuff is a lot!"

"Lemme tell you this, Gary. I've been in church my whole life, and I still don't know everything about the Bible or the mystery of God. God is infinite. But I know and believe this: Jesus Christ is the risen Son of God. Crucified, dead, buried, and resurrected! I'm saved 'cause I believe that!"

"Resurrection? That's about Easter, right?"

"Yeah, basically."

"So how does believing in the resurrection save you?"

The waitress returned with their orders, placing them on the table. "Here're your drinks, guys. You ready to order?"

"Not yet," Gary answered.

"Well, just holler if you need something else."

The waitress briefly distracted Esdell, but he could still see the curiosity and confusion on Gary's face. He quickly thought about how some people go through their lives celebrating Easter and Christmas, year after year, without really knowing the true meaning of these holidays. Now, here was Gary, wanting to know about the road to salvation. Just as quickly as he had this thought, he prayed that the words he was about to speak would bring clarity and better understanding to his friend.

Esdell took the Bible that was lying on the table explaining the concordance in the back and how to use it. He looked up the word *atonement* and was lead to the Old Testament and to Leviticus chapter five and verse number six that read:

As a penalty for the sin they have committed, they must bring to the Lord a female lamb or goat from the flock as a sin offering; and the priest shall make atonement for them for their sin.

He explained about how the shedding of blood by the priests through animal sacrifice was used as the atonement for sins; the making of amends for sins committed. They sat for nearly an hour as Gary asked questions and Esdell answered them. Then Esdell went to the New Testament to explain how Christ came to become the final sacrifice; the final atonement for sin.

"Christ was crucified and His blood ran down. It now covers us. When God looks down on us from above, He doesn't see our sins. He only sees the blood of his Son. It's because of His blood that we are saved! After he died and the final atonement was made, Jesus rose from the dead and returned to heaven to be with the Father. Jesus sits in heaven now, forever being our advocate and intercessor. He's always pleading our case when we ask for forgiveness as believers. Does that make sense, Gary?"

"It's starting to. It's starting to."

"If you want a relationship with Christ, it's like any other relationship. You gotta work on it. You need to read the Bible, that's God talkin' to you. And you gotta pray, that's you talkin' to God.

"I hear ya, man, but I ain't never said a real prayer before. I don't know how," Gary admitted.

"It's not that hard, man. Just talk to Him. Remember that you're talkin' to the Most High God. Remember that and be humble. You can ask him anything. Give Him proper respect, ask Him to forgive you for your sins, give Him thanks, and then just talk to him. Okay?"

"Okay!"

"Well, I hope I helped you some. If you don't mind though, I'm gonna pass on dinner. I need to be heading to the house. You ready?"

Gary got the bill and laid money on the table to pay. "C'mon. Let's go."

They walked to Gary's car and then started the trip to Esdell's house. During the drive, they talked more about the Bible and also about some things that were going on at work. Shortly, they pulled up in front of Esdell's house.

"Thanks for the ride, Gary. See ya tomorrow." Esdell began to open the car door.

"Hold on a minute, Esdell." Esdell stopped. Gary clutched the top of the steering wheel with both hands and laid his forehead on them.

"Hello, God, my name is Gary, but I guess you know that already!" he nervously snickered. "Please forgive me for being a not-so-good person. Thanks for giving me a friend like Esdell. Please be patient with me while I try to be a better person. Thanks!"

Esdell put his hand on Gary's shoulder. "In the name of Jesus. Amen!" he added.

"Yeah. Amen. How's that?"

"Fine. God heard every word! One more thing. I encourage you to find a church. Church is family. A good church family with a good pastor is important for you to grow. See ya tomorrow, Gary!"

"Bye, Esdell. Thanks."

Enough had been said. The seed had been planted, and Esdell left it in the hands of the Lord to grant the increase.

Esdell walked into the house and found Karlena and Micah in the living room. Karlena was watching television, and Micah was sitting on the floor playing with his toys.

"Hey, y'all!" he said, walking toward Micah.

"Stop right there, Daddy!" Karlena ordered. "Stand right there!" She walked over to Micah, standing him on his feet. "Go see, Gramps! Call him, Daddy!" Esdell smiled and stooped down.

"C'mere, li'l buddy!" Cautiously, Micah took one step and then another, and another. He looked like a mechanical robot as he continued step by step, deliberately, until he reached the waiting arms of his granddad.

"All right! Look at you! You're walking!!"

Karlena beamed, clapping her hands. "Yay, Mick Mick! Yay!!" she cheered, almost crying.

"When did this start?" Esdell asked.

"Today at Grandma's. We were sitting in the front room, and he was standing, holding on to Grandma's leg, just sorta bouncing up and down. I was sitting in the big chair across the room drinking some pop, and Micah musta decided he wanted some. He reached for me and then just walked over to me! Turn him around," she said kneeling. "Come to Mommy, Micah!" Once again, Micah started with his Frankenstein-like walk back to his mother. Karlena picked him up and spun him around. "Mommy's big, big boy! You walked before your first birthday! Mommy's so proud of you!"

"That's too much! Let's see if he'll come back. C'mon, Micah, c'mon!" Esdell beckoned and back he came. Esdell picked him up and kissed his cheek. "Who's the biggest li'l man?" he sang.

"What?" Karlena questioned.

"That's the Micah song. I'll sing it for you one day!"

"All righty then! Oh, Daddy, we had dinner at Grandma's, and she sent you a plate. It's in the microwave."

"Okay, good. Kareem in his room?"

"Uh-huh. He's studying. Mick Mick, its time for bed. Let's go get ready for bed," Karlena said, taking Micah from Esdell. "Say night-night."

"G'night, li'l buddy!" Esdell bidded.

He went into the kitchen and looked in the microwave. There he found a plate that his mother had sent him. It contained mashed potatoes, green beans, and a huge slice of meatloaf. Esdell thought it was too late to eat such a large meal and decided just to eat the potatoes and green beans. He made a sandwich with the meatloaf to take in his lunch tomorrow. After tidying up the kitchen, he went upstairs to Kareem's room. He tapped on the door before peeking in.

"Hi, son. Can I come in?"

"Hey, Dad! Sure, c'mon in. What's up? Enjoy your nightout?"

"It was fine. How you doin'?"

"I'm good. Did you see Micah walk?"

"Yeah, I did! That boy's growin' up so fast. He's tryna talk, and now he can walk! Just eleven months old! Kinda reminds me of you."

"Did I walk early?" Kareem asked Esdell.

"You were just about the same age as Micah, 'round eleven months. Karlena walked at just over a year old. Your mama was glad that y'all walked a month apart. She was grateful that she didn't have to chase you both around at the same time! I sure wish she was here to see Micah!"

Kareem smiled.

"Oh, she sees him, all right! You best believe that!"

"You're right," Esdell agreed. "You look real busy. How's your summer class? Gotta test comin' up?"

"Not really! I'm tryna stay ahead of the game. This whole class concentrates on the Pentateuch. It's so detailed and so much info, I can't afford to fall behind. Mosaic and Levitical laws, lotta serious stuff in the first five books of the Bible, Dad."

"Oh, I know that's right, so I'ma let you get back to it. I'ma go watch a little TV after my shower, and I think I'll turn in early. We've been real busy at work, so I'm tired. G'night, son!"

"Night, Dad!"

Esdell completed his nightly routine, which ended with his prayer to God. He gave thanks for being allowed to live another day and prayed that he had pleased the Lord in his actions and deeds. He asked for forgiveness for any wrong he may have committed, and then he presented his prayer list, trying to call everyone he was praying for by name. It was a long list. He included Gary's name, his family, and his coworkers.

"In the name of Jesus. Amen," he said and then climbed into the beds and fell right to sleep.

* * *

Morning came quickly. Esdell stood, reading the morning paper at the corner bus stop. The bus pulled up, the door opened, and Esdell boarded.

"Mornin', Don!"

"Hey, Esdell. How you hangin'?" the bus driver asked.

"I'm hangin'! How 'bout you?" Esdell asked taking a seat.

"I'm hangin' in there too. Hey, I need to ask you something."

"What's that?"

"Somebody left their *Indianapolis Business Weekly* paper here on the bus, and I saw an article saying that they were selling your company. Is that true?"

"Well, we were told that the bosses were talkin' 'bout it. We thought we woulda heard 'bout the final decision by now, but we haven't heard yet."

"Think you gonna lose your job?"

"I don't know. It's possible. I just prayed on it and turned it over to God."

"That's all you can do! I'll be praying for y'all too," Don said. "This is a bad time for anybody to be losing a job. Hard times!"

"You sho' right about that!"

"Morning, ma'am," Don said as a woman boarded the bus. His attention and conversation then shifted to the new passenger, which was fine with Esdell because he was content to read his paper all the way to work.

Soon, Esdell got off the bus and made his way to work. As he walked into the warehouse, he noticed a limousine parked near the back door of the building.

Must be Mr. Moore. Today could be the day! Touch, Lord!

Hank was standing by the time clock.

"No need to clock in, just go straight to the break room!" he ordered. "There are no route assignments today."

"What's goin' on, Hank?"

"Just go in. Mr. Moore's here, and he'll answer all your questions."

Esdell followed the instructions of his boss. He bought a cup of coffee and sat down, waiting for the rest of his coworkers to join him. One at a time, the room filled. Gary found Esdell and sat next to him.

"I guess this is it! The big announcement!" Gary stated.

"Guess so. How you doin', Gary."

"Good, Esdell, good. I don't believe it, but I'm good!"

"I'm glad. Let's send up a little prayer now."

"Man, I worked on that prayer thing most of last night," Gary admitted. They both bowed briefly.

"You guys better pray, because we're all about to be unemployed!"

Esdell and Gary looked up to see the same menacing man that Esdell had had the dispute with the last time they had a meeting with Mr. Moore.

"Back on up, man. We ain't in the mood to hear from you today," Gary said, peering back at the man.

"What! You funny, man. I just know you not starting something with me!"

"Chill out, both of you!" Esdell interrupted. "We don't know what's gonna happen."

"We didn't have to clock in, and you saw we didn't have any runs today. They worked us like dogs all this week to get the final orders done in time to close the warehouse. You gotta see that, unless you blind," the man said.

"Let's all just wait and see what's gonna happen. It's out of our hands and God's in control," Esdell said.

The angry man smirked. "Aw, I see now. You're one of them Bible bangers, huh?"

Esdell rolled his eyes, he looked at the man, and then at Gary.

"I don't bang on my Bible, but I do stand on it!"

"Quiet, everyone! Quiet!" Hank said. He and Mr. Moore had entered the room just in time to stop the argument. "Let's get to it. Here's Mr. Moore."

Mr. Moore stepped forward but standing next to him was a young woman with long, light brown hair and green eyes.

"Good morning, everyone. I know that you all have been waiting to hear on the sale of the warehouse, and I apologize that the decision wasn't made sooner." Mr. Moore cleared his throat. "Ladies and gentlemen, I am not a young man. You know how long I have been in this business. I had always hoped that my children would want to continue with the company. They don't, and they want me to sell."

"Here it comes!" Gary said as he tensed up.

Mr. Moore continued, "I am sixty-seven years old, and after much thought and prayers, I've decided that I probably have a few good years left in me! I will continue to be the owner of Moore's Warehousing and Delivery Service!"

The sound of cheers exploded in the break room. Everyone began to hug each other and give high fives.

"Quiet, everybody, I'm not finished!"

Everyone quieted down to hear what else Mr. Moore had to say.

"There will be a few changes. I want you all to meet my daughter, Dawn Moore-Reyes. Out of all of my kids, it was my daughter who changed her mind and decided to stick it out with her old man. She will be the one who will be stepping up to take a more active role in running things. She will handle most of the day-to-day decisions. Dawn is fair, but Dawn is tough!" His daughter smiled but nodded her head. "I'll let her take it from here. Dawn." Dawn stepped in front of Mr. Moore.

"I will keep this brief and to the point. This company is not making much money, so it's necessary for us to make some changes. First of all, there will be a hiring freeze, no new jobs. Our number of employees will be decreased by attrition. If someone quits or retires, you will not be replaced. This mean those of you who stay will have more work to do. Secondly, your future raises will be determined by your work performance. In the past, you have received an automatic cost of living raise each year, not anymore. If you work well, you will be paid well. No work, no raise. There will be no more overtime, and there will be no more Christmas bonuses." The workers began to moan and murmur. "I know these changes may be hard for you to deal with, but they are necessary to keep this company up and moving."

"Sounds like job security to me," Esdell said.

Dawn looked in his direction. "For a little while, anyway, sir. Dad, did you have anything else to add?"

Mr. Moore stepped forward again.

"Thank you, Dawn. Well, I want to give you a little time to absorb all of this. I know you all are wondering why you didn't have to clock in and why you have no deliveries to make today. You were probably also wondering why the deliveries this week were so excessive. That was by design. I had Hank purposely do scheduling like that so you could have today free. Against the wishes of Dawn here, everybody take the day off, with pay! Enjoy your weekend. If you have questions later, give them to Hank."

Mr. Moore and Dawn left the room while mixed emotions ran throughout the break room.

"Do you believe that?" Gary asked Esdell. "What do you think about that?"

"I think we owe God a big thank-you! What do you think?"

"I think so too. Thank you!" he shouted. Gary then saw his angry coworker scoffing at the praise that he and Esdell were sharing. "I also think you better work on your attitude or you might be looking for a job!" Gary said to him. The mean coworker cursed and stormed away.

"Wanna hang out, Esdell? The day is young, and I feel like celebrating! We can go have breakfast or something."

"Thanks for the offer, but I think I'll just go home and chill."

"Okay, I get it. I'll take you home," Gary offered.

They exited the building, and Gary drove Esdell home. They were elated that they would not be losing their jobs. Esdell was especially happy for Gary. He knew that Gary had just learned what it meant to pray and to have faith. He was thankful that God had allowed him to see Gary get a good start on his spiritual journey.

* * *

Gary pulled up in front of Esdell's house.

"Thanks, man. You have a good time today and stay out of trouble!" Esdell said as he got out of the car. Gary waved and drove off.

Hmm, Kareem's home! Esdell thought when he saw Kareem's car in the driveway. When he entered the house, he saw Kareem sitting on the couch, dressed in his suit and tie as if he were going to work. Esdell's entrance startled Kareem.

"Dad! What're you doing home?"

"I was 'bout to ask you the same thing. I see you're dressed for work. You comin' or goin'?" Esdell questioned.

"Neither! I called into work for my sales calls to save myself a trip to the office and to save gas. They told me not to bother coming in. They fired me, Dad. I lost my job. They said I wasn't making enough sales."

Esdell shook his head. How ironic it was that his job had been spared and then he comes home to an unemployed son.

Why, Lord? he thought. "It's all right, Kareem. You didn't like that job no way! It's just a—"

"I know, Dad. It's just a faith test. I get that. I've been sitting here praying and just asking for direction. One door closed, so now I'll just wait on the next door to open. I get it!"

"All right. Ain't nothin' for me to say then!"

"What're you doing home this time of day, Dad?"

"Uh, they gave us the day off!"

"Wow, what a deal. Dad, did you get a chance to ask your boss if there was a job for me there at the warehouse?"

More irony! The very day that a job freeze was announced at Moore's, Kareem asked if they were hiring.

"No, son. They won't be doin' any hiring at my job for a while. In fact, we just had a meetin' about that today. The company's not doin' so great. We had to give up a few things here and there. But, thank God, we still got our jobs!" Esdell understood even more now the importance and the blessing of keeping his job. He would now have to help his son with his daily expenses.

"Oh well! I guess I'll get up here to my room, get on the internet, and see what jobs are out there!"

"Hold on, son! There's a reason that we both got a free day today. I think it's so we can spend it together. We never get a chance to do that. What do ya think about us just hangin' out?"

"I can't think of anything I'd rather do today, Dad!"

"All right then! We can do whatever you want. Got anything in mind?"

Kareem sat to think for a moment and then said, "Remember back when you'd take me to the park to teach me how to play basketball?"

"You know I do!" Esdell said with a smile.

"You got any game left, old man?"

"I got plenty game left, young blood. And any game you got, you got it from me!"

"Well, let's do this thang then! We can go to the church gym!" Kareem said, standing and posturing as if he were challenging his father to a fight.

"Let's change and be out then!" Esdell said, walking toward Kareem. "And don't be crying after I put this spankin' on you!"

They both laughed and went to their rooms to change. In a matter of minutes, they were in the car on their way to the church.

When they got into the gym, they saw two men shooting around at one end of the court. The men looked up, recognizing Esdell and Kareem.

"Hey, Reverend Brown, y'all up for a game?"

"You wanna play, Dad.?" Kareem asked.

"Sure! A little two on two sounds good!"

"Okay, yeah, we'll play!"

"Play to 32?" one of the men asked.

"Coo'!" Kareem agreed.

The game began slowly at first but escalated to a fever pitch in no time. The men played as if they were playing in the NBA finals. Esdell marveled at Kareem's athletic abilities. He'd never seen Kareem play basketball all out like this before. Kareem was impressed with Esdell's skills as well, thinking his father was in great shape and still had that game he was bragging about. Both Esdell and Kareem were over six feet tall, which gave them a clear advantage. They made a great team; playing almost telepathically.

"Shot, Dad! Good shot!" Kareem cheered.

"Rebound! Get it!"

"Foul!"

The basketball banter went back and forth and so did the score. Their opponents were not going down easily. The game was becoming more and more physical.

"Here, Dad, I'm open!"

Esdell's eyes zeroed in on Kareem standing under the basket. He looked left and right and then passed the ball to Kareem with precision; like threading a needle. Kareem caught the ball and elevated to slam dunk it into the basket."

"Woo! That's game!" Esdell screamed. "That's my boy! Woo! That's what I'm talkin' 'bout!!" He ran to Kareem, giving him a hard high five and a chest bump.

"Good game!" the men relented.

From the end of the bleachers, they heard someone clapping. It was Pastor Edwards who had been watching them play. They walked over to where he was sitting.

"What a game! Good job, y'all," Pastor Edwards commented.

"Thanks, Pastor," Kareem said.

"Kareem, I thought that was your car in the parking lot. I'm glad you're here. You just saved me a phone call. May I see you in my office?" Pastor Brown asked.

"Yes, sir!"

"Give me a few minutes to check my messages, and then come on in," Pastor Brown instructed.

"Okay." Kareem watched as the pastor left and then turned to Esdell. "I wonder what that's about."

"Oh no! It's time for the senior sister's aerobic class!" one of the men said. "Here comes Sister Collette Cummins, the cougar! Y'all know she be pinchin' booties!"

"Yeah, man, I know! She pinched me last Sunday when I was walking around for tithes and offering," Esdell admitted. "That woman's almost eighty years old. She needs to go sat down somewhere!"

"Hey, y'all!" Sister Cummins said, walking up to the group. "How you doin', Reverend Brown? You lookin' mighty fine, standing over there all tall and sweaty! Come give Sister Cummins a hug!"

Kareem grabbed her hands before she got too close and kissed her on the forehead. "I'm just fine, Sister Cummins. I gotta go talk to the pastor. You have a good day, now," he said, backing away from her, grinning. "I'll see you shortly, Dad."

Sister Cummins's attention turned to the remaining three men. "Y'all look pretty fine too!" She walked toward them, and they all simultaneously plopped down on the bleachers, protecting their back sides.

"Thanks, Sister Cummins. You look pretty good yourself. Looks like your aerobic class is workin'. Hey, they're 'bout ready to start!" Esdell was delicately trying to send Sister Cummins on her way. She was momentarily detracted when she looked in the direction of her upcoming class.

"They're starting on time for once!" she said.

"Well, gotta go!" Esdell quickly dashed toward the exit while she was looking away, leaving his two basketball opponents to deal with Sister Cummins. Before anyone could speak, he was out of the door and in the hallway. The men laughed and shook their heads in disbelief.

Esdell walked down the hall that led to the sanctuary. He entered quietly and looked around before he took a seat on a back pew. The sanctuary was usually filled with over three hundred people, and Esdell had never been there alone. There was a huge stained glass window behind the pulpit and choir stand. The mosaic picture depicted the cross with a crown hanging on it, and there was a dove flying above the cross with an olive leaf in its beak. The sun brightly showed through the window making its colors cast down throughout the sanctuary like a dancing rainbow. Esdell looked at the communion table that sat at the front of the church below the pulpit. He thought of all the things that had taken place at that very spot. He smiled when he thought about all the Christmas and Easter speeches he had recited there as a child. It was there where both he and his children professed their belief in Christ. He was married there. The bodies of both his dad and his Kenya had lain in state there; Kenya in a closed casket. Esdell shook his head wildly, wanting to dispel this memory. He then remembered how he had escorted his mother down the aisle at her second wedding, giving her another chance at love. Most recently, he witnessed his son accept his calling to preach the Gospel of Jesus Christ. So much of his life had been played out there where the communion table sat, in the front of the Road to Damascus Baptist Church.

I can feel Him! Esdell thought. *I can feel the presence of the Lord!* He bowed his head to pray. "Lord, am not askin' for anything today. I just want to thank you for this very minute. Thank you for letting me enjoy this day with my son. It did not have to be, and I give you praise!"

"Hey, Dad," Kareem said standing in the door. "You ready to go? I didn't know I was gonna be so long in Pastor's office." Over an hour had passed.

"It's fine. I've just been spendin' time with God here."

"I know that God is everywhere, but it seems like you can really feel Him here!"

"Yup, and I do. How was your talk with Pastor?"

"It was good! Check this out, Dad. He wants to start an outreach ministry to the Juvenile Corrections Center, and he wants me to head it up. Do you believe that?"

Esdell smiled and nodded his head. "I guess that's that door openin' you were talkin' 'bout."

"It's just amazing, Dad. I just lose my job today, then Pastor calls me in to head up a new ministry. I may not have had time if I was working, but now I can dedicate this time to this new ministry. It's amazing! I won't be earning money, but this opportunity will pay off in much greater ways."

"Yes it will, Reverend 'Reem. Yes it will! I'm proud of you, Son. God's usin' you in a mighty way. I know you gonna do a good job!"

"Thanks, Dad. Just pray for me!"

"I always do! You ready to go?" Esdell asked.

"Yes, I need to get home and make a call to the juvenile center to see what we need to do to start our ministry there. I should probably call the unemployment office too!" Kareem laughed.

"Well, let's get on home then!"

7

"No! Kenya, No! The bomber! Look out!" Esdell screamed in his sleep. "Oh my god, no!"

Kareem and Karlena, hearing their dad's screams, had met in the hallway.

"You heard that, Kareem?" Karlena frantically asked.

"Yeah!" he answered, entering his father's room. Karlena followed just behind him. When they entered the room, they saw Esdell violently tossing and turning in his bed. He was no longer screaming, but he was moaning.

"Kenya! Hmm! No! The bombs!" he whimpered. Then again he screamed, "No! No!"

"We should wake him up!" Kareem said, approaching the bed, but Karlena grabbed him by the arm.

"No! He's having a nightmare. Don't go near him. He could wake up fighting!" she warned.

"What should we do then?"

"Uh, call him! Daddy! Daddy, wake up!" she hollered. Kareem followed suit.

"Wake up, Dad!"

"Huh! Wha…What's the matter? What is it?" Esdell sat up in the bed. He was soaked with perspiration and was panting heavily. You could almost see his heart beating through is T-shirt. Once it was evident that Esdell was fully awake, Karlena ran to him and wrapped her arms around him.

"Daddy, it's okay! It's okay!"

"You're safe, Dad. It's all right!" Kareem reassured.

Esdell sat for a moment trying to collect himself.

"All right! I'm all right! Go back to bed! Leave me alone. I'm fine!"

The twins looked at each other and saying nothing, left the room, going back into the hallway.

"Let's go in my room," Karlena said, gently pushing Kareem in his back to lead him in that direction. She sat down on her bed. "Kareem, I'm worried! Dad's been having trouble sleeping, and now he's having nightmares!"

"I know! I've been hearing him through the walls. He's been moaning and talking in his sleep."

"He might have posttraumatic stress disorder."

"That make sense! Just now he was yelling mom's name and talking about bombs. What do we do?"

"It's weird that this is just starting with Daddy. I learned in my psych class that PTSD usually starts right after a traumatic experience. He's talking about Mama, and it's been years since she died."

"Maybe it's because he's surrounded by all of their stuff again since we moved in here. It could be bringing up memories that he can't deal with."

"He has never talked about what he saw in the war. He's been holding it all in."

"He said he'd never tell us about his experiences in Iraq. He doesn't want to put those images in our heads. But what can we do to help him?" Kareem asked again.

"Well, its past time for him to talk about it. If he won't talk to us, he may need to get professional help."

"You mean a psychiatrist?"

"I don't need no psychiatrist!"

The twins were alarmed to turn around and see their father standing in the doorway. "Y'all don't need to be talkin' 'bout sendin' me to some shrink!"

"Daddy, there's nothing wrong with seeing a therapist!" Karlena conveyed.

"I'll turn this over to God. He's the only therapist I need!"

"But, Dad," Kareem interrupted. "God can work through people."

"Don't start preachin' to me, boy! I know what God can do! Y'all go back to bed before you wake up Micah!"

Esdell stormed out of Karlena's room leaving them stunned and speechless. But he quickly returned. "I'm sorry, kids! I didn't mean to snap at y'all like that. I know y'all concerned about me, but I'll be okay.

I'm just goin' through a little rough patch now. I appreciate you guys checkin' on me. I'm fine. I'm fine. I'm goin' back to my room now."

Karlena looked at her clock as Esdell left her room. It was just after 3:00 a.m.

"Let's try to get back to sleep, Kareem. We can't do anything now."

"I don't know how I'ma get back to sleep after that! Good night, Karlena."

Kareem returned to his room. Karlena sat momentarily on the side of her bed, being thankful that Micah had slept through everything.

"Bless him, Lord. Give him peace!" she prayed. She turned off the light and lay back down, hoping to fall asleep.

Kareem, who had returned to his room, was also praying to God, asking that He would grant his dad peace. He lay listening for sounds coming from his dad's room. Their rooms were next to each other, so it was easy for him to hear sounds through the walls. It was silent. Kareem hoped that Esdell was falling asleep.

Esdell, however, lay in his bed trying to understand why he still struggled with bad dreams. He did just as his children had done; he prayed for peace.

"Lord, I thought I was getting better. What is it that you want me to learn from these dreams? I've tried to keep it from my children that I'm still strugglin' with Kenya's death, but now they know and will worry. It's time, Lord. It's past time for me to be over this. I count it done that you will quiet these bad dreams. Ease the minds of my kids. Please don't keep them up worryin' 'bout me. Please, Father! Amen!" Esdell rolled over on his side and closed his eyes hoping that sleep would come quickly and peacefully, but he continued to toss and turn.

*   *   *

Soon it was 5:00 a.m. It was Saturday, so at least Esdell didn't have to go to work.

What's the use? I might as well get on up, he thought. His body and clothes were musty because he had perspired so heavily from his nightmares, so he took a shower. When he was done, he returned to his room, dressed, and began to read his Bible. After reading for a few minutes, he decided he needed some fresh air, so he went outside to sit on his deck to read. Esdell read the entire book of James. It was reaffirmed that everyone would experience trials, but they would benefit him in the end. When he finished, he relaxed on the chaise lounger letting the sun shine on his face and feeling the cool breeze. He again felt the presence of the Lord and remembered how he had this same feeling that day he was alone in the sanctuary of the church. More confirmation that God is everywhere!

He drifted off to sleep but was soon awakened by the sound of Micah crying in the kitchen. Then he heard Karlena talking.

"Shhh, Micah, Gramps is on the deck sleeping. We want him to rest."

Esdell yawned and rubbed his eyes. He stood and went through the back door, entering the kitchen.

""Mornin', li'l buddy!" he said to Micah who was sitting in his high chair.

"Sorry, Daddy, I was trying to keep him quiet so you could sleep. How you feelin'?" Karlena asked.

"I'm fine, baby girl. Really, I am. I'm sorry 'bout this mornin'."

"No need to apologize. Me and Micah are about to eat some cereal. Can I fix you some eggs or something else?"

"No, thank you. But I could use some coffee. Strong coffee!"

"Me too," Karlena admitted. "I'll make some."

"Karlena, about this mornin', I…I'm not really ready to talk about it, but I don't want you and Kareem to worry. I'll work it out."

"Daddy, I can understand that you don't want to talk to me or Kareem, but please think about talking to someone."

"I told you this morning, I don't need a psychiatrist!" Esdell was raising his voice.

"Okay! Okay! But at least talk to Pastor Edwards."

"I'ma go get the paper." Esdell was clearly trying to avoid the subject.

"It's here on the counter," Karlena said, handing him the paper. He snatched the paper from her. Karlena knew that it was time to change the topic of discussion, and she knew just what to talk about next.

"Daddy, you know what's coming up next week, right?"

"What?" Esdell said, trying to calm down.

"It's Micah's first birthday! I know you didn't forget that!"

"Li'l buddy, you about to be the big 0-1! How 'bout that?" The scowl that seemed to be imbedded on Esdell's face was replaced by a huge smile. He went to Micah and lifted him out of his high chair. "You are such a good boy. We should give you a big party!"

Karlena sighed, feeling relieved that her dad's mood had been lightened.

"I was thinking about that. Micah's only gonna be one. He won't remember a party. I was thinking that we would just have the family over and have ice cream and cake. It'll be like a really small party. Besides, it's only been a month since we had that big barbeque for Grandma and Pops. Is that okay?"

"Whatever you want. Uh, will you be inviting Jeff and his parents?"

Jeff was Micah's absentee father who had never wanted to be a part of his son's life. He had even denied being Micah's father until a DNA test proved that he was. Karlena had filed for child support, but Jeff barely worked at any job long enough for her to receive anything. His parents were quite elderly, so Karlena would take Micah to their home from time to time so he could get to know his grandparents. Jeff lived with his parents but was always conveniently out when they came to visit.

"I'll invite them. I really want them to be here, but I don't think they'll come."

"All you can do is ask them. It's the right thing to do, and I'm proud that you keep tryin'. Micah should know his people."

Karlena shrugged her shoulders. "I agree, Daddy." She then looked at the floor.

"What's wrong, baby girl?" Esdell asked.

"If Jeff doesn't start coming around, what will I tell Micah when he gets old enough to start asking about his father? We never had a real relationship. He pretended to be my boyfriend until he…He was my first and still my only. It was just that one time. I still feel ashamed about that."

"Karlena, we talked about this already! God has forgiven you, so that's that! There ain't no better mother than you. You love Micah so much. You try so hard to do the right thing. You just keep doin' what you're doin'. If there's anything missin', you got us to take up the slack!"

"He's got a really good role model in you, Daddy. I'm grateful for that." Karlena poured water into the coffeepot and turned it on. "This'll be ready shortly. Are you sure you don't want me to fix you some breakfast?"

"I'm sure. I got one more question though. You gonna invite Joseph too?" Karlena smirked and crossed her arms.

"I sure am! Joseph may be just my boyfriend, but he was more of a dad to Micah on the first day we met than Jeff has been in a whole year!"

"Okay then. But, Karlena, don't deny your ole dad a chance to fire up his grill. I can at least queue up a few hot dogs and throw in some chips for Micah's first birthday."

Karlena smiled. "Fine, Daddy!"

Kareem slowly entered the kitchen, scooting his feet and rubbing his eyes.

"Mornin', everybody. What's up?"

"We're having a little get-together for Micah's birthday next week," Karlena answered.

"Whatever you decide, I'm down. Which one of you is fixin' breakfast?"

"You're on you own," Esdell said as he went to pour himself a cup of freshly brewed coffee.

"You okay, Dad?" Kareem asked.

"It's all good, son. No worries."

* * *

The week went by quickly, and it was again Saturday and time for Micah's birthday party. Esdell and the twins had made the house ready for the family. He took great pride in his large backyard and made sure that everything was trimmed up nicely. Karlena had decorated the deck again and had purchased a decorated yellow cake with chocolate icing. Everything fell into place easily since the party was just a small gathering. Everyone was out on the deck enjoying a sunny June day. All of Esdell's family was there. Joseph had come to the party and brought a gift, but he had to leave early because he was scheduled to work. Even though Karlena had invited Jeff and his family, none of them showed up. Micah, of course, was none the wiser. He was walking from person to person, practicing his new skill. He was no longer content with just sitting in his high chair. It seemed that everyone was getting the biggest kick out of just watching him walk. He was dressed in navy blue shorts, a light blue tee-shirt, and sandals; a new birthday outfit purchased for him by his mommy. He almost seemed to model his clothes as he walked around.

"Anybody want another hotdog?" Esdell asked.

"Not me! I'm ready for cake!" Sammy said licking his lips. "Bring it on!"

"There goes Junya, the munch monster!" Christine said.

"Let's open the gifts!" LeAnn suggested. Her big sister, Celeste, looked at her, putting her hands on her hips.

"You act like you're getting something, LeAnn. All these gifts are for Micah!"

"I know that!" LeAnn snapped back.

"I think that's a good idea, LeAnn. Micah, baby, come to Mommy and let's open your gifts." Karlena held out her hands and Micah walked over to her.

Karlena sat on the floor of the deck and sat Micah on her lap. LeAnn handed the gifts to them one at a time, and Karlena helped Micah tear open each package. Everyone ooh'd and aah'd at each gift, but Micah was just enjoying ripping the paper. He had received enough clothes to outfit him for the summer, and plenty of toys, including a toy basketball goal from Esdell. His great-grandma, Grace, was a big believer in reading to a child early, so she and Isaiah brought him books. After all the gifts had been opened, Sammy spoke up again.

"*Now* it time for cake!"

Karlena went into the kitchen and brought out Micah's birthday cake with one candle stuck in it. She sat it on the patio table. She stripped Micah down to his diaper and put him in his high chair. She then put a pointy Happy Birthday cap on his head. LeAnn passed the hats out to everyone and insisted that they each wear one. Esdell lit the candle, and everyone sang "Happy Birthday," Stevie Wonder style.

"Blow, Micah, blow!" Karlena instructed. Micah blew several times, but it took a gentle blow from his mother's lips to help put out the candle.

"Yay, Micah!" everyone cheered and clapped. Karlena gave Micah the first piece of cake before serving everyone else. Micah tore into it with both hands, and it was not long before almost his whole body was covered with chocolate icing. Everyone laughed at the sight of Micah gobbling down his birthday cake, enjoying every bite.

"Oh my goodness, Mick Mick, you're a messy punkin'!" Karlena said, wiping Micah's face and hands with a wet cloth. "Let's go get you cleaned up." She took him from his high chair and went in the house on a straight course to the bathroom. As she approached the stairs, the front doorbell rang. She went to the door and looked through the peephole.

"Oh, my god! Incredible!" she whispered. She opened the door. "Hi, Jeff, come in." It was Micah's father. He entered the house arrogantly, walking in as if he owned the place.

"Wus up, Karlena? Aw shoot, look at Michael."

Karlena rolled her eyes and sighed heavily. "Say hello, *Micah*. His name is Micah, not Michael!"

"I know! I was jus' playin'. Wus up, li'l nigga? Looks like you been grubbin' on some cake."

"Uh, no you won't! Don't call him that—ever!" Karlena was speaking softly but deliberately through her teeth. She did not want to yell at Jeff and was trying very hard to keep her cool for Micah's sake.

"I'm jus' playin'!"

"Well, stop it! Stop playin'. Micah, say hello to your father. Say hi." She took his hand a waved it. "We're just finishing up out back. C'mon on out and speak to everyone. I'll fix you a plate."

"No, I'm coo'. I came to bring shawty a gift from Mom and Pops, and a li'l somthin' from me." Jeff handed Karlena an envelope. She looked at it, and it was obvious to her that the envelope was once sealed but had been opened. She read the printed card and then the handwritten message.

"Happy birthday, Micah. This might not be much, but it is sent with much love from Grandma and Grandpa. God bless you!" Karlena turned the card upside down and shook it as if she were expecting something to fall out. "Was there money in here, Jeff?"

"Was suppose to be. You know they old. They musta forgot to put it in there."

"Must have!" she said with disgust.

"Here man! This from me." Jeff handed Karlena a sack. She put Micah on the floor, and he held on to her leg to steady himself, and then he walked toward Jeff.

"He's walkin' already?" he said, stepping back.

"Yes he is. You don't have to move away. He won't bite. You can pick him up if you want to. Micah's very friendly." *But I should probably teach him not to talk to strangers!* she thought.

"No, I'm coo'. I ain't tryna let him get chocolate on my gear!"

"Come here, baby, let's see what's in the sack." Karlena took Micah by the hand and led him toward the dining room. She sat down and put Micah in her lap. Jeff stood over them.

"Sit down, Jeff." Karlena stuck her hand in the bag and pulled out a plastic watergun, which had clearly been purchased from one of the dollar stores. "Oh, look at this!" she said, immediately putting it back in the sack. She would have no part of giving Micah a gun, plastic or not.

"What's wrong? You don't like it?" Jeff asked.

"Well, it's the thought that counts. The question is: what were you thinking? Jeff, I'm just really into educational toys for him at this age. I'm glad you came over though. It means a lot that you came to help celebrate our son's first birthday. Thank you."

"Yeah, right. I need to holla at cha 'bout somethin'." Karlena looked at him, narrowing her eyes. Jeff leaned forward in his seat. "Uh, I...uh... filed my taxes a few months ago, and I been waitin' on my refund check. I called the IRS to see why I ain't got it yet, and they said they sent it to you. You get it yet?"

Karlena stared blankly at Jeff for a second with her mouth open.

"Oh, I see. So that's why you're here. Not for Micah, but for money! Well, no, I haven't received a check yet. The government runs a little slow, but it's good to know that it's coming!"

"I need that cash, girl. When you get it, I'ma need you to sign it ova to me!"

"You're jus' playin' again, right? When and if I get that check, it's going straight on Micah! I'm surprised you even held a job long enough to be able to file taxes!"

"Naw, I ain't playin'!" Jeff said, raising his voice. "I need a car, and I want my money!"

"Are you freakin' kiddin' me, Jeff?" Now, Karlena was raising her voice as she stood up, placing Micah on her hip. "You have not done one thing for this baby! You didn't even know his name. You owe Micah this money, and he will get it. I'm not giving you one penny! Are you serious? This is your son, and I would think you would want the best for him. How can you look at his face and not want to do better, to be the father you can be?"

Jeff stood up. "I ain't tryna hear that. That's *your* son!"

Karlena shook her head as her eyes began to fill with tears. She fully realized now, without a doubt, that Jeff was not planning to ever claim Micah as his own.

"You're right! He's mine. He doesn't even know you! You weren't around when he was born, when he got his first tooth, or took his first steps. His first word was mama! He's mine! I'm taking care of him, and that includes keeping the money that's owed to him by his jacked up father!"

"You gonna give me that paper!" Jeff yelled, grabbing Karlena's arm, almost causing her to drop the toddler. This scared Micah, and he began to cry.

"Get your hands off me!" Karlena screamed, standing Micah on the floor.

"Is there a problem here?" Suddenly, out of nowhere, Esdell was looming in the doorway. "I just know you ain't got your hands on my daughter! What the hell is your problem, boy!" He angrily approached Jeff. Karlena picked up Micah and stepped between them.

"I'm all right, Daddy! Go back outside, please!" she begged.

"Not a chance. You take Micah upstairs. I need to have a little conversation with this boy!"

"I got cha boy, ole man!" Jeff said.

"Jeff, be quiet, just leave. Please!" Karlena pleaded. She lowered her voice because she knew her brother, her uncle, and her grandfather were outside, and if they heard what was going on, they could come in the house too. Things could become far worse.

"I told you to go upstairs, Karlena. Take Micah upstairs and clean him up. I got this. Go now!"

"Daddy, I need you to go back outside, now. I'm okay. We're just having a little misunderstanding."

Esdell turned and looked at Karlena in a way that made it clear that she needed to do what she was told. She knew that there would be more of a problem if she stayed, so she reluctantly took Micah upstairs.

"What?" Jeff said defiantly, glaring at Esdell who smiled and nodded his head.

"Why you here, boy?"

"I got business with Karlena. It ain't got nothin' to do with you! And I don't 'preciate you rollin' up on me like you gonna do somethin'! And I ain't no boy!"

"You whatever I call you! You got nerve comin' in here puttin' your hands on Karlena like that. Dangerous, boy, real dangerous!"

"I ain't scared of you!" Jeff said.

"Okay, but lemme tell you somethin'." Esdell lowered his voice and bit his bottom lip. "It *is* my business when you come in my house, messin' with *my* daughter. I been givin' you the benefit of the doubt, tryna give you time to grow up and stand up to your responsibility. But you just showed me what you're made of. If you don't want Karlena and Micah, just leave 'em alone. If you don't mean them no good, they don't need you. I'll take care of them. They gonna be all right! So, leave now, before...Just get out, boy!"

"Look, I already done told you don't call me boy and that I ain't scared of you! I'll go when I'm done talkin' to Karlena! You betta back up off me!"

"Oh, you're done! Since you don't come around, you don't really know nothin' about me, so let me tell you some things. I been in a war, and I've seen and done some real bad stuff. Things that would make a li'l punk like you pee his pants. Things that affected me in a bad way. Now, my kids already think I got PTSD!" Esdell walked a little closer to Jeff. "Boy, I could snap your neck and break your back before you could blink an eye and get away with it! Don't mess with me and definitely don't mess with my family! You been warned. Now, I'm tellin' you again, you're done and GET OUT!" Esdell's voice was like that of a growling lion and the expression on his face threatening. He started to shake with anger. If Jeff was not scared before, he was now! He backed away and quickly left without saying a word, slamming the front door. Karlena heard the door slam and ran downstairs.

"Daddy?"

"He's gone! Micah all right?"

"Yeah, he's in his crib. What happened?"

"You don't have to look so worried," Esdell said. "I didn't lay a hand on him. I'm not proud of what I said though. I just had to clear up a few things. Why'd he come over here anyway?"

"For no good! He's no good at all, Daddy." Karlena did not want to replay the unpleasant events in her mind, nor did she want to anger her father any further. "He hasn't changed. I've been praying that he would become a dad to Micah, but I see it's not gonna happen."

"Well, keep prayin' for him. We can't change him, only God can do that. But until he can prove he's changed, he ain't welcome here!"

"I feel ya, Daddy. I'm gonna go give Micah his bath."

"And I'm gonna get back out there to our guests." Esdell looked at the floor while Karlena went back up the stairs. He thought about how he had threatened Jeff and felt just slightly guilty. So he made a small petition to God.

"Lord, forgive me, but those are my babies!"

8

Esdell came downstairs to find Kareem sitting at the dining room table, which was covered with books and paperwork.

"Hey, son, 'bout done?"

"Yeah, I'm just putting the finishing touches on my sermon for the juvenile center and making sure I have all the paperwork in order." Kareem had quickly complied with his pastor's request to start a ministry to the juvenile corrections center. "I've sent in the applications from the church volunteers. They all cleared their background checks and have had the required tuberculosis shots. I wasn't expecting that one, but it was good that the center made it easy by sending a nurse to the church. I'm glad you're involved, Dad. You ready?"

"Oh, yeah!" Esdell was excited to say. "This is a great idea, and I think that we can do some real good at the juvenile center. They're so many lost boys and girls down there. I'm glad to be a part of it. Proud of you too, man. You jumped on this with both feet."

"I feel like this is why God called me into the ministry. To help people close to my age. I hope I do a good job. I've been praying, fasting, meditating, and studying. I really want to bring these kids hope through Christ."

"I know you'll do a real good job. God's gonna use you in a mighty way!"

Kareem raised his right hand. "To God be the glory!"

Esdell sat at the table and began to read some of the research that Kareem had done to use in his sermon. He read how some teens were heavily involved in drugs, sex, theft, and even murder. There was a lot of information about gang activity, a subject that Kareem was really focusing on, considering his near involvement.

"This is some scary stuff! Now, I'm even more convinced that the church is needed at the center. Those boys and girls need help!"

"We'll only be ministering to the boys. I had to choose between the boys or girls to talk to, so I chose the boys. After all, they are the future heads of household."

"That's the word, Reverend 'Reem!" Esdell agreed. "That's the word!"

"You doin' any good down here, Kareem?" Karlena and Micah had just come down the stairs.

"He's workin' on it. Come see Gramps, Micah." Karlena put Micah on the floor so he could walk over to Esdell. "That's my big boy!" Esdell lifted him up to sit him on his lap.

"Kareem, here's a paper I wrote on drug addiction. I thought it might help you with your sermon," Karlena offered.

"You wrote this? Can I trust these facts? You probably didn't get more than a C on it!" Kareem joked.

"Boy, please! I got an A on this paper. My research is solid! Shoot!"

"Okay!" Kareem laughed. "Thanks, sis. I'm almost finished with this sermon, but I can probably use it later."

"It's too bad you're not going with us to the center, Karlena. Your medical knowledge could've been real helpful," Esdell said.

"I wanted to, but Kareem said no."

"That's best, I think. We'll be ministering to young boys, and they don't need to be uh…uh…distracted!"

"You think I'll distract them?" Karlena said, crossing her arms with a slight smile on her face.

"Yeah, I do! They might not pay attention to me because they'll be lookin' at that big ole head of yours!"

"Whatever, Kareem! I know what's up!" she responded, putting her hands on her hips.

Esdell chuckled. "It's all right to admit you gotta fine sister. She's beautiful. She looks just like your mama!"

Karlena smiled broadly. "And Mom *was* fine!" Karlena looked at Esdell's face and saw that sadness was taking the place of the smile that was once there. "But Micah's a handsome boy 'cause he looks like his gramps. Don't cha, Mick Mick?"

Micah smiled and bounced on Esdell's lap. He always seemed to like it when his mother called him Mick Mick. His playful reaction returned the smile to Esdell's face.

"Who's as cute as he can be, just because he looks like me? It's Miicahhhh!" Esdell sang.

"What was that?" Kareem asked.

"It's some song Daddy made up for Micah. I've only heard bits and pieces of it. That last verse was something else." Karlena giggled. "Maybe someday you'll sing the whole thing for me, Daddy."

"Maybe, someday!" Esdell teased giving Micah back to Karlena. "C'mon, son, we'd better get a move on. We don't wanna be late our first time at the center. See y'all later!"

"Okay, Dad, I'll drive," Kareem said. "Bye, big heads!"

"I got yo' big head, Kareem! Get on outta here! I know you'll do good," Karlena encouraged. "Y'all be careful!"

Esdell and Kareem left the house, and in no time, they were turning into the parking lot of the juvenile detention center. They entered the facility and checked in at the security desk.

"Good afternoon, I'm Reverend Kareem Brown from the Road to Damascus Baptist Church. We're here to have a service with a group of your boys today."

The security guard looked at the schedule to find the church's name.

"Yes, Reverend Brown. I need everyone in your group to sign in and go through a security check. Is it just the two of you today?"

"No, there'll be four more coming. We're a little early, but the others will be here soon. Can we wait out here?"

"That'll be fine. Just come back to the desk here when everyone else arrives."

"Thank you. Let's go have a seat, Dad."

The men took a seat in the waiting area of the center. There was a clear view of the parking lot where they watched police cars driving in and out and families coming and going from court appearances for their children. They witnessed people crying and others speaking out in frustration. There was not a smile to be seen.

"What a sad place this is," Esdell commented. "It makes me realize how blessed I've been that you and Karlena didn't have to come this way."

"Dad, it could've been me. That's why this is so important to me. I almost joined that gang 'cause I thought God had turned his back on me. We always say that God will never leave you nor forsake you. I realized that just in time. Now I have to help these boys realize it too."

"I know you'll make a difference here."

"Dad, if I can reach one, if I can help bring just one soul to Christ, it'll be enough for me. At least for now!"

Esdell nodded his head in agreement and then continued to watch the activity in the parking lot. Shortly they were joined by the other members of the church. Kareem directed everyone to the security desk. The group entered one at a time through the security door. Each person had to remove their shoes and was frisked for contraband. Even their Bibles were scanned for concealed weapons. Once everyone was cleared, they were led in to what appeared to be a conference room. At the front of the room, there was a lectern and five chairs that faced more chairs where the boys would obviously sit. The group appeared to be a little nervous because no one really knew what to expect. The door of the room opened, and a security guard entered with eleven boys following him. The boys were all wearing socks and were walking with their hands behind their backs. At the end of the line, there was another security guard.

"Detainees, be seated!" one of the guards ordered. "Direct your attention to the speakers; you speak only when spoken to. Is that understood?"

The young men acknowledged their instructions and sat in seats arranged in three rows. Most of them sat erect in their seats, while a few of them slouched in rebellion. Kareem approached the podium opening his Bible and spreading out his sermon across the surface.

"Good afternoon, young men. I'm Reverend...uh, my name is Kareem Brown. We're from the Road to Damascus Baptist Church, and we're all happy to be here. Um, I think I'll let the rest of the group introduce themselves." Each member stood and gave their names and expressed why they had chosen to come to the juvenile center.

"Thanks, everyone. Now we would like to meet you! If you want to tell us how you came to be here, that's fine. If not, that's fine too. Just tell us your name. Let's start over here with the young man on the end," Kareem invited.

Most of the boys just gave their names. They understandably did not want to talk about what they had done that had caused them to be in the juvenile detention center. They reached the last person who was a dark-skinned boy with braids. He had a large keloid scar that started from just under his chin and went back to under his right ear.

He remained in his chair, muttering his name.

"Kofi."

"Stand up, Kofi!" the security guard commanded. "Say it again!"

"My name is Kofi!" He stood just long enough to give his name and then flopped back down in his seat.

"Okay. Thank you, everyone. Do any of you have any questions for us?" Kareem asked. The room was silent. "Good enough. Well, I do have a word from God for you!" Kareem opened his Bible and began to briefly scan his sermon notes. The silence was broken by a loud, aggravated sigh from Kofi.

"Watch it, Kofi!" the guard cautioned.

"What's on your mind, man?" Kareem Asked.

Kofi sat up in his chair. "Why are you all here? Does it make you feel better about yourself to come talk to all us poor, misguided juvenile delinquents? I can only speak for myself, but I'm not interested in lis'nen' to you. You can't speak for God!"

The church members moaned in disapproval.

"That's it, Kofi, you're outta here! Let's go!" The guard stood over Kofi and directed him to the door.

"Hold on, officer! It's fine!" Kareem defended. "Please let him stay. Why do you feel like that, Kofi?"

"I listened to that Jesus stuff all my life. I listened before, and I believed, but look at me! Look where I'm at! Look where we all are! You see this scar?" Kofi pointed to his neck. "Where was God when I got jacked up and cut up on that parking lot? My daddy just up and left me and my mama for no reason. Where was Jesus, God, whoever then? Doesn't look like Jesus is helping me any!"

Kareem closed his eyes, smiled slightly, and shook his head. He was experiencing a moment of déjà vu. The words that Kofi had spoken sent him back to a similar conversation he'd had with his grandmother. He, too, had thought that God had forsaken him.

"Man I've been where you're at! I remember saying that God had done nothing for me! My mother was dead, killed at war. My dad was nowhere around because he was off fighting in that same stupid war. I just knew he was gonna end up dead too! I got beat up by some gang bangers because I didn't join their gang. But God spoke through my grandmother who told me to keep on praying. But I had to believe that God would hear and answer my prayer and bring my dad back home safe and unharmed. And he did it. That's my dad sitting right here next to me!" Kareem pointed to Esdell who was hanging on his every word. "I could've been killed by that gang, just like you could've died when someone slit your throat. Yeah, look where you are. You're here and you're still alive! You could've died, but you didn't! I ain't perfect. I've made mistakes and will keep making them. I just have to keep believing that God has got my back!"

When Kareem admitted that he, too, as a preacher, had doubted God, that he had been beat up by gang members, the young men began to open up about their own personal circumstances and the things that caused them to be arrested. Kareem did not use the sermon he had prepared for them. He closed his Bible and put away his notes. These young men did not need to be preached to that day; they needed to be heard. Everyone from the church shared a time in their lives when they felt distant from God.

"Life is always going to have its ups and downs, its ends and out. But God has plans for us." Kareem reopened his Bible. "Let me read you something. 'For I know the plans I have for you,' declares the Lord, 'plans to prosper you and not to harm you, plans to give you hope and a future. Then you will call on me and come and pray to me, and I will listen to you. You will seek me and find me when you seek me with all your heart. I will be found by you,' declares the Lord, 'and I will bring you back from captivity...' That's from the book of Jeremiah twenty-ninth chapter, verses eleven through fourteen."

"My mom use to read me that same verse!" Kofi said with widened eyes.

"All right then!" Kareem said loudly. "This is a word from God, and I am sharing it with you all! You may be imprisoned now, captive, but call on God, pray to Him, and He will listen. Look for Him with all your heart, your sincere and opened heart, and you'll find Him. Just believe, fellas. Just believe!"

"Sorry, Reverend, but your time is up. I hate to cut you off, but it's time for the boys to get back," the guard stated.

The young men had intently listened to what Kareem had said. They stood and applauded as they left. Kofi was bringing up the rear, waiting for his turn to exit. He stopped and looked Kareem in his face as if he were searching for something more. Kareem looked back into Kofi's eyes and felt a connection and blurted out.

"I'll come back to see you personally if you want me to!"

"K!" Kofi simply said as he left the room.

Esdell clapped his hands slowly but loudly and was joined by the rest of the church members.

"Job well done, son! You was fire!"

Kareem sighed. "To God be the glory! Thanks, Dad! Thank you, everybody! Thanks for coming!"

They left the conference room and walked down the hallway through the security doors talking about what they had experienced with the young men. Each member congratulated and encouraged Kareem, telling him that Pastor Edwards would truly be proud of him. He humbly accepted each compliment but always gave God the glory.

Kareem and Esdell were walking through the waiting area toward the exits when Esdell saw a familiar face.

"Hope?"

Yes, it was Hope, sitting humped over in a chair in the waiting area as if she were waiting just for them.

"Oh, hi. What're you doin' here?" Hope said softly. She was not her usual flirtatious self.

"We just had a service with a group of boys here. Kareem spoke, really good too. Did you meet my son at the barbeque?"

"Not officially. I saw him, but we weren't introduced. Hi, I'm Hope Shah."

"Kareem," he said, extending his hand to shake. "Glad to meet you, Ms Shah. Sorry we didn't get a chance to meet at the party."

"So, Hope, how come you're here?" Esdell inquired.

"I came to see my son. He was probably in the group you met with."

"Is his name Kofi?" Esdell asked.

"Yes!" Hope said. "How'd you know?"

"He looks a lot like you. Don't you think, Kareem?"

"Now that you mention it, Dad, yes, they do favor a lot. We had quite a discussion with young Mr. Shah."

"Actually, his last name is Thomas. I hope he wasn't any trouble. He has kind of a attitude problem," she said shamefully.

"Uh, well, I plan to come back and see him. I think we made a little connection." Kareem did not want tell Hope that Kofi had, in fact, been a problem.

Hope smiled slightly. "That'd be nice. Kofi doesn't have many friends, any that mean him any good, anyway. Thanks."

"Hope Shah!" the security guard called. "Come to the desk, please!"

"It was nice seeing you. Excuse me." Hope went to the desk.

Esdell and Kareem watched Hope as she went toward the security desk. Kareem started toward the exit, but Esdell did not move. "I'll meet you at the car in just a minute, Kareem."

"What's up, Dad?"

"I don't know, but I'ma hang back for a minute. I'll catch up with you."

"All right then."

Esdell continued to watch Hope as she talked to the security guard. At first, he could only hear a word here and there, but she began to speak louder. It was evident that Hope was becoming upset by the conversation. "I've been waiting over an hour. I deserve an explanation! What happened?" she asked.

"You getting loud with me isn't going to help you! There's been an incident and all visitations for the rest of the day have been cancelled. You'll have to reschedule. I'm sorry, Ms Shah, but you should've come earlier like you originally scheduled," the security guard answered.

"My car broke down, and I couldn't be on time. I had to take the bus. This is ridiculous! I want to see my son!" Hope yelled.

Esdell quickly went to the security desk. "C'mon, Hope. Go with me!"

"I wanna see my son! I wanna see my son!" she cried.

Esdell took hold of Hope's wrist and pulled her away toward the exit.

"Let me go!" She snatched away from him but then forced herself to calm down. "I'm sorry. I don't want to start trouble. Is there anyway you can make an exception. May I see him for just a few minutes?"

The security guard shook his head. "Like I said before, I'm sorry, but you need to come back another time. Call back to arrange your next visit."

Hope hung her head and was obviously trying to fight back tears.

"Let's go, Hope," Esdell said, pushing her gently on her back. She walked to the exit slowly, as if all the fight was taken from her; she said nothing. They walked out to the parking lot just as Kareem was pulling up. "We'll take you home," Esdell volunteered. "Where do you live?"

"Don't start actin' like you give a crap about me! I came on the bus, and I can go back on the bus!" Hope's was now directing her anger toward Esdell. He opened the back door to the car.

"You don't need to be on no bus. You just mad now. Just get in the car!"

Hope climbed into the backseat; Esdell closed the door behind her and then got into the front seat. "Where do you live?"

"On Georgetown Road. Way on the west side," she muttered.

Kareem knew how to get to Georgetown Road, so he got on the interstate and headed west. No one spoke. Both Esdell and

Kareem intuitively knew to be quiet, giving Hope the opportunity to compose herself.

Kareem drove to the correct off-ramp and exited the interstate and asked, "Which way now, Miss Hope?"

"You sound like your daddy, calling me Miss Hope. That's funny. Just keep straight." She forced a smile.

"Hey, you know what. I'm kinda hungry. Y'all wanna get somethin' to eat?" Esdell said.

"I could eat," Kareem agreed. "How 'bout you, Miss Hope?"

"To be honest, fellas, I could eat too."

"All right then! My treat. Where you two wanna go?"

"Doesn't matter to me, Dad. Miss Hope?"

"Wendy's," she answered.

Esdell smirked. "I can afford a little better than that!"

"I need some comfort food and nothin' cheers me up like a Chocolate Frosty from Wendy's!" Hope confessed.

"There's one just ahead, Dad," Kareem noted.

"Okay. Fine with me!"

They went to Wendy's. The men ordered hamburger meals. Hope ordered the largest frosty available, but nothing else. They ate, making small talk. Esdell wanted to give her more time to collect herself.

"Feelin' any better now?" he asked.

"Yeah, I guess. I'm sorry 'bout makin' that scene back at the juvenile center, but I haven't seen Kofi in almost a month. He already thinks I've abandoned him 'cause I was supposed to see him last week, but couldn't make it 'cause I had to work. When he called me, he was…" She stopped talking and put a spoonful of the ice cream frosty in her mouth. She then asked, "How was he?"

Esdell looked at Kareem, gesturing him to answer.

"Physically, he seemed fine. Personally, I don't know him, but I could tell that he's a pretty angry young man. I told him I'd be back to see him, and I will definitely do that!"

"Seems like Kareem reached a few of them boys, and your son was one of them. I'm really proud of the way my son spoke today."

"You should be. It must be nice havin' a preacher for a son. That tells me a lot about your parenting skills, Esdell. Just like Kofi being in jail must tell you something about mine."

"What do you mean?" Esdell asked.

"Kofi's been in and out of trouble for the past couple of years, more time in than out. I must've failed somewhere. I don't know. I may not've done the best I could, but I did the best I knew. It just wasn't enough."

"Let me ask you something. What sorta things did you teach Kofi?" Esdell took a bite of his burger, waiting for an answer.

"What kinda question is that?" Hope was put off by the inquiry.

"What did you teach him?" he repeated. "It's a simple question."

"Well, the kinda stuff any mother would teach their kid: to respect his elders, study hard in school, brush your teeth…Where you goin' with this, Esdell?" Hope was becoming irritated.

"Just work with me here a minute. You don't have to answer this one if you don't want to, but what did Kofi do that landed him in jail?"

"He was caught riding in a stolen car with a known gang banger, and Kofi had a gun on him! Not that that's any business of yours!"

"Okay then! Now, I've heard you list a few of the things that you've taught Kofi, and I'm sure you taught him more lessons than that, but just when did you teach him to hang around with criminals and carry a gun?"

"That's a stupid question! I never did! What's your point, E. Brown?" Hope's irritation was turning to anger.

"*That's* my point, Miss Hope!" Esdell said sarcastically. "You never taught your son to do wrong. You said yourself you did the best you knew how to do. You shouldn't blame yourself that your son went wrong when you taught him right! He made his own decisions. Now, he may've had some bad influence, but that wasn't you, was it?"

Kareem sat quietly, smiling. *Game point, Dad!* he thought.

"No!" Hope said. "I told him to stay away from those thugs he was hangin' with, but he wouldn't listen to me."

"We parents blame ourselves when our kids get in trouble. I blamed myself when my single teenaged daughter got pregnant 'cause I wasn't around. I thought that if I'd been here, it wouldn't have happened. My kids were taught the same things that you taught Kofi. They were raised to fear God too. We do the best we can Hope, and then we just turn them over to Him."

"Well, I taught Kofi about God. My dad is a missionary! I took Kofi to church, but we stopped going when I started working two jobs. His dad wasn't never around to help me with him. I was lucky he stuck around long enough to sign the birth certificate."

"You divorced?" Esdell asked.

"Nope, we never got married. I've been a single parent Kofi's whole life. His daddy is no good. I don't even know where he is because he's dodging the child support order. Kofi's only seen him once when he was fifteen. He seemed to get worse after that. I think we're better off without him."

"If you don't mind me saying, Miss Hope, it's hard not having your father around," Kareem interjected." I went through plenty changes when my dad was overseas. It wasn't his choice to be gone so much, but it really affected me! I thought about joining a gang myself. I became disrespectful to everybody. But by God's grace, Dad came home and my faith was renewed. Kofi just needs to know that someone believes in him. I know that you do, and once I get to really know him, I think I'll come to believe in him too."

"So you really meant it when you said you'd visit him in jail?" she asked.

"I meant it!" Kareem affirmed.

Hope smiled with belief and contentment as they finished their food. "I've really enjoyed this, fellas. I really needed it."

"I've enjoyed it too, but its time we get you home. You 'bout ready?" Esdell asked.

"Yeah, I'm ready."

They left Wendy's restaurant and Hope gave Kareem directions to the apartment complex where she lived, which was only a few minutes away. They talked the whole way, and Hope was impressed with the honesty of both men. They were transparent when talking about the mistakes they had made and were emphatic when they talked about how God had graced them. Soon, Kareem was parked in front of Hope's apartment building.

"Here you are, Miss Hope!"

"Thanks, Kareem. I'm glad that you're gonna mentor Kofi. It won't be long before he's eighteen. If he doesn't change his ways, the next time he gets in trouble, he could be charged as an adult. Maybe end up in prison. Thanks for the Frosty, Esdell. Now you know one of my weaknesses!" she joked.

"Not a problem, Hope. Let me walk you to your door."

"You don't have to. I'll be just fine. Bye, y'all, and thanks again!" Hope got out of the car and trotted to her front door. Esdell and Kareem watched her until she was safely inside and then started on their way home.

9

Esdell opened the front door, responding to the ringing bell and leaving his dining room table that was covered with papers and books.

"Hey, man, c'mon in!" It was Karlena's boyfriend, Joseph.

"Hey, Mr. Brown, how you doin'?" Joseph asked.

"Keepin' it movin', man. Just keepin' it movin'. I was just lookin' through my syllabus and my textbooks." The summer had passed quickly and all of the Brown family was returning to school. Esdell was a great artist and was pursuing a degree in graphic design. "I just left the bookstore, and I can't believe I paid almost $200 for just two books! It's cheaper to just stay stupid."

Joseph laughed in agreement. "Education is expensive! Karlena's not here, is she? I didn't see the car in the driveway."

"No, she got hung up at the campus bookstore. The lines were real long! She probably won't be home for another hour or so. You can wait if you want to. You want somethin' to drink? Karlena just made a big pitcher of green tea."

"Green tea? You like that?"

Esdell shook his head. "Not really. I'd rather be drinkin' a big ole glass of red Kool-Aid with lemons, but future nurse Karlena is trying to detoxify us."

"Thanks, but I'll pass. Mr. Brown, can I talk to you about somethin'?"

"Sure! Sounds serious. Let's sit." They went and sat on the living room couch. "What's up?" Esdell asked.

"You know how we were just talking about how expensive it is to go to school?" Joseph asked.

"Yeah."

"Well, I recently had a conversation with my grandparents. They knew I was in school, and they just found out that I'm majoring in journalism."

"Okay."

"They own a small publishing company, and they want me to come work in their proofing department and be trained in all areas of the business. I didn't consider it at first because I'm just starting my third year of college, but then they made me an offer that I just can't refuse. They'll pay for the rest of my college education, but I'll have to transfer from Indianapolis City College, here, to Southern."

"Oh, I see. Well, Southern Indiana University is a good school, I guess, but I don't know much about it. You and Karlena can still visit. It's just a few hours away."

"Mr. Brown," Joseph started slowly, "it's Southern University in Louisiana."

"Oh, wow. That's different." Esdell paused for a minute. "Well, y'all will keep in touch through e-mail, and Facebook, and Twitter, and whatever else y'all young people do, and you'll have to see each other when you're home for the holidays."

"Mr. Brown, my grandparents want me to train in the business because they want me to eventually take it over. After I work there a couple of years and graduate from college, they're just gonna give me their business. I'll be permanently moving to Louisiana!"

"I see. So now you're worried about Karlena."

"Yes, sir. I don't know how she'll take it. I don't want to hurt her, but this is the opportunity of a lifetime. I'd be a fool to pass it up!"

Esdell scratched his head, "You're right. The rest of your education paid for and a business of your own when you're done. You can't pass it up. How do you feel about it? Leaving Karlena, I mean." He stared Joseph in the eye. "Are you thinkin' 'bout proposing marrying her and takin' her with you?"

"Can I be honest with you, Mr. Brown?"

"I expect the truth, Joseph."

"Even though Karlena is my girlfriend, she's more like my friend who's a girl. Me and Karlena are really just best friends. We barely see each other because our work schedules clash. She's busy at work, school, and taking care of Micah, and trying to do her part here. We've been together for months, and we haven't even taken our relationship to the next level, even though I wanted to."

Esdell was uncomfortable with the direction the conversation was going. "TMI, Joe! Too much information! I ain't tryna hear that!"

"I know, but believe me, I've never tried to convince Karlena to do anything she didn't want to do. I've totally respected her boundaries, but it ain't been easy! She's got a little baggage when it comes to men, I think. She's not tryna get caught up again like she did with Micah's daddy."

Karlena and Joseph had met when they were both registering for classes at Indianapolis City College. Joseph had become a comfort to Karlena. He was very supportive of her in the place of Micah's absentee father. They dated and Joseph was always a welcomed guest at all their family functions. Esdell had always assumed their relationship was romantic.

"Do you love her?" Esdell asked.

"Again, let me be honest. We love each other, but we're not in love. She's my closest, dearest friend. She's so sweet and thoughtful. She's hardworking, devoted to her son, her family, and her God. She's super intelligent and wise beyond her years, and on top of all of that, she's fine! She's almost perfect. It's weird. With all of that, I'm not romantically in love with her, but I *do* love her. Does that make sense?"

"It does. Well, when you gonna talk to her about movin'? You shouldn't wait."

"I'm not gonna wait. I'll be leaving the end of next week." Joseph rested his forearms on his thighs and hung his head. "I'm gonna miss her so much. And Micah, my man Micah! I hate to think about not seeing that li'l brotha grow up! I love him too. But he's young. He'll forget me quickly. Outta sight is outta mind like they say. I just don't want to hurt 'em, either of them."

"I appreciate you talkin' to me 'bout your plans. You've been really good for Karlena, and I liked you from the beginning. Who knows what the future holds for y'all? You want me to tell her?"

"Naw, I got it. I need to say my good-byes to her and Micah myself. I think I'll call her now and see if we can hook up later tonight. Maybe I'll take her out to dinner or something."

"That'd be nice. Micah's over to Mama's and is stayin' the night so y'all can be alone."

Joseph pulled out his cell phone and placed his call to Karlena.

"Hey, girl! I'm at your house. I wanna take you out to dinner. I need to talk to you about something. How long before you'll be home?" He listened to her response. "Okay. I'ma make a run, and I'll you meet back here in about forty-five minutes then. See ya then. Bye." Joseph stood up and straightened his clothes. "Thanks for hearing me out, Mr. Brown. I think I'll say my good-bye to you now." Esdell stood also and the men exchanged a testosterone-filled hug. Esdell escorted Joseph to the door and slapped him on the back.

"Take care, man. God bless you!"

"Thanks, Mr. Brown. I'll miss you too!"

Joseph walked onto the porch, and Esdell closed the door behind him. He was concerned about how Karlena would take the news about Joseph's leaving, and he simply asked God to touch the situation. He was hopeful that Karlena would see that Joseph's leaving was the best thing for his future.

A few moments passed, and Kareem was coming in the house.

"Hey, Dad, was that Joseph that I passed just now?"

Esdell sighed heavily. "Yeah, it was! He just gave me some good news and some bad news."

"Really? What's going on?" Kareem asked.

Esdell proceeded to tell Kareem about the conversation he'd just had with Joseph.

"Wow, Dad. How you think Karlena's gonna take it?"

"I don't know. I hope she'll be all right. Karlena's strong though."

"Yeah, she is. Well, I've got some good news!"

"Well, spill it, man. I could use some good news!"

"Come in the kitchen with me! I need something to drink."

Esdell followed behind Kareem. "Drink some of that green tea your sister made!"

Kareem did, pouring himself a full glass. He took a big gulp before he spoke.

"I just got out of a meeting with Pastor Edwards, and he told me that he was really pleased with the way that the ministry to the juvenile center was going. He said he had been hearing good things about me. Guess from who."

"Well, some of that good stuff he heard came from me!" Esdell confessed.

"Well, thank you for that, Dad, but he got a letter from Kofi!"

Kareem had been true to his word. He had visited Kofi in the juvenile center many times. They had actually become friends. Kareem was helping Kofi study for his GED and was prayerful, that through his biblical teaching, he was also helping Kofi renew his hope in Christ.

"Really? Kofi wrote a letter to the pastor? Wow!" Esdell was surprised.

"He's not the only one to write the pastor. Miss Hope wrote to him too!"

"Hope? Again, I say wow! Have you talked to Hope?"

"Not directly. We seem to just miss each other at visitation times, but Kofi says she's doing well. Dad, Pastor showed me the letters, and they were very encouraging to me, and they impressed the pastor. They impressed him so much that he made me youth pastor of the church!"

"What? Really? That's great, son! Congratulations! I'm so proud of you!"

"Wait, there's more! The church is gonna pay me! I am actually gonna get paid for doing the work of the Lord! I'll be making more than I make now on unemployment!"

"All right, now!"

"Wait, Dad, there's more!" Kareem exclaimed. "The church is even gonna give me tuition reimbursement if I keep at least a 3.0 GPA at Bible college! Do you believe that? God is awesome!"

"Oh, my Father, how great thou are! Kareem, see, all you had to do is hold on and look how He's blessed you! Pour out them blessin's, Lord! Pour 'em out!"

"Whew!" Kareem sighed. "Think about it, Dad, both me and Joseph were blessed today in a way we hadn't even thought about. Both of us will have our schooling paid for!"

"Oh yeah! God's good like that!"

"I can't wait to tell Karlena!"

Esdell's mind returned to concern he had about how Karlena would react to the news about Joseph leaving. "I know she'll be happy for you, but don't tell her about Joseph. He wants to tell her himself."

"Oh, I won't. By the way, Dad, speaking of Kofi. He's got a hearing coming up, and I'm going to court with him. He could use a show of support, so I thought I would ask the juvenile ministry members to go too. Will you go?"

Without hesitation, Esdell responded, "Of know I will! When is it?"

"It's during the week. It's two weeks from Wednesday. Will you be able to get off?"

"I can take a vacation day. It'll be fine."

"Uh, Dad, Kofi says that Miss Hope's been asking about you. He thinks she's feelin' you! What d'ya think about that?"

Esdell tilted his head and firmly pressed his lips together. "I really don't know. I have to admit though, I've been thinkin' 'bout her off and on since we took her out to Wendy's that day. I even drove by the flowershop where she works with the intention of checkin' on her, but I didn't. I just drove on by."

"How do *you* feel about *her?*"

"I think she's a nice woman with issues, and I think if things were different, I could…It's not the right time now."

"You're still not over Mama, are you?"

"I will *never* get over your mother!"

Kareem knew that he had hit a nerve, so he moved to change the subject as he did not want to be responsible for his father having more nightmares.

"Okay. When do you think Karlena will be home? Is Micah with her?"

Esdell knew why Kareem was redirecting the conversation.

"I'm sorry, man. I didn't mean to snap at you. Son, I've never loved anyone like I loved your mom. I pray that you and your sister find the kind of love that we shared. I don't believe that anyone will ever take her place. And in answer to your questions, your sister is out buying her books for class, and Micah's over Mama's."

An uncomfortable silence overtook the room. Kareem did not know what to say next. Esdell was having mixed feelings. He was sorry that he had become angry with Kareem, and then he was upset with him for remotely entertaining the idea that someone could ever take the place of his Kenya. But as he thought, Esdell became angry with himself because he had, in fact, thought about Hope from time to time, and now he was trying to dismiss the idea that he could be interested in her. But he was, and he felt guilty about it.

The telephone began to ring and Kareem jumped to answer it. He was relieved that awkwardness was being cut short. He looked at the caller ID.

"Hello, Grandma! How are you?" He listened as she spoke. "Dad, Grandma wants us to come over and eat. Karlena just called her. She's going out with Joseph."

"Let's roll!" Esdell answered; also glad to be pulled from an unpleasant situation.

They left the house and were soon at Grace's. They walked in the back door and were greeted by the smell of salmon croquets. Grace, Isaiah, and Micah were sitting at the kitchen table waiting on Esdell and Kareem to arrive.

"That was quick! Y'all must be really hungry!" Isaiah remarked.

"Hey, Grandma. Hey, Pops!" Kareem said.

"Hey, everybody. Mama, smells good as always!" Esdell turned his attention to Micah. "Hey, li'l buddy, you bein' a good boy?" He kissed him on top of the head.

"Hi, boys. Y'all wash up and sit down. We're ready to eat," Grace directed.

They did as they were told, and then Isaiah blessed the food. They began to eat and the dinner discussion ensued. Esdell talked about what was happening with Joseph, and Kareem was ecstatic to tell about his appointment at church.

"Goodness, y'all have had a busy day!" Grace commented. "Kareem, I'm 'bout to bust. I'm so proud of you. God is so good!"

"Yes, He is, Gracie!" Isaiah agreed. "So what'll your duties at the church be?"

"Well, Pops, I'll continue with the juvenile ministry to help it grow, and I will oversee the children's church and Bible studies. I'll be supervisor over the youth department director too!"

"We didn't even talk about that, son," Esdell said. "Being youth pastor is a big responsibility, but I know you can handle it!"

"I know he can too! To God be the glory!" Grace praised.

They continued to talk until they had all finished eating. Grace started to clear the table.

"I'll help you with this, Mama. You guys go on in the living room. Pops, it's time for your favorite show *Wheel of Fortune!*"

Isaiah stood up and then removed Micah from his high chair. "Micah likes it too. C'mon, Micah, we gonna go watch the wheel spin!" He looked at Esdell and could sense that he wanted to be alone with his mother. "You come to, Kareem. You smart, you can help me and Micah solve the puzzles."

"Okay, Pops." Kareem complied and left the kitchen with Isaiah and Micah.

"Mama, I'll wash and you dry." Esdell scraped the food remnants into the trashcan and then ran the dishwater. He put the dirty dishes in the sink and began to wash them, rinse them, and then hand them off to Grace.

"Anything new goin' on with you, son?" Grace knowingly asked.

"You know me way too well, Mama. Can we sit for a minute?"

Grace dried her hands and again sat at the kitchen table. She did not say a word. She just waited on her son to begin.

"Mama, I…I've been having a lot of trouble sleeping. I've been havin' a lot of bad dreams, dreams about Kenya."

"I see. What're the dreams about?" Grace asked.

"Dreams about her dying. I keep seeing her…" Esdell stopped. He did not want to be graphic. "I keep thinkin' 'bout how it was for her when she got killed. I pray for peace at night, but God hasn't seen fit to grant it to me yet."

"There must be somethin' you supposed to be learnin' from this, or maybe God is buildin' a great testimony in you."

"I believe that too, but there's somethin' else."

"Go on, Esdell, I'm lis'nin," Grace urged.

"Mama, how was you able to fall in love with Pops after you loved Daddy so much?"

Grace smiled. She recalled a conversation she'd had with her granddaughter LeAnn. LeAnn could not understand how Grandma could start dating Isaiah and just stop loving her Paw Paw who was now in heaven. The advice she had given to her, she would now give to Esdell.

"Son, the heart is a muscle, and it's like all your other muscles. The more you work it, the stronger it gets. Lovin' keeps the heart busy, and you can love so many people at the same time. You can love them, but in different ways. Your heart is big enough to hold all that love. LeAnn didn't like it much when me and Isaiah started seeing each other. She just couldn't understand how I could just forget her Paw Paw like that. I had to explain to her that I still loved my Samuel, but with the heart that God had given me, I could love Isaiah too. I even had to tell Isaiah that he didn't take Samuels place in my heart, but he had a place of his own. Are you interested in somebody?"

"I kinda think so," Esdell confessed.

"And you feelin' guilty about it?"

"I kinda think so," he repeated.

"Don't! God means for us to be happy and to be at peace. We all loved Kenya, baby, I know I did, and I know she'd want you to be happy too. It's not good that you still mournin' over her. You've closed up your heart makin' it weak, robbin' yourself of happiness. If you're interested in somebody, it's all right! Work that heart muscle by openin' it up and lettin' more love come in. Kenya's in a better place and you know that. Esdell, if there's somebody that can help bring you happiness, I got room enough in this ole heart to love her too. More love, more muscle makin' a stronger heart! Don't feel guilty, son. Just keep prayin' and believin' and watch what He'll do for you!"

"Thanks, Mama. Let's get these dishes done." Esdell stood to return to sink, but then looked at the back door when he heard it opening. Karlena was walking into the kitchen.

"Hi!' she simply said.

"Hey, baby girl. You're back early. You okay?" Esdell asked with concern.

"I will be, Daddy. It is what it is," Karlena responded. A tear was forming in her eye. "I'm really gonna miss Joseph. What do you do when someone you love goes away?" Now there was a stream of tears flowing from her eyes.

"You'll keep in touch. I know you will!" Grace consoled.

"We will. Uh, how was Micah today, Grandma?"

"Sweet as pie. He's watchin' TV with Isaiah and Kareem. I'll go get him for you," Grace said knowingly. "You feelin' sad and you need your baby to hold!"

Esdell put his arm around Karlena. He had paid special attention to the fact that Karlena said someone she loved was going away. He now knew that she felt more for Joseph than she had let him know.

"It's okay, baby. I know how it feels to lose someone you love. Do you love him?"

"I do, Daddy, but I didn't realize how much until now...now that he's leaving."

"Did you ever tell him that, Karlena?"

"No. He knows I care about him, but I always kept our relationship platonic. Maybe that was a mistake. Maybe I should've—"

"Ahem!" Esdell loudly cleared his throat to keep Karlena from going any further. He did not want her to say anything that might embarrass her later. "So, do you think you should tell him how you really feel?"

"No, it'll only complicate things. I don't want him to think that he has to choose between me and his future."

"You may be his future. God only knows. But like Mama said, you'll keep in touch. Somewhere down the line, it'll end up the way it's supposed to!"

"Yeah, you're right," Karlena agreed. "He wanted to come in to say good-bye to everyone, but I sent him home because he's got to be at work early in the morning. He said he'd call everybody before he leaves. He's leaving next Friday morning. If I can get off from work, I think me and Micah's gonna see him off." Karlena rubbed the tears from her cheek and sighed heavily. "The Lord gives and the Lord takes away."

"Hold on to the 'gives' part of that, sweetheart! God will give you just what you need, when you need it!"

"Here's your li'l man!" Grace said as she reentered the kitchen carrying Micah. "There's Mommy, Micah!"

Karlena reached for Micah and he leaned into her waiting arms.

"Right now, Daddy, this is what I need!" She hugged her baby boy and covered his face with kisses.

10

"There ain't no way I'd miss it! I'll be there! Thanks for includin' me, man! Bye!" Esdell hung up the phone. "That's all right!"

"It's time to go, Dad." Kareem looked at Esdell and noted the big smile on his face. "What's up, Dad? Who was that on the phone that's got you smiling like that?"

"That was Gary from work. He called checkin' on me to see why I didn't come to work today 'cause he wanted to talk to me."

"Something going on at the warehouse?"

"Gary's gettin' baptized and he wants me to come. He found himself a church and now he's gettin' baptized. I'm real happy for him."

"Good for him! Are you goin'?"

"Oh yeah, no doubt. You ready to head out?" Esdell asked.

"Yep, but I told Karlena that you'll need your car today because I need to go up to the church right after court. I've got some stuff I need to work on in the church library."

Esdell and Kareem were going to the juvenile court to Kofi's hearing. Kareem had arranged with some of the members of the juvenile detention center ministry to meet at the court to support Kofi as he appeared before the judge regarding his arrest for joyriding and being in possession of a firearm. Today was the day that he could be sentenced, and Kareem hoped that if the church would go in support, it might promote leniency from the judge.

"Micah, baby, come back here!" Karlena yelled from upstairs and then the sound of her running down the hall could be heard. She then came down the stairs grasping Micah in her arms. "Kareem, you left the baby gate open! Micah almost fell down the stairs!"

"I thought I closed it! You're okay though, right Micah?" Kareem asked.

"Thank God I saw him and caught him before he got to the stairs. You need to be more careful! You know this boy's as fast as a cheetah!"

"You're right. Sorry, sis."

"He's okay," Esdell reassured. "Karlena, I'll be straight home with the car after court in case you got somethin' to do today."

"I have no plans for today, Daddy. I don't have to work, and I don't have a class, so I'm gonna enjoy my day off with my little Mick Mick! Joseph is supposed to Skype later, so I'll be right here."

Joseph had made his way to Louisiana and was settling in. Esdell had installed Skype on the computer to help Karlena feel closer to Joseph across the miles. She and Micah had gone with Joseph's family to the airport to see him off. Karlena was strong; it was not the tearful good-bye that she had anticipated. She had prayed for a pleasant farewell, and her request had been granted. She understood from the beginning that the opportunity that had been given to Joseph was a great gift from God, and she was not going to make it difficult for him to leave by making a scene at the airport. The couple had decided to remove the title they had placed over their relationship as boyfriend and girlfriend. They were now simply friends. Karlena had come to realize through their conversation at the airport that Joseph loved her differently than she loved him. Along with making his transition to Louisiana easy, she wanted him to be free to date, so they amicably agreed to break up.

"No need for you to hurry home, Daddy," Karlena said. "I hope everything goes well for Kofi. I'm praying for him."

"Keep sendin' them up, baby girl! I'll see ya later. Be a good boy, Micah!" Esdell said, grabbing his jacket and leaving through the front door.

"Bye, you guys!" Kareem echoed as he followed Esdell out the door.

* * *

As Esdell drove onto the parking lot of the courthouse, his eyes perused the lot looking for cars that belonged to some of the church members.

Looks like we're the first to get here, he thought to himself. He and Kareem parked next to each other and walked together into the building. As soon as they entered, they were met by Hope.

"Hi, hello! You're here! I'm so glad!" She briefly but tightly gave both men a hug. "Is the rest of the ministry still coming?"

"Yes, Miss Hope, most everybody's coming," Kareem guaranteed.

"Good, I'm glad!" Hope turned her attention to Esdell. "Hi, Esdell. Thanks so much for coming. Nice to see you."

"Its nice to see you too, Hope." Esdell looked Hope directly in her eyes. His gaze verified that he was genuinely happy to see her. "How you feel?"

"I'm really nervous. I just want Kofi to get outta here. Do you think he's ready, Kareem?" she asked.

"Kofi has come a long way! I think he'll do just fine!" Kareem assured.

"I just hope being in jail didn't make him worse than he was. He's easily influenced. If he's be hangin' around the wrong crowd, he could be worse!" Hope feared.

"Don't talk like that, Hope!" Esdell protested. "We hope and pray for the best. This time in jail was probably the best thing for him. It may have kept him out of harms way!"

"Miss Hope, I've spent a lot of time with Kofi. We've talked about a lot of different stuff," Kareem said. "We've talked about the issues he has with his dad, and even you. We've studied together, prayed, laughed, and cried together! He's way different from the young man we first met."

"I hope he's not just frontin' so he can get out. Kareem, no matter what, I thank you so much for all you've been to him."

Kareem put a reassuring hand on Hope's shoulder. "Kofi's a good dude, Miss Hope. I've been praying for him, and I've turned this whole day over to God. He's in control, and the ultimate judge here."

Soon, Esdell, Kareem, and Hope were joined by the rest of the church members.

"Let's have Kareem pray before we go in," Esdell said. "Will you lead us in prayer, son?"

"Yes. Let us join hands." Hope planted herself between Kareem and Esdell, holding their hands tightly as Kareem began to pray. "Heavenly Father, we come humbly, thanking you for this day. You know why we are here today, Lord. We turn this situation over to you, and we claim the victory on behalf of our brother, Kofi. We pray his heart has been changed. We pray that you have touched him in a mighty way. Now, Father, I ask a special blessing on Kofi's mother, Sister Hope Shah." Kareem squeezed Hope's hand a little tighter. "Give her strength, understanding, and peace. Let her know you will always be with her and Kofi no matter the outcome today! Strengthen everyone in this circle and continue to bind us all together in Christian love. Amen!"

"Amen!" the group repeated, and they all went into the courtroom and sat down to wait for court to start.

"All rise!" the bailiff ordered. "Be quiet and come to order. Court is now in session with the honorable judge Levi Burrus presiding!"

After the judge took the bench, everyone again sat down. They sat through the few cases that were before Kofi's and witnessed onlookers rejoice or cry over the verdicts of the young people on trial. The judged seemed harsh but fair. It was difficult to guess which way he would go when it came to Kofi.

"The court now calls case number 86: State of Indiana versus Kofi Thomas," the bailiff announced. "All involved parties please step forward!"

Kofi was brought into the courtroom by a guard who escorted him to where his court-appointed attorney was standing. Kofi looked around the room, and it was apparent that he was happy to see all of the people who had come to support him. He looked at Kareem who gave him a thumbs up. He then looked at Hope who had her fists clenched in front of her mouth.

Everyone set up straight in their seats as Judge Burrus reviewed the documents concerning Kofi's case. He was stone-faced. He looked at Kofi over his black rimmed reading glasses, sighed heavily, and turned a page. He shook his head as if he were disgusted with what he was reading. Hope was watching his every move; trying to read his face. She whimpered. Esdell put his arm around her shoulders.

"Touch now, Lord, in the name of Jesus!" he prayed. "Hold on, Hope."

"What a busy little bee you've been, Mr. Thomas!" the judge stated. "Let's take a look at your school record, shall we? Hmm, failing grades, truancy, insubordinate to authority, and then finally expelled for fighting. Possession of marijuana. You were detained by police for suspected gang activity, but released, and now arrested for gun possession while riding in a stolen car! Yes, busy, busy bee indeed! For the prosecution?"

"John Stanton for the prosecution, Your Honor!"

"Elizabeth Douglas for the defense, Your Honor!"

"Talk to me, counselors! We'll start with Mr. Stanton!" the judge directed.

"Your Honor, you have already read the indisputable facts from the file of the defendant. There's not much that needs to be said after that. It's apparent that Mr. Thomas is on the road to even more serious, possibly violent crimes. At the age of seventeen, his criminal record is already extensive. It is my recommendation that he be sentenced and sent to the Plainfield Correctional Facility where he will no longer be a threat to society and can start the rehabilitation process. I move for at least a minimum sentencing of five years! I have nothing more. As I said, the file speaks for itself!"

"Dear Lord!" Hope gasped.

"Shh!" Esdell warned.

"Short and to the point! Thank you, Mr. Stanton. Ms. Douglas!" Kofi's attorney stood and walked toward the judge's bench.

"Judge Burrus, it's true that my client has been a problem in the past. In fact, he had to be isolated at one time while in the juvenile detention center for fighting!"

"That's not helping!" Hope moaned. She began to shake.

"Steady, Hope," Esdell whispered. He pulled her closer to him. He could feel her tremble. It felt almost like an electrical vibration. Esdell continued to hold her in an effort to brace and to calm her, but as he felt her body quiver, a strange feeling began to build within him. He dismissed it, blinking his eyes as if he was trying to come out of a trance.

"Your Honor," Ms Douglas continued, "along with all of the papers documenting Mr. Thomas's criminal activity, I'm sure you found personal letters and letters of recommendation from many of the people here in the courtroom that have come to support him. The members of the Road to Damascus Baptist Church. He has been mentored by the youth pastor of this church. Those papers should also show you that Mr. Thomas has almost completed all the requirements for his General Equivalency Diploma, testing above average. He has not received less than a B on any of his tests. I have here, Your Honor, affidavits from Reverend Kareem Brown, the GED instructor, and even one of the guards of the juvenile center that all attest to the great strides this young man has taken. The prosecution says that—"

The judge raised his hand to quiet the defense attorney. He quickly scanned the affidavits and letters. He then signaled for Ms Douglas to continue.

"The prosecution wants this young man to be put in prison so he will no longer be a danger to society, so he can start rehabilitating. I would submit that his rehab has already begun. The man you see here today is not the same man that committed the crimes on that rap sheet! He has been changed, changed by something or somebody greater than you or I!"

"Amen!" the courtroom shouted.

"Order! Order!" the judge said as he pounded his gavel. "Let me take a moment here to read more of these affidavits."

The courtroom was silent except for the sound of turning pages. The judge's face reacted to whatever he was reading. He frowned and then he smiled. He shook his head and, at one point, chuckled. He then put down the papers, leaned back in the large, high-backed leather chair, and crossed his arms. He sat quietly in deep thought.

"I can't stand this!" Hope softly exclaimed.

Esdell took hold of both of Hope's hands in his. "We claim the victory, Lord, right now in the name of Jesus. Claim it, Hope. Claim it!"

The members of the church silently prayed when they heard Esdell's plea to the Lord. As the righteous people prayed, they felt the presence of the Holy Spirit sweep through like a tsunami.

"Kofi Thomas, stand up!" the judge directed. "Do you have anything to say before this court?"

Kofi slowly rose to his feet. He looked at the judge, Kareem, and then his mother who was tightly holding hands with Esdell. He then looked at the rest of the people in the court.

"I'm sorry!" Kofi began. "I'm sorry for every minute of worry and grief I've caused my mother. I apologize to anyone I have ever done wrong to. I ask for forgiveness from all these people. I mean that. But if y'all don't forgive me, I'll just have to live with that, but it don't matter, because I learned to ask for forgiveness from God. As long as I'm coo' with Him, well, the rest will come later. Kareem—I mean Reverend Brown taught me that. Judge, I am different, but I know I gotta long way to go. I'm better, Judge Burrus. I ain't what I used to be. I'm better. That's all I gotta say. Thank you." Kofi sat.

"That's all we have, Your Honor!" Ms Douglas said.

The judge again peered over the top of his glasses. "It is my decision that Mr. Kofi Thomas be released with a probationary period of eighteen months!"

"Oh my god!" Hope screamed. "Thank you, Jesus!" The congregation of the church cheered and yelled amen in agreement.

"Quiet! Order!" the judge yelled, again banging his gavel. "Mr. Thomas, the stipulations of your probation are as follows: you will be required to wear an ankle monitor for the first six months. You must show that you are either gainfully employed or in school to complete or further your education. You will be assigned a probation officer to whom you must report each week until otherwise ordered. You will make said officer aware of your location should you move. You are not allowed to leave the state of Indiana without permission. All other stipulations will be made known to you at your first meeting with your probation officer. Do you understand these terms, Mr. Thomas?"

"Yes, sir! Thank you, sir! You won't regret this, Judge Burrus!" Kofi promised.

"Make sure I don't! Don't let me see you in my court again!" the judge barked and banged his gavel. "Next case!"

Kofi hugged his attorney. "I can just leave? I can just go?"

"You need to go back to the juvenile center until all the paperwork can be completed. You can't leave today, but tomorrow, you're a free man!" she assured. "Now go hug your mother!"

Kofi followed the instruction of his lawyer and ran to Hope.

"Kofi! Kofi! My baby!" Hope cried.

Esdell and Kareem shook the hands and hugged the members of their faithful church members and then turned to watch the reunion of mother and son with huge smiles on their faces.

"What happens now, Ms Douglas?" Esdell asked.

"Kofi has to go back to jail, just for tonight. He'll be released tomorrow to his mother."

"Thank you, Ms Douglas. Thank you so much!" Hope gushed.

"You are most welcome. Kofi, you need to go with the guard now. You'll see everyone tomorrow. I have to leave myself. Good-bye, everyone."

"Good-bye, Ms Douglas! Thanks again!" Kofi said and then gave his mother another hug and gave both Kareem and Esdell a knuckle punch. He smiled as he was led away by the guards. "See ya tomorrow, Mama!" he yelled.

"I love you, Kofi. See you in the morning!" Hope watched as Kofi disappeared through the courtroom doors and then all but collapsed into a nearby chair. "He's getting out!"

"Praising God right now, Miss Hope!" Kareem rejoiced.

"So am I! More than ever. Like I should have been all along!" Hope cried.

Esdell took Hope by her hand and pulled her up from the chair. "C'mon, Hope. Let's get outta here. Thanks, everyone!" He then guided her arm to lock inside of his and escorted her out of the courtroom out to the parking lot where everyone gathered. They all praised God for the blessing of Kofi's pending release, and then they all went to their cars to go to their respective homes.

"Dad, I'm going to the church now. I can't wait to tell Pastor the good news! See you at home," Kareem said as he turned to Hope. She leaped on Kareem hugging him firmly around his neck.

"I have no words, Kareem. Thank you for everything you did!"

"Thank you, and praise God, Miss Hope! I'm so grateful that everything turned out so well."

He gently pushed Hope away. "See ya later, Dad." Kareem went to his car, leaving Esdell and Hope standing alone in the parking lot.

"Did you get your car fixed, Hope, or do you need a ride?" Esdell asked.

"I could use a ride, if you don't mind," Hope answered. "My coworker brought me, but he couldn't stay. It'll take me a hour to get home on the bus, and it'll be dark by the time I get home."

"Let's go, then."

Esdell and Hope talked all the way to her apartment complex. They were elated with the way everything had turned out at court. Esdell continued to praise God for the blessing of Kofi's release. Soon they arrived at Hope's place. Esdell walked Hope to her door. As they approached her front door, there was the sound of something crashing on the inside.

"What was that?" Esdell asked.

"I don't know." Hope cautiously unlocked her front door. Esdell stepped in front of her.

"Let me go in first!" As he stepped through the threshold, Hope flipped on a light switch that was just on the inside wall. Suddenly, a cat ran from the kitchen into the bedroom.

"Woodstock, you bad kitty!" Hope chastised. "I should've known it was you. I bet he was on the countertop again!" She walked into the kitchen. "Yeah, uh-huh, just like I thought. It's okay, Esdell." She walked out of the kitchen holding a broken coffee mug.

"So, you're a cat person!" he smirked. "Didn't know that!"

"Why? You gotta a problem with cats?" she asked, tossing the broken mug into a nearby trashcan.

"No, not at all! I just didn't think you'd have a pet with the way you work and all."

"I got real lonely with Kofi being in jail. My cousin, Dameon, is the only family I have here, and I don't get to see him much. I just gotta few friends. I needed someone, something. So I got a cat. They're real low maintenance. They do good by themselves. He's good company. Kofi's in for a surprise. He hasn't met my little kitty-cat yet."

"You've gotta a nice place here, Hope," he complimented.

"Thanks! Have a seat. You want something to drink?"

"No, I should get on home. It seems like everything's okay. I'ma head on in."

Hope walked toward Esdell and looked up at him. "Thanks for the ride, and thanks for today. Y'all bein' there helped so much. You supported me, emotionally and physically. I probably would've fallen on my face if you hadn't been there to hold me up. Thank you!" Just like she had done with Kareem, she hugged Esdell tightly around the neck, standing on her toes to reach him. He clinched her waist. Then she released him and slowly lowering herself. Then she began to cry. She buried her face in his chest.

"Go 'head, Hope, let it all out!" Esdell urged. "Let it out. You been through a lot today, but it's over now. You go 'head and cry." She sobbed as Esdell gently held her. She soon stopped and again looked up at him. Esdell looked down into her eyes. He slowly lowered his head as Hope raised hers. His heart pounded. He softly pressed his lips to hers but immediately stepped back. "I'm sorry! I gotta go."

"Please don't go, Esdell. It's all right! Please stay!"

"I can't, Hope. I can't! Please understand!"

Esdell rushed back to his car while Hope watched in disbelief from her front door. He quickly drove from the apartment complex.

"What did I just do?" he asked himself. "Forgive me, Kenya!" Esdell sped onto the onramp of Interstate 70 east and drove like a criminal being chased by the police. When he had put distance between himself and Hope's apartment, he calmed down. *I'd better slow down*, he thought to himself. *What is wrong with me?*

All manner of thoughts were running through his head, but above all, he was feeling guilty. He had made it up in his mind that he could never be with another woman. Even though Kenya was dead, he felt as if he had been unfaithful to her. He drove around the city in a daze trying to shake the shame he felt. When he had finally composed himself, he returned home and entered the house. The downstairs was quiet, so he went upstairs and started toward his bedroom. Karlena was with Micah in her bedroom when she heard his footsteps in the hallway.

"Is that you, Daddy?" Karlena asked.

Esdell stopped and then went into Karlena's room. "Yeah, it's me."

"How did it go?"

"What? How did what go?" Esdell asked defensively.

"What's the matter with you? What happened at court?"

"Oh, that! He got probation, and he'll get out tomorrow."

"Great! That's wonderful!" Karlena could tell that something was wrong with Esdell. He still appeared dazed even though he thought his demeanor had returned to normal. "What's going on with you, Daddy?"

"I'm just real glad Kofi's gettin' out of jail. It's real upsettin' seein' all those kids in trouble so young. Did you have a good day off with Micah?" he asked.

"I did! We just finished talking to Joseph on Skype. He's doing really, really well!"

"That's good."

"He says he really misses us. His conversation was different."

"How so?"

"Well, Joseph has always been very kind to me. He's a fo' real gentleman, but tonight, he wasn't just kind, but he was sweet and tender.

"He said he didn't realize he'd miss me so much. Missing the water, well dry, that kinda stuff! How can I go on with my life and even consider dating anyone when I know he's feeling like that?"

With this question, Esdell's forgot about what he was going through. It was now all about Karlena.

"You two broke up, right?"

"Technically, yes! But I still feel like he's my boyfriend."

"Karlena, you're attached emotionally to Joseph. You just don't forget that kinda feelin'. But he's miles away. It's hard to keep up a long-distance relationship. When y'all broke up, you freed each other to date other people. You don't have to feel guilty or like you're cheatin' on him. But I will tell you this: God has His own plans for you. If He means for ya'll to be together, it will be, and if he has someone else in mind for you, that will be. Like always, just pray on it!"

Karlena licked her lips. "Daddy, Joseph invited me and Micah to come to Louisiana for Thanksgiving. I think I wanna go."

"Oh really!" Esdell said with a protesting tone.

"He lives with his grandparents for now, and he says they have plenty of room in their house for us. Me and Micah will have our own room. Joseph and I wouldn't be sleeping together, if that's what you're thinking!"

"That's *not* what I'm thinkin'! I'm not feelin' y'all bein' away from the family on a holiday!" He picked up Micah and gave him a kiss. "You ain't tryna leave Gramps on Thanksgiving, are you, li'l buddy?" He placed him on the bedroom floor. "I realize you're a grown woman. I can't stop you if you really wanna go. You gotta enough money for that kind of trip?"

"Joseph's willing to pay for our trip. If he can get the plane tickets now, that'll be cheaper. It'll be Micah's first plane trip, won't it, Mick Mick." Karlena look at the place where Esdell had set Micah, but he wasn't there, and then there was the sound of something crashing. "Micah where are you?" She ran into the hallway in time to see Micah disappear quickly down the stairs. "MICAH!" she screamed running toward the staircase, but Esdell passed her in the hall. He leaped down the stairs and picked up Micah.

"You're *okay*! You're *okay*!" he said.

"Give him to me!" Karlena ordered. She looked at Micah, looking for any sign of injury. "You left the gate open. I keep telling y'all to CLOSE THAT GATE!" She looked at Micah, and he was laughing.

"Maaa!" Micah gurgled.

Esdell looked around and saw Micah's tricycle lying near the front door.

"He musta pushed the tricycle down the stairs and went down after it. He probably just slid down the stairs on the carpet. Whew! Thank you, Lord."

As the adults tried to downshift from panic mode, Micah was laughing like it was all a game.

"Micah, you scared Mommy half to death." Karlena hugged him tightly.

"Sorry, Karlena, my mind was a thousand miles away. I'm so sorry!" Esdell apologized.

"He's not hurt. That's all that matters. Sorry for yelling at you, Dad."

"I deserved it."

Karlena started back up the stairs, not saying another word to Esdell and went into Micah's room. She sat in the rocking chair and rocked her baby. It was she, however, that needed to be nurtured, not Micah. Esdell looked in the room and apologized again.

"I'm really sorry!"

"He's fine, Daddy. It's fine."

"I'm goin' to my room. I got homework to do."

Esdell tried to study, but recalling the events of the day were far too distracting. First, there was the court trial, then the encounter with Hope, and now Micah's fall. His mind raced, he began to sweat. The sound of that tricycle tumbling down the stairs and Karlena's screaming returned his thoughts to war. He thought about gunshots, bombs, and the sound of wounded men yelling. All of this, of course, sent his thoughts to Kenya's death.

Three hours had passed. Kareem had come home, and Karlena had told him about Micah's fall. He knocked on Esdell's door.

"Can I come in, Dad?" he asked.

"Sure! C'mon in, son."

Kareem saw that Esdell's clothes were wet from perspiration. He knew exactly what was happening, but he did not know what to do. He did not want to make things any worse. He decided to avoid talking about what had happened to Micah.

"Pastor told me to tell you hello. He was real happy about Kofi. Uh, I got a lot of studying done in the church library. It's got a lot of good books."

"Yeah, okay," Esdell answered. "Kareem, go to bed. I know what you tryna do. Don't worry about me. I'm good. You ain't gotta tiptoe around me."

"You sure?"

"I'm sure. Now, go on to bed! I'ma go to bed myself."

"All right, Dad. Good night!"

Kareem went to his room and reviewed his homework before he got into bed. As he lay there, he could hear the sound of his father moaning through the walls as he had heard so many times before. Everything that happened that day had prompted another night of bad dreams.

"Kenya! No Kenya!" Esdell called.

"Lord God, please give my father a peaceful night's sleep," Kareem quickly prayed and then turned on to his side, pulling the covers around his neck.

Esdell continued to toss and turn but eventually fell into a deep sleep and began to dream.

* * *

He was walking through a dark forest toward a light that shined brightly ahead of him. He began to run quickly, desperately trying to get to the light. When he reached the bright light, he stopped running. The light was so bright, it was almost blinding and it frightened him. He then walked into a great pasture where he saw a flowing river that was as clear as glass. It had a golden bridge crossing over it. He walked aimlessly, trying to understand where he was. As he walked around, taking in the beauty of the pasture, he felt a calmness coming over him. The grass was as green as emeralds, and when he touched it, it was as soft as velvet. There were brightly colored tropical flowers throughout the field. He walked to the river and watched it flow. The splashing water appeared as diamonds.

"Esdell!" a soft voice said. "Esdell!" the voice again called to him. He walked in the direction of the voice. He looked ahead; his mouth fell open.

"Kenya, is that you?"

"Yes, Esdell it's me!"

He couldn't believe his eyes, but it was Kenya standing there before him. She was wearing a long bright white gown with a gold sash tied around the waist. Her skin was like shiny copper. Her eyes appeared as dark amber, her lips red as rubies. Her brown, naturally curly hair fell past her shoulders with one side pulled behind her ear, being held back by a bright pink hibiscus flower. Her beauty was as bright as the light that shined throughout the pasture.

"What is this place, Kenya? Is this heaven?"

"It is, my love."

Esdell started toward Kenya but she held up the palm of her hand, signaling him to stop.

"I can't believe it! Oh my god! Kenya!"

"It's good to be with you, Esdell. I would ask how you are, but I already know. But I must ask you, why are you so troubled?"

"I miss you, Kenya. It's so hard trying to live without you! You were taken from me so quickly and so horribly. I keep seeing your body after you were killed, and I can't shake it!"

"It's not good for you to be this way, Esdell. I watch you toss and turn in your sleep and see those terrible dreams you have. I don't like it."

"I miss you so much, Kenya," he said again. "I look at Karlena every day and see your face. It's a blessing and a curse at the same time. Won't you come back and be with us?"

"Did you not just recognize this place as heaven?" she asked. "Look at me. I'm whole again and resting in peace here with God. The brightness you see here is His glory! No, I don't want to come back, but I'm with you, Kareem, Karlena, and Micah every day."

"You've seen Micah?"

"Yes! And he's just fine; not hurt one bit! What a good and lovely boy he is. And just like you singin' that silly little song of yours, he's handsome just like you!" She smiled knowingly.

Esdell was amazed to imagine that Kenya had not missed one day in the life of their family.

"You're so beautiful, Kenya. There will never be anyone who can take your place. I don't know if I'll ever be the same."

"Don't believe that! You should take your own advice, the advice that you gave Karlena. Don't you believe that God can grant you peace? I know you are a man of great faith. Its one of the many things I love about you." Kenya opened her arms and Esdell ran to her, resting his head on her breasts. She pressed her ruby red lips to his forehead.

"My sweet, sweet love, Christ said 'Peace I leave with you; my peace I give you. I do not give to you as the world gives. Do not let your hearts be troubled and do not be afraid.' Christ has already given you peace. You have so much love to give. That didn't stop when I was called home, here, to be with Jesus. He loves you just like I do. You still have faith in the all powerful God, don't you?"

"Of course I do!"

"God wants you to have joy, love, peace, and hope, and so do I."

Kenya held Esdell tightly and again kissed him on his forehead. He could feel all those torturous memories calming within him with that kiss. "It's all right, Esdell. I'm fine. Go back now and know the peace that God has given you."

"But I want to stay here with you! Can't I stay?" he begged.

"Don't be silly. It's not your time yet. There is much left for you to do. Many lives have changed because of you and many more *will* be changed because of you. You must go now, Esdell. I'll wait here for you all. Good-bye!"

Esdell watched Kenya as she walked toward the river to the bridge. She began to cross over it. Halfway across, she stopped, turned around, and blew him a kiss. She then removed the bright pink hibiscus flower from her hair and tossed it into the flowing water.

"Wait, Kenya, come back!" he yelled, but she kept walking into a mist that enveloped her. He could no longer see her.

*   *   *

Suddenly, with a big swoosh, Esdell seemingly fell to earth. He gasped deeply and then he opened his eyes trying to bring himself to full consciousness. He sat up panting, his heart was rapidly beating. "Oh my Lord!" He blinked his eyes and continued to pant. Slowly, his breathing returned to normal. He sat still trying to fathom what he had just experienced. Then he knew that God had answered his prayer; finally granting him peace. Yes, Kenya was gone, but what Esdell already knew had been confirmed: she was happy, whole, and was resting with the Lord, and he would, indeed, see her again.

"Thank you, Lord. Thank you!" He lay back down and stared at the ceiling. He meditated on his dream, committing every detail to his memory. He thought of how beautiful Kenya was as well as her surroundings. Finally, his eyelids became heavy and he drifted off to sleep, calmly and peacefully. Those horrible dreams of Kenya's death would vex him no longer.

11

The Thanksgiving holiday had come and gone and it had been really different for Esdell and his family. After much discussion, he relented to Karlena's desire to go to Louisiana to be with Joseph. She was gone for five days, and the house was very empty without her and Micah. Not only was Karlena and Micah gone for the holiday, but so was Grace and Isaiah. Isaiah had an elderly aunt and uncle in his home state of Georgia, and he wanted to spend Thanksgiving with them. They were the last of his father's generation. Grace, of course, was concerned about leaving her family and did not want to go, but she understood the sense of urgency felt by her husband. So Esdell, Kareem, and Sammy had a small Thanksgiving dinner with Christine and her daughters at their apartment. They had a good time, but they all had to admit it just was not the same. They were deliberate in giving God thanks and to praise Him for all he was in their lives. Greater praise was given when everyone returned home safely. Karlena, Grace, and Isaiah were full of stories from their Thanksgiving travels. Though they, too, missed being at home, they were all happy that they had made their journeys.

Through the days gone by, Esdell was constantly replaying the scenes from his dream in his mind. He continued to ponder on what it all meant, but one thing he knew for sure, it was meant to bring him peace of mind, and that it had done. With that peace of mind, Esdell found himself thinking more and more about Hope. He always knew of her circumstances because of Kareem's ongoing relationship with Kofi. He finally admitted to himself that he was attracted to her. The question was now what to do with this realization. He had loved Kenya so much and had held on to her so tightly, he did not know how to approach the prospect of a new relationship. He was woefully out of practice when it came to romancing a woman, so he prayed on it and just kept a wait-and-see attitude.

* * *

Christmas was approaching along with the end of the school semester. Esdell and the twins were all studying and preparing for final exams. Esdell walked into his house carrying a large sack.

"What's all that, Dad?" Kareem asked.

"I went to the art supply store on lunch today to buy some charcoal and pastel pencils I need for class, and while I was there, I picked up some canvass and some oil paints. I thought I'd get a head start on my class next semester and try my hand at painting. But now I gotta hit the books and get ready for my first test."

"Hmm. How was work?"

"It was good. Gary reminded me that his baptism's this Sunday afternoon. He wants to make sure I'ma be there. Wouldn't miss it!"

"I might go with you, if you don't mind."

"Man, Gary would love it if you came! He's been wanting to meet you."

"You were a great witness for Christ, Dad. You were a big influence on his connecting with God."

"I just told him what I knew, and the Holy Spirit did the rest!"

Esdell turned his head in the direction of the sound of Micah's stomping footsteps as he came from the kitchen. Karlena followed closely.

"Hi, Daddy. Micah, go see gramps."

"Hey, li'l buddy!" Esdell greeted as he scooped him up. "How you doin'?"

"Micah, say gramps," Karlena prompted.

"Dae!" Micah responded.

"No, say gramps!" she instructed.

"Dae! Dae!" Micah said again.

"Dae? That's so cute!" Karlena said. "I don't know why this boy wants to call you Dae. I don't know where that came from."

"Its all right by me. You can call me Dae if you feel like that, Micah. What kinda day you have, baby girl?" Esdell asked.

"Pretty good. It got even better when I came home. First, I saw that Kareem had ordered Chinese for dinner! Then I talked to Joseph. Daddy, you got plans for tomorrow night?"

"Just studying. Why? What's up?" Esdell asked.

"Joseph told his parents to sell me his car if I wanna buy it! I was hoping you'd go with me to look at it."

"Joseph doesn't want his car?" Kareem asked.

"No. He doesn't need it. He's driving one of his grandparent's cars. They had three!"

"Man, Joseph's grandparents are ballers!" Kareem exclaimed.

"You got that right! You should see their home! They were just gonna give him the car, but Joseph insisted on working it off at the publishing company. That's just the way he is!" Karlena said with an adoring look in her eye.

"How much?" Esdell asked.

"Twenty-eight hundred."

"Twenty-eight hundred?" Kareem yelled. "That car's only four years old. Shoot, if you don't buy it, I will!"

"That's a good price," Esdell agreed. "Even if there's somethin' wrong with it, it's worth gettin' fixed. Sure, we can go look at it, but you got $2,800 Karlena?"

"You know I don't! I can pay half without completely wiping out my bank account, and they're willing to take payments on the rest."

"You really don't have to look at it, Dad! Joseph took really good care of that car. You better go get it before they decide to sell it to someone else!" Kareem suggested.

"He's right, Daddy! I used to tease Joseph by saying he took better care of that car than he did of himself! But I don't have to worry about them selling it to someone else."

"Why's that?" Kareem asked. "He's giving *you* a deal 'cause he could make more if he sold it to a stranger! If things get tight, he might consider selling it to somebody else. I know that ride's worth at least twice as much and more than he's selling it to you for."

"Like I said, he won't sell it to anyone but me. We talked about me getting my own car when I went to see him Thanksgiving. I told him it was getting cold, and I didn't want Daddy taking the bus all winter, and that it was kinda hard scheduling our jobs and classes with us sharing a car. That's when he offered me his car. He woulda given it to me, but he still owes twenty-eight hundred to his parents because they paid it off for him to save him interest. That's how he decided on the price. Plus, he said it made him feel like he was still looking out for me."

"Now, ain't that just the sweetest thing?" Kareem mocked. "Like Aunt Christine would say: *Woo, woo, woo!*"

Esdell sat for a moment, chuckling at Kareem. Then he said, "Well, thanks for lookin' out for me, Karlena! It's pretty cold on that bus stop, but I enjoy riding the bus. Anyway, I'll tell you what, you pay half, and I'll pay half. It'll be an early Christmas present."

"Really, Daddy?" Karlena exclaimed. "Thank you!" She threw her arms around him, nearly smashing him and Micah.

"You're welcome! You're welcome! Now let us go!"

"Man, Karlena, you're lucky! I wish someone would buy me a car!" Kareem said.

"Excuse me, dude, but Grandma *gave* you a car. It might notta been new, but it didn't cost you a dime!" she retaliated. "And don't even act like you're jealous that Daddy's giving me half. He paid for your summer class, remember?

"Kids, don't y'all start that competition mess! You've got money from your mom just like Kareem. Both of y'all been blessed, so just count them and be grateful!"

"I'm just playin' with Karlena. I'm happy for you, sis. All I want is a ride every now and then! Don't forget your brother when you're rollin' tuff in that ride!"

"Anytime, bruh! Well, almost anytime!" Karlena corrected.

"Yeah, whatever! Anyway, I'm going to the church library. I gotta a paper due and more studying to do. See y'all later!" Kareem pulled his coat from the living room closet. "See ya, Micah! Say bye-bye!"

"Bye-bye!" Micah said as he waved to his uncle as he left.

"You give Joseph's parents a call and tell 'em we'll be there tomorrow. Ask if they want cash, or if they'll take a check. Make sure they got the title and all," Esdell advised. "Joseph's bein' awful generous, awful generous!" He gave Karlena a questioning look.

"Whaat?" Karlena squealed, smiling. "Why are you looking at me like that?"

"I think there's more to this than you sayin'. *Dae's* 'bout to go eat him some eggrolls. Li'l buddy, you go back to your mama who knows exactly what I'm talkin' 'bout!"

Esdell went into the kitchen and fixed himself a plate and then sat at the table to eat. Not only were there eggrolls, but a large container of shrimp fried rice and broccoli stir-fry. Karlena had followed him into the kitchen and still had a silly grin on her face. She sat next to him.

"Daddy, is there something bothering you about me buying Joseph's car?" Karlena asked.

"No. It's too good a deal to pass up. The car ain't the issue, it's the reason behind it. I think more happened on y'all's trip to Louisiana than you're tellin'. You got somethin' you wanna tell me?"

"Like what?"

"I think it took Joseph to move away from you for him to realize how much he really cares about you." Esdell recalled the talk he had with Joseph before he left. He said that he didn't romantically love Karlena; he only loved her as a close friend. Now, it seemed that the romance was being aroused long distance. "Y'all back together?"

Karlena smiled, shook her head, and then looked at the floor. "Um, not really. Well, sorta. I don't know. Uh, it's complicated!" Karlena seemed totally confused about their status. "Daddy, I swear you're a mind reader! Joseph and I spent a lot of time talking when I went to see him. At first, he said that he kinda feels like he abandoned me and Micah. He knows that I was being careful about allowing Micah to become attached to him. I'd told him that I wasn't gonna be the kind of single mom that just went from man to man trying to find a husband. He said he feels guilty about leaving us and that he just wants to make sure we're all right and taken care of."

"I think that's my job. For now, anyway," Esdell asserted.

"He did say that he now realizes that he loves me. *Now* he realizes it, when he's a million miles away!"

"So, what're you gonna do now? Did you tell Joseph how you feel about him?"

"He knows I love him."

"Do you really?"

"Yeah, I really do, and it's the first time I've been in love, Daddy, and I'm nervous 'cause Joseph's so far away. I'm afraid he'll find someone else even though now he says he loves me. Then what would I do?"

"Lick your wounds 'til they heal, then move on! That's somethin' I'm tryna learn myself." Esdell lowered his head. "Tryna learn how to move on!"

Karlena slightly tilted her head. "Is there something *you* wanna tell *me*?"

"No! At least not yet! We ain't talkin' 'bout me! Karlena, if God means for y'all to be together, you will be. Life's short and tomorrow's not promised to nobody! I thought me and your mama would be together a lot longer than God gave us." He paused trying to gather his thoughts. "I don't really know where I'm tryna go with this, but please don't waste time. Set a goal! Don't just be dreamin' about a life you might have with Joseph, being satisfied with a few crumbs here and there. Don't tie up your life."

The more Esdell spoke, the clearer the meaning of his dream of Kenya became. He had tied up his life loving a woman who had gone home to be with God; a woman who would not come back to him if she could. "Just think and pray hard on what you want and be sure to let the boy know how you feel!"

"Well, I'm definitely not gonna look to find anyone else now. I'm just gonna give him a little time."

"You don't need to look to find anybody. The man who finds a wife finds a good thing. That's Bible! Someone'll find you, girl, so don't wait too long on Joseph."

"I hear ya, but like you said, I'll keep praying and let God tell me when it's time to 'move on,' Daddy."

"He'll do it. We always talk about prayin', but it's the best way to understand what God's plan is for us," Esdell agreed.

Esdell finished his meal and went to his room to study, but after his talk with Karlena, he wondered if he should tell his children that he may be ready to start dating. Thoughts of Hope filled more moments of his time than he ever thought any woman could. Yet he was still resistant. Maybe he was only interested in her because she had first approached him. No, that wasn't true. Several women at church had pursued him, but he had ignored all of those advances. Well, he had ignored Hope too! He was making himself dizzy going back and forth.

Get your head in these books! he thought. He read through his notes from class, but it was hard for him to stay focused. He forced himself to concentrate until he was actually engrossed in his lessons. He studied for more than two hours, repetitively reading his notes and his textbooks. *If I don't have it now, I never will! Bring it back to me, Lord!* he thought as he closed his books and put his papers away. He yawned and stretched and then began to think about the conversation he had with Karlena. He had to concede that it was a real possibility that his baby girl could go to be with Joseph. He played all sorts of scenarios in his mind but then fought to dismiss them all. After that, he found himself thinking about Hope. He laughed at himself and then prepared to take his shower. On his way to the bathroom, he met Kareem in the hall.

"Get your paper done, son?" he asked.

"Yeah I did. I feel an A on the way!" Kareem bragged. "Hey, I got some good news!"

"Always down for good news! What is it?" Esdell questioned, following Kareem into his bedroom.

"Kofi called me and he completed his GED courses. He got his diploma!"

"That's just great!"

"I'm so proud of him. He's really turning his life around."

"I'm proud of him too. I'm also proud of you! You were a big influence on him, Kareem."

"Hey, I'm just taking after my dad. Look what you did for Gary. You introduced him to Christ."

"I ain't takin' credit for that! God just did what he does!"

"Yes, He did, but you were the instrument," Kareem corrected.

"Um, I'll bet Hope's really proud of Kofi, huh?" Esdell asked, looking away from Kareem.

"Oh yeah! Miss Hope's about to pop with excitement. You should hear her!"

"I wish I could." A look of embarrassment crept across Esdell's face. Kareem noticed immediately. "What's up, Dad?" he cautiously asked.

"Can I tell you somethin', man to man?"

"Absolutely!"

"I'm feelin' Hope," Esdell said just above a whisper.

"Are you serious, Dad?"

"I hope you okay with that, even though I'm still tryna figure out if *I* am!"

"Are you kiddin' me? I am totally D-O-W-N with it! It's about time!"

Esdell sighed with relief. "I wasn't sure how you'd feel about me bein' with somebody besides your mama."

"No one could ever take Mom's place, but, Dad, it's time! Past time!"

"I don't want you and your sister to feel like I'ma let someone come in between us. I was just gone too much while y'all was growin' up. It's important to me that we always be close."

"You really need to quit talkin' about that, Dad. That's in the past, and frankly, I'm kinda tired of hearing about it!"

Esdell's mouth flew open.

"I don't mean to be disrespectful, but it's the truth. I don't know a better father than you! Nothing and nobody could ever come between us because that's not us! We're family, bonded and God-fearing!"

"You right, but I feel I need to make every minute count, 'cause it won't be long before y'all will be out with your own families."

"Listen to you, you got me moved out and married with kids, and I don't even have a girlfriend!"

"Well, since you brought it up, are you interested in anybody?"

"Who? Me? Naw, I'm like the apostle Paul. I don't have time for a woman now. I got work to do for the Lord," Kareem declared. "But we're not talking about me. We're talking about you! Kofi told me that Miss Hope is always asking about you. He's a little skeptical though, 'cause he says Miss Hope makes bad choices when it comes to men. He really doesn't know you, so he's not sure about you either. He just doesn't want her to get hurt."

"He don't have to worry about that. I'd never hurt her. I've been thinkin' about her a lot, a whole lot!"

"Then you need to stop trippin'! She's thinking about you and you're thinking about her! It must be meant to be if you guys are all up in each other's heads and you don't even see each other. It seems to me that this is a relationship in the making if y'all would *stop trippin'*!"

"I did kiss her that night I took her home from court," Esdell softly confessed.

"What? For real? What happened?"

"It was...not good. I ran. I actually ran away from her. She must think I'ma punk!"

"Evidently not, if she keeps asking about you." Kareem smiled. "Now me, I'm the one who thinks you're punkin' out! Dad, you've found someone you like and that's a good thing!" The very words that he had spoken to Karlena earlier in the evening were now being spoken to him by his son. He could only smile and shake his head. "Stop running, Dad. If you wanna be with Miss Hope, it's cool with me, and I know Karlena's cool with it too!"

"I can't hardly take it when you give *me* advice!"

"Now, I think we need to get Karlena in here."

"No, we don't!" Esdell disagreed. "Why?"

"I'm about to take away another excuse you'll use for not seeing Miss Hope. I can see you now saying that you're gonna wait to see how Karlena feels."

"No, Kareem. Karlena's dealing with her own stuff right now. She don't need to put this on her!" Esdell protested, but Kareem ignored him. He immediately left his bedroom and returned quickly with Karlena.

"What's going on?" she inquired.

"You remember Kofi's mama, Miss Hope, right?" Kareem asked.

"Yeah. She was at Grandma's anniversary party back in the spring. She had on a pink dress and we were wearing shoes alike."

"Figures you'd remember her whole outfit! Anyway, Dad's gotta thang for her, and he's gonna hook up with her!"

"Delicately put, son!" Esdell responded.

"Yay!" Karlena yelled, clapping her hands. "It's about time, Daddy! Now I'm mad 'cause you two been holding out on me! How long have you been thinking about this, Daddy?"

"I think maybe too long. Is this really okay with you, Karlena?"

"It really is! You need someone. I know how you feel about Mom, but, like we were talking about, it's time to move on."

Once again, Esdell's own words had returned to convince him. Now all of his excuses were gone. At first there was his dream, and now it was permission from both of his children. Complete validation.

"See, Dad, I told you! We're cool with all of this. Now what's your excuse? Huh? Huh? Don't have one do you? I didn't think so!" Kareem chattered. "Go for it, Dad. Me and Karlena ain't even gonna block!" The twins burst into laughter.

"Look at his face, Kareem! What's the matter, Daddy?" Karlena chuckled.

"Aw man, I don't believe it! I'm actually nervous!" Esdell admitted.

"It's all right, li'l fella!" Kareem joked. "You been outta the game for a long time, but you'll be fine!"

"You really will, Daddy. Miss Hope is a lucky woman. She'd better be good to you, or she'll find herself answering to me!" Karlena kissed Esdell on his forehead and gave her brother a knuckle punch. "Daddy's gotta girlfriend! Daddy's gotta girlfriend!" she chanted as she skipped out of Kareem's room.

"That girl's got issues!" Kareem said. "I hope some of yours have been taken care of. You good?"

"I think I will be!" Esdell affirmed. Now he had to decide what his next move would be. The possibility of being in a relationship had met the approval of his children, but he knew that for him to be totally comfortable with it, he would have to go into fervent prayer.

12

Friday at 6:00 p.m., Esdell approached the timeclock in the warehouse after a hard day of work. He saw Gary going into the locker room. Esdell clocked out and then followed in behind him.

"Hey, Gary, how's it going? You ready for Sunday?"

"As ready as I can be!" Gary said with a smile. You're still coming, right?"

"You know it! Kareem and I will be there," Esdell affirmed. "Sunday at four o'clock."

"You know where the church is?"

"North Meridian Methodist Church? Sure do!"

"I was wanting to ask you if you'll be okay coming to a Methodist church with you being Baptist and all. And the church is predominately white."

Esdell scowled slightly and looked at Gary. "Man, have you met me? You know that stuff don't matter to me, it being Methodist or white! You should know me better than that!"

"*Okay,* I'm sorry. I'm glad you'll be there to support me. I never went to church before now. This is a big step for me!"

"How did you decide on Meridian Methodist?"

"It's weird!" Gary said. "I made a delivery to a pet store that's across the street and the church marquis said, "We'll see you here next Sunday." I didn't think nothing of it. I made my delivery and went on to my next stop. A week later, I had another delivery to the pet store and the marquis said, "We missed you last Sunday, so please come on the next!" When I came out of the pet store, I saw a man standing in front of the church, and next thing I knew, I was pulling into the church's parking lot. The man was the pastor, and he invited me to come to service. I've been going ever since. It's weird. I've passed that big ole church a thousand times but never paid it any attention."

"That's not weird! That's God! He sent you where you could grow and where He can use you," Esdell said, slapping Gary on the back.

Gary continued, "I went to one service and the pastor preached on that song 'Amazing Grace.' He spoke on each verse of that song, and it seemed like he wrote that sermon just for me. Deep! But, Esdell, I wonder why God sent me to a Methodist church. After all, it was you who started talking to me about Christ. You'd think He'd send me to a Baptist church like yours."

"Gary, I don't think God's about denomination. I think He's tearing down the divide!" Esdell declared. "God's gettin' his army ready to fight the war against Satan and his legions. When we go to war, we're all just Christians! No Baptist, Methodist, Pentecostal, Catholic, or whatever! We're all gonna be Christians in the army of the Lord! Man, don't get me to preachin' up in here!"

"Too late for that!" Gary laughed. "Anyway, I'm going under the water! I thought I was just gonna get some water poured on me! What's the difference? Do you know, Esdell?"

"Again, it's a denomination thing. Some religions feel like complete submersion, or goin' under the water, as you said, is the only way because Jesus was completely submerged. Others think any kind of washing by water will do, as long as the water flows on the head. But either way, if you believe that Jesus is the risen son of God, you're already saved. The baptism shows your obedience to God, and it's a outward show of your inward profession. It represents the death, burial, and resurrection of Christ and the death and burial of your old, sinful life, and your resurrection to a new, saved life. That's what I've been taught my whole life."

"I believe all of that! So, what else you got planned for the weekend?"

"I gotta be on campus by seven tonight to take my last final. Man, I'm so glad Karlena got a car 'cause now I don't have to rush tryna catch the bus, or worry about her having to take the bus. Hey, I got a A on my art history test. Did I tell you that?"

"No! Congrats, man!" Gary said, giving Esdell a high five.

"Thanks. I'm ready for this English test tonight! Then it's winter break! Tomorrow morning I'm gonna put up the Christmas tree, and then me and the kids are gonna start decorating. It's our first Christmas in our house, and I'm kinda excited! Then I'll see you on Sunday!"

"You gotta full weekend, so I'm gonna let you go so you can get to campus. Thanks again, Esdell. You've been a good friend to me!"

"No thanks needed. Bye, man, I'm out!"

Esdell went to his car and set course for school. He arrived on campus and went to his classroom to take his English test. He completed it quickly and left confident he would receive a high grade. With that, the end of the first semester was done. His mind was now set on the Christmas holiday. He made plans all the way home.

He entered the house and was happy to see that Kareem had brought up the Christmas decorations from the basement. The boxes, which had previously been in storage, were clearly marked but looked worn. Esdell hadn't seen the decorations in years. He paused for a second but then smiled. He smiled because he knew he would not be saddened by the sight of the Christmas decorations that Kenya had purchased.

"Daddy?" he heard Karlena call from upstairs.

"Yeah, it's me!

Karlena came down the stairs. "Hi!"

"Hi" Esdell returned her greeting. "Micah sleep?"

"Yes. How'd you do on your test?" she asked.

"I think I did real good. Probably gettin' an A, and definitely not getting any less than a B. "

"All right, Daddy! Uh, I didn't cook anything. We just all ate sandwiches. Kareem ate and went—"

"Down to the church!" Esdell finished Karlena's sentence. "That's my boy! I ain't worried about dinner. I'm not really hungry. I'll just eat some crackers and cheese or something. I see Kareem brought up the Christmas boxes."

"Yeah, and look at this!" Karlena went to the dining room table and then picked up a tree ornament that was a little black girl dressed as a nurse holding a Teddy bear. "It's my nurse ornament Mama bought me! I thought it was lost, but it's been in one of the boxes all these years. Oh, I've missed you, baby nurse!" She kissed the little ornament.

"Girl, you're silly!" Esdell chuckled. "I remember you always told your mama that you wanted to be a nurse and that's why she bought that for you. Now you're studying to become one! How 'bout that! Well, tomorrow, when we put up the tree, she'll be the first ornament on it!"

"I found Kareem's little fireman ornament too. He used to wanna be a firefighter. Who woulda thought he'd end up being a preacher? I guess he's on fire for the Lord though, huh?"

"You can say that for sure!" Esdell agreed. Father and daughter chatted for an hour or so and then went to bed.

*   *   *

First thing the next morning, Esdell, Karlena, and Kareem began to decorate their home for the Christmas holiday. Micah watched with great interest from his playpen. He was fascinated by the lights and all the sparkling ornaments. They worked together to put up the tree, and Karlena was delighted to put her little nurse on the tree first. Once the tree was up, the men put lights on the outside of the house, and Karlena continued working on the inside. She had just put a red tablecloth on the dining room table when Esdell and Kareem reentered the house.

"Looks nice in here, sis," Kareem complimented.

"Thanks! Y'all get finished outside?" Karlena asked.

"We did," Esdell responded. "We just put lights around the gutters and some on the shrubs. We kept it simple. You need help?"

"I'm pretty much done. I need a centerpiece for the table though. I found an artificial poinsettia in the box, but it's all smashed up."

Esdell paused for a minute and then an enlightened look came across his face. "I'll go get something. I'll be right back!"

In a manner of minutes, Esdell was parking his car in front of While They Yet Live Flowers. He sat in his car as he looked into the large picture window in front of the shop where he could clearly see Hope. *Good, she's working today. Thank God!* he thought. He watched her as she worked assembling a floral arrangement. 'That's so pretty. She's so pretty!' Esdell watched intently as Hope's skillful hands crafted the flower piece. *I'd better get in there before she calls the police thinking I'ma stalker or something.* He took a deep breath, exited his car, and walked into the shop. A jingling bell alerted Hope that someone was entering the shop. She looked up to see Esdell standing in front of her.

"Esdell," she said softly.

"Hello, Hope. How ya doin'?" he asked.

"What're you doing here?"

"Uh, I'm looking for a Christmas centerpiece for our dining room table. Can you suggest something?"

Hope squinted her eyes and nodded her head. "Oh, I see! Sure. Did you have anything in mind?"

"This's nice." Esdell pointed to the piece that he had watched Hope work on. "You do good work!"

"Thank you, but this arrangement is a special order. It's not for sale. Let me show you something else." Hope came from behind the counter and walked to a large display of poinsettias.

Esdell tried hard not to stare, but he couldn't help himself. Under an apron, Hope was wearing a pair of black jeans. The pant legs were tucked inside of a pair of flat, black suede, knee-high boots. She had on a red sweater that defined her voluptuous figure. In the holiday spirit, she was wearing a Santa Claus hat.

"These are always a nice touch. We sell a lot of 'em and as you can see, they come in different colors," Hope said and then waited for a response, but Esdell said nothing. "Well, do you see anything you like?"

"Yes, I do!" Esdell suggestively answered, but he immediately changed the tone. "Uh, these *are* nice. There's a red tablecloth on the table. Which one do you think is best?"

"I would go with a white one. I can add some Christmas picks to it if you like to make it a little more festive," she suggested.

"That would be great. I'll take a white one then. How long do these things live?" Esdell asked.

"If you keep the soil moist and keep it in a sunny room, it'll last through Christmas with the colored leaves. The colored leaves will eventually fall off, but the plant will grow new green ones. They can live for a long time if you don't mind a plain, green poinsettia."

"You really know your stuff, Miss Hope! Yeah, this big white one will work just fine."

"Good choice. Would you like me to add some Christmas ornament picks?"

"Sure, whatever you think will look good. You decide. I trust your judgment."

Hope took the plant back to the counter and began to add festive, holiday ornamentation. Esdell said nothing to her as she concentrated on her craft. In just a few minutes, she was done.

"Is this okay?" she asked.

"Looks really good! How much do I owe you?"

"That'll be $26.75," Hope calculated.

Esdell paid for the plant, then asked, "I hope I can remember how to take care of this thing. What if I have questions?"

Hope picked up the store's business cards and handed to Esdell. "If you have any questions, feel free to call us."

"Thanks," Esdell said, looking at the card. "Uh, this is the number just for the shop? What if I have a question after hours? Is there a number where I can call you?"

"E. Brown, what're you doin'?" Hope huffed. "Don't come up in here playin' with me! I'm tryna work and you're about to make me lose my professionalism. What do you want?"

Esdell sighed heavily and scratched his head. "Hope, I was tryna be smooth, but I see that ain't workin'. That was my sloppy way of asking for your phone number. I'd like to call you sometime."

"You wanna call me? What for?"

"I'd like to get to know you better. I know I've acted a little strange in the past, so…"

"A little strange? A lot strange is more like it!" Hope interrupted.

But Esdell continued, "Sooo, if you'd rather not be bothered, I'll understand."

Hope stood and just stared at Esdell for a moment. She paced back and forth behind the counter and then returned to stand face to face with him. She took the business card from his hand and wrote her phone number on the back of it.

"This is my home phone," Hope said and gave the card back to Esdell. "I'm not giving you my cell phone number 'cause I'm not gonna pay extra for you to waste my time!" She paused. "Don't play with me, Esdell! Please don't!"

"Oh, I ain't playin', girl! I'll call you tonight if you don't mind!"

"I don't. I'll be home by seven."

"I'll talk to you later then. Bye!" Esdell started toward the door.

"Uh, E. Brown, you're forgetting your poinsettia! That *is* what you came for, right?" Hope said smiling.

Esdell went back to get his plant. "Thanks, Miss Hope, I got *all* that I came for!"

He left the store and got into his car. "Whew! Whoa now!" He blurted and then began to drive back home.

Was it coincidence or fate that Karlena needed a centerpiece to complete her Christmas decorating and that Hope worked at a place that could fill that need? He believed it was fate. He recalled their previous encounters and thought how ridiculous he had appeared in the past. His mind began to race.

It's a miracle the woman even talked to me, much less gave me her phone number. She must think I'm crazy! What am I gonna say to her when I call her? Man, she's pretty! "Ahhh!" he yelled aloud. "Help me, Lord!"

He smiled and turned up the radio in the car. Esdell sang all the way home. When he arrived at home, he practically skipped in the front door carrying his newly purchased plant. Karlena and Kareem were sitting on the coach in the living room watching TV as Micah was taking a nap upstairs.

"Hey, Daddy, whatcha got there?" Karlena asked.

"It's a poinsettia for the table," Esdell answered setting it on the dining room table. He turned it around trying to determine the best side to display.

"That's nice! It's perfect! Where'd you get it?"

"I bought it from the flower shop where Hope works."

"Hope?" Karlena questioned. "The Hope you gotta crush on. Hope? Did you see her? What happened?"

Esdell blushed. "Yeah, I saw her. She sold me this plant and fixed it up for me. She did a good job, didn't she?"

Kareem looked at his father with a smirk on his face. "Yeah, it's beautiful. Anything else happen?"

"Well, as y'all would say, 'I got them digits!' I'm gonna call her later."

"Go 'head, Dad! I knew you had it in you!" Kareem exclaimed.

"Now the question is, what will I say when I call her?" He paused for a minute. "But you know what, kids? I ain't even gonna worry 'bout it. I'm just gonna go with the flow. This thang is already worked out."

"Y'all don't have a 'thang' yet," Karlena corrected. "But you will. I know you will. I'm happy for you! Just be honest with her. I know you will be! She's a lucky woman who doesn't know yet just how blessed she is!"

"Thanks, baby girl. It's been a long time comin', and I'm not gonna rush into anything. But I'm ready for a change."

Kareem walked over to Esdell and hung his arm around his neck. "All I wanna know, Dad, is did you get yo' mack on?"

"Son, I was a white hot mess!" Esdell laughed.

"Well, Pops, you might've been a mess, but you were effective! You on your way, Dawg!" Kareem said, giving his dad a knuckle punch.

"Did you whip that smile on her, Daddy, or did you just turn on that deep, sexy voice?" Karlena kidded.

"Uh, a little of both!" Esdell answered immodestly with a smile.

"Oh yeah, you got your mack on! All right, Dad!" Kareem said. "Sit down! You gotta tell us what happened!"

Esdell sat in the living room with his children and told them the whole story of him and Hope, starting with the first day he met her at the flower shop. He told them how he saw her again at Gordon Food Service the day he shopped for his parents' anniversary party and how she showed up at that very party. Then Kareem became a mentor to her son, Kofi, through the juvenile prison ministry. The more he talked, the more he knew that this pending relationship with Hope was meant to be. Everything had fallen into place, in spite of his early resistance to every situation. He told them about everything except his dream. That was something he would keep to himself for now.

* * *

Before Esdell knew it, it was close to seven o'clock. He was getting nervous and began to feel butterflies in his stomach. He went to his bedroom and set on the bed with the phone in one hand and the business card in the other. Should he call her right at seven, or should he wait until a few minutes later? He had punched in Hope's number before he answered his own question. The phone began to ring.

"Hello?" a man's voice answered.

"Hello? Uh, may I speak to Hope, please?"

"Who's calling?" the man's voice aggressively asked.

"Esdell Brown," he answered cautiously.

"Oh, hey, Mr. Brown. This Kofi. What's up?"

"Hey, Kofi! What's up with you? I heard you got your GED. Way ta go, man! Congratulations!"

"Thanks! Thanks a lot!"

"So, what're you gonna do now?"

"I know I wanna further my education, but I'm not sure what I wanna do or be."

"What do you like to do? What's fun for you?"

Kofi chuckled. "Well, what I used to do for fun just got me in trouble! I'm not tryna go back there! I just want to make a good living. I ain't smart enough to be no doctor or nothing like that."

"Don't sell yourself short, Kofi. A year ago, did you see yourself with a high school diploma?" Esdell asked.

"A year ago, I didn't even see myself alive!"

"But look at you now. You got your GED and making plans for your future! I know you're good at something!"

"Well, I can draw a little bit, and I like working with my hands. I liked working in the woodshop when I was locked up."

"You draw, really? So do I. And you like working with wood. Ever think about being an architect or a carpenter? You can design homes and build them. Or furniture, you can design furniture. Being a carpenter is a noble profession. Jesus was a carpenter, ya know."

"Ah yeah! You're RK's dad all right!"

"RK?"

"Reverend Kareem. I call him RK, and you talkin' Jesus just like he does!"

Esdell chuckled. "Oh, I see. Well, if you like, the next time I'm on campus, I can get you some course info from the School of Architecture or the School of Arts."

"Coo'! Thanks. You wanna talk to Ma? Hold on a minute. Hey, Ma. Phone!" Kofi screamed. "Nice talkin' to you, Mr. Brown. One more thing."

"What's that, Kofi?"

"Be right wit my mama!"

"Nothin' less, Kofi!"

"Hello? I got it Kofi," Hope answered.

"Bye, Mr. Brown." Kofi clicked off.

"E. Brown, aren't you the punctual one? It's straight up seven! Were you eager to talk to me?" Hope asked.

"Yeah, I was! Did I call too soon? If you just got home, you can call me back once you get settled."

"No, you're fine. I've been home for about a half hour. How was your day, Esdell?"

The way Hope called his name made Esdell almost quiver. "It was very good. It started off busy, but it's ending up great! How 'bout you, Hope? I bet you were nonstop busy today."

"Yes, I was. It's gonna get busier the closer we get to Christmas, then it'll slow down until Valentine's Day. Then, it's off again!"

"How do you like working at the flower shop?" Esdell asked.

"I like it just fine," Hope answered.

"You like working at the flower shop or at GFS the most?"

"Oh, the flower shop, no doubt. I like watching things grow, and I like creating different floral designs."

"Hmm, Kofi was just telling me how he likes workin' with his hands. I see where he gets it from!"

"I guess."

"You did a real good job on the plant you sold me. My daughter, Karlena, just loved it. It looks really good on our dining room table. Your coworker told me you made assistant manager at the shop after just six months. I see why. You're very talented."

"Thanks. Nice of you to say so. But I don't plan on being assistant manager for very long though."

"Why's that? You plan on finding another job?"

"No! I plan on buying the shop. I'm gonna own the whole place some day! Yup, I'm gonna buy it!" Hope boasted.

"Really? All right, now, Miss Hope!"

"That's part of the reason I work two jobs. That and trying to keep a roof over me and Kofi's heads."

"It's great that you have a goal like that. You seem determined, and if you got your sights on that shop, claim it as yours!" Esdell encouraged. "I'll pray on it with you."

"You'll pray for me?"

"Of course I will. It wouldn't be the first time I prayed for you, Hope. You and Kofi."

"Thank you. That means a lot to me. You gotta dream, Esdell?"

"Well, I wanna get my college degree. I'm over forty and shoulda had it by now, but I won't quit 'til I get it. Most of all, I wanna see my children succeed. I see Kareem as a great pastor of a church someday. Karlena's studying to be a nurse, but I see her as a doctor."

"So you dream for yourself and your children? Look at you, Papa! I know what you mean though. I wanna see Kofi succeed too. I'm so proud of him for getting his GED. There's gonna be a ceremony with a cap and gown and everything. I almost cry every time I think about it. I thought I'd see him in jail or in a coffin before I'd see him graduating."

"You should be proud and thankful to the Lord that you'll see the latter!"

"You're so right!"

Esdell and Hope continued talking, mostly about their jobs and their children, especially the friendship between their sons. Though Kareem was only a few years older than Kofi, Hope was amazed at Kareem's maturity and the positive influence he had on Kofi. The more the two of them talked, the more they discovered what they had in common. Their conversation was pleasant and lighthearted, as if scripted by God to ease any tension that may have been between them.

"Hey, Ma!" Kofi interrupted. "I'm hungry! Are you gonna cook, or should I order something?"

"Hold on a minute, Esdell," Hope said. "Kofi, I'll be off here in a minute. I'm sorry, Esdell. What were you saying?"

"Man! We've been talking for over two hours!" Esdell noted. "I should let you go so you can see 'bout Kofi."

"He's a big boy. He can…" Hope paused. "You know, I should go fix him something to eat. Another one of my goals is to be a better mother to my son and to be a little more attentive. He deserves that much from me. I haven't been the best mother."

"You've been better than some moms, I'm sure!"

"You're so sweet, Esdell. Will you call me again?"

"I will! I really have enjoyed talking to you, Hope. And, uh, I'm sorry."

"Sorry for what?" she asked.

"I'm sorry for actin' so stupid with you! Forgive me?"

"Yes. Well, I'ma go now. Talk to you soon?"

"Definitely! Good-bye."

"Okay, bye, Esdell." Though both of them had said good-bye, like two giddy high school students, neither of them disconnected the call.

"Hey, Hope, you still there?" Esdell asked.

"Yes, I was waiting on you to hang up!"

"I'm waiting on *you* to hang up!" They both burst into laughter. "What're you doin' tomorrow evening? Would you like to go to dinner with me?" Over their entire conversation, they had not talked about dating or trying to develop any kind of relationship. Hope was pleased by the invitation.

"Why, E. Brown, are you askin' me for a date?"

"Yes, Miss Hope, I am! How 'bout it?"

"I'd love to," Hope said softly.

"I'm goin' to see a friend of mine get baptized tomorrow at four o'clock. How 'bout I pick you up after that? It'll most likely be around six thirty. I'll call you when I'm on my way."

"That's fine. You remember where I live?"

"Oh yeah!"

"Well, I'll see you then. Now, I'm hangin' up for real! Bye, Esdell."

"G'night, Hope. See ya tomorrow."

A date being definitely set up for Sunday evening reassured both Esdell and Hope that they would be continuing their dialogue. They simultaneously hung up. Esdell smiled with satisfaction.

I gotta date! he thought to himself. He jumped up and went into Kareem's bedroom and knocked on the door.

"Come in!" Kareem said. Esdell entered. "What's up, Dad?"

"That's Mack Daddy to you! Tomorrow, after Gary's baptism, I gotta date with Hope! Whew!" Esdell spun around and then jokingly flopped to the floor as if he had fainted.

"You go, Dad." Kareem smiled as he looked down at his father lying on the floor. "You go, boy!"

13

Sunday started off as it normally did, with Esdell's family rising early to go to Sunday school, followed by worship service. Pastor Edward's sermon was very inspirational and Esdell tried to concentrate on it, but his mind wandered to the day's pending events. The day started off the same but the end was going to be anything but normal. He had Gary's baptism to attend and then there was the much anticipated date with Hope. Before those two things, however, he had Sunday dinner with the rest of the family.

As they did every Sunday after church, Esdell, Karlena, Kareem, and Micah went to his mother's house to have dinner. As the serving bowls were being passed around, he could only imagine how they would take the news of his starting to date. He wasn't really sure how to tell them.

"Would you pass me the gravy, Grace?" Isaiah asked. "Babe, this roast is delicious. It's so tender. My wife sho' can cook!"

Grace smiled broadly. "You say that every Sunday, Isaiah, and I never get tired of hearing it! Here ya go, honey," Grace said, giving the gravy bowl to Esdell to pass. She then noticed how empty his plate was. "Here, Esdell, have some potatoes," she insisted, giving him the bowl. Esdell took the bowl and put a very small amount of potatoes on his plate.

"The church sure looked nice today. The deaconesses did a great job decorating the church for Christmas. Those poinsettias they set around the pulpit were so pretty," Christine said.

"We have a beautiful poinsettia on our dining room table, don't we, Kareem?" Karlena inserted. She smiled looking at her brother knowingly. It now seemed that the decision on when to tell the family about his date was being made for him. Esdell darted his eyes in the direction of both of his children, warning them to be quiet. The deliberate stare caught Christine's attention.

"What's that look for?" she asked. "Something going on?"

"Here, Christine, have some more potatoes!" Esdell passed the bowl to her. It was obvious that he was trying to quiet her as well.

"Hmm. Thanks," she said, narrowing her eyes. She then turned her attention to Karlena. "So, Karlena, tell us about your plant. Is there something special about it?"

"Karlena, taste the roast. Pops says it's really good. Taste it and tell me what you think. Put some in your mouth!" Esdell blurted.

"Why you tryna shut the girl up, Esdell? What's going on here?" Christine asked accusingly.

Esdell looked at the face of everyone sitting around the table. Kareem and Karlena sat with smirks on their faces while the rest of the family had questioning looks on theirs. Esdell shifted in his seat, looking at the twins as they grinned at him. He scowled.

"Go on, Dad," Kareem urged. "Tell 'em."

Esdell said nothing, but his expression made it evident that he was avoiding something.

"What up, Big E? Somethin' you need to tell us?" Sammy asked.

"What is it, son?" Grace asked. "Your plate's almost empty, and next to Junya and Kareem, you eat more than anyone at the table. Don't you have a appetite today? Something botherin' you?"

"No, Mama, nothing's bothering me, but now is as good a time as any to tell y'all," Esdell said. "The reason I'm not eating much is 'cause I've gotta dinner date after we leave Gary's baptism."

Christine sat up straight in her chair. "Say what? You gotta date? With who?"

"That's with whom, Mom," Christine's daughter Celeste corrected.

"Whatever, li'l girl!" Christine retorted. "Stay outta grown folks business. Are you hookin' up with someone from church? I know! I bet you're going out with Sister Cummins"

Esdell laughed. "The bootie pincher? You too funny, Christine." Every one laughed right along with Esdell.

"I think you two would make a good couple!" Sammy added. "She just need a little love! But I bet I know who you're goin' out with. Is it Dameon's cousin, Hope?"

"You on it, Junyam" Esdell verified.

"All right, bruh!" Sammy approved. "Y'all remember the woman that was helping my friend Dameon when he came to DJ at Ma's anniversary party? That's who he's going out with!"

Everyone paused for a moment trying to remember what Hope looked like. Christine was the first to recall her.

"Oh, I know! It was that woman in the hot pink dress. She was cute! How'd you hook that up?"

"It's a long story," Esdell said. "But it's good one. I'll tell y'all someday, but right now, I just need all y'all to pray for me. I ain't been on a date since Kenya died. I hope I don't do nothin' stupid."

Christine laughed. "It's you! You can't help but do something stupid!"

Grace interceded, "Don't start, Christine. I think is good that you're brother is starting to date again. Where you taking her, baby?"

"Mama, I really don't know. If she has a preference, I'll let her decide. If not, then I guess it's your favorite restaurant, Down Home Chews."

"Good choice," Isaiah said. "That's where I took Gracie on our first date!"

"They all know that, Isaiah, and they don't need to hear that story again!"

Everyone began to groan in agreement. The story of Isaiah and Grace's courtship had been shared by Isaiah more times that anyone wanted to hear. It was well-known.

Esdell listened and laughed as his stepdad proceeded to tell the story again. It was a true love story that told of how someone could find love for a second time. He realized now how much he could learn. He had to be open to finding love. His mother never thought she would ever find another love after his father died, but she did, and now she was remarried and very happy. He wasn't thinking about marriage, but he thought he was ready for at least a casual relationship.

The banter continued well after dinner. They joked about Isaiah retelling his story, and kidded Esdell about his date. Christine continued to make digs at Esdell about him being out of practice when it came to the dating game. Samuel offered up his expertise as a supposed lady's man on how to entertain a woman. Christine reminded Sammy that he was on lockdown due to his relationship with her friend Danielle, so he was out of practice himself. Christine's daughters, Celeste and LeAnn, listened intently, finding all this talk amusing.

"Hey, Dad, we'd better get moving!" Kareem said, looking at his watch. "It's three thirty already."

Esdell checked his watch, too, and stood up. "It sure is! Well, fam, it's been real, but we gotta go. Y'all lift Gary up in prayer. It's a big day for him! And, uh, pray for me too!"

"You'll do fine, bruh!" Sammy encouraged. "The Brown men got it like that when it comes to women. Do yo' thang, player!"

LeAnn jumped to her feet, running to give her uncle a hug. "Uncle Esdell, this lady is really lucky to have you for a date. You're so handsome and so smart! I know she'll have a good time and so will you!"

"Thank you, LeAnn. You're too sweet!" Esdell took a deep breath. "Well, everybody, I'm out!"

"Details, I'll want details!" Christine insisted.

Sammy had to chime in. "If you need some help, just hit me up on my cell. I'll give you some pointers!"

Esdell and Kareem said their good-byes and started their trip to the North Meridian Methodist Church. Taking separate cars, Kareem followed Esdell through the streets of Indianapolis to the church. It was a relatively short journey, taking only about fifteen minutes to get there.

They pulled into the parking lot and were surprised that there were only a small number of cars there. They had no problem finding a spot to park near the side entrance of the church. The church was made of gray stone with three steeples; the tallest one being a bell tower. It was an old church that had been a part of the Indianapolis skyline for decades. They approached the building wondering where they should actually enter it. A couple passed them, so Esdell and Kareem simply followed them as they seemed to know exactly where to go. They followed the couple as they passed what was obviously the sanctuary of this old majestic building. Esdell's steps slowed as they passed by, looking into the large room with over one hundred pews.

"Beautiful!" he remarked. "God's house!"

"C'mon, Dad. This way," Kareem said, keeping an eye on the couple that they had been following.

They finally entered into a chapel that housed the baptismal pool. There were more people seated there than expected. Esdell looked around trying to spot Gary. A woman wearing a black and red dress greeted them, giving them a program and inviting them to sit wherever they pleased. They sat three rows back from the pool, making sure that Gary would see them when he came out. And he did!

Gary came out wearing a white baptismal robe. He walked quickly over to Esdell and Kareem.

"Esdell, you made it!"

Esdell stood up. "Lookiin' good, man. How ya feelin'?"

"I'm excited. So excited! I been praying and studying and I'm ready! I'm ready to show everyone that I've accepted the Christ. Thanks for comin'."

"I wouldn't have missed it. This is my son, Kareem," Esdell introduced.

"Good to meet you, Reverend Brown! I feel like I know you already!" Gary said, extending his hand for Kareem to shake.

"Good to meet you too. Just call me Kareem." Kareem firmly grabbed Gary's hand and pulled him toward him to also give him a hug.

Gary took a deep breath, "Well, I'm supposed to sit on the front pew. There's two kids getting baptized. I'm the only adult. I thought I would be embarrassed, but I'm not!"

"And you shouldn't be!" Esdell agreed. "Heaven is rejoicing! Me too!"

Gary smiled broadly. "There's a short ceremony before the baptism and then there's a small reception after. See you guys later!"

Esdell and Kareem sat down and glanced over the program. Shortly, the woman who had given them the program stood in the choir stand and began to sing "The Lord's Prayer." She had a perfect soprano voice and sang with such spiritual emotion that it almost brought the two men to tears. When she had finished her solo, Esdell and Kareem applauded enthusiastically with shouts of "Hallelujah!" Their voices echoed throughout the chapel. The congregation turned to look at them, smiling. They were, perhaps, used to more controlled praise.

The pastor of the church spoke briefly ending with the reading of Matthew 3:16.

"And Jesus, when he was baptized, went up straightway out of the water: and, lo, the heavens were opened unto him, and he saw the Spirit of God descending like a dove, and lighting upon him. And lo a voice from heaven, saying, 'This is my beloved Son, in whom I am well pleased.'" He then entered the baptismal pool and called each candidate one by one. Gary was last. He stepped into the water. The pastor crossed Gary's hands over his chest.

"Now, by the profession of your faith and your obedience unto God, I baptize you, my brother, in the name of the Father, and of the Son, and of the Holy Spirit. Amen!" He cast Gary backward into the water and raised him quickly. He then gave Gary a towel. Gary dried his face then raise his arms high, clenching his fist as if in victory. He looked at Esdell; his face was beaming.

"Amen! That's all right, Gary! Praise God!" Esdell said, standing to his feet and applauding. He was not concerned about what the rest of the people thought. He stood in support and encouragement of his friend. "Amen!"

The church echoed him. They all applauded the newly baptized Christians. The pastor bowed to pray, giving thanks for all that had taken place. He invited everyone to the church reception hall to enjoy refreshments and fellowship.

"Well, Dad, are you gonna go to the reception?" Kareem asked.

"For a li'l bit," Esdell answered. "I wanna talk to Gary and then I'ma head on out to pick up Hope. I wanna be at her place by six."

"It'll take Gary a while to dry off and get dressed, but you've got time."

Then the woman who had greeted them and who had sung "The Lord's Prayer" approached them. She thanked them for their enthusiastic response to her solo. She chatted with them about Gary and about their church in general. She again invited them to the reception, but Esdell asked her if it was all right for him to look around. He wanted to go back into the main sanctuary. She told him he was more than welcome to do so, and also told them where to find the reception hall.

Esdell and Kareem went into the sanctuary and sat on the back pew. The ceiling arched and the stained glass windows where lined on both sides. Esdell was in awe.

"It's amazing" he remarked.

"What's that, Dad?"

"How I feel the Holy Spirit here, just like I feel it at our church. It just proves what I always thought. God ain't into denominations, he's just into salvation!"

"You're so right about that. I think that would make a good sermon. I'ma have to work on that one!"

The two men chuckled and sat for a few more minutes enjoying their surroundings and then went into the reception hall. Gary spotted them as they came in.

"Oh good, you waited! I thought you guys had left! Let me get you some punch."

"No thanks," Esdell declined. "I got somewhere else to be. I just wanted to wait and congratulate you! How ya feel?"

"I feel just wonderful! I wanted you to meet my pastor, but he's gone. Another time, maybe!"

"Maybe so!" Esdell said. "Well, I gotta go. I'll see you at work tomorrow, Gary, and, Kareem, I'll see you at home later."

"Okay, Dad. Have fun!" Kareem chuckled and gently punched his dad on his shoulder.

Esdell smiled broadly, took a deep breath, and went straight to his car. Once on the inside, he bowed his head and prayed. He first gave thanks for everything that had taken place up to this point, especially Gary's baptism. Then he asked God to bless the evening with Hope. He prayed that things would go smoothly, and that he wouldn't act or say anything out of place. He called Hope and told her he was on his way.

*   *   *

On the drive to Hope's apartment complex, Esdell tried to plan what he would talk about with her. One thing he knew for sure was that he would not discuss their kiss the day after Kofi's hearing. They had not discussed it before, so he saw no need to bring it up now. By the time he pulled into the complex parking lot, he had decided it was silly to try to script the evening, and that he would just let it flow on its own. He parked his car and started toward Hope's apartment. As he approached her front door, he popped a breath mint into his mouth. He tugged at his overcoat and knocked. After just a few seconds, Hope's son, Kofi, answered the door.

"Hey, Mr. B. C'mon in." Kofi smiled slightly and closed the door behind Esdell once he was inside. "Ma, Mr. Brown's here!" he yelled. "Move out the way, Woodstock! Stupid cat. Have a seat. That dumb cat thinks he owns this couch."

"So I take it that you're not too fond of your mom's cat," Esdell observed.

"Not really, but I put up with him 'cause Ma loves him so much. She said he kept her company when I was locked up. Anyway, she should be out soon. She prolly still all up in the mirror. She's kinda excited about tonight. How 'bout you, Mr. B? You excited to take out Ma?"

Esdell, sitting on the couch, rubbed his chin. "I am, but to be honest, I'ma little nervous. I haven't been on a date in a long time. Hey, Kofi, congratulations again on getting your GED.

"Thanks!" Kofi beamed. "So where you takin' Ma?"

"We're goin' wherever she wants to go!"

"Then what?

"Depends on what she wants to do after. This evening is all about her!"

"What you plan on gettin' out of it?"

Esdell was starting to feel like a teenaged boy being interrogated by a suspicious father. "Just some nice conversation with a nice woman, someone I want to get to know better. That's all! I'm not gonna try to take advantage of her, if that's what you're worried about!"

Just as Kofi was about to ask another question, Hope came into the living room.

"Hi, Esdell," she said.

Esdell stood up and turned to look at her. She was wearing all black with a bright pink flower brooch accenting a turtlenecked sweater. The flower was somehow familiar to Esdell, but he could not put his finger on why. Her earrings were large hoops, also bright pink. Her hair was put up in a French roll, and her bangs were curled with tendrils alongside her face. Her soft, sweet scent filled the room. Esdell blinked his eyes because he felt himself staring.

"Hi, Hope. You look very nice."

"You're looking pretty good yourself. Well, I'm ready!"

Esdell found himself staring again.

"I'm ready, Esdell," Hope repeated. "Are you?"

"Yeah, uh, yes, I am." He took the black leather coat she had draped over her arm to help her put it on. "Well, Kofi, we're out. Don't worry, she's in good hands."

"You just be sure to keep those good hands to yourself!" Kofi warned.

Hope smiled, rolled her eyes, and shook her head. "Where are we going, Esdell?" she asked.

"Wherever you want, Hope."

She walked to the door with Esdell following close behind her. "I'd really like to go to Applebee's. It's not real fancy but I like it!"

"Okay then, let's go!" Esdell said.

"Good night, son. I should be home before time to go to work tomorrow!" She joked. Kofi merely waved.

They walked to Esdell's car; he opened the door for her and closed it once she was safely inside. On their way to the restaurant, Esdell talked about his day. He told Hope about the church service, dinner at his mom's house, including the ribbing he had taken from his sister and brother. He told her about Gary's baptism. He also confessed how he had been looking forward to their date. Hope admitted that she, too, had been looking forward to their evening together. She talked about her day and conceded that it was uneventful in comparison to his. She asked questions about Esdell's church because she had no church home of her own. She knew that Kareem was the youth pastor at their church, so she was very interested in hearing about the Road to Damascus Baptist Church. Esdell, of course, was eager to tell her all about it. This consequently led to an invitation for Hope to join him one Sunday. Esdell took a slight detour through downtown to look at the Christmas lights. He drove them around the Monument Circle that housed Soldiers' and Sailors' Monument and was the center of downtown Indianapolis. The monument itself was close to three hundred feet tall, straight up and down, and was decorated annually with lights. At Christmas time, it was known locally as the world's largest Christmas tree. The surrounding downtown area was beautifully decorated as well. Hope was almost childlike as she viewed the holiday lights.

"You know, I've been living here for ten years, and I've never been down here at Christmas time. It's pretty!"

Esdell smiled when he noticed the look on her face.

"When we were little, my mama and daddy would pack all us kids in the backseat of the car, and we'd ride down here and all around the city just looking at the lights. Gas was a whole lot cheaper then, and it was a fun thing to do that didn't cost much."

Esdell drove two laps around the Circle and then drove to the restaurant. The hostess seated them immediately, and within minutes, a waitress came to take their drink orders. They looked over the menus, decided what they wanted to order, and began to chat while waiting for the waitress to return for their orders.

"I have to admit" Hope began, "that I never saw myself on a date with you especially after that little kiss incident!"

There it was; the one thing that Esdell had decided he was not going to discuss. He looked at Hope and took a sip of his drink. He said nothing.

"What was that all about anyway?" she asked. Again, he said nothing.

"Are you ignoring me, E. Brown?"

"Are you gonna call me E. Brown every time you get irritated with me?"

"Probably! One thing you need to know about me is that I don't like being ignored, and I don't like being cut off when I'm talking!"

"That's two things, Miss Hope," he corrected.

"Are you gonna call me Miss Hope when *you're* irritated with me?"

"Prolly!" he said. They chuckled. "I must've seemed pretty lame that night, huh?"

"Yup!" Hope quickly agreed.

"I was goin' through some things then. I think I got 'em all worked out now."

"I hope so! Oh, here comes the waitress."

The waitress took their orders. Hope ordered a crispy chicken salad with a baked potato. Esdell ordered shrimp Alfredo with a side salad. They continued their conversation.

"So, Hope, you said you've only been living here for ten years. Where did you live before?"

"All over. I've been all over the US. I was born and lived overseas for the first nine years of my life."

"Really? That's interesting. How were you born overseas?" Before she could answer, the waitress brought their food.

"Hmm, that pasta looks good. I should've ordered that!" Hope said. She picked up her fork to take a bite of her salad when she noticed that Esdell's head was bowed to bless his food. She lowered her fork and bowed as well. She hoped that Esdell had not noticed her omission.

"Wait!" Esdell said. "Didn't you mention once that your dad was a missionary? Is that how you were born overseas?"

"Yeah, that's right! My dad's African but went to school here in the States. He went to Howard University. That's where he met my mother. They fell in love and got married."

"So your last name is African? I thought it was different. I never heard the last name Shah before."

"Uh-huh. Kofi's name is African too. It means born on Friday."

"Was Kofi born overseas too?"

"No, he was born in Chicago. My mom and dad taught in a school there for a while. When they got their next missionary assignment, I didn't want to go. I decided to stay in the States instead of returning to the mission. I lived in Chicago for two years, met Kofi's dad, and got pregnant. I could tell baby daddy wasn't gonna do right by Kofi and just wanted to get away from him. My cousin, Dameon, was living here and convinced me to move to Indy. Kofi' dad visited us once, a few years ago. He left, and we haven't heard from him since. I've raised Kofi by myself. That man didn't care about Kofi or me."

"So you were born in Africa?"

"Yes."

"What made you decide to stay in the States instead of going back with your mama and daddy?"

Hope swallowed a mouth full of potatoes. "Well, I just got tired of all the running around. My daddy's mission in life is to teach math and to teach Jesus. We were always poor and never had anything. I went to college, but I didn't finish. I just got tired of traveling. I wanted to settle down! Make some friends! Mama wanted me to come back when I wrote her I was pregnant, but I stayed."

Hope continued to tell about her life. She was "worldly" in more than one sense of the word. Esdell was intrigued but not judgmental.

"Boy, that's some story, Hope. You've seen and been through a lot. But living in Africa must have been exciting. Where in Africa were you born?"

"Nairobi, Kenya."

"Wait, what?" Esdell said, lowering his fork back down to his plate. "Where?"

"Nairobi, Kenya," she repeated.

"You're from Kenya? You're from Kenya!"

"Yeah, something wrong with that?" Hope asked defensively.

Esdell's thoughts jetted back to the dream and the words that his Kenya had spoken to him.

God wants you to have joy, love, peace, and hope, and so do I.

God wants you to have hope, and so do I, he repeated in his mind. *I want you to have Hope.*

"Oh my god, you're from Kenya!" Esdell stared at his plate, twirling his fork in the pasta. He could not believe it. Had Kenya meant this Hope? Not expectation, hope, but Hope Shah? He was barely breathing. He looked at the hot pink flower on Hope's sweater and suddenly remembered the bright pink hibiscus flower that Kenya had pulled from her hair and tossed it into the flowing water in his dream. Had this flower found its way back to him through Hope? Could this be even more confirmation?

"What did I just tell you about ignoring me, E. Brown? You got something against Kenya?" Hope huffed.

"No. No, that's not it at all. My deceased wife's name was Kenya. If this ain't the most ironic thing I've ever seen."

Now it was Esdell's turn to tell his story. He told Hope about how he had met Kenya, about their marriage, and the birth of their children.

He had told Hope that he was a widower, so he even told her about how Kenya had died. He stopped short of telling her about his dream, however.

Hope was just as interested in Esdell's story as he was in hers. What an evening it was turning out to be.

Just as they finished their dinner, it had begun to snow, so Esdell ordered coffee to warm them up before they left. Then the waitress brought the bill.

"That was really good, Esdell." Hope slid the bill in front of her. "It looks like I owe around fifteen dollars." She reached for her purse.

"What're you doin'?" Esdell asked sliding the bill back to himself.

"All I have is a twenty, so I'll leave the tip too."

"You don't have to leave anything. I got this!"

"I thought we were splitting the bill."

Esdell pulled his wallet out, removed a debit card, and signaled for the waitress. "Where'd you get that idea from? I asked you out, girl. Put your purse away!"

"Okay then!" Hope said contently. She acted as if she were surprised.

After the bill was taken care of, Esdell again helped Hope on with her coat. When they exited the restaurant, he offered his arm to escort her to car in the slippery snow and held her hand until she was in the car.

"Hey, we didn't get dessert. Wanna stop and get a Frosty?" he offered.

"A Frosty? You remembered that I like Frosties. That's so sweet. Thank you, but no. I'm full. I think I should get in. It's getting late, and I have to open the shop at six in the morning. I need to get to bed."

So Esdell drove directly to Hope's apartment. The ride home was simply a critique of the restaurant, its food, and its service. Esdell parked the car in the complex lot and rushed to open the car door for Hope. Again, he offered his arm to escort her across the snow to her front door.

"Here you are, Hope, safe and sound."

"I'd invite you in, but like I said, I've got a early day tomorrow."

"Next time, maybe."

Hope smiled. "Will there be a next time?"

"If you want it."

"I do," she said smiling even more broadly. "Esdell, thank you for the sweetest evening I've ever had. This must be what it's like to be treated like a lady! Whoever says chivalry is dead has never been out with you. You've been a perfect gentleman. So different from what I'm used to."

Esdell put his hand under Hope's chin to lift her head looking her directly in her eyes. "Okay?"

"Yes," she whispered.

He put his arms around her waist. He was determined to do it right this time. He kissed her softly, once, twice. Then he pulled her closer to him and kissed her deeply. Then two more pecks on the lips.

"That was better. So much better!" she said softly. Suddenly the outside light came on, and she heard Kofi loudly clearing his throat just inside the door. "That boy's a mess! Night-night, Esdell. Will you call me?"

"Absolutely!" Esdell said.

"Hold on a second." Hope went into her purse and pulled out a business card and a pen. She wrote on the back of it and gave it to Esdell.

"What's this?" he asked.

"It's my cell phone number. I wanna be sure you can always reach me!"

Esdell chuckled and gave her another gentle kiss. "Good night, Hope."

Hope unlocked the door and went inside. Esdell returned to his car. Once he left the apartment complex parking lot, he yelled.

"Woo-hoo! Git down like you live, Big E! Yes!" He banged on the steering wheel. "Yes!"

This ride home from Hope's place was far different from the first. He could not wait to tell Kareem and Karlena.

14

Esdell's first date with Hope was just a couple of weeks before Christmas. It was a very busy time at both of their places of employment, so they spoke on the phone often, but had just one more dinner date. They were not able to spend Christmas together, however, because Hope's parents had returned to Chicago to visit some old friends and Hope had gone there to see them. Kofi, after getting special permission from his probation officer to travel out of state, went with her. They stayed in Chicago until after the New Year. The Browns, as usual, gathered at Grace's house. They had a big Christmas dinner and exchanged gifts. The biggest gift to Kareem and Karlena was their dad's newfound happiness. Though Esdell was normally positive and upbeat, the smile on his face seemed broader, his face seemed brighter, and his heart seemed lighter. The nightmares had ceased.

Karlena had received another special gift. She was pleasantly surprised with a visit from her ex-boyfriend, Joseph, who had not told her he was coming home for the holidays. His visit was only for a few days, but they had made the most of it, spending much time together. At the end of his visit, they agreed that they would try to renew their relationship long distance. They knew it would be difficult, but Joseph confessed he couldn't bear the thought of Karlena dating other people. Karlena was elated because she felt the same way. She remembered that her father had told her, more than once, that if God meant for them to be together, they would be. She had finally told Joseph how she felt, so they had convinced themselves that they would work it out somehow.

The New Year came in quietly. The Browns went to watch night service at church the way they always did. Esdell was especially prayerful and thankful. He testified how God had given him inner peace, and how he was anxiously waiting to see what the Lord had planned for him. After an empowering sermon from Pastor Edwards, they were all ready to face the New Year.

The Monday after watch night service, Esdell returned to work, putting in a full day of deliveries before returning to the warehouse. As he clocked out, his cell phone rang. He pulled the phone from his pocket and looked at the caller ID. It was Hope, so he quickly answered.

"Hey, you! What's up? Where are you?"

"Hey, yourself!" Hope responded. A smile could be heard in her tone. "We're back! We just got home."

"Praise God! I've been praying for traveling grace for you both."

"Thank you!"

"How was the drive back?"

"It was okay. We ran into some snow just outside of Chicago, so the two-and-a-half-hour trip turned into almost four. Did you miss me?"

"Yes, I did," he answered as he clocked out and then walked to his car. "I missed you too. What you got going on tonight?"

"I'm headed to school. I gotta class."

"Dang it! I wanted you to come by and meet my parents."

"Your parents are here?" Esdell inquired.

"Uh-huh. They came home with us for a short visit. Then they're flying out from here to Florida and then they're taking a ship to a mission in Haiti. What time you get out of class?"

"Nine o'clock, but I got a discussion group after that. I won't be done 'til after ten."

"Hmm. That's bedtime for Mama and Daddy. Well, if not tonight, maybe later in the week? I'm working both jobs tomorrow, so I'll check my schedules and see when I'm off. Maybe we can all go out to eat or something."

"Just let me know."

"I will. Well, I'ma go and help Mom and Dad get settled in. I'm so excited about them being here! Then I've gotta go get Woodstock from the vet's. I don't wanna pay another day to board my little kitty!"

"Tell everyone I said hello, including your little kitty. I'm glad you're back. See you soon. Bye."

"Okay. Bye-bye."

Esdell drove to school, smiling. He had missed Hope while she was gone, and he couldn't wait to see her. When he got to campus, he stopped by the registration office to pick up the brochures from the school of art and the school of architecture that he had promised Kofi. His class time and the discussion group went by quickly, so he found himself back home in what seemed to be no time at all.

The house was quiet as he entered. It was ten forty-five, so he assumed everyone was sleeping. He climbed the stairs and stopped to listen at Kareem's door and heard his television. He tapped on the door and peeked in.

"Hey, son. Everything all right?"

"Hey, Dad," Kareem said as he sat up in his bed. "Yeah, everything's fine. I'm just waiting on the news to come on. I wanna catch the highlights from the Colt's game. What's up with you?"

Esdell entered Kareem's room and sat down. "Hope and Kofi are back."

"Yeah, I know. Kofi called me. He's really excited that his grandparents are visiting. He wants us to meet them."

"Hope said the same thing. Maybe we can have them come over here. Hope has to check her schedules to see what days she's off. We can meet her parents, and she can get to know Karlena."

"That's a good idea. We can talk about that tomorrow, I guess. Karlena was really tired tonight. She put Micah to bed at eight thirty and crashed out herself about an hour later. I know she'll be good with it though."

Esdell and Kareem continued to talk up until it was time for the sports broadcast. They watched it together, and then Esdell went to his room. He stopped to listen at Karlena's door before entering Micah's room. He watched his grandson sleep for just a few minutes. Everyone was safe and sound, and his home was peaceful. He was thankful.

He slept soundly through the night and rose early the next morning to find over an inch of fresh fallen snow on the ground. He washed up, shaved, dressed, got the newspaper from the porch, and went into the kitchen to make coffee. He skimmed the front page of the paper and then paused to send up his morning prayer. After that, he went upstairs to Karlena's room and knocked on her door.

"Ahem!" Karlena cleared her throat. "Yeah, come in."

"Mornin', baby. I just wanted to let you know that it snowed last night. You might wanna get on up and get an early start. I don't know what kinda shape the roads are in."

"Okay, Daddy. Thanks." Karlena yawned.

"Uh, Hope's parents are in town, and she wants me to meet them. I was thinking about inviting Hope and her family over for dinner one day this week. You haven't got the chance to really talk to her. It'll be a good chance for y'all to get to know each other a little."

Karlena sat up in her bed. "That's fine with me. I'm off on Friday, and I don't have a class. That's really my only free day."

"Hope is checking her schedules today. I hope we can work it out. Get on up now. I'll clean your car off for you. I'm out. Have a good day."

"Thanks. Bye, Dad."

True to his word, Esdell cleared off all the snow and ice on Karlena's car before he cleared his own. It was a cold, brisk January morning. The frosty air smelled fresh and clean. He smiled slightly and paused briefly to view the beautiful, wintry landscape of his neighborhood. He put his hand on Karlena's car.

"Hedge of protection, Lord," he prayed, and then he was off to work.

As he drove to the warehouse, he was relieved to see that the Indianapolis Department of Transportation had been on the job, and the snow had already been plowed from the main streets. He entered the warehouse, clocked in, and went to dispatch to get his delivery assignments for the day. He took his paperwork into the break room to map out his route. He smiled when he saw that Hope's shop was scheduled for a delivery. Gary came in, and they chatted briefly before they started their workday.

"You be careful out there today, Esdell," Gary advised.

"You too, Gary!" *Hedge of protection round us all today, Lord!* Esdell prayed.

He started his route, and before he knew it, it was lunchtime. He had purposely worked it that his stop just before lunchtime was While They Yet Live Flowers. He stopped and bought lunch for himself and Hope.

Entering the parking lot, Esdell drove around to the back of the strip mall to make his delivery. After he had backed into a parking space, he rang the doorbell. Hope answered.

"Hey! I was hoping you'd be making the delivery today!" She gave Esdell a big hug. "I missed you. C'mon in out the cold!"

Esdell carefully balanced the bags that held their lunch.

"I missed you too. Here, I bought you a sandwich and a Pepsi," he said, entering the back room of the shop.

"Thanks! But, E. Brown, you need to know that I'm a Coke drinker!"

"Well, I won't hold that against you," he kidded. "How's your first day back?"

"Not too bad! I'ma have to eat this at the counter because Mark, my coworker, is out making a delivery to Methodist Hospital. You can't be behind the counter but sit right here next to the door."

Esdell sat on a stool that was in the back room while Hope stood behind the counter. They enjoyed their sandwiches as they caught up on each other's news. They discussed what they had done over the holidays and imagined what they would have done if they had celebrated together. Mark came back from his delivery and unloaded the truck. Mark remembered Esdell from when he had first come into the shop and how Esdell had dismissed the suggestion that he might be interested in Hope.

"Someone must've had a change of heart!" Mark joked.

"Someone really did!" Esdell acknowledged.

Hope looked at them curiously but couldn't address the exchange between the two men because someone had come in to make a purchase. She simply gave a little scowl, shook her head, and then tended to her customer.

Mark joined the couple on their lunch hour eating a meal he had brought from home. Hope explained, in little detail, how she and Esdell had become friends through the relationship of Kareem and Kofi. The more personal information was intentionally left out. After lunch, Esdell collected and threw away the trash and prepared to finish the day's deliveries.

"Did you find out about your schedules yet?" he asked Hope.

"I did, and they stink! I'm working here all week, and I get off at four every day. We're closed Sunday, and that's my only day off. I called GFS. I'm working Wednesday through Saturday six to ten since I'm closing up. Sunday I get off at six. I'm only free tomorrow night. I guess dinner is out, huh?"

Esdell thought for a second. "That's messed up! Karlena's only day off this week is Friday. She's working two til six on Sunday. Wanna try to get together then? We can go out to eat, so nobody will have to cook."

"I don't know, Esdell. I'm so tired after working at GFS. I probably won't be good company."

"Girl, you and them two jobs!"

"Kofi says two jobs are for two people, but I got thangs to do! I need both my jobs."

"Well, you think about it, and if you feel like it, we'll try for Sunday," Esdell said as he started to leave.

"Hey, Mark, will you take the counter for a few minutes?" Hope asked.

"Sure thing," Mark responded.

Hope walked Esdell outside to his truck. She crossed her arms in an effort to ward off the cold air. "Call me later?"

"Yeah," Esdell answered. He bent over and kissed Hope on her forehead. "Get back in there before you catch cold. I'll talk to you later."

"Bye, and you be careful on the road." Hope gave Esdell a smile in answer to the little peck he had given her.

Esdell drove the rest of his route thinking that it was a shame that Hope had to work so hard, but he remembered that she'd told him that she wanted to buy the flower shop someday. On top of that, she was taking care of Kofi and running a household. It occurred to him how amazing Hope was.

Esdell only had a study group after work, so he was home by eight. Kareem was sitting on the living room floor playing with Micah when Esdell entered the house.

"Hey, y'all. What's up?" he asked.

"Hi, Dad! I'm just hangin' out with my nephew. Karlena's not back home from school yet. What kind of day did you have?" Kareem asked.

"Pretty good. I had lunch with Hope, and we couldn't come up with a day for us all to get together. Everybody's so busy!"

"How long are her parents gonna be here?"

"I don't know, but we'll work it out, if anyway possible." Esdell swooped Micah up in his arms. "Hey, boy. How's my li'l buddy?"

"I tore it up in the kitchen tonight, Dad! I fixed hot dogs with chips!" Kareem laughed.

"Works for me," Esdell said. He put Micah back on the floor and ate his dinner quickly. He showered, dressed, and then called Hope.

"Hello?" Hope answered.

"Hey, it's me," Esdell responded. "You okay?"

"Just fine. How 'bout you?"

"Oh, I'm good. You free to talk now, or are you busy with your family?"

"I can talk. Mama and Daddy are playing Scrabble with Kofi. They love that game. They have a travel game that they take with them everywhere. Kofi didn't want to play, but Dad insisted saying that it'll help him keep his mind sharp. I wish I had a dollar for every game I've played. Do you play Scrabble?" Hope inquired.

"As a matter of fact, I do! We'll play one day. So, how long your parents gonna be here?"

"Oh, man! They'll be here longer than expected. There was a small earthquake in the part of Haiti where the mission is, and they can't get there until they clear the roads. I guess the mission is in a pretty remote spot. They had to reschedule their flight. They're really anxious to get there though."

"That's too bad! What a tough break for the Haitian people. God bless, 'em! I'll lift them up in prayer."

"I know you will. So now it's no big deal if we can't all get together this week. We have more time."

As it turned out, Hope's parents, Mr. and Mrs. Shah, stayed with her for over a month. They met Esdell, his children, and his grandchild, and they shared a few visits. They were beautiful God-fearing people and were really glad to see that their daughter was dating someone who loved the Lord as much as they did. They let Hope know how proud they were that their daughter seemed to be doing well. Hope's parents often spoke of the different missions they served, and Kareem was intrigued by their stories. Kareem had always compared himself to the apostle Paul. He had studied his missionary journeys and had even written a paper on him for one of his classes in seminary school. Esdell could see the impression that the conversations with Mr. and Mrs. Shah were having on his son. Would they be adding "missionary" to Kareem's resume? Esdell could see that was a real possibility.

Karlena and Hope finally got the chance to meet more formally, and they hit it off immediately. Karlena enjoyed Hope's sense of humor and the way she interacted with her dad. It reminded her of the way that Esdell and Christine kidded around with each other. Most of all, Karlena appreciated the way Hope interacted with Micah. She found herself tearful at one point, thinking this would be very close to the way her mother would be with her son.

Karlena also got the chance to meet Kofi for the first time, and he was taken with how pretty she was. She caught him eyeing her once almost lustfully. Kareem saw it too and quickly but delicately put him in check. Kofi was so embarrassed, but Karlena eased his concerns, joking that she knew he couldn't help himself because she was "so fine." Everyone laughed at this little episode, so all was forgiven.

Valentine's Day was approaching. Hope was extremely busy at the flower shop, and Esdell had not spent much time with her. He had planned a special evening with Hope. Unfortunately, he had to change his plans when he found out that her parents were leaving the day after Valentine's Day. He realized that Hope would want to spend as much time with her parents as possible. So he took everyone out to dinner so they could all enjoy the Shahs' last day in Indianapolis.

After Valentine's Day, Esdell, along with Hope and Kofi, drove her parents to the airport. Kareem exchanged information with the Shahs and promised to keep in touch with them. Esdell, Hope, and Kofi watched as the plane took off, and Esdell comforted Hope as she sadly waved good-bye to the ascending aircraft.

When they returned to Hope's apartment from the airport, she invited Esdell in. When they entered, Kofi started toward his bedroom when Esdell stopped him.

"Hey, Kofi, here's the brochures from the school of art and architecture that I promised you. We been so busy, I forgot to give them to you before. They gotta lot of info on what it'll take to get each degree."

"Thanks, Mr. B. I 'preciate cha! I'll go look at 'em now! Night. Y'all behave out here!" Kofi laughed as he went to his room.

"Git on outta here, boy, before I bop you one!" Hope warned with a giggle. "That boy is a mess! Sit on down, Esdell. Can I get you something to drink?"

"No thanks. Come sit down." Esdell patted the spot next to him on the couch. "Your parents are real nice people. I'm glad I got a chance to meet them."

"They're very special. I'm glad they got a chance to meet you too. They really liked you, Esdell. You're the kinda man they always wanted me to date."

"If you say so," Esdell said, almost blushing. "Kareem was real interested in their lives as missionaries. Do you miss that life?"

"Not at all! I wanted to settle down. I didn't like all that moving around."

"Still, I'm sure that your parents and their work must've had some influence on you."

"Of course it did. I learned how loving God means you have to love others. We always served the poorest people. It was hard. When I find myself feeling sorry for myself, or having a pity party, I remember the people who wouldn't have even had clean water if it wasn't for missionaries. How they wouldn't have gotten even a little education if it wasn't for Daddy and Mama. It makes me grateful. Keeps me praying too."

"Can I ask you something, Hope?" She nodded. "How come you don't go to church?"

Hope hung her head slightly. "I know I should go. I was going, almost on the regular, but money got tight, and I had to get that second job. I feel guilty about it, especially after Kofi took that bad turn. I need to do better, I know."

"Hope, I need to talk to you about something."

Hope's body tensed up. "I don't know that I like the sound of this. What's up?"

Esdell licked his dry lips. "You say you love God, so do you believe that Christ is the risen son of God?"

Hope frowned. "Yes, of course! I've never been asked that before. Are you holding it against me that I don't go to church? Why you ask me that?"

"I just had to hear you say it. And for the record, I ain't judging you. But now, I got another question. Do you like me?"

"What? That's a dumb question. You know I do. Can't you tell?"

"Well, one thing I know about women is that you can't take nothin' for granted. So, Miss Hope…"

Hope's body tightened even more. "Oh no, not the Miss Hope! What is it? Spill it, E. Brown!" Her eyes rolled upward. *He's about to dump me!* she thought.

"Well, Hope, I like you too. Like I said, I've learned not to take nothin' for granted when it comes to women." Esdell licked his lips again. "Hope, you've made a big difference in my life these past few months. I just can't tell you! I want us to be…I wanna know if…if you'd consider being my girlfriend?"

Hope's tensed body relaxed. "E. Brown, if you ain't the cutest thing!" She began to chuckle.

"I'm glad you're amused, but that ain't the response I thought I'd get!" Esdell sat back on the couch, crossing his leg and arms. He was clearly insulted.

Hope gently took his hand. "Esdell, it would be my greatest honor, my greatest pleasure to be your woman. I laughed because no man has ever asked me before. They just took it for granted, like you said. I keep forgetting that you're a gentleman and a *real man*. I never had one of them before either. That's why my parents loved you. Thank you! Yes! You is my man now, and I is yo' woman!" Hope said in jest. "Now, can we seal the deal with a kiss?"

"You betta know it!" Esdell said, leaning in until their lips met. He then backed away to display a big smile. "I's got me a girlfriend!"

Hope laid her head on Esdell's chest as he put his arm around her. Their relationship was now clearly defined. A few tears fell from Hope's eyes and she sniffed. Esdell leaned to look at her face.

"Hope, you're crying! What's wrong?"

"Never had anyone treat me like you do. I thought you were gonna leave me and now I'm your girlfriend. I'm just happy, that's all."

"I'm happy too. You deserve so much more than me." He kissed her again. "Hmm. You'll have to get to know the rest of my family now."

"They all seemed nice enough when we met at the anniversary party. Why you sounding all skeptical? It's not me, is it?"

"That's the last time I wanna hear that kinda talk from you! No, it's not you. They're nice enough. They just crazy! I hope you're ready for 'em!"

"You came from them, so they gotta be like you. I can't wait to meet them!"

"Be careful what you wish for!" Esdell said as he hugged Hope tightly. "Man! We're a couple!"

15

Esdell quickly spread the word about the new exclusive relation-ship between him and Hope. The twins were so happy for their dad but were not at all surprised by the announcement. He, of course, got plenty of humorous feedback from his brother and sister.

"Go 'head, playah, playah. Get yo' pimp on!" Sammy Junior kidded.

"I can't wait to meet this woman. She's either desperate or crazy to hook up with your sorry behind!" Christine said.

His mother was happy to hear the news. She had long thought it was past time for her son to find a new romantic interest, and his stepdad was in total agreement with her.

It was proving very difficult to arrange a time for everyone to get together. Esdell and his children were working and going to school. Hope was working two jobs. Sometimes days went by before Esdell and Hope would even see each other, but they talked on the telephone every day. They giggled and carried on like teenagers whenever they spoke. Their personalities began to blend with every passing day. Hope's calloused exterior began to soften with the sweet and gentlemanly treatment she received from Esdell. Esdell had let loose of the emotional shield he had placed around his heart. For the most part, they were comfortable with each other.

Then finally, Hope got a whole weekend off from both jobs. Esdell was quick to invite Hope and Kofi to come to church and then to the family's Sunday dinner.

"So, I can come pick y'all up," Esdell offered over the phone.

"No, that's all right," Hope said. "I'll drive and we'll meet you at church. I know you go to Sunday school, and honestly, I don't want to get up that early. I wanna sleep in a little."

"I understand. Service starts at eleven. I'll wait for you out front and park your car for you. Do you need directions?"

"No. Kofi's been there with Kareem before, remember? And thanks, but I don't need valet parking either. Just wait for us out front like you said. Was your mother okay with our coming to dinner?"

Esdell chuckled. "Are you kiddin'? Mama's been waiting for this day. Ain't no tellin' what she'll fix for dinner. Be sure you bring your appetite!"

"What can I bring?"

"Girl, you better not insult my mama by bringing something your first time to her house! By the way," Esdell cautiously began, " can you cook?" Hope was silent, but then started to laugh. "What's so funny?" he asked.

"I can cook, in more ways than one!" Hope answered suggestively.

Now it was Esdell that was silent. "Um, I just wondered. I love to eat. You have to know how to fix a good meal!"

"They used to say, back in the day, 'The way to a man's heart was through his stomach.' Now you get there a different way!"

"Yeah, uh-huh! Like I said, I love to eat, so I need to test you skills in the kitchen!" he said playing her off.

"Okay. Whatever, Mr. Old Fashion. Will I see you on Saturday?"

"Sure. You wanna go to the movies?"

"No. I'ma cook! You have dinner with me and Kofi. You'll see what kind of culinary skills I have!" Hope boasted, dropping her risqué tone. "Can I cook? You'll find out! What would you like?"

"Surprise me!" Esdell answered. "Do *you* want *me* to bring anything?"

"Just yourself. Be here around six. Well, sweet'nin', I'm sleepy, so I'll talk to you tomorrow, and I'll see you on Saturday. Good night!"

"Bye, Hope," Esdell said, then hung up the phone. "That woman's a mess!"

* * *

Promptly at 6:00 p.m. on Saturday, Esdell was knocking on Hope's front door. She quickly answered.

"Right on time. C'mon in!"

"Something smells good," Esdell said as he entered carrying two sacks. He saw Kofi sitting on the couch. "Hey, Kofi, how you doin'?"

"I'm good," Kofi answered. "How're you, Mr. B?"

"I'm good too."

"I hope you're hungry, Esdell. I fixed chopped steak with onion and mushroom gravy, mashed potatoes, and steamed broccoli. I have cherry cobbler for dessert. I even bought you some Pepsi."

Esdell smiled. "Thanks! Here, I brought some ice cream. It'll go good with that cobbler. And I rented a movie." He gave Hope both sacks.

"Well, everything's ready," she announced. "Let's eat before the food gets cold. We're eating buffet style." Hope put the rented movie on top of the TV stand and put the ice cream in the freezer. Then she grabbed a plate and headed toward the stove, but she stopped suddenly. "Will you bless the food, Esdell?"

They bowed and Esdell gave thanks for the meal. They all fixed their plates and sat down at the table. Good food and conversation ensued. Esdell was pleased to find out that Hope, in fact, was a relatively good cook. He laughed as he asked Kofi if his mother had actually cooked all that food, or if everything had been purchased from the GFS frozen food section. Hope was offended. She had cooked almost everything but had to laugh when she served the cherry cobbler. She admitted she did buy it from GFS.

"Did you get enough, Esdell?" Hope asked.

"I did. Thanks, it was really good too." Esdell patted his slightly bulging stomach.

"Yeah, Ma, that *was* really good," Kofi agreed. "Mr. B, before y'all watch the movie, can I talk to you about school? I looked at those pamphlets you brought me, and I got a few questions."

"Sure, what's up, Kofi?"

Kofi had many questions about the classes required to major in art or architecture. Esdell was able to answer a lot his questions on art. As they reviewed the brochures, they discovered that both courses of study had several classes in common. Hope had positioned herself on the couch, leaving the men to talk.

"Hold on a minute, Mr. B. I got something to show you!" Kofi said eagerly. He left the room and then returned with a notebook in his hand. In it, there were drawings that he had done. He was so excited to show his work, he did not notice a few pages that had fallen out just outside his bedroom door. In the book, there were sketches of furniture that Kofi had designed, landscapes, and buildings. There were some pictures that seemed oddly placed. There was a picture of broken chains, an uncaged bird, and a picture of graduation regalia. Hope sat on the couch watching as Esdell and Kofi talked. She smiled to herself, being pleased to see their interaction. She had never heard Kofi hold a conversation on this serious level.

"Hope, have you seen these?" Esdell asked. "Come look."

Hope stood and started toward the table but noticed the pages that had fallen on the floor. She scooped them up and went to the table. She looked first at the drawings in the notebook. She complemented Kofi on his work but wondered why he had never shown her his drawings. As the men continued to talk about classes and Kofi's notebook, Hope became noticeably quiet. She had stepped back to look at drawings that were in her hand. Her mouth dropped opened. These drawings were dark and eerie. These drawings depicted Kofi's life and his true inner thoughts. These torn out pages showed a self portrait of Kofi that showed the scar on his neck where someone had once tried to slit his throat. There was another picture of himself where he was standing alone in a tunnel. There was light coming from one end, but a strong wind was blowing him in the opposite direction toward the darkness. These drawings portrayed violence and desperation. There was even a sketch of a woman, obviously Hope, standing as money rained down on her as Kofi stood just out of reach watching and begging.

"Whatcha think, Ma?" Kofi asked with pride. He turned to see his mother looking at the torn out pages. He gasped and snatched them from her hand.

"What are those, Kofi?" she asked with a shaky voice. "Why...You never said a word. Is this how you feel about your life?"

"Well, uh...ya know," Kofi stammered. "I guess I never showed them to you 'cause I didn't think you'd be interested." He passed the pictures to Esdell to see. He viewed them quickly but said nothing.

"Is this woman with the money comin' down on her supposed to be me? What does this mean?"

"Yeah, that's you. You just wantin' money and caring nothin' about me," Kofi started. "But I don't feel that way no more. Look at this picture of the broken chains and the bird that was freed from his cage. That's me! I feel free from all that bad stuff. I don't feel that way no more!" Kofi proclaimed. "I gotta high school diploma, and I'ma try to go to college! I got real dreams now, Ma! That's why those pages are torn out! I don't feel that way no more!" Kofi balled up the torn out pages. Hope managed a weak smile and picked up the notebook to look at furniture designs.

"He's got real talent, huh, Esdell?" Hope asked.

"Yes, he's very, very talented. There's real potential here," Esdell encouraged.

"Kofi, I'm glad that you've decided to go to school. I'm glad you got dreams and I'ma be there, doing my best to help them come true. We're gonna work all this out together. I'ma be better, Kofi, I promise," she said, placing her hand on Kofi's face.

"You already better, Mama. I see how you've changed. And I'ma start working on my dreams. I think I want to take a class in the summer just to see how it goes, and maybe try to go full time in the fall." Kofi looked at his mom. "I'll need help trying to get some financial aid." Kofi turned to look at Esdell. "Can you help us, Mr. B?"

"You know I will! Remember this, Kofi," Esdell started, "a dream is just a dream until you start workin' toward it, then it becomes a goal! Whatever you need, my man!"

"All right then! Well, I'ma go to my room. G'night, y'all." Kofi stood to go to his room.

"You don't wanna watch the movie with us?" Esdell asked.

"Naw, you guys go 'head. I'ma leave you two alone. Y'all behave out here!"

"Night, Kofi," Esdell said.

"Good night, son," Hope said watching as Kofi went to his room. She went back to the couch, flopping down on it and crossing her arms. "What movie did you rent, Esdell?" There was a worried look on her face.

"What's wrong?" he asked.

"I was a rotten mother! Money was very important to me but now that Kofi's going to college, I'll need those two jobs more than ever." She sighed heavily. "I wanted to buy the flower shop someday. Now that money I saved will have to go toward Kofi's education. It's fine. I'll do what I have to! I promised him I'd be better."

Esdell sat on the couch next to Hope. "Like he said, you're already better. And like I said, I'll help you check into financial aid. You're a single parent, head of household. I know you'll be able to get some help. As far as the shop is concerned, what God has for you is for you. If you're meant to buy the shop, God'll make a way for you to do that and send Kofi to school too!"

"Think so?"

"I'll pray so! There's a scripture in Jeremiah that says God knows the plans He has for us, and they are good plans, not evil ones."

"'To give you a future and a hope,'" Hope quoted. "That's one of Mama's favorites. Jeremiah 29:11. I used to read it to Kofi. Humph, I'm surprised I remember it."

"Hope, the word is in you. It comes back to you when you don't expect it, when you need it."

"I guess. How often do you read. The Bible, I mean."

"I try to read something every day. Don't always do it though."

"You probably don't need to. You probably got the whole book memorized." Hope managed a little smile. "I wish I could get some help from Kofi's daddy, the deadbeat sperm donor! He's never lifted a finger to help me."

Esdell shook his head. "I know what you mean. My grandson's father is the same way. Karlena's supposed to get child support, but he can't keep a job long enough for her to collect. I wanted to put a hurtin' on that boy once, but I didn't. You'll have to do for Kofi's dad like we do for Micah's, and that's pray that God will change him. We need to pray that they both get a mind to stand up to their responsibilities!"

"I doubt that there's much chance of that. I ask myself all the time what I even saw in him. He didn't look that good, didn't treat me like nothin'! I guess that's what being lonely will do to you. I was really, really lonely after I stayed in Chicago when Mama and Daddy left. I took all his crap just so I could say I had somebody!" Hope paused. "Oh, I'm sorry, Esdell. I'm sure you don't wanna talk about my old boyfriend!"

"It's okay, Hope. It's good to get it out! We all need to talk through our hang-ups. If we don't admit what's wrong, we can't fix it. I know that first hand. But can I ask you something?"

"What's that?" Hope reluctantly asked.

"Did you love him? Do you miss him at all?"

Hope thought for a second. "In a way, I guess I did love him, but the only thing I miss is his being a dad to Kofi. Hell, Kofi is the only good thing that came out of our relationship, and I almost blew that!"

"How?"

"Esdell, I'ma be totally honest with you, okay?"

"Always, Hope. Always be honest with me!"

"I was no more than sex to Kofi's daddy and I know that. When I told him I was pregnant, he immediately said it wasn't his. He called me a slut. Said he knew he wasn't the only one I'd been with. I almost got an abortion. I was on my way to clinic when something told me to go back home."

"That 'something' had to be the voice of God, Hope. And you listened. And you're right. Kofi is the good thing that came outta that relationship. He may have been a problem before, but I know that boy's gonna make you so proud!" Esdell reassured.

"Thanks. He's making me proud now with all this college talk." Hope became silent and looked away from Esdell.

"What?" Esdell asked. Hope answered just above a whisper and Esdell could not hear her. "What did you say?"

"I *was* a slut," she shamefully responded. "I've been with more men than I wanna admit. You need to know this about me, Esdell. But I'm clean. I've been tested, and I'm clean!" Hope waited for Esdell's response.

"Miss Hope," he started, "you're not that way now, are you?"

"No."

"We all got things in our past that we're ashamed of."

"Like you've ever done anything wrong, Mr. Religious!"

"Hey, it ain't like I just fell off the holy wagon this mornin'! I was young once, and I did my share of dirt. I had my share of women before I met my wife. I was blessed to meet her while I was still young. I love God and I loved her. Those two things made me get right real quick. God forgave me for my sinful ways, and Kenya never gave 'em a thought. God has forgiven you too, and I ain't thinkin' about nothin' or nobody you did before you met me!"

"Well, uh…" Hope started.

"Well what?" Esdell asked.

"Nothing," she responded.

"We're being honest here, Hope. Remember?"

"Its nothing I want to talk about now." She sighed heavily. "You're my boo, E. Brown. You are some kinda special!"

Esdell put his arm around Hope and tightly pulled her to his side. "I'd betta be your boo! You're special too, Hope. You been workin' through a lot. Although you may think you've been doin' it alone, God has always been with you. He's helped you make the right decisions and do the right things."

"I don't know why! I all but turned my back on God."

"Grace and mercy! Nothin' but grace and mercy. Maybe you faked left for a minute, strayed away, backslide, or whatever, but once saved, always saved. God kept you. You got the Holy Spirit inside you. The Bible says if you draw close to God, he'll draw close to you. You're turning back to him, and he's gonna meet you more than halfway. You believe that?"

"Yeah. The grace and mercy is evident, and I see it every day! I thank God for keeping me." Hope sighed again. "I guess that's what's been wrong with me all this time. I kinda put God on hold. But things will be better now. I do believe that! I have to! It's only by His grace that I'll be able to help Kofi with his schooling!"

"Now that's the way to talk! He'll work it out for you. Hey, what d'ya say we watch the movie now?"

"Sure." Hope put the movie in the DVD player and the couple cuddled on the couch as the movie played. It was a comedy, which was a good thing because it lightened the somewhat somber mood that was in the room. They laughed so much that Kofi came out of his room to find out why they were laughing so hard. He joined them and watched the movie until its end.

"Man, that was a good one!" Hope said. "I haven't laughed that much in a long time. My cheeks hurt!"

"Mine too!" Kofi agreed. "I'm tired from laughing so much, I'm going to bed! Night, Mr. B. I'll see you at church tomorrow. We're still going, Ma?" Kofi asked as he stood up.

"Yes, sir! C'mere, son." Hope stood up and extended her arms. Kofi gave her a curious look but walked toward her. She hugged him. "I'm so proud of you, Kofi, my college boy!"

"Thanks, Mama," Kofi said, returning the hug. "More of this right here, Ma. Lots more of this!" He then started for his room, and once he got to the doorway, he said, "I loves ya, Mama!" He never turned around. He simply went into his room and quickly closed the door behind him.

"He said he loves me!" Hope said in amazement. "I don't think he's ever said that before! We're gonna be all right, aren't we?"

"Oh, yeah!" Esdell said as he stood up and stretched. "I need to head on home. I need to go over my Sunday school lesson. You be on time in the mornin' now."

"We will." Hope locked arms with Esdell to escort him to the door. "I hope you enjoyed dinner. Now you see I can cook."

"Everything was good, the dinner, the movie, the company, and now this."

Esdell took Hope in his arms and kissed her good night.

"Hmm!" Hope moaned. "Oh, wow! Yeah, go on home. I'll see you in the morning, promptly at eleven."

"Bye, Hope."

"Bye, Boo!" Hope watched Esdell as he went to his car. She waved good-bye as he backed out of the parking space. She licked her lips, shook her head, and closed the door.

Esdell drove home thinking about the evening. Once he got home, he checked on his family, giving them a brief account of his dinner with Hope and Kofi. He then found his Sunday school book and studied the lesson. He showered and laid out his clothes for the next day. Finally, he knelt at his bedside to pray. He thanked the Lord for a wonderful day and was mindful to send up a special request for Hope. He climbed into his bed and drifted off to sleep.

He awakened the next morning before his alarm clock went off. He fixed breakfast and waited to be joined by Kareem, Karlena, and Micah. They shared the meal, dressed, and went to church.

It seemed as though Sunday school was dragging on forever. Esdell was eager to have Hope and Kofi come worship with him and the rest of his family. He had told them in advance that they were coming and warned his sister and brother not to give Hope any grief. Christine told him that she wasn't making any promises.

It was now ten minutes to eleven, and Esdell stood in the foyer of church, waiting on Hope and Kofi. He was talking to Sammy when Sammy's eyes gazed toward the door.

"There go yo' girl and her son right there," Sammy announced. Esdell turned and raced to the door to greet them.

"Hey, y'all!" He gave Hope a peck on the cheek and shook Kofi's hand. Some of the church members recognized them from the prison ministry and Kofi's court appearance and gave them both a hearty welcome. Sammy came over to greet them as well.

"Hey, now! Good to see y'all!"

"You remember my brother, Sammy, don't you?" Esdell asked.

"The man who kicked off my cousin's DJ'ing career? I certainly do!" Hope extended her hand. "How've you been?"

"Nu uh!" Sammy said. "This is how we do!" He gave Hope a big hug.

"Oh, wow! Thanks, Sammy. This is my son, Kofi," Hope introduced.

"What up? What up, man!" Sammy hugged Kofi too. "Glad to finally meet you."

"You too, Mr. Brown," Kofi said.

"Just call me Sammy, man. Uh-oh, here comes Christine and the girls. Y'all get ready."

"Hey, there!" Christine said, walking toward them.

Esdell stepped forward. "Hope, Kofi, this is my sister, Christine, and her daughters, Celeste and LeAnn."

"Hi. Good to see you all! Y'all look so pretty!" Hope commented.

"Thank you! You're Uncle Esdell's girlfriend?" LeAnn eagerly asked.

"Watch your manners, LeAnn," Christine warned.

"Yeah, watch your manners," Celeste repeated.

"And you watch your manners too! It's good to see you again and good to meet you, Kofi," Christine welcomed. "Y'all ready to go in?"

"Sure. Will your mother be sitting with us?" Hope asked.

"No. Her and Pops are in the choir, and they'll be in the choir stand," Esdell answered. "I see Karlena's already seated. Let's go in."

Everyone followed Esdell into the sanctuary. The usher, knowing the family, led them all to where Karlena and Micah were sitting.

"Hi, Miss Hope. Hi, Kofi," Karlena greeted. Hope and Kofi returned the greeting. "Kareem's up in the pulpit with Pastor. He told me to tell you he'll get with you later, Kofi."

Kofi looked toward the pulpit and saw Kareem looking and smiling at him. Kofi nodded his head.

"He looks real good up there. Real natural," Kofi said.

Shortly, they were joined by Sammy who had just come in. "Hey, everybody!" But there was not much time for conversation as the service was starting with devotion. The congregation sang a hymn, followed by alter prayer. The choir sang two songs, and then Pastor Edwards rose. He asked all the visitors to stand to be acknowledged. Hope and Kofi stood, hoping that they did not have to say anything. They did not. Pastor Edwards had the church welcome them and the other visitors with applause. After a few moments of fellowship, Pastor Edwards began his sermon. As usual, it seemed to custom made for someone in the congregation. He preached from Jeremiah 29:11–14, quoting,

> "For I know the plans I have for you," declares the Lord, "plans to prosper you and not to harm you, plans to give you hope and a future. Then you will call on me and come and pray to me, and I will listen to you. You will seek me and find me when you seek me with all your

heart. I will be found by you," declares the Lord, "and will bring you back from captivity. I will gather you from all the nations and places where I have banished you," declares the Lord, "and will bring you back to the place from which I carried you into exile."

Unbelievable! Hope thought. It was the same scripture that she and Esdell had discussed the night before.

As Pastor Edward preached, he explained how turning away from or not honoring God was a form of captivity and banishment. He explained that God would hear all the prayers of those who would repent and all who would seek him with all their heart. God had plans, good plans, for all who would do these things. Indeed, this sermon was custom made for Hope. She smiled in revelation. She was grateful that God had granted her grace and mercy over all the time she had been away from Him. When Pastor Edwards gave the call to discipleship, Hope seriously thought about joining Esdell's church. She liked the warmth of the members the way the choir sang, and she especially like the way that Pastor Edwards made the word so clear. But she kept her seat. Now was not the time, she thought. She knew that God would make it clear to her if this was to be her new church home or if His plans were to place her somewhere else.

The benediction was given and church was dismissed. More of the church members came over to talk to Hope and Kofi. Those who had not met them personally knew about them through the prayer requests and the testimonies of the members of the prison ministry. Kofi was overwhelmed with all the attention and well-wishes. When they all made their way out to the foyer, they were met by Kareem.

"What's up, y'all? Glad you could make it!"

"Hey, Rev!" Kofi responded.

Esdell noticed Grace and Isaiah standing in the foyer and called to her. "Mama, Pops, here's Hope and Kofi!" They went quickly to meet them.

"Hello, Hope, it's so good to see you! And this is Kofi! What a handsome young man!" Grace gave them both a big, warm hug.

"Y'all sure do a lot of huggin'round here!" Kofi exclaimed. He smiled as he embraced Esdell's mother.

"Kofi, this is my husband, Isaiah Willis," Grace introduced. Kofi went to Isaiah and did not bother trying to shake his hand. He hugged him.

"Well, hello to you too, Mr. Kofi!" Isaiah said. "Y'all ready to go?"

"Just a minute, Pops," Kareem said. "Pastor wanted to say hello to Kofi and meet Miss Hope. C'mon you two." Kareem led them away toward the pastor who was also in the foyer talking to a few members.

"Well, Isaiah and I are goin' on home so I can get dinner on the table," Grace said to Esdell. "Y'all take your time, and I'll see you at the house."

"We're right behind you, Mama," Sammy said as he ushered Christine and his nieces toward the door.

"Okay, Mama. We'll go home and change, and we'll see you in a while," Esdell said and then he turned to Karlena. "I think I'll ride with Hope and Kofi back to our house. You, Kareem, and Micah go on."

"Kofi can ride with us, and you and Miss Hope can ride together," Karlena suggested.

So, after all the good-byes were said to the members of the Road to Damascus Baptist Church and all the traveling arrangement made, Esdell and his family, along with Hope and Kofi, went home. Upon arrival, Esdell unlocked the front door and escorted Hope inside.

"Come on in, Hope. Have a seat anywhere you want."

"Wow, this is nice, Esdell. I've tried to picture what your house looks like. It's really nice."

"Thank you very much! I'ma go change, the kids should be here shortly." No sooner than Esdell had finished his sentence, "the kids" were coming in the front door. Kareem offered Kofi a seat, and then he, Karlena, Micah, and Esdell all went upstairs. Hope and Kofi sat in the front room and checked out the Browns' house.

"Oh, this croton could use some help!" Hope said.

"What, Ma?" Kofi inquired.

"That plant over there. It's called a croton. It looks a little sick!" she snickered.

"Clock out, Ms. Flower lady! You're not at the shop now!" Kofi joked. Hope noticed some pictures on the entertainment center and walked over to take a closer look. She stared particularly at one photo; a family portrait of the Esdell Brown family.

"This must be Kenya, Esdell's wife. She was very pretty. Beautiful, in fact."

Kofi joined his mother in front of the entertainment center. "Man, Karlena looks just like her! Yeah, she was pretty," he agreed. "Not as pretty as you though!"

"Thanks, son, but what else are you supposed to say?" Hope continued to stare at the photo. She picked it up. *They look so happy,* she thought. *The twins were cuties then and cuties now! Esdell's fine as he wanna be!* She placed the picture back on the shelf and looked at the rest of the pictures. There was another family portrait of Esdell, his brother and sister, and obviously his mother and father, Samuel Senior. There was also a picture of Grace and Isaiah. So many pictures! *One big happy family!* She walked around, peeking into the kitchen before returning to the couch. "This is a nice old house. Who would've thought houses could be this nice in this old neighborhood." She sighed. "So, Kofi, how'd you like service today?"

"It was coo'. I know a lot of people at the church, but that's the first time I've been to a service and heard Pastor Edwards preach. He was pretty good. How'd you like it, Ma?"

"I thought it was good. I haven't been to a service like that in a long time. That's how church is supposed to be! Everyone was so friendly. But I did catch a few of the women looking at me funny though!"

Kofi laughed. "Mama, Mr. B's a good lookin' dude in a church with a lot of single women. You were the competition! Yeah, they looked at you funny!"

"I guess." Hope began to wonder if she would be able to fit in with Esdell's lifestyle. He had a big, close family. Her family wasn't that big and not that close. He was a churchgoing man. She hadn't attended church regularly in several years. She wondered how much she would have to change if a long relationship with Esdell was her intent. In a few minutes, she would be having dinner with his mother. She now wondered how much and just what Esdell had told his mom about her. She was getting nervous, and she could feel butterflies beginning to flutter in her stomach. A feeling of shame overtook her. She was an unwed mother. She had not always been there for her son, often choosing other men over him. She had strayed away from the Lord. She began to dread going to Esdell's mother's home. She was now trying to come up with a reason not to go. She could use the queasy feeling that was intensifying in her stomach. She began to grimace.

"What's wrong, Mom?" Kofi asked, noticing the look on her face.

"I don't feel so good all of a sudden. My stomach is bothering me. Maybe I should go home."

"But Mrs. Willis is expecting us for dinner. We shouldn't stand them up!"

"I know, but I feel sick!" Hope protested. Her eyes then turned toward the stairs because she heard someone coming down. It was Esdell.

"Okay! Let's go! I'm hungry!" He looked at Hope and Kofi and could tell something was not right. "What's going on?"

"Mom says she feels sick all of a sudden and wants to go home," Kofi answered.

"What's the matter, Hope?" Esdell walked to Hope to comfort her. "Can I get you something? We've got all kinda medicine upstairs. What's bothering you?"

"It's my stomach!" Hope said, looking away from Esdell.

"We're ready!" Kareem and Karlena with Micah were now coming down the stairs.

"I don't think we're going. Mom's not feeling well," Kofi repeated.

"You can go on, Kofi," Hope said. "That is if somebody will bring you home."

Esdell looked closely at Hope and could tell something other than sickness was really going on.

"Huh, I'll bring him home. Y'all go on over to Mama's, and I'll be there after while."

"All right then, let's be out!" Kareem said, walking toward the door, being followed by Karlena and Micah.

"Are you sure you don't mind me going, Mom?" Kofi asked. "Maybe I should go home with you in case you need me."

"No, that's all right, son. I'll drive myself home and just lay down when I get there. And, Esdell, you go on too. No sense in your being late on account of me!"

"No," Esdell said, "I'ma make sure you're okay before I leave. Go on now, Kofi."

"Okay then. I'll see you later, Ma. Feel better." Kofi skeptically left.

"Now tell me what's really goin' on here, Miss Hope?" Esdell deliberately asked.

"What? I told you I don't feel well!" Hope answered defensively.

"Just last night we talked about being honest with each other, but here you sit, claiming to be sick. I don't think you're sick at all! What's up?"

"So now you're calling me a liar? I ain't gotta take this. I'm going home!" Hope stood and started toward the door.

"And now the big dramatic exit!" Esdell scoffed. "You need to come back here and talk to me! Don't just run away."

"Running away?" Hope stopped in her tracks. "You're the expert on that, not me!" She was referring to their rocky start; particularly the time Esdell ran from her apartment after they kissed.

Esdell paused. "Okay, I guess I deserved that. Come back, Hope, and tell me what the problem is. I don't wanna fight, I wanna help. What is it, babe?"

Hope's scowl turned briefly to a little smile. "You called me babe, first time term of endearment." She went back to the couch and sat down. "I was just looking at all the pictures over there. It's your whole life on display. So clean, happy, and wholesome. Not at all like mine. Leavin' my mama and daddy to stay in a city where all I did was whore around! Getting pregnant with no husband and neglecting my son. I don't deserve to be with you or your family!" She started to tear up as Esdell started to swell up.

"Not this sh—Not this mess again! Girl, you almost made me cuss!" He raised his voice and began to pace. "Just tell me what I gotta do. We had this conversation already! What kinda family you think I come from, where all we do is sit around and judge people? We don't do that! *I* don't do that! You told me about your past, and I don't care about any of that! So you had a baby outta wedlock. Well, that's the first time that's ever happened!" He said sarcastically. "Did you meet my daughter? Oh no, you haven't, because we sent her away in shame because she got pregnant with no husband!" His sarcasm continued. "Are you serious, Hope?"

"You need to stop yellin' at me, E. Brown! I'm serious about that!" she snapped back.

"Then don't give me nothin to yell at you about!" He took a deep breath to try to calm himself. He picked up the Bible that sat on the coffee table and flipped through the pages. He began to read:

This righteousness is given through faith in Jesus Christ to all who believe. There is no difference between Jew and Gentile, for all have sinned and fall short of the glory of God, and all are justified freely by his grace through the redemption that came by Christ Jesus. God presented Christ as a sacrifice of atonement, through the shedding of his blood; to be received by faith. He did this to demonstrate his righteousness, because in his forbearance he had left the sins committed beforehand unpunished. He did it to demonstrate his righteousness at the present time, so as to be just and the one who justifies those who have faith in Jesus.

"That's Romans 3 verses 22–26. That means nobody, *nobody*, is perfect. Jesus came and died so we can all be forgiven of anything. *Anything* we've done. Have you asked God to forgive you for all this trash you keep carrying around?"

"I guess so," she answered.

"You don't know? If you don't know, then do it now for sure! Ask God to forgive you!"

"You tryna be my pastor now? Be careful. You might wanna back up!"

"I'm no pastor. I just want you to know for sure that you are forgiven by God if you just ask him. He's the only judge that matters. What I think, my mama, or anyone else for that matter, doesn't matter when God forgives you. If you don't think you've asked him, then do it now. I'll leave the room. I'll help you pray. Whatever you need me to do. But, Hope, I need you to let this go! All that baggage you carry ain't gonna do nothin' but break your back! Cast all you burdens on Christ!"

"Esdell, when I think about you and the life you must've led, I don't think I'll fit in!"

"If you don't wanna be with me, if you're having second thoughts, just say so. Don't try to use your past to block me. We'll end it now before we get in any deeper."

Hope shook her head. Ending things with Esdell was the last thing she wanted. She was trying to think what to say next. Esdell was concerned about her silence.

"Is that it, Hope? Have you changed your mind about us?"

"No. No," she softly answered. "Esdell, you are absolutely, positively, without a doubt the best man that I've *ever* dated. I've known a lot of men..." Esdell rolled his eyes. "Let me finish!" she spoke a little louder. "I've known a lot of men, but none of them are anything like you. Sometimes I think I don't deserve you. Maybe you're too good for me. I think we might not be equally yoked. You know what I mean."

"Yeah, I do. And once again, that's *garbage!*" Esdell close his eyes and grabbed one of Hope's hands. "Heavenly Father, I come right now in the name of Jesus, standing in the gap for your daughter, Hope. I beg you,

Lord, to remove all these negative thoughts from her mind. Remind her she is your child, and there is nothing she has done that you won't forgive her for. Remind her of her upbringing by her parents that fear you and work tirelessly for you. She was raised to fear you too but may have briefly strayed. But now, she's turning back to you! I ask again, Lord, let her know she is forgiven."

"FORGIVE ME, LORD!" Hope yelled through tears. "Please forgive me, my God!"

"Right now in the name of Jesus! Amen!"

"Right now in the name of Jesus!" she repeated. "Right now! Amen"

"It's done, Hope! It's done!"

Hope cried and whispered, "Thank you, Father." She turned her tear-filled eyes to Esdell. "Thank you, Esdell."

"We not coming back here no more, Hope. I don't want to talk about this ever again!"

He held her while she slowly began to compose herself. Over twenty minutes passed before she finally spoke.

"Y'all 'bout to kill that plant!" She giggled. With those words, the subject had been changed and dropped. "It needs professional help!"

"Just my luck, I know a professional. What does it need, doc?"

"It's getting plenty of light." She sniffled "But it's probably getting too cold being that close to the front door. It is a tropical plant, you know."

"I do now. Karlena brought that plant cause of the colors in it. I'll tell her and let her decide where to move it. Are you okay now? Ready to go to Mama's? I'm hungry."

"Me too, but I need to go fix my face first."

"Sure. The bathroom is right up the stairs, there. The door's open." He watched her as she ascended the stairs. "Lord, that woman," he continued to pray. "If we're meant to be, please remove all doubts from her and from me. I believe you let me find her, so grant me patience! Amen!"

Once Hope finished freshening up, they went to Grace's house for dinner. They got there just as the food was being placed on the table. Esdell was happy that everyone was finally getting a chance to get to know Hope and Kofi. Grace, as usual, had prepared a delicious meal. She had prepared honey-glazed ham, macaroni and cheese, yams, green bean casserole and cornbread. After eating that large meal, there was no room for the lemon glazed cake and ice cream that was waiting for dessert.

In stead, everyone went into the living room to talk. They had discussed the church service during dinner, so now they were letting Hope talk about herself. She told them about how thankful she was that the church had embraced Kofi. She talked about how proud she was of her son because he was turning his life around. Christine asked a lot of questions, but none of them alluded to anything that could have been considered highly personal.

Kareem began to talk about his relationship with Kofi and Hope's parents. He had been in touch with her parents off and on since they had left. He was so excited to share their stories about the mission in Haiti. He could see himself doing this kind of work someday.

The time flew by as everyone talked and laughed. Even though Hope had been asked a lot of questions, she never felt as though she were being interrogated. All of Esdell's family seemingly liked Hope and Kofi and made them feel welcomed and at ease. When it was time to leave, Grace wrapped up two large pieces of lemon glaze cake for Hope and Kofi to take home.

"Good-bye, Mrs. Willis," Hope said. "I had a really nice time. The food was great. I hope to see you again soon."

Grace gave Kofi and Hope a hug as the rest of the family waved good-bye.

"She's a sweet woman," Grace whispered to Esdell.

He smiled and hurried to walk out with Hope. It was a wonderful afternoon, and another milestone in Esdell and Hope's relationship.

16

Esdell and Hope were enjoying their first Saturday together in weeks. It was continuing to be difficult for them to spend much time together with their work and school schedules. This Saturday was a long time coming. Esdell picked Hope up early and took her to breakfast. After that, they went to a nursery to shop for flowers to landscape his yard. It was a beautiful spring day in May and a great day for gardening. Hope had dressed for their breakfast date but not for working in the dirt, so Esdell was taking her home to change clothes. Hope removed the mail from her box before entering the apartment.

"Sit down, Esdell. It'll just take me a few minutes to change." She flipped through envelopes in her hand. "Oh! I've been waiting on this!" She ripped open a letter and began to read its contents. "Are you serious?" She continued to read. "You have gotta be kidding me!"

"What is it, babe?" Esdell inquired.

"Look at this!" Hope gave the letter to Esdell who skimmed it briefly and then sighed. Hope asked, "Do you believe it? I can't believe it! They turned Kofi down for financial aid! They say I make too much money! This is ridiculous. I took a second job to help make ends meet and now it's put me over the income limit for financial aid." She sat down at the table. Esdell continued to read the letter a little more thoroughly.

"Hope, they did give him *some* money."

"Three hundred dollars! That's barely enough to buy a book! Kofi's all set to go to registration in two weeks for his summer classes. He'll need eleven hundred dollars for just two classes!" She shook her head. "Woo, I need to calm down. This letter is bringing me and the whole day down real quick." She smiled slightly and licked her lips. "Praise God I've got the money. I've got more than that saved up. I guess I just gotta accept the fact that the money I'm saving to buy the flower shop will now have to go toward Kofi's education. But I sure was hoping to get some financial help."

"I can help you," Esdell said without hesitation.

"I should've known you would offer to help." Hope reached across and grabbed Esdell's hands. "I won't let you do that. You've got your own schooling to take care of. Plus, you need to be concerned about your own kids. We're gonna be fine. I've got the money, and I promised Kofi. He's got it made up in his mind that he's going to college, and I'll make sure he goes."

"If you want me to help, I will." He thought for a moment. "How much more did you need to buy the shop?"

"The owner will sell me the whole thing for eighty-five thousand dollars. I'm far from that."

"Did you think about getting a small business loan?"

"Sure, but my credit isn't the best, so, I was really trying to pay cash for it. He wanted to close the deal with me by the end of the year. He's been really patient. Maybe I should just tell him to try to sell it to someone else."

"Don't give up on your dream!" Esdell thought for a moment. "I'll cosign a loan for you. How 'bout that? Or I can chip in on what you've saved already."

Hope stood to kiss Esdell on his forehead. "You! One day I'ma get used to you just doin' you! I know you mean it, Boo, but me and Jesus, we'll work it out! Well, I'm done bummin' out over this. I'm gonna change, and I'll be right out."

Esdell was so pleased with Hope and her renewed faith. She had been going to church more frequently; as much as her schedule would allow. She seemed more at peace.

In a matter of moments, Hope emerged from her room dressed in old jeans and an old T-shirt. She was reading a text. "Hmm, Kofi wants to know if I'll need the car later. He wants to go to the mall."

"I got ya, girl. I'll get you wherever you need to go today."

"Okay, I'll let him know." Hope typed and sent her message and then they were on their way to Esdell's with a trunkful of flowers.

Over the past few months, Kofi had been released from probation. Esdell had helped him get his drivers' license, and now Kofi was free to come and go as he pleased. Esdell and Kareem had made themselves always available to Kofi. They were helping him to understand the importance of working on his relationship with God. They had also continued to encourage him to go to college and now that time had come. Esdell and Hope discussed Kofi and his pending college career as they drove to his house. By the time they arrived, however, Hope had changed the subject by planning where to plant all the things Esdell had bought.

Esdell unloaded the car and got his gardening tools from the garage. Hope immediately went to work. Hope had instructed Esdell on what perennial plants to buy. She had methodically planned where to plant them. With the plans she had made, Esdell's yard would always be in bloom during the spring and summer months. He had also purchased a gazebo that would be delivered later and would be placed near the back of his huge backyard. The structure had lattice sides, and it was Hope's plan to plant dark pink clematis bushes on each side that, by next season, would vine over it. He marveled at how hard she worked. He hung some floral baskets on some hooks on his front porch and then raked up dead leaves and twigs. He did most of the digging but concerned himself primarily with the lawn. Hope was in a zone. It was like she was burying her frustrations along with those flowers. Nearly four hours passed, and then they were done.

"When all these plants bloom, this is gonna be like the Garden of Eden!" Esdell beamed. "Thanks, Hope. You sure know your stuff."

"Thanks! It may not look like much right now, and maybe not even this season, but just wait 'til next year. It'll be beautiful! But now, I'm starving! You have to feed me. I don't work for free."

Esdell laughed. "Okay, where you wanna go to eat?"

"I can't go anywhere looking like this!" Hope brushed some soil from her jeans. "I need to go home and clean up. I know after I take a hot shower, I'ma just wanna relax, and I won't feel like going anyplace. Can we pick up something on the way to my place?"

"We can do that! I need to clean up myself. I'll take a real quick shower and then we can get whatever you want."

"Keep it simple. Burger and fries, work for me."

"And a frosty?"

"You read my mind!"

They both laugh and went into the house. Hope sat on the couch while Esdell was showering upstairs. She listened to the sound of the water running in the shower. She began to fidget as she waited for him to finish bathing. She stood to walk around the room. She looked again at the family pictures on the entertainment center. She shook her head. She noticed that the croton plant had been moved to the dining room table. She checked the moisture of the soil in the pot and pulled off one dead leaf. She returned to the couch to sit down, and in her mind, she started to arrange her furniture in Esdell's house.

"Silly, girl!" she whispered to herself. She then heard the front door opening. It was Karlena coming in with Micah.

"Hey! Miss Hope! So you're the one responsible for all the flowers in the yard," Karlena noted. "The yard looks great! The hanging baskets on the porch are so pretty."

"I'm glad you like it. It wasn't easy talking your daddy into buying all those flowers. Wait until you see 'round back. Micah! Hi, handsome boy!" Hope said.

"Hi!" Micah simply said, waving his little hand.

"What y'all up to this evening?" Karlena asked Hope.

"I'm waiting on your daddy. He's taking a shower, and then we're going to stop to get something to eat on the way back to my apartment. What about you?"

"I'm going to Skype with Joseph tonight. That's my boyfriend in Louisiana."

"I remember. How're things with y'all, if you don't mind my asking."

"I don't. We're doing the best we can long distance. That is if you don't mind an electronic romance." Karlena leaned in closer to Hope. "I have to admit though. I miss the feel and the smell of him. Ya know what I mean?"

"Oh yeah, I know exactly what you mean!" Hope agreed.

"Shh! Here comes, Dad," Karlena said, hearing footsteps on the stairs. "That's just between us, *okay?*"

"Gotcha, girl!"

"Karlena and Micah! How y'all doin'?" Esdell asked. "C'mere, li'l buddy."

"Dae dae!" Micah said, running to him.

"How was work, Karlena?" Esdell inquired.

"It was good, Daddy. Miss Hope just told me your plans for tonight. So have fun! I'll be talking to Joseph later. I'll tell him you said hi." Karlena picked up Micah and started up the stairs. "Bye, you guys!"

"Bye-bye," Micah repeated.

"See you later! Ready to go, Esdell?" Hope stood up to prepare to leave.

"Let's go!"

They stopped at Wendy's for carryout and then went to Hope's place. She really was hungry, so she just washed up so they could go ahead and eat. She then went to take a shower of her own, telling Esdell she would be out shortly. He watched the news on TV while waiting on Hope.

"Now that's better!" Hope had finished her shower and was now joining Esdell on the couch. "I feel so much better now that I've got all that dirt off me! I know I smell better!"

"You smell real, real good!" Esdell said, nudging Hope's neck with his nose. She turned her head to kiss his lips.

"Um, I wonder where Kofi is. He should've been home by now." She reached for her cell phone. "I'm gonna call him." Seconds passed. "Kofi, where you at?" She listened to his response. "You didn't say anything about going out with a friend. What friend?" Again she listened. "Kareem? Boy, why didn't you just say so. Y'all be careful and you don't be out too late! Bye!" She sighed. "Kofi and Kareem are going to the bowling alley to watch your church league bowl in a tournament."

"Oh yeah, that is tonight! You wanna go watch?"

"Not really. Let's just see what's good on TV."

"All right." Esdell reached for the remote on the coffee table, crossing slightly over Hope. She smelled him.

"You smell pretty good yourself! Um, looks like we got the night to ourselves, since Kofi's hangin' out with Kareem," she said, smiling and licking her lips. She turned her face toward Esdell for another kiss. He obliged her, but this kiss was different. Hope kissed Esdell passionately, rubbing him and pressing her body hard against his. Esdell began to respond, but suddenly stopped, pushing her away.

"Hope, stop! What're you doing?"

"What's the matter with you, Esdell?" Hope asked, breathing heavily.

"What's the matter with me? What's the matter with *you*?"

"It's okay, I'm your girlfriend! Don't you want to?"

Esdell stood up and walked across the room.

"I can't take this anymore!" she said in frustration. Esdell said nothing. Hope took several deep breaths. "*Okay*, E. Brown, you said you want to keep things honest between us! It's time for a reality check here!"

"*Okay*, run it!" Esdell said, keeping his distance.

Hope thought for a moment. "Um, I know you said you don't want to talk about my past again, but I gotta go there. Yes, I've been with other men. Partly 'cause I wanted to just have a man, and partly just 'cause I wanted it. Shamefully, but truthfully, my sex drive is high." She waited for a response from Esdell. There was none. "Esdell, boo, we been together for months now and you haven't…You act like you don't want me. I'm your woman, and I think it's past time we take our relationship to the next level." She paused. "Well, say something!"

"Whatcha want me to say?"

"Esdell, for months I've tried to be content with kissin' and cuddlin', but I want more. At your house today, I listened to the water running when you were taking your shower. I was picturing the water runnin' all over you and almost lost my mind. I'm your woman, Esdell. Don't you want me? Because *I want you*! There, I said it! Now, say something!"

Esdell paced a bit. "I'm a man, ain't I?" He walked back to the couch and sat down, leaving a cushion's width between him and Hope. "Yeah! Yeah, I want you. Fo' real though! I've been fightin' off thoughts and urges since the first day I saw you. But, Hope, I'm tryna do this thang right! I'm tryna be with you, be your man, and stay in the will of God! And it ain't easy. You so fine, Hope, and I'ma go on say it like I mean it. You sho' nuff sexy! You wanna talk about a shower? When you came out from your shower you smelled so good. Your skin was still a little moist, and it was so soft. It ain't easy for me either!"

"So what do we do? I'm trying to do better. I wanna stay in the will of God too. But He made us sexual beings. What're we suppose to do with that?"

"I went through this with my son, and I'm tryna remember what I told him so I can tell it to myself now!" Esdell tried to muster a chuckle. "Uh, I'ma man and you're a woman and God meant for man and woman to be together, but at the right time! It's not the right time for us yet, Hope. Where's your Bible?"

"I don't need you to read anything to me from the Bible now, man!"

"Hope, the word is always in order!"

"I know that! My reading the Bible is the only thing that's kept me from attacking you for this long!"

"Me too!" Esdell agreed. "The Bible, a lot of prayer, and some *cold* showers!" Again, he tried to chuckle. "Sexual immorality is all through the Bible. It's been with us since the beginning of time and—"

"I read all about that!" Hope said, cutting him off. "It says sex outside of marriage is wrong. I know all that! They say knowledge is power, but my knowledge of what the Bible says hasn't given me the power to fight my urges, Esdell!"

"But you said it yourself, you reading the Bible is what's got you through up 'til now. Um, this is where we gotta depend on the Holy

Spirit to bring us through. We need to be in that Bible right now, trying to renew our strength! We need to read and pray! We need to…"

Esdell looked at Hope as she sat with her arms firmly crossed, biting her bottom lip, and shaking her leg. It was clear she was not being too receptive to what he was saying.

"Man, Hope!" Esdell said, bowing his head. "I kinda feel like a hypocrite here because I feel like you do. I ain't been with a woman since Kenya died. I didn't wanna be. All I was thinking about was bein' a good dad to my kids. I wanted to make sure I helped them in every way I could. Everything was about my kids! Then I met you. I let you in a place that I thought was closed up forever. Now, yeah, I wanna be with you. I'm fighting my urges too! It's just not the right time."

"I know, we're supposed to be married! Married?"

"Uh, it's not time to talk about that either. I'm just tryna work through some things, clear my head, and completely throw away some ole baggage that I'm carrying. You've got me thinkin' thoughts I haven't thought in a long time! God help me!"

"Humph! God help us both!" Hope agreed. They sat for a while not saying a word. "Well, we may as well watch TV!" Hope said as she slid closer to Esdell to get the remote. Again, she smelled him. She looked him in his eyes and kissed him again, leaning him backward. Esdell groaned and sighed heavily.

"Woman, you sure make it hard on a man tryna live holy!"

17

Esdell walked around his backyard with a garden hose watering his lawn and all the flowers. He was taking good care of all the landscaping, making sure that all of Hope's hard work would not go to waste. He was careful to follow all of her instructions to keep his yard healthy. He walked around to the front of his house, watered the hanging baskets, and then sat down on the steps of his porch to water the grass. Karlena came out and sat next to him on the steps.

"I love the smell of water on the soil. Don't you, Daddy?"

"Yeah, I do! Don't know why though. Micah taking a nap?" he asked.

"Finally!" Karlena answered. "The older that boy gets, the harder it is to get him to go to sleep. He acts like he's afraid he's gonna miss something."

"He can do a lotta stuff he wasn't able to do before. He wants to explore, push the boundaries a little."

"He's pushing the boundaries all right. He's pushin' my buttons too!"

"That's my li'l buddy!"

"The yard is looking really good. I never knew you had a green thumb."

"It's not my thumb that's green. It's Hope's! I better keep this yard in shape. I ain't tryna answer to her!"

"I know that's right! Miss Hope don't play!" Karlena chuckled. "How you two doing, Daddy?"

"We're doin' all right! Taking it slow, but we doin' all right."

"She loves you," Karlena said.

"What? What makes you say that? Did she say somethin'?"

"No, I just got a feeling she does." Karlena stared out at the street and began to pat her foot.

"What's on your mind, baby girl?"

"You always know, don't you? You always know when me and Kareem got something to talk about."

"I'm lis'nin'."

"I'm going to take a vacation the week of Memorial Day, and Micah and I are going to visit Joseph."

"*Okay.*"

"I've got the time at work, this is the last week of school, and I've got the money to fly, and…"

"Karlena, I said okay. If you wanna go see Joseph, that's up to you. You a grown woman."

"Wow, I was expecting you to give me a hard time. You always want us all to be together on the holidays. You made such a big deal when I went at Thanksgiving."

"That was then, this is now. Things change. People grow up."

"And people get new girlfriends!" Karlena smiled and nudged Esdell. "You got Miss Hope to fill my spot now!"

"No such thing! Besides, it's prolly cheaper for you to fly to Louisiana than to pay your cell phone bill anyway. You and Joseph been burnin' up the phone lines!"

"True, true. I can't lie about that. We talk or Skype almost every day. Even with all that, I still miss him."

"Love'll do that to you. You go on down there, Karlena, and have a good time. We'll miss you. With the grace of God, we'll be right here waiting on you and li'l buddy when you get back." Esdell flipped a little water in Karlena's face. "You behave yourself!" He laughed.

The family, as a whole, really had no plans for the holiday weekend. Grace and Isaiah's anniversary would be the week before it, but they made it clear that they wanted to spend their anniversary quietly at home. Of course, Esdell would do some grilling and anyone that wanted to come over was more than welcome. Karlena and Esdell discussed Karlena's vacation in full detail while he watered the lawn. They laughed and enjoyed each other's company. Esdell relished every moment of his father-daughter time.

"Oh, I hear Micah calling me!" Karlena stood to go into the house. "Good talk, Daddy! Love you!" she said, dashing into the house.

"Love you too, baby girl!"

Esdell finished watering the lawn. He turned off the water and coiled up the hose on the side of the house. He returned to sit on his front porch. Oh, how he enjoyed his porch! He looked at his yard and up and down his neighborhood street. He thought of his family, and then he thought about Hope. It had been almost a year since he met her. He could not believe how his life had changed in the past couple of years. He thanked God for all that had taken place and prayed for His continued guidance. He prayed that God would continue to bless him and his family.

Just as Esdell was about to go into the house, Kareem pulled into the driveway. Esdell waited on him by the front door.

"What up, son?"

"You won't believe what's up, Dad," Kareem alluded. "How you feelin'?"

"Fine, I guess. Sit down and let's talk!" Esdell returned to his favorite seat on the porch. "This must be talk to Daddy day! Wut's up?"

Kareem took a deep breath. It was hard to tell if he was nervous or excited. "Dad, I just came from a meeting with Pastor..." he started.

"Okay," Esdell said.

"And both Pastor and I have been talking to Mr. and Mrs. Shah."

"Hope's parents, go on."

"The mission where the Shahs are is in need of a minister at the village church, and Pastor and I think I should go." Kareem waited for a response from Esdell. "Well, Dad?"

"Well, I don't know what to say! When did all this come up?"

"I knew I was going the day the Shahs flew out. God showed me then that was His plan for me."

"What about school?"

"It'll have to wait. I'll get my degree someday, but my theology education will now come from the work I'll do for the Lord in Haiti. I've prayed on this, Dad, and I'm going to Haiti. It's what I'm supposed to do."

"I can't argue with you on that. So when will you be going?" Esdell asked.

"Four to six months. There's a lot of paperwork involved, and I've got to get my inoculations updated, get a passport, that kinda stuff. I'll be taking this time to get everything in order here at home and at church."

Esdell stood up and held out his arms. Kareem stood and the two hugged. Esdell slapped Kareem firmly on his back. "I'm so proud of you, son. I knew that God had great things in store for you. I didn't know how, but I knew that he was gonna use you in a mighty way! Well, let's go tell your sister, who, by the way, is spending the holiday in Louisiana with Joseph. Whoever said that having adult children is easier than having babies lied," Esdell said as he walked into the house. "Karlena, come in here!" he yelled.

Karlena came in from the kitchen holding Micah by the hand. "Yeah, Daddy? Hey, Kareem, when did you get home?"

"Just a few minutes ago. I been outside talking to Dad."

"It must be the day for it!" she agreed. "What's going on, Daddy?"

"Let's sit down, everybody," Esdell directed. "Karlena, your brother... Kareem, you tell her!"

"Sis, in about six months, I'll be leaving. I'm going to Haiti."

"Haiti! What're you talking about, Kareem?"

"I'm going to be with Miss Hope's parents at the mission where they are. I'm going to pastor a church there."

"For how long? How long are you gonna be gone?" Karlena asked.

"For as long as it takes. God is sending me there, and he'll tell me when it's time for me to come home."

Karlena began to fight back tears. "What do you think about that, Daddy?"

"Well, it's just like I told you. Kareem is a grown man. He's makes his own decisions. This is different though. He's answering to God's call. This thing was decided for him. I wouldn't even start to talk against it. God's will be done!"

"Six months, huh?" Karlena contemplated. "I gotta a half a year to mess with you!" Karlena ran to her brother and put him in a playful headlock.

"Watch out, 'Lena. You don't want none of this! You better get her, Dad!" Kareem easily broke Karlena's hold on him. He picked her up and spun her around.

"Handle your business, Kareem! I'm going upstairs!" Esdell laughed and swatted Karlena on her backside as he passed her.

"Micah, come help Mommy!" Karlena blurted with a laugh. Micah came over and grabbed his uncle by the leg.

Esdell laughed when he looked at his children as they played in the living room. He went into his bedroom and sat in his chair and remembered when they used to wrestle around as little kids. He grinned as he thought how some things never changed. His face became serious when he thought about how some things change greatly.

"My Lord! Haiti!" he said. He bowed in prayer. "Heavenly Father, thank you for the man that you have allowed Kareem to become. He is truly your servant. I pray that you continue to let me witness the things that you have in store for him. Please, Lord, continue to bless my children as they grow. I pray that they are always be in your will. A lot of decisions are 'bout to be made here, Father, please guide us all. Keep us willing to obey. In Jesus's name. Amen." He sat to meditate on his prayer. He then thought about how his mother would react when she heard about Kareem going to Haiti, but his mind was immediately set as ease. It was his mother, Grace, who always knew God would call someone from their family to preach His word. Though Kareem would be missed, Esdell knew his whole family would support Kareem in his decision.

But for right now, he would rejoice in the time he would have with his children. Kareem's announcement, however, made him a little less agreeable with Karlena's trip to Louisiana. The Memorial Day Weekend would be one less holiday they would all spend together with Karlena being gone. Oh well, that wasn't going to stop him from firing up his grill and barbequing that holiday. He would open up his home to anyone that had a taste for his ribs and burgers. His mother, stepdad, brother, sister, and nieces knew they were welcome to come over if they wanted to, so now the thing to do is to invite Hope and Kofi.

Esdell decided to text Hope, asking her to call him. She was working so he would just wait for her to call when she was free. That did not take long.

"You rang, boo boo?" Hope asked when Esdell answered his phone.

"Yeah, I did. How you doin'?"

"Fine, but always better when I hear from you. I'm on break. What's up?"

"I'm tryna plan for Memorial Day weekend. I'ma grill. You and Kofi wanna come over?"

"We'll be there! Is the rest of your family coming over?"

"They gotta standing invite. They'll come through if they feel like it. My guess is they will." Esdell sighed heavily. "I got big news, Hope."

"What's the matter?" she asked with concern.

"Kareem just told me that he's gonna go to the mission in Haiti where your parents are to be the pastor of their church."

"Really? Mom and Dad never said a word! How'd that happen?"

"He's been corresponding with them ever since they left. He discussed it with Pastor Edwards, and they decided it's the right thing to do."

"Are you okay, Esdell? How do you feel about it?"

"I'll miss him. It'll be like losin' an arm, but it's God's will for his life, and I know it. Ain't no way I'll try to talk him out of it. It's in the Lord's hands."

"I don't know what I'd do if Kofi left, 'specially now that we're just now getting close. You must feel the same way."

"Sorta. I just trust and believe it'll be okay."

"He will be. I grew up in missions, you know. Mama and Daddy took good care of me, and they'll take good care of Kareem too. He's in good hands."

"I know that. Anyway, back to the BBQ," Esdell said changing the subject. "I'm Q'ing ribs and burgers and Karlena will fix…Oh, I almost forgot Karlena won't be here. She and Micah are spending the holiday with Joseph."

"Oh my goodness, Esdell! Karlena's leaving too?" Hope realized that he had to be saddened by the news from his children. "I'll bring some sides. Don't worry about a thing! We'll have a good time! I'm looking forward to it, spending the holiday with my man!"

* * *

Just days before Memorial Day, Esdell had sadly taken Karlena and Micah to the airport to fly to Louisiana. On the holiday, he rolled out his grill and prepared to barbeque. He put on the ribs and hamburgers just as he had planned. The rest of his family, along with Hope and Kofi, came with different dishes to make the meal complete. They all sat and talked while they waited on the meat to get done. Hope and Christine got to know each other better. Everyone observed they had a lot in common. Sammy joked that that was a good thing and a bad thing. It was a beautiful sunny day. The mood became a little somber when they talked about Kareem going to Haiti and when they talked about Karlena and Micah spending another holiday down south. But they laughed, played games, and delighted in what turned out to be a very good day.

Esdell's family all left just as it was getting dark, but Hope and Kofi stayed later. Kofi began to talk about starting school the very next week.

"Think about it, Mom, I'm 'bout to be a college student!"

"I know and I'm so proud," Hope beamed.

"Are you excited?" Esdell asked Kofi.

"Yeah, and nervous too! I haven't been in a real school for a long time. I hope I fit in."

"You will! I know you will," Esdell said. "I don't think I know anybody more determined than you. You got your mind made up and you gonna do real good!"

"I agree with Dad," Kareem acknowledged. "You were so excited after you left registration."

"Yeah, I was." Kofi laughed. "I didn't really know what to take. My counselor said to start with the basics, so I signed up for English 101 and Intro to Art."

"We worked that thing out, us and God. Everything's paid for and now my baby's set for summer school!" Hope said proudly.

"Me and RK drove around the campus. It's not as big as I thought, but it's still a little scary."

Hope smiled as she looked at her watch. "Oh, Kofi, we need to go! It's going on eleven o'clock! I gotta work both jobs tomorrow, and I need to get to bed."

"You and them two jobs!" Esdell lamented. "They keep cuttin' in on my mack time!"

"Whatever, man! Don't get me started on you and your classes at school! That's cutting in on your so-called "mack time" too! Give me a break!" Hope stood gathering her things in a large shopping bag.

"Hey, I'll be graduating with my associates next April! You won't be able to stand the mack I'ma put on you then!" Esdell joked.

"Promises, promises!" She laughed as she started toward the door. Esdell took the heavy bag from Hope and then walked her and Kofi to her car.

"Have a good day tomorrow, Hope." Esdell kissed her on her forehead.

"Thanks for having us! It was fun. You have a good day too." She pulled Esdell down to her face by his shirt to kiss him on the lips.

"Hey, nobody wants to see that! Let's go, Mom! Later, RK!" Kofi yelled to Kareem as he waved from the front porch. Hope shrugged her shoulders and got into her car.

"Talk to you tomorrow!" Esdell said, closing the door behind her.

"Bye, sweetie! Have a good night." Hope waved and drove off.

Esdell watch them until they had driven out of sight and then joined Kareem on the porch. "That *was* fun! I'm glad everybody gets along."

"Yeah, Dad, and I'm glad everyone is accepting the fact that I'll be in Haiti in a few months."

"It's not gonna be easy for none of us when you leave, but we all know that you gotta go. We ain't gonna question what God told you to do, not our place," Esdell said sitting down. He sat for a few minutes saying nothing. "You know what though? I gotta feelin' you leavin' ain't the only change that's about to take place around here."

"What? Are you making plans with Miss Hope? You two make a real good couple. Is love in the air?" Kareem curiously asked, nudging Esdell.

"Could be, could be!" Esdell answered, "But that's not what I'm talkin' 'bout. I gotta feelin' there's a gentle storm blowin' in from the south!"

"Huh?"

Esdell rubbed his eyes. "I don't think your sister is long for this house."

"What do you mean, Dad?"

"I was praying, as usual, for God's hedge of protection around you and Karlena while she's away and that's what the Spirit told me. Somethin' big is brewing between Joseph and her."

Kareem sat up straight in his seat. "Like what?"

"I got an idea. The Spirit is tellin' me to be ready! It's been a lifelong duty, workin' on my relationship with the Holy Spirit. It's something that I encourage everybody I talk to to do! It's important. That relationship gives you strength, makes you wise, and it gives you discernment! Know what I mean?"

"Yeah, I do. Could be marriage, Dad."

"That's what I'm thinking."

"Are you ready for that? I mean, if they do get married. Will you be okay?"

"Don't know yet."

"Well, I do! You'll be fine, Dad, like you always are."

Esdell stood up. "Well, I'ma go cover the grill and go get ready for work tomorrow. I'm glad it's a short week!"

"All right. I guess I'll head on in too. Need some help?"

"No, I got it."

"Well, g'night, Dad."

"Night, son." Esdell walked around to the backyard and put the cover on the grill. He then sat on the deck for a moment to think. He looked at his backyard and around his deck. He thought about all the work that he had put into this house in the short time that he and his family had lived there. He had made a home for his children a safe place, a place where they could live for as long as they wanted. He looked toward the sky.

"Is it true, Lord? Are both my children 'bout to leave?" He sighed. "Your will and your way, Lord!" He went into the house and made sure all the doors were locked and then ascended the stairs. He stopped at Kareem's door and touched it. He did the same at Karlena's and Micah's doorway.

"Your will and your way, Lord!" He showered, prayed, and then went to bed.

18

Though it was a short workweek, it seemed to Esdell like he had worked eight days instead of four. Since the warehouse was closed on Monday for the holiday, the deliveries were almost doubled. He entered his house on Friday evening very tired. The house was quiet. Esdell flopped down on the couch to sort through the mail. Just as he had finished reading, Karlena came in.

"Hey, Daddy!" she greeted.

"Hi! Where's Micah?"

"Grandma and Pop were going for a walk in the park and wanted to take him with them. I'll pick him up later. Anything in the mail for me?"

"Just a catalog," Esdell answered, passing it to her.

"What're your plans for tonight? Goin' out with Miss Hope?"

"No, she's working tonight, which is fine with me." Esdell sighed. "I'm so tired, I'd be poor company. I'ma take a shower, fix me a grilled ham 'n' cheese and just watch TV and wait on Hope to call me when she gets home."

"Okay! You got an exciting evening planned! I'm gonna change and go back over Grandma's. I'll eat over there. What's up with Kareem tonight?"

"I don't know. I look for Kareem when I see him comin'! He's all over the place tryna tie up loose ends and gettin' ready for his big move to Haiti."

"Dang! I still can't get with that! I've been with that boy since conception!" Karlena chuckled. "It'll be hard to say good-bye to my old wombmate!" She chuckled again.

"You funny," Esdell said, yawning as he rose from the couch. "Time to hit the shower." He patted Karlena on the head and went up the stairs.

He took a long, hot shower to relax his tired muscles. After he dressed, he sat on the side of his bed. Karlena knocked on his door.

"Daddy, are you dressed?"

"Yeah, baby girl. Come in."

"I'm headed back over to Grandma's. See ya later."

"See ya! Tell Mama I'll talk to her tomorrow."

"I will. Bye." Karlena waved and was then on her way. Esdell waved back and then stretched out on his bed. The next he knew, he was awakened by the sound of the doorbell. He was so tired, he had fallen asleep. He quickly gathered his wits and went to answer the door.

"Yeah! Yeah!" he shouted as he descended the stairs. "I'm comin'!" He snatched open the door without looking to see or asking who it was. When he opened the door, he was shocked to see Joseph standing on the other side.

"Hello, Mr. Brown!" Joseph said enthusiastically.

"Joseph! This is a surprise! C'mon in here, man!" Esdell gave Joseph a manly hug, slapping on the back. "What's up? Karlena didn't say a thing about you comin' home! Yeah, this is a big surprise! Glad to see ya!"

"Thanks! You look great, Mr. Brown," Joseph said, walking into the living room. "Actually, Karlena didn't know I was coming. I just flew in. I flew in to talk to you."

Esdell's mind flashed back to the previous time Joseph came to his house to talk. "Hmm. The last time you were here to talk, you told me you were moving to Louisiana and breakin' up with Karlena. Sit, let's sit." He gestured. "So?"

"Yeah, I remember that conversation!" Joseph said, licking his lips. "I'm about to eat some of those words right now!"

I already know! Esdell thought to himself, but he wanted to open it up for Joseph to continue. "Meaning what, Joe?"

"The last time I was here, I told you how I loved Karlena but only as a friend. I said I wasn't romantically in love with her. But all that has changed."

"I know! And now?"

"I love her! I miss her every moment I don't talk to her. I want to be with her and..."

"And?" Esdell questioned.

"And I want to marry her. I want to be her husband, and the father that Micah needs and deserves!"

"Marriage, huh? What did she say?"

"I haven't asked her yet. I'm coming to you old school! I wanna get your permission first, at least I hope so. I'm wanting to marry your daughter and take her and your grandson to Louisiana to live." Joseph waited for a response. "Mr. Brown, I know this is a lot and probably unexpected."

"Son, the only thing that's unexpected is that you came to me first." Esdell lowered his head. "God already told me this was comin', but I don't know, man! Kareem's going to Haiti and now you want to move the rest of my family 'way 'cross the country?" Esdell's voice was getting louder and Joseph was getting nervous. "You know you broke my baby's heart when you left, don't you Joseph? Now you want to marry her?"

"I *do* know that! It's the biggest regret of my life! It took my leaving to realize how much she meant to me! I love her! I love her in every possible way there is to love a woman," Joseph defended. "I've tried to make it up to her in word and deed. I was really hoping to get your blessing, but if not, I'm gonna ask her anyway! It's her decision!"

"My blessing? You tryna take my babies, and you want my blessing? Well, my blessing is what you get from me!" Esdell said with a wide grin. "I'm just messin' with you, dude. My daughter loves you, and I'd be proud to have you as a son-in-law!"

Joseph's face went from despair to delight. "Aw! You had me trippin'! Really, Mr. Brown? You good?"

"Yeah, I'm good. I'm good! Like I said, God told me this was comin'." Esdell lowered his head again. "He told me, but I see now that I ain't ready. Kareem asked how I'd be if all my kids left. Messed up. That's how I feel, messed up!"

"It's gonna be all right, Mr. Brown. I'm doing really well down south. I'll take good care of them both." Joseph reached into his pocket and took out a small box. "Look!" He opened the box to display a diamond ring. "You think she'll like it?"

"Wow! Oh yeah, she'll love it. Man, that's real bling! Must've set you back big time!"

"There's not a ring big enough to show Karlena how much I love her. She's priceless. She's matchless!" Joseph stared at the ring as if it were hypnotizing him. He snapped out of his trance when he heard a key in the front door. Karlena was entering. Joseph quickly closed the ring box and jammed it back into his pocket.

"Joseph!" Karlena said in astonishment. "What're you doing here?" Joseph rose to hug her.

"Hey, Micah! Karlena, baby, I need to talk to you."

"Uh, Micah, come go with Dae Dae," Esdell said, reaching for Micah. He took him upstairs into his room. He looked at his grandson and kissed him on his cheeks. He bounced him on his knee. He tickled his little belly and kissed him some more. "What am I gonna do without y'all? Not see my li'l buddy every day! Who's the biggest little man?" Esdell began to sing. "Who's the best in all the land?"

"Ahhh!" Karlena screamed from downstairs. "Yes, Joseph, Yes!"

"Way ta go, Joe!" Esdell smiled and then finished his little song. "It's Miiicah! Let's go see about your mama!"

Esdell and Micah went down the stairs just in time to see Karlena and Joseph in a tight embrace.

"Daddy, look!" she said, showing off the ring on her finger. "We're getting married, Daddy! We're getting married!"

"I know. Congratulations! I'm real happy for you both!" Esdell affirmed.

"We're getting married!" Karlena repeated running into Joseph's arms. He picked her up, hugging her tightly. "Oh, I gotta call Grandma! Ahhh!" Karlena screamed again, stomping her feet and spinning in a circle. She stopped spinning just as Kareem was coming in the door.

"What's going on in here? Karlena, I heard you screaming all the way outside." Karlena ran to her brother, grabbed him by the shoulders, and jumped up and down.

"Look at this! I'm engaged!" she yelled. Kareem looked at the ring and then turned to see Joseph standing near the dining room table.

"What's this?" Kareem freed himself from Karlena's grip and crossed the room to talk to Joseph. "Joseph, man, when did you get in town? Good to see you." He vigorously shook his hand. "What's this crazy girl talking 'bout? Really, man?"

"Good to see you too, Kareem," Joseph said. "She's not crazy! We're getting married!"

"Then you're the one who's crazy!" Kareem kidded. He noticed his dad. "You called it, Dad! Holy Spirit don't play! So what now?"

"I...I don't know! It just this minute happened!" Karlena was panting. "I gotta call Grandma!" she said again and ran to the phone. She dialed quickly. "Pops, let me speak to Grandma, please." She tried to calm down while waiting for her grandmother to answer. "Hello, Grandma, Joseph's here and guess what. We're engaged! Do you believe it? He came all the way here from Louisiana to propose!" Karlena walked into the kitchen leaving the men alone. Kareem went to his dad's side.

"You okay, ole man?" Kareem reacted to a slightly sullen look on Esdell's face. "You already knew, Dad."

"Yeah, I did, but it just got real. Didn't it, li'l buddy?" Esdell went to the couch to sit down. He bounced Micah on his knee. "Whatcha know 'bout that, Micah?" Esdell bit his bottom lip and shook his head. "Wasn't expecting this so soon. It just got real."

"Mr. Brown," Joseph started, "like I said, I'll take good care of Karlena and Micah. I'm doing well in school and learning more about the publishing business every day. The company will be ours. Karlena will work only if she wants to, not because she has to. I'll see that she finishes school too. I'll treat Micah like he's mine. I already feel like his dad. I love them both so much, Mr. Brown."

"I know you do." Esdell paused. "Where are you spiritually, Joseph? We've never talked about that." Joseph chuckled a little.

"I remember when I first met Karlena. She drilled me on that subject. She wanted to make sure we were 'equally yoked.' I go to church. My grandparents make sure of that, but I have to admit that I'm not as active in my church down south as I was here in Indy. I just don't have that kind of time anymore. But you best believe that I'm in church every Sunday!" Joseph looked at Esdell's face and could tell that he probably had not answered his question sufficiently. "I'm saved, Mr. Brown. By the blood of Jesus, I'm saved."

"Nuff said then!" Esdell said.

"Nuff said!" Kareem agreed. "So how soon are you planning to marry my sister, Joe?"

"That's up to her, but I'm not gonna be down with a long engagement!"

"I hope she doesn't wait too long. If y'all get married after I move to Haiti, I'm not sure if I'll be able to get back here for the wedding!"

"Wow!" Esdell exclaimed. "Wedding! It gets more real by the minute!" In his mind, he began to make financial provisions for a wedding. He then remembered that he had previously offered to help Hope with either Kofi's education or buying the flower shop. It was almost like he saw dollar signs with wings flying around the room. "Well, let's just wait to see what Karlena says about a wedding first. All that's gonna be up to her." He turned his eyes away from Joseph and Kareem and imagined his baby girl in a wedding gown; she would look just like his Kenya. He looked at Micah sitting on his lap. *Lord, all my babies gone. What will I do?* he thought. He could hear Karlena squealing in the kitchen as she talked to her grandmother. It was then he decided that whatever his baby girl wanted in the way of a wedding, he would provide.

After about ten minutes, Karlena came back into the living room. "Well, Grandma's crying. She said she was happy and sad. But mostly, I think she's happy for me. She asked me if I was going forward with my wedding plans."

"What plans? You already made plans?"

"Daddy, I've been planning my wedding since I was a little girl. I struggled with plans for a while after Mama died. I went to Grandma, crying that I couldn't imagine a wedding without Mom. Grandma told me she would be there with me, and she told me the same thing just now. Every girl wants a wedding, whether it's a big one or a little one. I'm no different. It's all right here." She tapped her temple with her index finger. "The only blank to fill in was who would be my groom, my husband. Now that blank has been filled in." She walked over to Joseph, and he put his arm around her shoulders; she hugged his waist. "Can I tell you my plans, Joseph?"

"Absolutely, baby!"

"I'll take Micah upstairs with me," Kareem said. "Come go with us, Dad. Let's leave these two alone."

"Right behind you, son." As they climbed the stairs, Esdell could hear Joseph and Karlena kissing and then Karlena began to cry. Esdell smiled.

"I'm gonna call and see if Hope is home."

"I completely understand, Dad. Go call your woman." Kareem took Micah into his room while Esdell went off to his room. He punched in Hope's number as he sat on his bed.

"Hello!" she pleasantly answered.

"Hey, Hope, what's up?"

"Not much. What's up with you? What's that tone in your voice? Did something happen?"

"Something definitely has happened!" Esdell confirmed. "Karlena's boyfriend came in town and became Karlena's fiancé!"

"What?" Hope paused. "He proposed?"

"Yup! They're getting married. Ain't that something?"

"I think it's great, but you don't sound too happy about it!"

"I'm happy for her. I'm just trying to process it all. They're downstairs making plans. She's talking about wedding plans. Man, I'm 'bout to become the father of the bride. Ain't that something?" he said again.

"Yes it is! And what a handsome father of the bride you'll be! Are you sure you're all right? You sound a little funny."

"Like I said, just tryna process everything."

"Well, let Karlena know that if she's planning a formal wedding, I can help her with flowers! Whatever she wants, I can get it for her wholesale, and I'll do all her arrangements for free! I can also get the food for the reception on my GFS discount."

"Hmm. Those two jobs of yours are really gonna come in handy. I can't wait to tell her."

"Being in the floral business, I've got all kinds of wedding contacts. Let her know I can hook her up."

"Sure will." Esdell, again, heard the doorbell ring, then he heard more squealing coming from the living room. "That sounds like Christine downstairs. Hope, let me call you back." They said their good-byes, and he started toward the steps. He met Kareem in the hallway.

"That didn't take long! Aunt Chris is here! C'mon, li'l man, let's goes see Tee Tee!" Kareem said.

"Good news travels fast, I see," Esdell said when they all reached the bottom on the stairs.

"I had just gotten over to Mama's when she was hanging up from talking to Karlena. She told me what happened. My niece is getting married!" Christine screamed and hugged Karlena. "A wedding, I can't get over it! I just had to see her face. Ahhh! My baby niece is getting married!"

"Just what we needed, more screamin'!" Esdell joked.

"We're getting married and getting married very soon," Joseph said.

"What? Did y'all set a date already?" Christine asked.

Esdell took a deep breath and held it as he waited on the newly engaged couple to answer. It was Karlena who responded.

"Joseph doesn't want a long engagement, and I don't either!"

"I would marry her tonight if I could, but Karlena wants a wedding," Joseph said.

Karlena walked next to Esdell. "Daddy, I want to get married on September 16, Mom's birthday."

The room went quiet as though everyone was paying homage. Esdell smiled and then hugged Karlena. Suddenly, Christine spoke up and broke the silence.

"September 16, that's in three and a half months! Girl, we need to get to planning!" Christine insisted.

"It's planned already, Aunt Christine! It's just a matter of putting everything in motion!" Karlena turned to face Joseph. "I have to confess,

I wanted a really big wedding when I was younger, but not now. I'm marrying the man I love, my first love! Not many people get to do that. I just want to become his wife. So small, sweet, and simple will do." Karlena looked at her dad and chuckled. "You can exhale now, Daddy!"

Esdell cleared his throat. "Well, all right then! Uh, I just talked to Hope, and she said she would help with flowers. She knows a lot of people in the wedding business. She wants to help. I'ma go call her back and tell her the date."

Esdell went back up to his room. He sat back down on his bed and looked up.

"Wow, Kenya, our baby girl's getting married!"

19

Karlena's wedding was a little over five weeks away. Karlena, her aunt Christine, Grandma Grace, and Hope did all the wedding planning. It was amazing how quickly things came together. Karlena's childhood plans of a large wedding party of twenty had been replaced with a wedding party of only six. She chose her cousins, Celeste and LeAnn, to be her bridesmaids. They would be dressed in silver halter gowns and shoes. Joseph had a little sister who she chose to be her flower girl. Joseph's older brother and Kareem were set to stand with him. The groomsmen would wear gray slacks and bowties and black tuxedo jackets. They made Micah the ringbearer in name only. He would be dressed in a little tuxedo but would sit with the family and not stand with the wedding party. Grandma did not quite agree with this decision because he was so young, but Karlena just wanted her son to be a part of her wedding in some way. Karlena selected an off-white sleeveless, satin wedding gown with a lace covered bodice, a fitted waist, and layers of organza over the A-line skirt. She would wear flowers in her hair; no veil. Joseph's tux was also off-white to match Karlena's gown. True to her word, Hope was handling all the flowers, which included bouquets, boutonnieres, and sanctuary decorations. All the flowers would be dark red, accented with silver ribbons. The wedding, of course, was to be held at the Road to Damascus Baptist Church, and Pastor Edwards, after marriage counseling, would perform the ceremony. Grandma wanted to save Esdell money by doing all the cooking for the reception, but everyone convinced her to just let the event be catered. Almost everything was done, and everyone was just waiting on the sixteenth of September to come. Esdell was taking Hope home after they had spent the afternoon together. He had gone to be fitted for his tux.

"Kofi, I'm home!" Hope yelled as they entered her apartment. "Kofi, you here?" There was no answer. "Humph, let me check my phone." She pulled out her cell phone, and sure enough, there was a text from Kofi. "Well, he's out with some friends." Hope slightly smiled.

"What you grinnin' about, girl?" Esdell asked.

"There was a day when Kofi's being out with friends would have worried me. I'd imagine him being out getting in some sort of trouble, but not now. He's changed so much, and I'm so thankful."

"Yeah, he's a good kid!" Esdell said as he helped himself to a drink from the refrigerator. "From crime to college! You were so proud when he got Bs on his first two college courses, weren't you, babe?"

"I sure was!" Hope answered as she shuffled through the mail.

"Hey, did you really think I looked good in that tux?" Esdell asked. Hope did not answer.

"It's not like I'm fishin' for compliments or anything, but did it look all right?"

Hope still did not answer. Esdell turned around and saw her standing with a letter in her hands. She was just staring at the envelope. "What's the matter?" he asked, walking to her side. "What is it?"

"There's a certified letter here from a Chicago legal firm. Kofi signed for it." She continued to stare at the envelope.

"Well, are you gonna open it?"

"I haven't lived in Chicago for years. What could it be after all this time, Esdell?" She laid the letter on the table. "What could it be?"

"You'll never find out if you don't open it." He put his hand on Hope's shoulder as she stared at the letter on the table. "Open it, Hope." Esdell picked up the letter and handed it to her. She slowly opened it and removed the letter to read it. She sat down at the table.

"Oh no, Kofi's dad died. He died last year." She kept reading. "Oh my god!" She jumped to her feet. "There was a one-hundred-thousand-dollar life insurance policy and Kofi's a beneficiary! Oh my god! Oh my god!" Then softly, she repeated herself, "Oh my god, Kofi's daddy is dead. Lord, forgive me. He's dead."

"Hope?"

"I sounded happy. I was practically celebrating. Even if he wasn't much of a dad, he was Kofi's father, and he was someone's son. All I saw was the money." Hope sat down to finish reading the letter. She exhaled heavily. "Listen to this. There's a copy of an e-mail he sent to the attorney."

I'm not proud of the life I've led. I have done things that I'm ashamed of, and even things I should have gone to jail for. I've done things that I regret. The biggest regret of my life is that I didn't have a relationship with my son, Kofi Thomas. I met him once, left, and never looked back. I didn't want to be tied down with a child. I didn't want the responsibility. In life, all I gave him was my name; nothing more. But now, at least through my death, I can give him something. I apologize to his mother, Hope Shah. She was a nice woman who deserved better than me.

Hope continued to read. "According to the attorney, he took out this policy years ago. His mother was the original beneficiary, but she died, so he made Kofi the beneficiary. He always thought he'd die young. He was always mixed up in some kinda mess."

"How'd he die?"

"It just says he died after a chronic illness. It also says they've been trying to locate me for several months. Hmm, he finally decided to do something for his son. I feel so bad now. I feel guilty about the way I first reacted."

"Don't. You didn't wish death on him. An unexpected hundred thousand dollars is enough to make anybody scream! You already asked forgiveness for that, it's done. What now?" Esdell asked.

"There're some forms here that Kofi and I need to sign and get notarized. Since he's eighteen now, they'll send a check payable to him in sixty to ninety days." Hope closed her eyes and shook her head.

"What?" Esdell asked.

"The Bible says the love of money is the root of all evil. Kofi's come so far. I hope this money doesn't make him lose his focus. He never had this kind of money before. This is a real game changer! He could…"

"You don't know what he'll do, so don't start speakin' life to bad thoughts."

"You're right. I wonder how soon he'll be home. Should I call him and tell him? No, I shouldn't. I'll just wait 'til he gets home." Hope said, answering her own question. Then she slapped the top of the table, smiling at Esdell. "And yes you did!"

"I did what?"

"You did look really fine in that tuxedo, bride's daddy! I can't wait to see you walking Karlena down the aisle!"

"Thanks. I can't wait to see Karlena as a bride. It took me long enough to get with that! My daughter: a bride and somebody's wife!"

"She's gonna be a beautiful bride. She's such a pretty girl. She'll be a good wife too. After all, she's survived in a house full of men and kept them all in check, including you, E. Brown!" Hope faked a hearty laugh and then her attention returned to the letter. She picked it up and read it again. Esdell simply watched. She studied the forms that needed to be completed. "Do you know a notary, Esdell?"

"Yeah, babe, our church clerk is one. You might wanna think about getting your own attorney or at least getting a financial advisor. Either can help you deal wisely with this."

"That's a good idea. I'm real anxious about how Kofi is gonna deal with this."

"It's all good," Esdell said. "Well, unless you think you need me to be here to help you talk to Kofi, I think I'm gonna head on home. I gotta let Karlena know how my fitting went."

"Like I said, she keeps all you guys in check! That's fine. You go on home, I'll be okay." Hope stood to walk Esdell to the door.

"See ya later." He gave her a little kiss.

"See ya!" Hope said, closing the door behind him. She looked up. "Oh, Lord, I'ma need your help big time with this!"

* * *

When Esdell arrived home after leaving Hope's apartment, he was eagerly met at the door by Karlena. As expected, she wanted a report on her dad's trip to the tuxedo shop.

"Hey, Daddy, how'd it go? Did you try on your tux? Did it fit okay?" Karlena questioned.

"Huh, good, yes and yes!" Esdell chuckled, answering all three questions. "And I'm doing good. How are you?"

"Sorry, Daddy. I'm just trying to tie up all the loose ends. Thank God for Aunt Christine! She's worked so hard on this wedding. So everything went okay?"

"Everything went well. Hope went with me, and she said the tux looked good on me. So, you can check me off your list. I even bought new drawers just for the occasion!"

"TMI, Dad! I don't need an update on your underwear! But thanks! I'm glad Miss Hope went with you. She's been a real Godsend too! Did she show you the pictures of the bouquets she's gonna make? They're gorgeous!"

"She's ordering the best. My baby don't play when it comes to flowers!"

"I know that's right!" Karlena agreed. "We're really close, Daddy. In a little over a month, I'm gonna be Joseph's wife! I'll be moving away."

"I know, baby girl. It's all I've been thinking about."

Esdell and Karlena took advantage of the fact that Micah was napping to talk again about the things that had taken and the things that were about to take place. After Joseph proposed, he told Karlena that he wanted to adopt Micah, and Karlena quickly agreed. She reluctantly met with Micah's father, Jeff. The meeting disgusted her. He, at first, was eager to sign away his parental rights and the responsibility of having a son. But after he thought about it, he tried to use it as a way to extort money from her. He said that he would sign the adoption papers only if she agreed to pay him five thousand dollars. He had not forgotten the tax refund he was forced to forfeit for back child support. His plan was to get that money and more. Though Karlena was disgusted, she was not surprised. Jeff was just being himself. Karlena simply said, "I knew I should have brought Daddy with me," and Jeff quickly relented and readily signed the papers when presented to him. Father and daughter went on to discuss the day of the nuptials. After the wedding, Karlena and Joseph had planned to spend their wedding night at the finest hotel in Indianapolis. They would spend Sunday with Karlena's family, and then on Monday morning, Karlena, Micah, and Joseph would take the flight to their new home in Louisiana. Karlena had packed and shipped most of her and Micah's things already. Everything else she could pack and take with her on the plane. What a long road it had been for Esdell and the rest of the family to accept that Karlena and Micah would be leaving, and that Kareem would be leaving some time after that. But they all welcomed it as God's will and found joy in it.

Later that evening, Hope called to tell Esdell about how it went with Kofi after he learned about his inheritance. He was, of course, excited! He spouted his plans on how he would spend the money, most of them materialistic. It was such a lot of money for such a young man to have all at once. He had even mentioned that he could now move out and get his own place. With all those dreams, Hope was relieved to hear that Kofi would use some of the money to continue his education. Esdell and Hope encouraged each other as they both lamented about the life-changing events that were affecting them. It was as life would have it; children grow up and start living adult lives. It was a blessing to Esdell. There were days, when he was at war, and especially after Kenya was killed, that he was not sure that he would even be alive to witness his daughter's wedding. Now, it was weeks away. Likewise, Hope counted the blessing that Kofi was going to college and now even had the money to pay for it. She had only seen incarceration or death in her son's future. They agreed that their God was great and worthy of more praise than they could possibly give him.

There then was a knock at Esdell's bedroom door.

"Hold a sec, Hope. Yeah?" he answered. "C'mon in!" Kareem entered with an odd look on his face. "What's up, son?"

"Dad, we need to talk," Kareem said with a serious tone.

"Huh, Hope, I'ma let you go. I'll talk to you tomorrow. Bye! Okay, what's going on Kareem?" Kareem looked at a letter that he was holding in his hand.

"My paperwork is all done. Everything's done. I…I've been cleared to go to Haiti in six weeks. The church needs me right away!" There was a loud silence.

"My God, my God," Esdell murmured. He stood and paced back and forth and then repeated, "My God, my God."

"I know, Dad, I know. It's just a week after Karlena's wedding." Kareem paused. "But we knew this was coming!"

"Yeah, we did. Me and Hope was just talking our kids growing up and moving away, now here you come. I was hopin' that you'd be here until after Thanksgiving, guess not! Oh well, what's a daddy supposed to do? 'Cept give his son a big manly hug. C'mere, son!" Kareem walked into Esdell's arms, and they firmly embraced. Esdell ended their hug by slapping Kareem on the back with both hands. "All right, now, Pastor Brown! I'm so proud of you and Karlena. And I'm so grateful that God allowed me to see my kids all grown up and 'bout to be on their own. I'm so grateful." Esdell stared off into space.

"Let me pray with you, Dad." Kareem grabbed his hands. "Lord God, we come to you now in the name of Jesus."

"In the name of Jesus!" Esdell echoed with his head bowed.

"We thank you, Heavenly Father, for everything that you have done for us and give the praise and honor that is due to you and you alone. Now, Lord, I come asking that you continue to strengthen and guide us in the days to come. I ask a special blessing on this, your son, Esdell, hold him fast! My sister and I are so blessed to have him as our earthly father. No better man could you have given us, and we are grateful! He has led us, instructed us, loved us, and prayed for us. Now you have given my sister and I new instructions. You have given me an assignment in a foreign land to minister to your people. Give me wisdom to lead and pastor them as you would have me to do. My sister will soon be married and will move across the country to live, bless her marriage. But, God, these things are not going to be easy for any of us, but we submit to your will."

"We submit!" Esdell repeated.

"We turn over all our concerns and worries to you. Let my father know that his children will be fine because you are our God. My dad has taught us your ways and all the good that he is, he has given to us. Hold him up, Lord. Hold us all, Lord, in your powerful, gracious, and merciful hands. We claim the victory and pray this prayer in the name of your son, Jesus! Amen and amen!"

"Amen!" Esdell sighed heavily. "Thank you, son. It's all good now!"

It truly was all good. To have his son pray for him was a gift to Esdell. It meant everything to hear Kareem go to the Lord on his behalf. The prayer had empowered Esdell, and the next five weeks went by with little sadness when he thought of his children leaving.

* * *

On Karlena's wedding day, Esdell was happy and prepared for the task ahead of him as father of the bride. He and Kareem entered the lounge portion the men's restroom at their church. Kareem reached for his dad's garment bag.

"I'll take it, Dad. I'll hang up our tuxes."

"Thanks, son. The sanctuary looks good! Hope had to get here pretty early to hang the floral arrangements. Don't know where she got the energy to do this after leaving the rehearsal dinner so late last night. Anyway, the real flowers were worth every penny. The church smells as good as it looks."

"Miss Hope definitely got skills *and* energy! I've been to a lot of weddings here, but the church has never looked this beautiful. I know Karlena's gonna be a snotty mess when she see it!"

"I think there's gonna be a lot of snotty messes around here today. I just hope I'm not one of 'em!"

"You want me to punch you if you start crying?" Kareem asked.

"No. Well, maybe, if I start sobbing!" They laughed at the thought of it.

"What's up? What's up?" Sammy asked, dancing into the lounge. "What y'all laughing at?"

"I'm glad you're here, Uncle Sammy. Me and you might have to punch Dad out if he starts crying today!"

Sammy burst out laughing. "Oh, just give me a reason, Big E. Give me a reason!"

"Play if you want to. I can take both of y'all right now!" Esdell pretended to spar with both his brother and his son. They shared a hearty laugh.

"Okay! Okay!" Sammy said. "That's enough! Christine sent me in here to check on y'all. She told me…make that, *ordered* me to tell y'all to get dressed and get in the sanctuary for pictures. She's actin' like a drill sergeant around here. Remind me if I ever get married, not to let Christine coordinate it!"

"I know she's trippin' hard! She's already bossy," Esdell agreed. "And now she has all authority over this wedding! Boy!"

Esdell and Sammy reminisced about other times their sister had shown her bossy nature. They were deep in their conversation when Kareem showed himself fully dressed.

"You guys just keep on talking 'bout Aunt Christine. I'm dressed and going to sanctuary. She's not putting my name on her hit list!"

"Hey, I'm already dressed!" Sammy defended. "It's Esdell who's in trouble."

"You know y'all ain't right! Go stall her and I'll be dressed in five minutes!" Esdell said, dashing toward his tux. In just a little less than ten minutes, he entered the sanctuary fully dressed. Christine pointed out that his bowtie was crooked, and she went to adjust it.

All of the wedding party, except for Karlena posed for the many pictures that the photographer took. They each complimented each other on how good they looked. Esdell hugged his nieces, Celeste and LeAnn, stating they looked like princesses. No sooner that the photography session was over, guests started to arrive. Christine rushed everyone back to their dressing rooms. She kept a close eye on her watch as she was determined that the wedding would start on time. At 2:15 p.m., the ceremony began. Joseph's mother was escorted in by his dad. Grandma Grace was escorted in as the mother of the bride by her husband, Isaiah. She was dressed in a dark red gown and in black and silver shoes. The guest all smiled with approval when she entered. They were followed in by an usher who was carrying Micah, the honorary ringbearer in his little tuxedo complete with a little red boutonniere.

"Aw!" The room said in unison. Then Pastor Edwards entered, followed by Joseph and the groomsmen. Next, Celeste and LeAnn entered. Celeste sashayed in as if she were a runway model, while LeAnn walked in methodically, trying to stay in time with the music. The ushers pulled down the runner and Joseph's little sister came in dropping red rose petals for Karlena to walk on. Esdell stood nervously just outside the sanctuary doors staring at the floor. Then a shadow appeared over the spot at which he was staring. He looked up and Karlena was walking toward him accompanied by Christine. Esdell gasped and tears immediately formed in his eyes.

"Where dem boys when I need 'em?" he jokingly whispered to himself. He blinked his eyes to push back the tears. "Karlena! Karlena, when I saw your mother on our wedding day, I swore I'd never see a more beautiful bride. I was wrong! Beautiful doesn't begin to describe you. Baby girl, you are breathtaking! You look just like your mom!" Karlena's gown gently hugged her body, demurely showing off her figure. Her hair and makeup were perfect; her lips being red, matching the red rose bouquet she held in her hands. She smiled broadly.

"Thank you, Daddy. You look very handsome."

"Okay, you guys, it's time!" Christine instructed, touching both of them. "You both look great. Now get on down that aisle!"

"Are you ready, honey?" Esdell asked.

"Ready, Daddy!"

The ushers opened the doors, and Pastor Edwards signaled for the congregation to stand. Joseph adoringly fixed his eyes on Karlena as she walked toward him on Esdell's arm. When Karlena and Esdell reached the front of the church, they went to a silver candelabrum that was decorated with red and white roses and held a single candle. There was a decorative lighter that was ornately tied to the candelabrum that Esdell unfastened and handed to Karlena.

She lit the single candle and said, "In remembrance of my mother, Kenya Brown, whose beautiful spirit is always with me. I love you.

Mama and I know you are here today." Esdell then escorted Karlena to her waiting groom.

Pastor Edwards began to speak, "We are here today to join in holy matrimony Karlena and Joseph. Who gives this woman to be wed to this man?"

Esdell responded, "I do!" He kissed Karlena on the cheek and presented her hand to Joseph. He then stepped back and took his seat next to his mother and the rest of the family. Hope was sitting in the row behind him. She leaned forward and caressed his shoulders to comfort and reassure him. He patted her hands to let her know that he was just fine. Esdell watched the nuptials almost in a daze. The ceremony seemed to fly by. The couple made their vows and opted to take communion in remembrance of Christ. This sacrament would also symbolized that Christ would always be at the head of their marriage. They exchanged rings.

"I now pronounce you husband and wife," Pastor Edwards announced. "What God has joined together, let no man put asunder! Joseph, you may kiss your bride!" The couple kissed as the audience applauded. It was done. Esdell had given away his baby girl. He forced a smile as the wedding party started the recessional. Kareem playfully shook his fist at Esdell as he passed him to remind him that he would still punch him if needed. This made Esdell chuckle.

After the ceremony, more pictures were taken. It had been a beautiful ceremony, and Karlena was glowing. Once the pictures were done, the bridal party departed for the reception hall. Hope's cousin, Dameon, acted once more as DJ for the Brown family. He announced the wedding party as they entered the room as the guests applauded. After a delicious meal, the newlyweds cut the wedding cake, and then Karlena and Joseph had the first dance. After that, it was time for the father/daughter dance.

"C.mon, baby girl, let's show 'em how it's done!" Esdell and Karlena glided around the room like professional dancers. "Are you pleased with your day, Karlena?"

"It almost exactly like I dreamed. Thank you, Daddy. I'm so happy! This day, this moment, and this dance with you will be something that I'll remember for the rest of my life!"

"Me too, and I'm happy that you're happy!" Esdell said as he twirled Karlena around.

Joseph approached them. "I'm cutting in Mr. Brown! Or can I call you Daddy B?"

"I kinda like that!" Esdell consented. "Karlena, dance with your husband."

Karlena hugged and kissed him. "I love you so much, Daddy! I may be Joseph's wife now, but I'll always be your baby girl!" With that, she turned and took Joseph by the hand. And they danced across the room. Christine signaled for the rest of the guest to join them on the dance floor. Esdell started toward his table but was met halfway by Hope.

"Dance with me, E. Brown! We've never danced before."

"Why sure, Miss Hope!"

"You did really good today, Esdell, giving your daughter away, I mean. You hung in there like a champ! I'm proud of you!"

"I did, didn't I?" Esdell agreed. "It started off hard, but it's ended up real sweet. Karlena's happy, God's in his heaven, and all's right with the world." He smiled at Hope. "Dameon is jammin' with the music, and you doin' all right on this dance floor! Thanks, baby, for all your hard work. Everything looked great, thanks to you."

"Well, thank you, sir. You are most welcome. It was truly my pleasure."

"The flowers were beautiful." He paused. "You're beautiful!" Esdell paused again. "You're beautiful, and I love you!" Hope stopped dancing and looked at Esdell with her mouth open.

"Esdell, I think you're getting caught up in the day, this wedding and everything. I'ma let you slide with that."

"Girl, you ain't gotta let me slide with nothin'! I love you!" Dameon changed the music to an up-tempo song, but Esdell and Hope continued in their slow dance posture.

"I love you too!" Hope declared. They kissed in the middle of the dance floor to the cheers of everyone. Karlena looked up to see her father kissing Hope.

"All right, now, Daddy!" she said with an approving smile.

20

Sunday afternoon, Esdell lay on his back in his bed thinking. Saturday had been quite a day, so he decided to stay home from church and just relaxed. He replayed the events of the previous day: the marriage of his daughter and his declaration of love to Hope. Both events made him smile but left him wondering what the next days would hold. He knew that Karlena and Micah was on their way to Louisiana the first thing Monday morning. He had taken a week vacation so he would be available to take them to the airport and to give him time to recoup from the weekend. He dreaded what his house would be like without his daughter and his grandson in it. No more li'l buddy and no more baby girl. He knew he could talk to them every day but acknowledged it wouldn't be the same. He turned on his side. There, lying next to him sleeping was Micah. He had kept him while his mom and her new husband enjoyed their wedding night. Esdell gently patted Micah on his back. He shook his head and sighed when he shifted his thought of Kareem's pending departure. He sent up a quick prayer asking God for strength. He decided not to dwell on Kareem but to focus on Hope.

"Ah yeah!" he said with a grin. "But now what?" He loved her and she loved him. *Well, it's out now. I never woulda dreamt it*, he thought to himself. He had spent so much time mourning Kenya he had never envisioned himself in love with anyone else. But now he was. *Let's just see where we go from here. Dang, my baby girl and my li'l buddy and my son!* His thoughts and emotions ping-ponged back and forth. It was dizzying. He looked at his clock and realized it was close to time for them to go to his mother's house for dinner. The last Sunday dinner he would have with all of his family. He gave Micah a gentle shake.

"Wake up, Micah. Wake up, li'l buddy. It's time to go see mommy and Gran gran."

"Mama!" Micah whined as he woke up. Esdell sat up and put Micah on his lap.

"Who's the biggest li'l man? Who's the best in all the land? It's Micah! It's Micah!" Esdell sang. "Bet you're glad you don't have to hear that song anymore! I'ma sho miss singin' it to you. C'mon, let's go get ready. "Who's as cute as he can be? Just because he looks like me! It's Miiicaahhh!" Esdell finished his little song that he had composed for his grandson so many months ago.

They went into the hallway and proceeded to Micah's room. They entered the room and it was empty. Esdell had let himself forget that all of Micah's furniture and possession had been shipped to Louisiana. "Lord Jesus!" Esdell exclaimed. He went into Karlena's room remembering that she had left a duffle bag full of Micah's remaining clothes in her room. He looked around. Karlena's room was basically the same. She was leaving all her furniture. Esdell sat on her bed thinking that he would just leave her room the way it was. It would be a guest room. "Let's get you dressed, li'l buddy." Once he had dressed Micah, he drove to his mother's home.

As soon as they entered the house, the smell of fried pork chops greeted them. Everyone was there except for Karlena and Joseph.

"Look, it's Mr. Hooky-player!" Not only did the smell of pork chops greet Esdell and Micah, they were also greeted with a verbal jab from Sammy. "You missed a good time at church today. Everybody was still talking about the wedding yesterday."

"Well, it surely was something to talk about," Kareem said. "You did a good job, Aunt Chris."

"Thank you, nephew! Hey, Micah, come see Auntie Christine. Is your grandpa teaching you bad habits by missing church?" She reached for Micah. When she took him from Esdell, he put his arm around her shoulder.

"All jokes aside, Chris, you really did do a great job! I asked Karlena if she was happy with the way things turned out, and she was. It was a beautiful day, and I got you to thank for that!" He kissed her on the cheek.

"Well, you only say that because I saved you a boatload of money. Don't try to get all sentimental, you owe me big time, dude!"

"Whatever, Chris!" Esdell scoffed. "Just take the compliment and be quiet!"

"Some things never change! You children never stop messin' with each other!" Grace said, entering the room. "Hi, son, did you get you some rest? I hope Micah didn't keep you up last night. You know I woulda kept him."

"I know, Mama, but I wanted to spend time with my li'l buddy. Both of us slept well. How you doin' today?" Esdell asked.

"I'm good. Still flyin' high from yesterday. It was a beautiful day! My grandbaby was a gorgeous bride, my grandson and son were handsome, and I was a hot great-granny!" she said, popping her fingers. Everyone clapped their hands, egging her on. "Y'all stop that! Anyway, Isaiah left from church and went straight to the hotel to pick up the newlyweds, and they should be here anytime! Esdell, is Hope and Kofi comin' over to eat with us?"

"I invited her, but she said she didn't want to intrude on our last family day with Karlena and Micah."

"Well, that's just foolishness!" Grace argued. "That girl worked as hard as anybody on the wedding yesterday. She's more than welcome to be here today. She's like family!"

"I know, Mama, I tried to convince her, but she just wasn't havin' it."

"That's too bad. Okay, well, ladies, y'all come help me finish dinner so we can eat when they get here," Grace directed Christine and her daughters into the kitchen.

The menu was typical Grandma Grace. She went all out. Besides the pork chops, there was also baked turkey breast with dressing and gravy, macaroni and cheese, mashed potatoes, deviled eggs, a huge pot of collard greens, corn bread and rolls. For dessert, there was chocolate cake, and Karlena's favorite, peach cobbler and ice cream. Everyone was in awe trying to figure out when Grace had time to fix all this food.

When Isaiah arrived with Karlena and Joseph, they were met with words of congratulations, wedding night jokes, and growling stomachs, so the family went immediately to the dinner table. Kareem blessed the food, and the chow down began. As they ate, they, of course, talked about the wedding. Joseph and Karlena expressed their sincere gratitude to everyone involved.

"Yesterday seems like a dream, like a fairy tale," Karlena said. "I felt like a princess!"

"You looked like a goddess!" Joseph boasted.

"Aw, man! Don't say anything else to make that girl's head any bigger, Joe!" Kareem yelled. "She loved yesterday because it was all about her! If you didn't know already, my sister loves to be the center of attention."

"How could I ever be the center of attention when I've been sharing space with *your* big head since conception!" Karlena argued. "Boy, you

A MAN FAVORED IN HIS EYES

betta go on somewhere!" The twins began to banter, but Cousin LeAnn did not like it.

"Please don't fight! Both you guys are 'going somewhere' and you shouldn't be arguing!" The elephant in the room was outed. The family had been avoiding this subject all weekend, but now it was staring them directly in the face. "Kareem and Karlena are almost like a mom and dad to me, and Micah is like my little brother, and you're all leaving! Doesn't anybody care about that? You haven't said anything about it. What am I gonna do?" she tearfully asked.

Esdell put down his fork and scooted back from the table. "C'mere, LeAnn," he beckoned. She walked over to him and he sat her on his lap.

"We all care about that, and we're all sad that they're leaving. Probably no one will miss them more than me. They're my children. But let me tell you what I've come to know. God has a plan for everyone's life, and it's His plan that Karlena and Kareem move away. Now His plan for Kareem is pretty clear, he's goin' to spread the Gospel of Jesus Christ. You understand that, right?"

"Yes, sir." LeAnn sniffled. "I know he's gonna be a preacher, and people need preachers to learn about God and stuff, but what about Karlena and Micah? Why is God sending them away?"

"Well," Esdell started, "Karlena knows about God. She might not be a preacher but she can help people learn about God and stuff too. That's everybody's job, left on record by Jesus himself. We're supposed to help bring others to Christ. Or your cousin Karlena wants to be a nurse. She could be going to Louisiana to take care of someone or save someone's life. We don't know. But, LeAnn, we just have to be patient and prayerful that God will allow us to understand just what he has planned for any of us. I know they're movin' away, but we'll always be close. God is gracious and merciful. He'll keep us close! So try not to be sad, but be happy that God is using your cousins to make his will perfect. Okay?"

LeAnn nodded her head. Esdell took his napkin and dried her tears. "And think about this, won't it be fun to get on a plane to go visit?"

"He's right! You can come visit us anytime, LeAnn, as long as it's okay with Aunt Christine," Karlena said. "Daddy, you always know the right thing to say."

"That's good stuff, Dad. Good stuff!" Kareem agreed. "Now it won't be so easy to come see me, LeAnn, but Indianapolis is my home, and it always will be. My family is here, and I'll come home as often as I can."

The twins looked at each other knowing they were both thinking the same thing: that they had the best father God could ever provide. And with their twin connection, they both knew they all would survive their separation because God had, just at that moment, granted them all peace.

"I'm gonna miss these worrisome little brats myself," Christine smirked. "But it will be fun going to visit. Don't you think?" she asked her daughter who nodded her head again. "Do you feel better now, LeAnn?"

"Yes, ma'am, but I'd feel even better if I can have a double slice of chocolate cake for dessert!"

"Aw, way to work a guilt trip!" Celeste commented.

"You go finish your dinner," Grace said. "When you're done, Gran gran's gonna do you right. If my grandbaby wants a big ole piece of chocolate cake, then that's what she'll get!"

"Leave it to Grandma!" Karlena said. "She *will* dish out that comfort food!"

Everyone laughed in agreement and then continued on with the delicious meal that had been prepared for them.

After dinner was done and all dishes were washed and put away, the family decided to play games. They laughed, reminisced, and made deliberate plans on how they would be together in the future. But then it was time for the evening to come to an end.

"Daddy B," Joseph began, "it's past eleven, and I think Karlena and I are gonna go on back to your house. I hate to break this up, but we have an early flight in the morning."

"You're right, son-in-law," Esdell reluctantly conceded. "If I'm driving y'all to the airport in the morning, I'd better get home and get in the bed." Everyone stood up, seemingly in agreement with Joseph and Esdell, but no one moved toward the door. They all just stood silently staring at each other. Suddenly and quickly, Karlena ran into her grandmother's arms crying.

"Grandma, I'm gonna miss you so much!"

"Oh, baby, I'll miss you too!" Grace said, taking Karlena's face in her hands. "You're gonna do fine. You're a wonderful mother, and you're gonna be a wonderful wife. I'm so proud of you. You will be fine!"

"I'm wonderful because of you, Grandma! You taught me everything! Thank you for taking such good care of me," Karlena sighed. "I love you, Grandma!" She then began her good-byes, turning to everyone, individually starting with her cousins. She hugged Celeste and told her she could call her anytime to talk about anything. She kissed away LeAnn's tears, reassuring her that they would always be close. She hugged her pops, Isaiah, and thanked him for loving her grandmother so much and accepting the adult Brown children as his own. "You even put up with my crazy uncle Sammy living here with you and Granma." Karlena chuckled. She hugged her uncle who danced with her, spinning her around.

"I know you'll miss me more than anybody!" Sammy said as he dipped Karlena to finish the dance. "No one can make you laugh like me!" It was true; Karlena would miss her uncle Sammy's quick wit and sense of humor. She then turned to her aunt Christine.

"Aunt Chris, thank you for all you did for my wedding and for being part of my village, My mom, for as long as I had her, Grandma, and you have made me the woman I am." Karlena gave Christine the final hug. "I love all of you so much. I couldn't have made a better family for myself. I thank God for all of you. Y'all won't get a chance to miss me 'cause I'll be calling, texting, Skyping, e-mailing, or Facebooking somebody *every day*! Let's go, Joseph." Karlena pick up Micah and headed toward the door.

Everyone followed her as she walked out. Karlena turned to blow a kiss. "Love y'all!" The family repeated the sentiment as they watched as Esdell's family load into two cars and drive away.

It was a pleasant drive to Esdell's house as Karlena replayed in her head all the ways that she could keep in touch. She would always be a part of the family's lives even if it was only electronically. She and Joseph would try to come home at least twice a year, she thought. Her only concern was her daddy. She prayed silently to the Lord to remove his worry and to always be with him. She smiled.

I know you will, Lord, because you're good like that! Amen! She ended her silent prayer just as they drove into the driveway. They entered the house and were met by the packed bags that they had dropped off just before they went to Grace's. Karlena look at her dad's face, trying to read his mind.

"Oh, that reminds me," Esdell spoke, "I need to get Micah's bag repacked so it'll be ready in the morning."

He seems okay! Thank you, Lord! Karlena again prayed.

"Sooooo, what're the sleeping arrangements for the night? You bunkin' with me, Joe?" Kareem asked with a sheepish grin on his face. Joseph did not answer. Everyone stared at Esdell waiting on him to reply.

"What y'all lookin' at me for?" Esdell responded. "Kareem, you're more silly that the law allows! It's obvious! You go to your room, Micah's with me, and Joseph and Karlena will sleep in her room! Everybody coo' with that?"

"Works for me, Daddy B," Joseph said with relief.

"All right then, but we not tryna hear no newlywed noises coming from your bedroom, Karlena!" Kareem instigated.

Esdell jumped to their defense. "Mind your business, boy! Now, let's all hit the sack. We got a very early day tomorrow!"

They slept through the night though Esdell did his share of tossing and turning, being careful since Micah was again sleeping with him. He woke with a start. Someone was knocking at his door.

"Daddy, we need to get moving. Can I come in?" Karlena asked.

"Yeah, huh, come in." Esdell yawned.

"I need to get Micah up and dressed!" she said as she gently picked him up. "Wake up, Mick Mick, it's almost time to leave. See you in a few, Daddy." She grabbed Micah's bag and left the room. Esdell leaped to his feet. He washed his face, dressed, and went downstairs. Joseph had already packed their luggage into the car.

"We're all set, Daddy B. We need to hurry. We'll barely have enough time to check in," Joseph advised.

"I didn't realize what time it was," Esdell said. "The sun's not even up yet. Let's load up. Kareem, are you coming?"

"Here I come, let's go!" Kareem came down the stairs, took Micah from Karlena to put him in his car seat. Everyone followed him out. "Joseph, you, Karlena, and Micah sit here in the back, and I'll ride shotgun!"

With everyone buckled in, Esdell drove to Indianapolis International Airport. No one spoke, so he turned up the radio to break the silence. All too quickly, they were pulling into the unloading area at the airport. Due to airport security, Esdell and Kareem could not go to the boarding gate, so Esdell parked the car just outside the airline terminal door. He helped Joseph with the bags as Karlena watched him from the curb. He saw her from the corner of his eye but did not look directly at her, but he knew he had to.

"Well…" he started. Karlena gave Micah to Kareem and threw her arms around her father's neck.

"Bye, Daddy, I'll call you as soon as we get settled!"

Esdell kissed her cheeks and forehead. He freed one arm so he could take Micah. He hugged them both. He kissed Micah.

"You be a good boy for mommy and daddy, okay, li'l buddy. Dae Dae loves you!"

"Hey, y'all give me some of that love!" Kareem ordered. He also hugged and kissed them. He turned to Joseph and shook his hand. "Take care, man. God bless you! Take good care of my sister and my nephew!"

"No doubt, brother-in-law. I got this! Daddy B…" Joseph said. "Don't worry about a thing. The only two people that will take better care of Karlena and Micah is you and God himself. They're my world now! You can believe that!"

"Oh, I do!" Esdell hugged Joseph and whispered in his ear. "Take care of 'em. Don't mistreat them! Call me for anything!" He stepped back. "Go on, y'all. You still have to get through security before you board. Love y'all!" He raised his hands as if to bless them. "Hedge of protection, Lord. Hedge of protection!"

"Bye, Daddy. Bye, Kareem. I love you!" Karlena waved.

"Love you!" Esdell and Kareem repeated. They watched them as they disappeared through the terminal doors.

"Man, that was just a little rough. You okay, Dad?" Kareem asked.

"Yeah. It's all good!" Esdell looked at Kareem and he had tears in his eyes. "Hey, looks like it was more than a *little* rough on you. You need me to punch you?" The two men looked at each other and laughed and got back into to car. "I'll tell you what, son, I'm gonna take you to breakfast!"

"Yeah, Dad! How 'bout you and me just hang out today?"

It was an offer Esdell would no way refuse. He had just said good-bye to one of his children, and by the end of the week, he would have to do it over again. He was going to spend every minute with Kareem. It was another reason he had taken the week off.

"Let's go to IHOP. I gotta taste for some blueberry pancakes. How's that sound?"

"Sounds good to me, Dad, let's do it!"

Off they went to the restaurant. When they got there, they were quickly seated as it was still very early. The waiter kept the coffee flowing as the two men enjoyed pancakes, eggs, bacon, and hash browns. They talked about Karlena's new family and imagined how her home would be in Louisiana. They even made a little bet as to how long it would be before Micah would have a little brother or sister. Esdell was perfectly fine with the thought of more grandchildren but hoped that Karlena would finish her education first. Kareem talked about his soon-to-be new home in Haiti. He admitted to being excited and also nervous. The furthest away he had ever been was Georgia. He also admitted that he was still a little unsure he was up to the call of pastoring in a foreign land. Esdell was quick to address this concern.

"Son, you already know that God sent you there, so you're already equipped with all you need to make His will perfect. Plus, God is God in Indianapolis or Haiti. Do what you do, teach Christ and just be the good and kind man that you are! Stay with what you know to be true, and you can't go wrong!"

Kareem smiled and nodded in agreement as he took a sip of coffee. Esdell felt his cell phone vibrate and reached in his pocket to answer it.

"It's Hope. Hey, baby! Good morning!"

Hope was calling to check on him after Karlena left.

"I'm fine. Matter of fact, I'm havin' a good time with Kareem at IHOP. We just gonna hang out today. I'll call you later when you get off work. Okay? I love you too! Bye."

"Yeah, about that, Dad. You and Miss Hope, that's a real good thing! My little boy's all grown up and all in love and stuff!"

"Boy, you silly, but you're right! I'm *all* in love and stuff! It's funny though, I never saw it coming," Esdell confessed. "When I think back to when I first met Hope, she was the last one I ever thought I'd be fallin' for. She was so much like Chris, it was scary!"

"I can see that," Kareem agreed. "She and Aunt Chris do have a lot of traits in common. Both of them are just a little mouthy!"

"I would get you for talkin' 'bout my woman and my sister if you weren't tellin' the truth!" Esdell chuckled. "Hope has a mind of her own, and she don't bite her tongue. That just makes her honest. And, you know, the fact that I wasn't tryna be in a relationship, we were both honest! We were ourselves, none of that phony stuff that a lot of couples start off with tryin' to impress each other. Yeah, my girl is honest, and that's just one of the things I love about her." He paused. "I love her! I really do! We've shared some real-life events in the short time we've been together. Humph!" Esdell seemed to go into deep thought.

"Well, what now, Dad?" Kareem asked.

"Now? Now we go home and figure out what we gonna do the rest of the day!"

"I know what I wanna do, take you to the hoop before I go! You up to it, or are all those pancakes weighing you down?"

"I could beat you after a full Thanksgiving dinner with double dessert!"

"I'm not from Missouri, but you gotta show me!" Kareem challenged. "Church gym?"

"Church gym! Let's go home and change!"

When they arrived to the church gym, the doors were locked because it was so early. Kareem, being youth pastor of the church, had a key, so they were able to get in. The gym was empty, so it was going to be a game of one on one. It was, as expected, a very competitive game; neither man wanting to be outdone by the other. They were loving it to the fullest. They talked and laughed and they stuck to their plan: to play a good game of B-ball, and to spend the day together.

21

"Okay, Karlena, I'll talk to you tomorrow. Love y'all, bye!" Esdell said, ending a call with his daughter. It was Tuesday afternoon, and this was the second phone call he had received from her since she had flown out the day before. Karlena had decided that she would call him every day. Esdell knew that this practice would most likely be temporary, lasting only until she was comfortable in her new surroundings. That was fine with him. If he talked to her and Micah every day, it could keep him from missing them so much. He laughed to himself when he thought about how Micah was trying to talk to him on the phone. Esdell then turned his attention to the books on his desk. Though the weekend seemed like a dream, with Karlena getting married, her moving to Louisiana with Micah, and his profession of love to Hope, it was time to get back to reality. It was a new semester, and he was back in school. By the end of the next semester, he would have his associate degree, and it was time to study. He was taking three classes: computer graphics, color theory, and advanced algebra. He reviewed his class notes, praying that he had not bitten off more than he could chew. He kept himself encouraged as he drove into his books. He had been studying for several hours when he decided to go fix something to eat. He had just finished making a sandwich when he heard Kareem come in.

"Dad?" Kareem yelled.

"In here, son! Makin' a sandwich. You want one?" Esdell offered. Kareem walked into the kitchen.

"No thanks, I'm not hungry." Kareem sat down at the kitchen table. "I had the final meeting with the missionaries that are going to Haiti with me, and we had a big lunch."

"How'd that go?"

"Well, a bus has been chartered to take us to Florida, and then we'll fly out of Miami to Haiti. But we've been scheduled to pick up some other missionaries in Georgia. Because of that, we'll be leaving on Friday instead of Sunday."

"Friday? Man!" He sighed heavily. "Uh, you know Mama was planning another big good-bye dinner on Saturday for you," he said, trying to hide his disappointment.

"I know, but I don't need a dinner. We just did that day before yesterday for Karlena, so we really don't need to go through that again. I just want to leave quietly." Esdell turned up one side of his face in a half a smile.

"Now you know that ain't hap'nin'! You already said that cell phone service and internet access is practically nonexistent where you'll be in Haiti, and you'll probably have to landline call once a week. There's no way you're gettin' out of here without a big family good-bye!"

"That's why I'm visiting everybody individually between now and Friday, one-on-one time. That's the way I want to do it."

Esdell listened to Kareem's farewell plans. He had already called his aunt Christine and was going to have dinner with her and his cousins, Celeste and LeAnn, that night. He would spend Wednesday night with his grandparents and his uncle Sammy. On Thursday, he would Skype Karlena and then spend the day with his father.

"What about Hope and Kofi?" Esdell asked.

"I'll call them sometime between now and Friday."

"What time you pullin' out Friday?"

"Five in the morning. Would you take me to the bus station?"

"Sure. Y'all gettin' to me with these early morning departures! Sounds like you got it all worked out though." A look of confusion showed on Kareem's face.

"You're surprisingly calm, Dad. I was expecting a bigger reaction to this news!"

"Kareem, God gave me peace!" Esdell said. "I'ma miss you, sure enough, but I got all faith that you and your sister will be safe in His care. Have you talked to Pastor Edwards?"

"Just left him. We talked, we prayed. It was good. He was really encouraging." Kareem sighed, "Well, I need to get going. I'll see you later tonight."

"You'd better call your grandma and tell her what's up," Esdell said.

"I'll call her from Aunt Chris's." When Kareem got to the front door and opened it, he was startled when he found Hope standing on the other side preparing to ring the doorbell. "Hey, Miss Hope. C'mon in! Dad, Miss Hope's here!" Kareem yelled. "I was just on my way out."

Esdell entered the room. "Hey, babe, I wasn't expecting you. Everything okay?"

"Hi! I know I should've called, but I need to talk to you before I go home. Is that okay?" Hope asked.

"You don't have to call. Just come!" Esdell said. "What brings you over?"

"I've got some big news;" she started. "I couldn't wait to tell you!"

"I've got news too, but I'll let Dad tell you," Kareem said. "I've gotta get going! See y'all later." He exited, waving as he left.

Esdell took Hope by the hand and led her into the living room to sit down.

"What's up?" he asked, but he kissed her before she could answer. "Hmm, that's what a man needs after a long day of studying. Now, tell me your news." Hope kissed him again.

"It's also what a woman needs after a hard day at work!" She kissed him again. "Uh, anyway, Kofi got his check from his father's insurance policy today, and it was more than we thought. Even after all the taxes were taken out, he still got over one hundred thousand dollars!" She began to bounce her knee up and down. "Guess what he wants to do with his money," she soberly asked. The look on Hope's face gave Esdell any number of guesses as to how Kofi wanted to spend his newfound wealth, but he said nothing. He simply shrugged his shoulders. Hope was now biting her bottom lip.

"What, Hope? What's he gonna do with all that money?"

"He wants to buy me the flower shop! Do you believe that?"

Esdell was confused by Hope's expression.

"Are you upset? I thought you were 'bout to tell me that he was plannin' something really stupid!" Esdell confessed. "What's wrong with that?"

"That's his money. His daddy finally decided to do something good for Kofi, and I can't take that away from him. But how unselfish is that?"

"That's probably one of the most unselfish things I ever heard of, and that's coming from a young kid. So the problem is—"

"I can't take his money. He really put me on the spot though."

"How's that?"

"He came to the shop and Bill, the owner, was there. Kofi told him he wanted to buy the shop for his mama. He made him an offer. I told Bill we'd get back to him. We had to talk about it. He reminded me time was running out because he's ready to sell. Kofi's at home waiting for me to discuss it. I think I'm gonna turn him down. I can't do it. What do you think, Esdell?"

"Miss Hope, I can understand that you want Kofi to spend his money wisely, and you're right, y'all should talk about it. But it sounds to me like a blessin' and a answer to a prayer."

Esdell put his arm around Hope's shoulder and they talked for a half hour about this wonderful gesture. "One thing to consider," Esdell continued, "don't block a blessing meant for Kofi 'cause you won't let him bless you. Go home, talk about it, pray together on it, and then decide."

"Okay. I will." Hope stood up, preparing to leave. "Oh, wait! Didn't you have some news about Kareem?"

"Oh yeah, that!" The couple sat down again and Esdell told Hope that Kareem would be leaving very early Friday morning. He gave her the schedule that Kareem had set for himself, and she was upset that he was not planning to see Kofi but planned only to call him.

"Esdell, I know time is short and you want to spend every possible minute with Kareem, and I don't want to intrude on that. But do you think we could come over Thursday? Kareem has been the driving force in Kofi's life ever since the first day they met at the juvenile detention center. It would kill Kofi if he didn't see him before he left. Do you think you could convince Kareem to spend a little time with him?"

"I'll tell him you're coming over. It's fine, and you won't be intruding. Go on home and talk to Kofi about buying the shop and let him know what's up on Thursday. We'll see you both then."

Hope left, and when Kareem returned home, Esdell told him that Hope and Kofi would be coming over Thursday to say good-bye. Kareem had no objection to the change of plans. He really did want to see Kofi before he left.

Kareem's visit with his aunt and cousins was very pleasant, and he called his grandma like he said he would. It seemed that everybody was more at ease with his leaving since Karlena had gone before him. They were like his dad, at peace, and he thanked God for that peace. He did, however, have to explain to his cousins that they would have to go old school to communicate with him. He would call them when he could on the "old timey phone," and they would have to write each other. Christine thought it would be great for her daughters to learn how to write a good old-fashioned letter.

"Y'all be good girls!" Kareem instructed. "Help your mom and don't give her a hard time! I love you girls so much!" Christine assured him she had everything under control, including her girls! When he left, he hugged and kissed them all, reminding them that they should always pray for each other.

Kareem stuck to the schedule he had set for himself. Wednesday, he spent the day with his grandparents, and Grandma fixed a big dinner. He should have known that there was no way he was getting out of Indianapolis without one more big home-cooked meal from his grandma Grace. She asked a lot of questions about the mail and how to ship things because she was already planning to send packages to Kareem and his church. Pops thought it would be a good idea for their church to send contributions to Kareem's church on a regular basis, and he planned to talk to Pastor Edwards about it. Grace pulled out family albums, and they reminisced about the years Kareem and Karlena stayed with her. She beamed as she watched Kareem grow through pictures. Now he was going to be a pastor and was doing it in Haiti. It was a wonderful evening, but it was a little sad because Sammy had to work and missed the dinner. Kareem would try to see him tomorrow. When it was time to leave, there were a few tears and a big long hug from Grandma that he would hold in his heart forever.

"I always knew God would call someone from this family to preach his word," Grace said. "I'm so proud of you, Kareem, and I'm so thankful that God allowed me to see you work in your calling." Pops offered up his well-wishes with a little grandfatherly advice and told Kareem he would always be in his prayers.

Thursday morning, Esdell and Kareem had breakfast on the back deck. Since it was mid-September, the leaves were beginning to change color, but it was still warm outside. The yard was beautiful and still full of blooming perennial flowers. It was just how Hope had planned it when she landscaped Esdell's yard earlier. There would always be something in bloom until the first frost. It truly reflected Hope's gardening skills. After breakfast, Kareem finished packing and cleaned his room. He then sat at the computer to Skype with Karlena.

"Our townhouse is looking pretty good. You should see how Joseph had Micah's room set up, Indianapolis Colts blue and white," Karlena

A Man Favored in his Eyes

said. "We may be in New Orleans Saints country, but my husband is still a die-hard Colts fan!"

"He'd better be! Dang, Karlena, it's weird hearing you say my husband!" Kareem admitted. "My sister's married. How you liking it?"

"Loving it! All five days of it!" Karlena chuckled. "How about you? Are you ready for your big trip?"

"I'm as ready as I'm gonna be. The Shahs have tried to prepare me for the poverty and disparity of Haiti, but I'll have to live it for myself. I've been doing some research too. Pray for us, Karlena!"

"Without ceasing, bro." The twins talked for almost an hour, making a pact that they would talk as often as they could and write each other at least once a week.

"Love you, sis!"

"I love you too, Kareem. Be careful and God bless. Good-bye," Karlena said, ending their Skype session.

Kareem found Esdell watching television in the living room and set down next to him. Neither of them spoke; they sat quietly staring at the screen, but then they simultaneously looked at each other. Kareem aimed his fist toward Esdell and gave him a knuckle punch. They both smiled and resumed watching TV. Before too long, the doorbell rang. Esdell rose to answer it.

"That's probably Hope and Kofi." When he opened the door, Sammy barged in.

"What up, dudes?" Sammy said with a boisterous tone. "I know you wasn't tryna get out of here without seeing your favorite uncle!"

"Now way, unc!" Kareem said. "I did send you a text earlier. I'm glad you came over."

"What y'all doin' up in here, just watchin' TV? That's no way to spend your last night in town!"

"We just havin' a little quiet time, but I see we can forget that now that you're here, Junya!" Esdell snickered. Again, the doorbell rang.

"I'll get it, Dad." Kareem opened the door, and this time, it was Hope and Kofi. Hope entered and immediately gave Kareem a big hug.

"Hey!" she sang.

"Hey, Miss Hope! Hey, Kofi, y'all come on in!"

"Hold the door!" a voice yelled from outside. Walking up the sidewalk was Christine with her girls, Grace and Isaiah!

"Aw, man, what're you guys doing?" Kareem asked as everyone entered.

"Looks like a party to me!" Sammy declared.

245

"We had to get the family together before you left," Grace said. We got pizza, pop, and cookies. And I packed you a goodie box to take with you on the bus. It's ham and cheese sandwiches and more cookies. Should be enough cookies for everybody."

"Grace been baking cookies all day!" Isaiah announced. "You got chocolate chip, peanut butter, and oatmeal raisin! I gotta admit, I done had my share of 'em!" he said, rubbing his stomach.

"Figures!" Esdell remarked. "Mama, you somethin' else."

Grace smiled, looking at Hope and Kofi. They appeared uncomfortable.

"Hope, it's good to see you!" she said. "Kofi! You're lookin' good, young man. How've you been?"

"Thank you, Mrs. Willis," Kofi responded. "I'm doing fine. How 'bout you?"

"Fine, just fine." Grace turned back to Hope. "How're you, Hope?"

"Good, Mrs. Willis," Hope answered. "I wasn't expecting everyone to be here. I'm sorry if I'm intruding."

"No such thing!" Grace stated.

"Girl, you need to quit!" Christine added. "You dating my brother, you stuck with us now. Besides, you gonna need all the support we can give you to put up with that boy!"

Esdell started to answer back but LeAnn quickly jumped in to stop the pending argument. "Okay! Let's eat some pizza. I'm hungry!"

"I'm with you, sis!" Celeste said.

Sammy also chimed in. "Ah yeah, it's on now!"

Esdell got some plates, glasses, and napkins from the kitchen. Sammy turned on some music and danced around as he stuffed his mouth full of pizza. The evening really had turned into a small party. They ate, talked, and laughed. Sammy loved to dance, and before long, he had almost everyone up dancing too. Grace paid extra attention to Hope and Kofi. She had made it her business to make them feel welcomed. She asked Hope how she got Esdell's yard looking so pretty, and Hope was eager to talk about it. Kareem stepped back to absorb everything that was going on. He had claimed he did not want a big deal made over his leaving, but now he was honestly happy that Thursday turned out the way it had. Kofi, noticing that Kareem was standing alone, went over to him.

"Hey, RK, can I holla at you for a minute?"

"Yeah, let's go out on the porch." They slipped out the front door. "What's up, Kofi?"

Kofi stood, wringing his hands and pressing his lips together.

"RK, I don't wanna come off like no punk, but I gotta tell you some things. Straight up, even though you not that much older than me, you're like the dad I never had. You saved my life! You showed me I could be a better man. You had faith in me. You never gave up on me, and I...uh, love you, man!"

Kareem smiled. "I love you too, man! You've come a long way by the grace of God. Remember that! It was Christ that saved you, not me! You let Him in your heart. I just introduced you to him. I have faith in you, and you have faith in God! That's an unstoppable combination! Your belief in Christ is what made you a better man."

"Okay, but you and your dad have made life so much better for me and Mom. Y'all showed us how to be a family. Y'all taught us how to forgive and love each other. And you did teach me how to depend on God. I still gotta lot to learn about all that though. RK, we'll keep in touch, right? I mean, I don't wanna lose you as a friend."

"No way that's happening, Kofi. I promise you to keep in touch!" Kareem patted Kofi on the back. "Now, promise me something."

"What's that, RK?" Kofi asked.

"All that stuff you say you need to learn about God, I want you to promise me that you'll keep working on that. Keep reading your Bible and try to go to church more often. Take good care of your mom. Can you promise me that?"

"Fo' sho'!" Kofi assured. "I guess we better get back in the house." Kareem wrapped his arms around Kofi before he could get in the house. Kofi stood with his arms hanging to his side. He slowly lifted his arms to return the embrace.

"Ah yeah, let's get back in there!" Kofi sniffled.

"Here they come!" Esdell said as they reentered. "We were lookin' for y'all. Hope says she has some news! Go ahead, honey!"

"Y'all see my handsome son over there?" Hope started. "That generous young man is giving me a gift that's just second to the gift of me being his mom. He recently inherited some money, and he is fulfilling my dream. He's buying me the While They Yet Live Flower Shop!"

"So, you decided to take it! Well, go 'head, Ms. Business Owner! Congratulations!" Esdell said. Hope clinched her fists in front of her mouth.

"I can't believe it! The shop is mine!" She started to cry. "Kofi, thank you! I know I've said it a thousand times already, but thank you!"

"Mom, stop all that!" Kofi ordered. He wanted her to stop crying because he felt himself choking up.

"Kofi, that's the most generous thing I've ever heard. It just validates what we were just talking about," Kareem remarked. "Your faith in God has changed your heart and made you a better person. Good job, man!"

Everyone complimented Kofi in agreement. They each thought this was a phenomenal gesture. They commented that most men his age would most likely have squandered the money away. All the praise made Kofi uneasy.

"Thank y'all, but I don't think I really deserve all this. It's my mom. She's the one that deserves all the compliments. She was willing to sacrifice all the money she was saving to buy the shop to put me through college. Then all of a sudden, I get this money from a dad I didn't know. He didn't do right by me or Ma. But with this money, he's helping us both!"

Kofi was putting some of his inheritance money with the money that his mother had saved to buy the flower shop. He was also paying her back all the money she had already spent on his education. He would still have enough money left to finish his education and buy an inexpensive car. He had planned to get his own place with the money, but there wouldn't be enough to do that now. Hope let him know that he always had a place to live. He could live with her for as long as he wanted.

"Hey, y'all, I got a couple of bottles of champagne in the fridge left from Karlena's wedding. How all the legals celebrate with a toast?" Esdell offered. Everyone was on board with the offer. Esdell took the two bottles from the refrigerator and poured a glass for all the adults. The youngsters were satisfied with toasting with a glass of pop. They all raised their glass as Esdell began his toast.

"Here's to the newest business owner in Indianapolis, Ms. Hope Shah, and her new shop. Congratulations! May you and your business continue to grow and prosper." They drank and then Esdell offered up another toast. "And here's to my son, reverend...excuse me, *Pastor* Kareem Brown! He is my son in whom I am well pleased! May God bless and keep you!" The room agreed.

"Here, here!" they all said. The congratulations were shared between Kofi, Kareem, and Hope.

It had been a joyous evening, but it came to an end when Kareem reminded everyone that he was leaving very, very early in the morning. Of course, there were lots of hugs and kisses and just a few tears. Kareem said his final good-byes, and then he and Esdell went to bed. Esdell was surprised with how well he slept.

At 4:30 a.m., the men arrived at the bus station. Kareem quickly found the bus that would take him and the other missionaries to Atlanta and then to Florida. He put his luggage in the baggage compartment beneath the bus and then began to introduce himself and his dad to his fellow travelers. He made immediate friends of the passengers when he gave them his grandmother's cookies to go along with their morning coffee. At 4:55, the bus driver announced it was time to get on board.

"Well, Dad, it's time to go. Take care of yourself, old man!" Kareem gave Esdell one of those manly, backslapping hugs.

"Good-bye, son! Call me when you land, if you can."

"I will. I will. Well, let me get on board." Esdell put both his hands on Kareem's shoulders.

"God, keep your hedge of protection around my son. In Jesus name!" he quickly prayed. Kareem got on the bus. Esdell watched it until it had driven out of sight.

The drive home was a silent one, but when Esdell entered the house, the silence was overwhelming. He sat on the couch and looked around recalling all the noise and activity that used to take place in his home. They were all gone now; Kareem, Karlena, and Micah. He would live in the house he had bought to care for his children all alone. He thought that maybe he would move into an apartment because he would no longer need all this space. He dismissed this idea. His children would always have this house to come home to!

"Maybe I'll get a dog!"

22

In the two months since Kareem had left, Esdell was still adjusting to the change in his household. He prayed daily for his children's safety, especially Kareem. He had only talked to him a few times since he left. Communications to the town were Kareem now lived was more limited than Kareem had thought. Kareem kept to his word by calling as often as he could and writing every week. He confessed that he thought his young age would be a problem with his congregation, but his new church welcomed him with open arms. He was becoming very close to the Shahs and his new church members. Karlena started off calling every day, but as expected, the phone calls decreased with each week she was in Louisiana. She was still calling twice a week, however. Karlena was learning her way around the city, making new friends, and learning how to be a wife. She would join Joseph at Southern University the following semester. As for li'l buddy, Micah, he was stealing the hearts of his new great-grandparents and everyone who met him. Esdell, after a couple weeks of the twin's departure, decided to do some rearranging in the house. He moved into Karlena's old room, which was the master bedroom with a connecting bathroom. Micah's room was turned into a studio/office where he worked on his art and studied for his classes. The remaining two rooms were just bedrooms that would welcome and house anyone that needed a place to stay, especially his kids.

One Saturday while Esdell and Hope were out, he decided to go to the humane society. He went there with the intent to adopt a dog but ended up coming home with an eleven-pound, two-year-old, black-and-white, male tuxedo cat. Hope had convinced Esdell that a cat would be best since he worked and went to school. Once he brought the cat home, Esdell found that he was pretty much self-sufficient and did well by himself, so Esdell named him Solo. Solo adapted to Esdell easily and was good company for him.

Now, Esdell was at Hope's flower shop preparing for her grand opening.

"Pull your side up a little, Kofi!" Hope directed. "Okay, that's good! That's good! Tape it!" Esdell and Kofi were working together to hang a banner in the flower shop window. Once it was secure, they descended their ladders and walked out onto the parking lot to stand next to Hope. The sign read: While They Yet Live Flower Shop. Under new ownership. Hope Shah–Proprietor.

"That's real impressive, Miss Hope!" Esdell declared.

"The sign looks real good, Mom," Kofi agreed. Hope looked at her watch.

"Oh, it's almost time to open. I need to get in there and make sure everything's ready for the reception," she nervously added. She then quickly walked into the shop with Esdell and Kofi following close behind. Now that Hope owned the shop, she had quit her second job at GFS so she could devote her time to the success of her business. Everything she had ever thought she would do as the owner of the shop she had done. She added new products and services. She did some remodeling and rearranged the setup of the store.

"The shop looks so good, Hope. You got everything under control," Esdell said.

Hope was skeptical. "You really think so? You think I got enough hors d'oeuvres? Did you call Pastor Edwards to come bless the shop? I probably need more cups! Oh, I need the window cleaner! The front door has smudges on it! What about—"

"Ma! Ma! Ma!" Kofi yelled. "Chill out! You're driving yourself and everybody else crazy! It's all good! Calm down!"

"You're right, son!" she pretentiously agreed. "Oh, look at that! Where's Mark? Mark!"

"Yes, Hope?" Mark asked, coming in from the storage room. Mark, Hope's former coworker, was happy to continue to work for her after she bought the shop. He had worried that he would lose his job under the new ownership, but Hope assured him his job was not in jeopardy because he was a good and dependable worker. But now, he appeared a bit irritated because Hope continued to find things wrong with the appearance of the shop, and she kept giving him things to do. "What's the problem now?"

"With it being so close to Thanksgiving, I think you should put out more of the ceramic pumpkin and turkey flowerpots. It wouldn't hurt to maybe display some of our Christmas products too."

"And put them where, Hope?" Mark asked. "If I put one more thing out, we'll look more like a dollar store than a flower shop! Everything looks fine the way it is! Sheesh!"

"Hope, why don't you go take a break and sit down?" Esdell suggested. "People will be arriving soon, and you don't want to be all sweaty when they get here."

Hope gasped. "I look sweaty? I should go freshen up! Do I look all right? How's my hair? I should put on some more lipstick!"

"Ma! Cut it out!" Kofi again yelled. "Way ta go, Mr. B!" Kofi got behind Hope and gently pushed her toward the storage room. "C'mon, Mom. There's a Coke back here that's calling your name."

"She's an absolute wreck, Esdell!" Mark commented. "I'm so stoked for her though. She deserves this shop. Lady Luck was on her side!"

"Lady Luck didn't have nothin' to do with this," Esdell disagreed. "God's grace was on her side."

Mark nodded his head. "Okay, man, if you say so!"

"And I do! Hope's come a long way since she's turned back to Christ. You know, the Bible says you can do anything 'cause He makes you strong!"

"Is that right?" Mark asked.

"Yep! If you haven't tried Him, you should check him out!" Esdell saw someone approaching the door. "The guests are starting to arrive. We can talk more later, if you want to."

"Maybe so," Mark replied. "I'm gonna take care of the guests until Hope comes back."

"I'll go check on her." Esdell went to the storage room and saw Kofi standing just outside of the restroom with a bottle of Coke in his hand. "She all right?" Esdell asked.

"I guess so. You really messed up when you told her she was sweaty." Kofi huffed. "She'll probably come out of there wearing a prom dress now!" They laughed.

Esdell tapped on the restroom door. "Hope, baby, guests are starting to arrive. You 'bout finished?"

"Oh, shoot! I'll be out in a minute," she yelled. "Wait for me!"

Esdell stood outside the door, patiently waiting for Hope to come out. She finally emerged, and the scent of cologne followed her.

"Wow, you smell good, Mom!" Kofi said.

"Oh no, I've put on too much perfume!" Hope turned to reenter the restroom. Esdell gently grabbed her wrist.

"Hope, you smell good, you look good, and the shop looks good! You have got it *all* together." He kissed the palm of her hand. "Now, let's get on out there and welcome your guests!" Hope took a deep breath and nodded. She and Esdell walked hand in hand into the store.

"Hi, everyone!" she said. She walked around to welcome each person.

All of Esdell's family was there, and some of his church members. Hope's coworkers from GFS and a few of Esdell's coworkers were also in attendance, along with some of Kofi's friends. Even Karlena called to wish Hope well. Pastor Edwards came to pray over Hope's new business, asking God to prosper and bless it. Hope proudly showed everyone around her store. She pointed out the changes she had made. She had divided her shop into different sections. There was a seasonal section, where an upcoming holiday would be highlighted. There was a birthday and baby section. Then there was Hope's favorite, the wedding and romance section. Each area offered gifts to go along with floral arrangements. She was eager to share her future plans, which included a souvenir and sports section. Hope was also considering wedding consultations.

"You look tired, Hope!" Esdell observed after a couple of hours. "You 'bout ready to shut this thing down?"

"I really am, but I don't want make people leave if they're not ready to go," she responded.

"It'll be okay. Here, I'll get their attention, Hey, everybody, may I have your attention please? Hope has something to say."

"Thanks, Esdell. I want to thank you all for coming," she began. "I want to thank God for all that he has done. And I have to thank my son, Kofi. He is the one who's responsible for making my dream come true through his generosity!" Kofi seemed to be embarrassed, so he waved her off. "He's just being modest, but thank you again, again, and again, son!" Hope said, locking arms with Kofi. "And before you leave, please help yourself to one of the chocolate rosebuds in the vase on the counter as a token of my appreciation for being a part of this day, and take as many of my business cards that you want and be sure to pass them out." She giggled. "Thanks again for coming, be careful going home, and God bless! Good night!"

After all her guests had departed, Esdell stayed to help Hope, Kofi, and Mark clean up.

"Quite a night, Hope. You were so worried, and look, everything turned out great!" Esdell commented.

"It was nice, wasn't it?" she agreed as she tied up a garbage bag.

"I'll take that, Hope," Mark said, taking the bag from her. "I'm gonna take all the trash out to the dumpster. If you don't have anything else for me to do, I'm headin' home!"

"No, we're done here. Thanks for everything!"

"No problem, boss. I'll see you Monday morning!" Mark yawned. "See you next time, Esdell. Maybe we can finish our conversation."

"Anytime, man!" Esdell agreed, waving to Mark as he left. "I think we're done, Hope. You ready?"

"Yeah, let's go. Kofi, make sure the front door is locked!"

"I just locked it, Mama. Let's go!" Kofi, Hope, and Esdell walked to the storage room to exit out the back door. Hope turned to view her shop one more time. She smiled broadly as she punched in the alarm code and then locked the door from the outside. "I don't believe it!" she said.

"God sho is good, ain't he?" Esdell knowingly asked. "C'mon, girl, it's time to go!"

Esdell escorted Hope and Kofi to their car, kissed Hope, and wished them both a good night. He then got into his car for the drive home. He reflected on how happy Hope looked; the smiles that lit up her face throughout the reception. He thanked God for her blessing. She had been through so much in her life, and Esdell felt she was so deserving of this wonderful gift from the Lord.

I'ma do everything I can to keep that smile on her face, he thought. *I love that woman. I do, I really do!* Esdell was still amazed that he had once again found love. He did love her, and there was no denying it! He didn't want to. He was happy and in love again. He then began to make plans for himself and Hope for the holidays. Neither Karlena nor Kareem would be home for Thanksgiving or Christmas, so he wanted to include Hope and Kofi in his holiday plans.

* * *

During Thanksgiving and Christmas, Esdell took Hope and Kofi to his family's holiday dinners. It was like they had been a part of the family for years. There was almost relentless teasing from Sammy and Christine about Esdell and Hope's relationship, but the couple took it in stride.

Once Hope was completely comfortable around Esdell's family, she showed that she could dish it out as well as she could take it. She and Christine had plenty of fun ganging up on Sammy Junior. Kofi proved to be Sammy's best ally. The teasing back and forth between the four of them was always a source of hilarity. There were also sad moments as they all missed the twins. They all had to be satisfied with the calls they received from them on each day.

New Year's Eve came, and everybody, including Kofi, who wanted to go out and party, went to watch night service at Road to Damascus. It was always a special night for Esdell and his family as it was the anniversary of the night Kareem announced his calling to preach the Gospel. The service, as always, was full of high praise and worship. Different members of the church testified to the goodness of God, expressing how they had been blessed throughout the year and giving thanks for being allowed to see another year approach. Esdell, though he did not stand to speak, gave thanks in his heart and mind for the peace God had given him when his children left and for Him keeping them safe. He again gave thanks for Hope coming into his life. Hope fought off nervousness to give her own personal testimony. She was thankful that her son had become a college student and turned away from a life of crime. She gave thanks for her shop, and she thanked God for Esdell. Pastor Edwards gave a powerful sermon and then opened the doors of the church to discipleship. Hope stood and walked to the front of the church. She had visited many times and now was finally going to become a member. Then the unexpected happened; Kofi followed behind her. Hope shouted in joy and thankfulness. God had blessed her over the past year and now her son professed his renewed faith in Christ and wanted to be baptized. The congregation applauded loudly. Esdell rushed to his side.

"All right now, Kofi! Praise God. Hallelujah!" Esdell shouted.

After church was over, Esdell went to Hope's place.

"What a night! What a year!" Hope yelled from her kitchen. "Esdell, I got some wine chilling. Would you like a glass?"

"Yeah, babe, but just one glass!" he said. "Kofi, I can't wait to talk to Kareem! He's gonna be so proud of you!"

"I couldn't help it! I just felt something. I don't really know what," Kofi confessed.

"Nothin' but the Holy Spirit, Kofi," Esdell said. "It fills you up!"

"I'm getting baptized. Do you believe it?" Kofi asked.

"Kofi, I believe it! Man, I can't *wait* to talk to Kareem!" Esdell repeated.

"When's the last time you talked to him, Esdell?" Hope asked.

"Christmas day. It may be another week or so before he calls again though."

"I know Haiti is a poor country, but you would still think that with modern technology, that communication would be better!" Hope expressed.

"I did call his cell when he first left," Kofi said, "but we only talked a few minutes before the call got dropped."

"Yeah, I know. That happens a lot when I try to call your grandparents, so I just wait for them to call me," Hope declared as she brought Esdell his glass of wine.

"Thanks," he said. "But it's getting better though. Kareem wrote that more cell towers are going up closer to the town where he lives."

"I hope so," Kofi said. "I really would like to talk to him more often. Like now, all I wanna do is call him and tell him about tonight! I could really use his advice. I'll never forget the day y'all came to the juvenile center. I was a real pain in the butt then. I 'member RK talking to me, telling me that God hadn't forgot about me. You know what I remember most of all?"

"What's that?" Esdell asked.

"He told me he would come back, and he did! He kept his word. He came back just for me! He talked to me and stood by me all the time I was in jail, through my hearing, on up to the day he left. Never had no man do that for me before."

"Well, Kofi, I know you and Kareem are really close, but if you need anything, you can always come to me," Esdell offered. "I know I can't replace him, but I'm here for you."

"I know, Mr. B. You and RK both all right with me! Thanks." Kofi sighed heavily. "Hey, y'all wanna play spades?"

"Uh-oh, Esdell, we're in trouble now. Kofi's is a real card shark!" Hope advised.

Esdell laughed loudly. "We'll see 'bout that! He don't want none of this! Get the cards and deal 'em up!"

Hope was right. Kofi proved to be very skilled at the game of spades. Esdell said it was a good thing that they were not playing for money. They played cards until 2:00 a.m. and then Esdell went home to find his cat, Solo, sleeping in the middle of his bed. Esdell sent up his prayer and climbed into bed. He lifted Solo and petted him. He did not think he would enjoy a cat as much as a dog, but found that his cat was good company, and as Hope said, he did not require much attention. Esdell laid Solo at the foot of his bed and drifted off to sleep.

He began to dream and saw a large, bright pink hibiscus flower floating in a stream. He had dreamt of this same flower many months ago and had accepted it as sign from Kenya freeing him from any obligation he felt he had to her and to go on with his life.

When Esdell woke up on New Year's Day, he felt a need to paint the flower of which he had dreamt. He went into his studio and pulled out some painting supplies he had bought a while ago and hoped that the paint had not dried out. He placed a canvass on an easel and began to sketch the hibiscus blossom. It was if he were compelled to draw it. Sammy called him to ask him what time he was coming over to eat. Grace prepared the traditional New Year's Day dinner of black-eyed peas and cabbage. She had fixed corned beef and fried chicken and made hot water cornbread. As inviting as that sounded, Esdell declined the offer, asking that they save him a plate. Hope called asking what his plans were for the day, and he told her he was working on something, and he would call her later. He was totally engrossed in his project. Several hours passed and he had not even eaten. He called Hope and apologized for waiting so long to call her and, because of the late hour, that he would see her tomorrow. She was disappointed that she had seen him on New Year's Day, but wished him a good night. He fixed himself a small snack and went to bed.

After work the next day, he returned home and resumed his project. Hope called saying she had had an exhausting day, and she was too tired for them to visit. He was actually glad to have this time become available so he could keep painting.

"We can get together tomorrow, Esdell," Hope said. "I'm so tired. It seems like I'm working harder now than I did when I was working two jobs."

"Okay, that's fine," Esdell said almost dismissively.

"You seem awfully eager to get off the phone, E. Brown. What you doin' over there?"

"I'm working on something." Hope did not say anything. Esdell speculated on what her silence meant and what she was thinking. "I'm working on something for you! You'll see. Okay?"

"Okay. I'll talk to you later," Hope said reluctantly.

"I'll call you or come by tomorrow," he promised.

Hope's apprehensive tone made Esdell determined to finish his painting quickly. So after coming home from work the next day, he finished the painting. He stepped back to admire his eighteen-by-twenty-four-inch masterpiece. He smiled broadly. He was well pleased with his work, feeling sure that he had truly duplicated the flower in his dreams. He had combined both pale and bright pinks, magenta, yellow, white, and smidgens of black in the single blossom. The leaves were lime and forest green and the background was different shades of blue, like the stream in which the flower floated.

"That's it!" he whispered, wiping sweat from his face and smearing paint on it at the same time. "That's it, Solo. Whatcha think, boy?" Solo lay sleeping in a chair in the studio and raised his head just to acknowledge his name had been called. He wagged his tail, lowered his head, and went back to sleep. "What do you know? I think it looks real good. I can't wait for Hope to see it." Esdell suddenly remembered all the times he had seen Hope in magenta or hot pink. "Wow!" he simply said. "She *was* meant for me! That's what this color means!" He called her. "Hope I got something to show you. Can you come over?" She agreed and was shortly at his front door. He led her upstairs to the studio to show her his painting.

"Stand here," Esdell directed. "This is what I've been doin' the past few days. There's a story behind this painting, and someday, I'll tell it to you. But I painted this for you, and I hope you'll hang it in your shop. He turned the easel around so Hope could see his finished product.

"I love it!" she said. "You painted this for me to hang in my shop?"

"Yes, it's for you! It's *all* for you!" Hope hugged and kissed Esdell, ignoring that he was covered with paint and smelled of turpentine.

"I know just where I'll hang it! I love it, Esdell, and I love you! Let's go hang it now!"

"No, not now. It's gotta dry, and I wanna have it framed." Esdell looked again at the finished product. "Hmm, I might add a few more touches."

"But, babe, it's perfect," Hope insisted. She watched Esdell as he studied the painting. She then trusted his judgment. "But, you're the expert. I'll wait if you say so."

Esdell ended up working on the painting for a good while longer. Kofi's baptism came and went to the delight of his mother. Every day that Hope worked, she imagined Esdell's piece hanging in her shop. As she patiently waited for the finished product, she cleared the space where it would hang. Finally, Esdell called to tell her he was done and the painting was completely dry. Hope rushed to pick it up, saying she would have it framed. She had it put in a gold frame with glass to protect it from the moisture in the store. The place of honor in the flower shop was behind the counter. She made sure it hung perfectly. She placed a vase of bright pink roses beneath it and vowed there would always be live flowers there to help showcase the painting. All of her customers admired it, often inquiring where they could purchase a print. She was proud to say, "This is an original painted for me by my man! But maybe I can hook you up!"

This little advertisement by Hope created an opportunity for Esdell that he had not considered. A few of Hope's customers commissioned Esdell to do paintings for their homes and businesses. They were customized, one of a kind pieces that opened a potentially profitable pastime for him. He was doing something he loved to do, pretty much at his leisure, and was getting paid for it. Sweet! Kofi would sometimes go to Esdell's house just to watch his technique. This helped Kofi to decide to major in art at school. Their mutual love of art and the time they spent together brought them closer. When Kareem finally called, he was happy to hear that his father was now becoming a father figure to Kofi. It was a relationship that Kofi needed and Esdell adored.

23

Esdell, dressed in a dark navy blue suit with a white shirt and lavender tie walked into the beautifully decorated reception hall at the church. He smiled broadly as his mother, Grace, approached him.

"There's my college graduate!" she chirped.

The school semester had ended, and he had received his associate's degree in graphic design. He had, at first, dismissed the idea of all the pomp and circumstance of a formal graduation. After all, it was only an associate's degree, but his mother and his girlfriend convinced him not to ignore the fact that he had achieved his goal. They would not let him discount all that he had accomplished all while holding down a full-time job and in the midst of numerous life-changing events. So he agreed to take part in the commencement services with his classmates, wearing his cap and gown proudly. Grace and Hope also insisted on an open house. Esdell agreed to that too, but insisted they keep it small.

The room was decorated in Esdell's school colors, crimson and gold. Mylar and latex helium filled balloons were in every corner of the room. Large votive lamps held red burning candles and set inside gold and white chrysanthemum flower rings. They set on round mirror tiles, making beautiful centerpieces on each white linen covered tables.

"Hope has done it again!" Esdell bragged. "The tables look real good!"

"That girl of yours got talent!" Grace agreed. "Where is she?"

"She stopped in the restroom to freshen up. Kofi's outside talkin' to somebody he knows from school."

Karlena, Micah, and Joseph had flown in just for the occasion. Kareem had a lot going on at his church, so he couldn't get away. Esdell lingered at the entryway, waiting for Hope to join him. She came out dressed in a cream pencil skirt and a tangerine satin top with freshened lipstick and brushed hair.

"Hey, Miss Grace," Hope said. "We made it!"

"The sisters on the church culinary ministry took care of everything. The food's all set up and ready to serve," Grace announced. "Looks and smells good, don't you think, Hope?"

"Yes, ma'am! It's making me hungry!"

"Well, the guest of honor is here, and we can eat if he's ready! Are you ready to eat, son?"

"Let's do it!" Esdell walked to the buffet table and invited all his guests to join him in line.

It was another Brown family occasion. One thing that was a well-known fact was that the Browns would take any and every opportunity to be with family and friends. They were genuinely loving people who simply loved people. Their Christ-like ways were always evident, and people enjoyed being around them. Even the family antics, joking and playing just made a day with the Browns that much more fun.

Esdell filled his plate with chicken drumettes, baked beans, and potato salad. He sat down at a table and was soon joined by his family, Hope and Kofi. Christine sat across from him staring.

"Why you lookin' at me like that?" he asked her.

"I just can't believe your big head actually graduated from college. I didn't think you had that much sense!"

"That's 'cause you ain't got enough sense to recognize good sense!" he countered.

"Uh-uh, bruh! You can't be a college student and still saying stuff like 'ain't got'! You gots to be using your edumacation!" Sammy added.

"Both of you need to be quiet!" Christine answered back "You both are talking like you never saw a day of school in your life. I've got impressionable young ladies here!" She nodded her head toward her daughters as they laughed.

And once again, they were off! The whole table and the tables around them laughed at the way that the Brown siblings made fun of each other. Kofi thought it was amazing that they could talk about each other and no one was ever really angry. He loved that about the Browns. They carried on with their cheerful debate when Joseph, who had been busy on his iPhone, interrupted.

"Hold up, everybody!" he said loudly.

"Wut up, Joe?" Sammy asked. "Did you get to another level on some game?"

"No, I gotta call for Daddy B!"

"A call for me?" Esdell asked as Joseph passed him the phone. He looked at the screen.

"Congratulations, Dad!" It was Kareem looking back at him with a huge grin on his face. "Way to go, old man. You did it. How does it feel?"

"Hey, man! It feels good! It feels good." Esdell had to admit. "How you doing? I'm surprise Joseph was able to connect with you!"

"I'm okay. I'm in Port-au-Prince today. Reception is much better here! I had a meeting with some city officials and some local businessmen. I'm trying to get funding for a new water system in my town. I wish I could've been there today to see you walk 'cross that stage! I'm real proud of you, Dad!"

"Thanks, son," Esdell said modestly. "But listen to you. Sounds like you're busy with some really important stuff. Good for you!"

"Hey, I don't want to talk about me. It's all about you today. How's the open house going?" Kareem asked.

"Well say 'hi' to everybody!" Esdell turned the phone around to scan those sitting at his table and tables around it. Every one waved and screamed greetings as they came into view.

"Hi, Kareem! Tell mama and daddy I said 'hello'!" Hope yelled. Esdell then walked around the room so the rest of his guest could say hello as well. He then returned to his table.

"Well, that's just about everybody! They all glad to see you! Me too!"

"I was at the right place at the right time. God is good like that!" Kareem said. "Well, I gotta go now. I gotta go pick up some supplies and get back to the mission. Congrats again, Dad. Thanks, Joseph! Talk to y'all soon!"

"Bye, son. Love you!"

"Bye, Kareem!" everyone shouted.

"Thanks for that, Joseph." Esdell handed Joseph back his phone. "It was like he was here."

"You're welcome, Daddy B. I'm glad I could get through," Joseph said.

After a few hours, the open house ended. Esdell collected his greeting cards and gifts, and then took Hope and Kofi home. He returned to his house to be greeted by Solo at the door. He picked him up and went upstairs to his room. He put on some sweat pants and a tea shirt and sat to read cards and open gifts. Esdell made a list of all the people he would need to send a thank-you card, including his mother and girlfriend who hosted his reception.

That was so nice, he thought. He immediately went into prayer thanking God for the day and all that had taken place. He had graduated; he spent time with his children, even if one visit was by phone. "God, you are great, and I praise you greatly in the name of Jesus. Amen." Esdell's thoughts turned to the work that Kareem was doing in Haiti. He wondered what he could do to help with the water situation in the village. The church was already sending clothing, health, and hygiene packages to them, thanks to a program started by Isaiah and Grace, but he thought they could, perhaps, do more. He sent up an addendum to his prayer asking God for direction.

"Well, Solo, how 'bout a little TV before we hit the hay? The kids are stayin' at Joseph's parents tonight, so it's just you and me." Esdell grabbed a bag of kitty treats off his nightstand. "Here ya go, boy!" Solo meowed in anticipation of his snack. Esdell chuckled to himself. "I never woulda thought I'd be a cat owner and lovin' it. But here we are!" He reached for the remote and turned on the TV. He lifted Solo onto his lap and stroked his head. "Here we are!"

The next day, early Sunday evening, Esdell sat on his deck with Karlena, drinking ice-cold tea and lounging in the cool breezes.

"It's so nice out here, Daddy. I love and miss this deck. We have a patio outside our townhouse, but it's not the same." Karlena paused. "It's quiet too. Micah's at Grandma's and Joseph's at his parents. It's just you and me." She paused again and watched Solo walk along the deck's railing. "Oh, and Mr. Solo. I still can't believe you gotta cat!"

"He's my pal. He's good company, when he wants to be!" Esdell laughed. "But he don't hold a candle to you, baby girl. I'm glad we can spend a little time together before y'all leave." He sipped his tea. "You still gettin' used to life down south?"

"Yeah. But you know what? I miss snow! I never thought I would, but I do! Hopefully, if we can come up for Christmas this year, it'll be a white one!"

"Maybe I'll come down there this Christmas. I worry about y'all spending so much money flying back and forth."

"We fly pretty cheap, it's not so bad. So, Daddy, what're plans now that you've got your associate's degree? Do you think you'll go back for your bachelor's now?"

"Maybe later, but not right away. I'm gonna take a break. Can I tell you what I been thinkin' though?" he asked.

"Please!" Karlena answered.

"Well, you know that I've been doing some commissioned artwork. I kinda think I wanna do a few pieces and maybe display them at some of the art shows 'round town. What you think?"

Karlena's face lit up. "I think that's the best ideas ever!" she exclaimed. "You can even do your *own* art show. And you could do a catalog or a book or something, and me and Joseph could publish it! We can hang some of your pieces in our offices and hook you up with some businesses in Louisiana! You can even start your own web site!"

"Whoa! Listen at you go! I've been thinkin' about it, but I didn't think that far ahead. But I did think to include Kofi. He works real good in pencil and charcoal. Maybe we can do a show together."

"Daddy, y'all could work this! You really could! I'ma get a pad and pen. Me and you are gonna make some real plans!" Karlena darted into the house. Esdell found himself getting excited.

When Karlena returned, the two of them sat at the patio table writing down ideas for Esdell's potential venture. Once they started, the ideas flowed like water. When they were finished, Karlena went to the computer to put all their ideas in a document. Esdell leaned over her as she looked at different sites on the web to help devise a game plan. Soon, Joseph came in with Micah. Karlena shared the plans that she and Esdell were making. Joseph, being very business minded, was just as enthused as they were, agreeing with Karlena that this was a very feasible plan. Karlena put Micah to bed as the two men discussed the financial end of things. Joseph made suggestions on what might be the most cost-effective way to pursue the venture. Esdell listened intently to what Joseph said, and they both recognized that he would have to keep his full-time job for now. It would take some time before he would show profit from the sale of his pieces, and he would need that income from his job to fund all his supplies.

By the time Karlena and her family were ready to go back home, the plans were complete. Again, Esdell had taken them to the airport.

"Daddy, promise that you won't sit on the plans for your art show and all the other things. Don't make me have to come back and get on you!" Karlena warned before they boarded the plane.

"I promise. I'm going over to Hope's right now, and I'll be talking to her and Kofi," Esdell assured. "Thank y'all for all your input! Y'all have a safe flight. Call me when you get home!" Once again, he gave them all hugs and waved good-bye as they entered airline doors.

He went straight to Hope's apartment. He eagerly shared all the ideas he, Karlena, and Joseph had devised. Kofi was fascinated. "You really think we can do this, Mr. B.?" Kofi asked. "I mean, do you think I'm good enough to do an art show?"

"No doubt, Kofi!" Esdell assured. "You do real good work! Now remember, we just tryna get our names out there to start. We may never really make a lot of money, but we can show our God-given talents. If we acknowledge that he is the source of our gifts and give Him praise, there's no tellin' where he'll take us!"

"I don't know about you, son, but I'm excited. I'm lovin' the thought of you two working together. Aren't you?" Hope asked.

"I am!" Kofi admitted. Esdell and Hope clenched each other's hands in agreement. They again went over the plans that had been made.

So Esdell continued going to work, faithfully driving his delivery truck. He began to buy art supplies for himself and Kofi as they both started working on their pieces. Esdell's mind was on his latest project after he clocked out from work and was walking from the warehouse to his car. His thoughts were interrupted by a familiar voice.

"Hey, Esdell, wait up!" It was his coworker, Gary, calling for him.

"Hey, Gary!" Esdell answered. "What's up? I thought you woulda been gone already."

"I been waiting for you. I need to talk to you!" Gary said excitedly. "You gotta minute?"

"Yep!"

"You remember the young lady that I brought to Hope's grand opening of the shop?" Esdell quickly flashed back to that night and he recalled Gary introducing him to a petite young lady named Carolyn who had reddish hair and green eyes. He nodded.

"Yeah, she was a cute little thing. Carolyn, right?"

"Yeah, that's her!" Gary confirmed. "You ain't gonna believe this, but we're getting married!"

"What?" Esdell said. "Uh...uh, congratulations, man! This is a surprise. Y'all haven't been together that long, have you?"

"Only a few months. I met her at church when I joined the choir. I swear, man, it was love at first sight. I fell for her hard and quick! I knew right away that she was going to be my wife. When a man finds a wife, he finds a good thing!"

"All right, Gary, quote that scripture now!" Esdell slapped Gary on the back. "I'm happy for you. When's the big day?"

"Pretty soon. That's what I wanna talk to you about. Do you think Hope can consult on the wedding? Her business card said that was one of the new services of her shop."

"I don't see why not. You got her card. Give her a call and set up an appointment."

"Okay, I'll have Carolyn call her. Will you tell Hope to expect her call?"

"Yes, I'll be talkin' to her later. Congrats again, Gary."

"Thanks, man! See ya later." Gary shook Esdell's hand as they went to the parking lot.

Later that evening, Esdell called Hope. She answered the phone, sounding very tired.

"Hi, there," Hope yawned. "How was your day?"

"Fine," Esdell answered. "The question is: how was your day? You sound pooped."

"I am. Hard day at the office! Since I decided to stay open later for the summer months, it's been very tiring."

"You're still learnin' every side of owning your own business, but I know you're handlin' it!"

"I'm trying," Hope yawned again. "I'm tryna hang!"

"You not havin' regrets are you?" Esdell asked.

"No, not at all. Like you said, I'm still learning."

"Well, I'm glad to hear that 'cause some more business is coming your way."

"Really? What?"

"My buddy from work, Gary, is 'bout to take that walk!"

"He's getting married? Really?"

"Yeah, he is, and his fiancée is gonna be callin' you to set up an appointment."

"What does she want me to do for her? Her flowers?"

"Gary said she wants you to consult."

"Oh yeah?" Hope's tone perked up. "This'll be my first wedding consultation. When're they getting married?"

"I don't know, but Gary said it'll be pretty soon. You interested?" Esdell asked.

"Absolutely! I need to get studied up!"

"I know you'll do fine. Just wait 'til she calls so you'll know exactly what she needs you to do," he suggested.

"Nuh-uh, I'm getting off this phone and getting on the computer right now! See you later, boo!"

"Bye!" Esdell laughed as he disconnected from the call. "Go gettem, baby!"

As it turned out, after Hope had spoken with Gary's fiancée, Carolyn, she found that the wedding was going to be pretty simple. They met with Hope, and she immediately began to coordinate their special day. While working at the flower shop, Hope had made several contacts with different types of vendors. When she was working out the plans, she came up with an idea and went by Esdell's to talk to him about it.

"So what's your big idea, Hope?" Esdell asked her.

"I want you and Kofi to put your heads together and design Carolyn's wedding invitations and programs. I want her and Gary to have something really different," she eagerly proposed. Esdell sat for a minute.

"Wedding invitations? That's a little girlie for us, don't you think?" Esdell asked.

"Girlie? Uh, who painted that beautiful *hot pink* flower that hangs in my shop? I think that was you! C'mon, Esdell, you just got a degree in graphic design," Hope continued "You know how to do templates, and you *and* Kofi can draw like crazy. This is not a problem!"

"Well, yeah, but that flower was inspired!" Esdell said.

"Yeah, and I'm still waiting to get the full story on that inspiration, but another time."

"Well, Kofi drawing flowers and landscapes and stuff could be real interesting. That ain't really his style," Esdell said, recalling Kofi's portfolio. "But I'll talk to him and see what he says."

Esdell talked to Kofi, and he was reluctant about doing a wedding. He, too, thought doing wedding invitations was a little "girlie," but he would give it a try. Hope met with Carolyn and Gary and later told Esdell and Kofi what they had in mind. They collaborated and came up with a few things to show the engaged couple who quickly made their selections.

When the programs were passed out at Gary's wedding, Esdell and Hope sat quietly listening to the comments on how beautiful they were. They appeared to have lace corners atop the mauve colored paper and accented with delicate lily of the valley and printed with bronze colored lettering. The guest immediately turned to the back of the program to read the acknowledgements to find out who did the programs and who did the decorations. It brought them great pleasure to see all their names in the list of vendors and to hear the approving comments of the guests.

"Listen to them, Esdell," Hope whispered. "We're a hit. I feel a lot of business coming our way."

"God is good!" Esdell proclaimed.

This idea of Hope's inspired Esdell and Kofi. They decided that they would actually try to start a small business. They had worked well together and their talents blended like coffee and cream. The invitations and programs were just the start. Esdell and Kofi designed a line of general and customized stationary and greeting cards. They specialized in African American artwork. They developed a web site, got business cards, and began advertising. They called their business "Rapture" at Kofi's suggestion because it meant joy and delight. But more importantly, he chose the name because he now believed in the rapture at the return of Jesus Christ. Even though they were developing their greeting card business, the two men never lost sight of their original plan of having an art show and continued to work toward it.

Hope also had been motivated by the success of Gary's wedding. She took an online course, becoming a certified wedding consultant and event planner in just a few months; just in time for the wedding season.

"We're about to get really busy, boys!" Hope said to Kofi and Esdell. "I hope you're both ready!"

"Yeah, Ma, we're ready! You know me and Mr. B got skills. We stays ready!" Kofi bragged.

"All to the glory of God, Kofi," Esdell reminded. "Never forget, all we are and all we do is to the glory of God! But we do got skills!" he agreed, giving Kofi a hard high five.

24

Kofi sat in Esdell's car in the underground parking lot of the Circle Centre Mall of downtown Indianapolis looking at a pamphlet. Many months had passed, and the time had come. After a lot of hard work and fervent prayer, it was time for their art show. It wasn't like they had originally planned however. They had planned to have a show that showcased their work exclusively. But after some of their work had been seen by a curator, they were invited to be a part of a large art exhibit that was being held at the Indianapolis Artsgarden. The Artsgarden, a glass dome structure, curved ninety-five feet into the air over a major intersection of downtown. Being attached to the mall, it was an impressive attraction of Circle Centre. The facility offered an elegant environment for any event. The venue was perfect for an art show, and it was more than either of them had hoped for. It was an opportunity that Esdell and Kofi would not pass by.

"You ready, Kofi?" Esdell asked. "We should get in there. Your mama's in there waiting on us."

"Yeah, I'm ready, Mr. B." Kofi started to open the door but paused. "I can't believe we're at the Artsgarden! Can you imagine how much it would have cost us if we'd tried to get this place on our own? Man!"

"Yeah, I'll bet it's pretty pricey, but thank God we're here."

Kofi continued to stare at the pamphlet. On the inside, there were pictures of all the artist that were participating in the gallery. He saw his picture and one of Esdell, listing them as featured artists.

"Yeah, we're here!" Kofi boasted. "I'm so hyped! I never dreamed of nothin' like this. I always thought I was gonna end up in jail. In jail or dead!"

"Yeah, but look at cha! God kept you. God is good!"

"You're always sayin' that! It took me a long time to believe it, but I do now, no doubt! RK and you really changed my life when y'all turned me on to God. Mom tried, but back then, I wasn't tryna hear her. You guys came along and stuck with me and made it clear, drove it home!"

"Hey, man, the scriptures say Jesus knocks at your door, and all you gotta do is let him in. You let him in!"

"Yeah, but y'all showed Him where I lived!" Kofi laughed. "You can play it off all you want to, Mr. B. I know you try to humble and all that, but you and RK made a big difference in my life. I'll always remember that and always tell you how thankful I am about it. After RK went to Haiti, I wasn't sure what I'd do. You was right there! You helped me with school and believed in my art. Now my work is hangin' in the Artsgarden! *And* we got our little greetin' card hustle. Yup, God is good!"

"All the time, Kofi!" Esdell agreed. "Well, we need to get in there. And you know what, Kofi?"

"What's that, Mr. B?"

"I'm hyped too! We worked so hard and here we are!"

Esdell and Kofi had worked feverishly preparing for this show. They threw themselves into their work. Their pieces had been framed and prints had been made of a few.

They left the parking lot and walked to the elevator that took them to where the show was taking place. It was a beautiful afternoon. When the elevator doors opened, the sun shined brightly through the glass walls of the Artsgarden. Both men gasped in response to the appearance of the room.

"Jesus!" Esdell exclaimed. "It looks like the glory of God himself is lightin' up this room!"

All Kofi could say was, "Whoa!"

"Whoa is right, son!" Hope, who had arrived early to prepare both of their booths, greeted Kofi and Esdell with short hugs. "Well, if it isn't Pablo Picasso and Michael Angelo!" she kidded as she escorted them to their booth and art display.

"Table looks nice. You almost outdid yourself!" Esdell stated. "You are the hostess with the mostess!"

"This is such a high-class place and you two are high-classed artist. I had to do it up just a little. I really didn't do much! Look at this place! Look at these beautiful, live tropical plants! Need to find out who their distributor is."

With the Artsgarden being all glass and temperature controlled, it was like a large terrarium, letting in plenty of light that helped all the potted plant grow large.

"It looks…" Kofi started. "Like you said, Mr. B, like the glory of God is all through here! Like the garden of Eden!"

They walked around together looking at the work of some of the other artist. Some of the art hung on portable drywalls or peg boards and some set on easels. It was a great exhibit, featuring the work of many local and a few national artists. There were tables with light refreshments in one corner of the room. There were paintings, sculptures, handmade tapestries, and jewelry.

"Mom, this is somethin', huh?" Kofi said as they returned to the booth he and Esdell shared. They had only seven framed pieces between the two them to display, but it was their best work. Some were old, some were revisions, and some were brand new. They had created a wall that displayed the sketches and painting, and on the table that Hope arranged, they displayed some of their greeting cards and invitations. The table sat to the side and also laying on it was a catalog that was designed by Joseph's publishing company, just as Karlena had promised; brochures and order blanks included.

As the guest entered, they meandered around the showroom. Impressive and awesome were words that were constantly tossed around. Esdell borrowed the painting he had done for Hope to display, but this piece was not for sale, nor was there a print. This piece was done exclusively for Hope, and it would not be duplicated. Though all the artwork was being appreciated, it seemed the center of attention was Kofi's creation titled *Transitioned*. He had combined and recreated the drawings he had done, and Esdell had seen a few years earlier. The charcoal sketch was that self-portrait profile of Kofi showing the scar of his once slit throat. At the back of his head were gang members with knives, guns, and drug paraphernalia. His face was turned and lifted up toward the sun rising over the horizon; his eyes closed, a satisfied smile, and that scar on his throat clearly evident. Within the beams coming from the sun were broken chains, flying birds, graduation caps, and praying hands. The thing that one could miss if they did not look closely was camouflaged in that scar on his neck. It appeared to be an image of Jesus on the cross. Kofi was depicting his transition from the darkness of sin to the light of salvation. Hope noticed that a man stood staring at this picture. He had been there for quite a while. She approached him.

"Like it?" she asked, looking at the piece with him.

"Interesting!" the man answered, turning to Hope. She then recognized him.

"Judge Burrus!" It was the judge who presided over Kofi's case. "How are you, sir?" She shook his hand as her eyes darted looking for Kofi. The judge looked at her.

"Um, I'm sorry. You have me at a disadvantage. You are?" the judge asked.

"I can believe that. I'm Hope Shah. You presided over my son's case a few years ago. Kofi Thomas? You sat over a lot of cases that day. Over the hundreds of cases that you've heard, I can't expect you to remember his. But I remember you. You let my son go. In spite of his terrible record, you let him go!" The judge stood silently, thinking.

"I remember. He had that large group of church members supporting him. I still remember some of the statements in their letters. They made the difference in my decision. How *is* Kofi?'

"Judge, he's doing just fine! This piece you're looking at is Kofi's work!" Hope stated with great pride.

"Really? It's very telling, and it's very good! Is this what Kofi's doing these days?"

"Yes, this, and he's in college and has started a small business with my boyfriend. Thank God. And thanks to you too, Judge. You trusted him and gave him a chance. And like he told you that day, he's better. *So* much better!"

"Now, that's what I love to hear! Is he here? I'd like to talk to him."

"And I want you to talk to him, but I don't see him," Hope said, again looking around. "Oh, he can't be far. I'll call him. No, wait! There he is! Kofi!" Hope signaled for him to come over and he came quickly. "Kofi, this is—"

"Judge Burrus!" Kofi called his name before Hope could get his name out. "Good to see you, sir!"

"You too, son. I've been hearing good things about you," the judge said, extending his hand for Kofi to shake. "I'm loving your work, here. I see the story unfolding, and it looks like it has a happy ending!"

Kofi and Judge Burrus talked about Kofi's journey. The judge was no less than impressed by the story that Kofi had to tell. As they spoke, Esdell joined them, happily adding his two cents to the story. Kofi and the judge continued to talk as Esdell and Hope talked to the different people who visited the booth.

"Kofi, you've done well. I'm proud of your progress." The judge turned and look at Kofi's drawing again. "I want to buy this. How much?"

"What? You wanna buy this?" Kofi was surprised. "Judge Burrus, you giving me a chance to prove myself is a debt I can never pay back. Uh, you can have it!"

"No!" the judge contested. "How much?"

"Mr. B!" Kofi called.

"Yes, Kofi?" Esdell asked, walking over.

"Judge Burrus wants to buy this, but I just want to make it a gift to thank him."

The judge shook his head. "You're in business now, young man, and you need to always make good business decisions. I know you've set a price for it." He looked on the table where he found a price list. He saw Kofi's *Transitioned* listed for $350.

"Underpriced, but considered it sold!" Judge Burrus said, taking out his check book. Kofi stood with his mouth hanging open.

"All right, Kofi, your first sale!" Esdell congratulated. Kofi was still speechless. Esdell spoke for him. "Uh, Judge, since this is part of the exhibit, we're under contract for all our pieces to stay on display until the show is over. We can deliver it to you later, or you can come back and pick it up after the show is over."

"I'm going to look around some more, then probably grab a bite at the restaurant downstairs. I'll be back!" the judge decided. "Just don't sell it to anyone else."

"Don't worry about that, Judge," Esdell said. "It will be marked as sold! Congrats, Kofi!" Kofi still stood in a daze.

The judge turned to him. "Kofi, I'm going to hang this in my office. It will remind me that all black kids don't wind up in jail and that I still got it when it comes to reading young people. I'll be using you and this drawing as an example of hope. It's a great piece, son. Here's your check." He handed it to Kofi. "Here you go, Kofi. Now say SOMETHING!"

"Judge, you just changed my life again! You have made me a *professional* artist!" Kofi declared.

"I consider it an investment. Keep up the good work, and I'll see you later. Good to do business with you."

Hope gave the judge a receipt, and they all watched him walk to the next exhibit. Hope smiled at Kofi and gave him a hug of congratulations.

"I sold it!" Kofi finally spoke in disbelief. He had mixed emotions about selling his piece. It felt like he had just sold his child. After all, it really did tell the story of his teen years, and he had put a lot of who he was into that self-portrait. Kofi blinked his eyes and sighed deeply. "I'm pro now, dawg!" he said, fanning himself with the check.

"You go, son!" Hope cheered.

It turned out to be a good night for both men. Kofi sold his self-portrait. Esdell had done a painting in various shades of blue of sun beams breaking through dark, stormy clouds, which sold shortly after. The crux of Esdell's and Kofi's contribution to the Artsgarden exhibit was that their work depicted hope, promise, and the glory of God. Their spiritual pieces were well received by the art critics of Indianapolis. All of the brochures were passed out as well as their business cards. Several people were interested in having family portraits done by both artists. Before they disassembled their booth, Esdell, Kofi, and Hope held hands to pray, giving thanks for all that he had done.

The next day, Esdell called Karlena to give her a report of how the art show had gone. She, of course, wanted to come, but Esdell talked her out of it. She and Joseph had done the catalog, so they had already seen all the pictures that Esdell and Kofi had to offer.

"Sounds like your show was a success, Daddy. Are you disappointed that you and Kofi didn't have a private show?" Karlena asked.

"No, not really. I did want our own show at first, but we're unknown in the art world," Esdell conceded. "We probably woulda only had family and friends show up. This way, hundreds of people saw our work. It was a real nice event. They even had an open stage with poets and dancers!"

"I wanted to be there! I just wanted to come to support you guys. Anyway, Daddy, you might have been unknowns going in, but the Naptown art world knows you two now! Did you talk to Kareem yet?" Karlena asked.

"I tried, but the call didn't go through. You know how it is."

"Yeah, but I thought the reception was getting better over there."

"Just a bad day for the phones, I guess. Could of been a storm or something. Hey, let me talk to my li'l buddy!"

Karlena put Micah on the phone. He had turned into quite the little chatterbox. Esdell could now have an actual conversation with him. Micah was excited to tell Dae Dae about his new toys and the little dog that lived in the townhouse down the street. He always asked about Solo, though he really didn't get to play with him much when they visited. Solo would hide from Micah most of the time, and Micah spent much of his time looking for him.

When Karlena got back on the line, Esdell remarked about how well Micah was talking. He told his daughter that he needed a playmate to talk to, hinting that it was time for a little brother or sister.

"Not right now, Daddy." Karlena laughed. "I wanna finish school first. You need to talk to Kareem. It's time he got married and started a family!"

"Girl, you know your brother is married to the church, but feel free to suggest that the next time you talk to him!"

Esdell and Karlena finished their phone call when Esdell's doorbell rang.

"Gotta go, baby girl. Hope's here. She's bringin' dinner."

"Okay, tell her hi for me. Love you, Dad. Bye!"

"Love you too. Bye, sweetie!" Esdell then answered the door.

"Hi, babe!" Hope sang as she entered the house. "I got chicken with all the fixin's! Let's eat while it's still hot!" Esdell kissed her on the cheek.

"It smells good." He took the bags and went into the kitchen. He took out some plates and forks and served the food. Hope said grace and they ate.

"This was really good," he said. "Good choice. Oh! I meant to tell you, I was talking to Karlena when you came in, and she said to tell you hi."

"She doin' okay?"

"Yup, just fine. I wish you could hear Micah talkin'. Li'l buddy's a li'l trip!" Esdell laughed. "You 'bout done?"

"All done! You wanna watch TV or something?" Hope asked.

"In a minute, but I wanna show you something first."

Esdell led Hope downstairs into the basement. They descended the stairs, and he showed Hope around.

"I've never been down here before. Lotta space and a lotta, uh, stuff." Hope observed.

"Yeah, its kinda junky, I admit. There's stuff I need to get rid of." Esdell sighed and looked at a box that he knew was packed with Kenya's things. "For one reason or another. But I want you to look pass all the mess. I see a office, a workspace for me and Kofi's business. It a full basement we could put everything down here!"

"I can see it! It's a good idea!"

"My family can do the work. We remodeled Ma's basement, and we did most of the work on our house. Brown's got talent!"

"Me and Kofi got talent too! I know he'll think it's a good idea. I'll talk to him when I get home."

Esdell and Hope started to devise a plan to turn his basement into a business office. Esdell planned to move his studio from Micah's old room downstairs. There was enough room for Esdell and Kofi to have their own workspace, store art supplies and office equipment, and conduct appointments with potential clients.

Hope was right in assuming that Kofi would be in agreement with turning Esdell's basement into an office space. It was a matter of days before Esdell started cleaning and clearing it out. He wanted to get most of the things moved out before the actual remodeling started. When Esdell came across the boxes that he knew held Kenya's belongings, he went through them quickly; just long enough to make sure there was nothing of value or anything that the twins might want was enclosed. He surprised himself when he realized that he spent little time reflecting on his marriage. There were moments of sentiment, but they did not last long. He packed up all of her things in boxes. He kissed his hand and patted the top of each box with it, as if to kiss them all good-bye. Then he set them out on his front porch for a local charity group to come pick them up. There were things that belonged to Kareem and Karlena that he set to the side. He called Karlena and described them. She didn't want them as she had taken all she wanted or needed when she got married and moved. So they went to the charity group as well. Once again, he tried to call Kareem, but could not get through. So he repacked his things in boxes, labeled them and put them to the side. Hope came one day to help him.

"Have you talked to your parent's lately, Hope?" Esdell asked.

"Yes, I have. I talked to them yesterday as a matter of fact. Why?" she asked.

"I've been tryna get Kareem for a long time with no luck. Just a little concerned."

"Don't be. You know what it's like trying to call over there. Mama and Daddy were doing good. Matta fact, they were telling me how much progress Kareem was making getting the new water system for the village! He's been traveling a lot, according to what Dad said. I'm sure he's fine," Hope reassured. "Hmm. Not much light down here," she continued. "I'm gonna order a Cast iron plant, mother-in-law tongue plant, and probably a Chinese evergreen plant to put down here. They do pretty well in darker, damp places. You'll need a few grow lights though. I have some you can have."

"Look, Hope, like Judge Burrus told Kofi, you're in business and you need to make good business decisions. We'll pay for whatever you order for us, and we'll pay for the grow lamps too."

"Boy, please!" Hope opposed. "Even though I'm paying him back, my son bought that business for me. My son is *your* business partner and anything that comes from *my* shop for your office will be at no charge, E. Brown!"

"My bad, Miss Hope! Didn't mean to insult you!" Esdell put his arm around Hope's waist and rubbed his nose across Hope's ear. "But I love it when you call me E. Brown! Sometimes you call it flirty, sometimes it's nasty. Either way, I love it!" He hugged her tighter.

"Back up!" Hope playfully pushed him away. "Let's get back to work!"

Work on the basement continued each day Esdell got home from work. Hope and Kofi help most nights and over the next few weeks. The once dark and dank cellar was remodeled into a working office place. They carpeted the area where they would meet with their customers with plush reddish brown carpet. They found bronze leather furniture at a secondhand store that looked barely used. Once it was cleaned, it looked like new. They had prints made from some of their pieces and hung them. They painted a mural of the downtown Indianapolis skyline at sunrise in the middle of the largest wall. They then bordered it with woodwork so that it looked like a large office window. It was so realistic and brightened the room so much, you almost forgot you were in a basement. Hope's plants made perfect accents along with glass and ceramic vases. Esdell and Kofi had their own work space and decorated it according to their own taste.

"Mr. B, we lookin' good down here!" Kofi said.

"Yeah, I think we're 'bout done. We just need to get the half bath installed, but we can do that later."

"What did Mrs. Willis think when she saw it the other day?"

"Oh, Mama loved it! Chris did too, believe it or not. She saw the muraland had to give it up!" Esdell said as he reached into his pocket to answer his cell phone. "Oh, it's Kareem. Finally! Hey, Kareem!" he answered.

"Hello? Hello? Helloooo! Hmm, the call got dropped." The disappointment was evident in his voice.

"Try to call him back! He's gotta be somewhere where he's gettin' a signal!"

Esdell did. The phone rang and then a screeching sound.

"Didn't go through. Man, it's been weeks and weeks since I last talked to him!"

"He's okay though, he just called. He talk to Karlena or anybody?" Kofi asked.

"Mom. I know he's okay. Mama talked to him and your grandparents been givin' Hope reports on him. It's just that I ain't talked to him. Need to hear my boy's voice. Ya know?"

"Yeah, 'cause I wanna talk to him too."

"Hedge of protection, Lord," Esdell said for the millionth time.

"What's that, Mr. B?"

"Just my quick prayer askin' God to protect my loved ones."

"Hedge of protection!" Kofi repeated.

"You guys down there?" Hope was yelling from upstairs. "I let myself in. I got pizza, c'mon up and eat!"

"Right on time. I'm starvin'!" Kofi lead the way upstairs to the kitchen. By the time they reached the top of the stairs, Hope had dealt out the paperplates and was opening the box to serve up the pepperoni pizza.

"Sit down and dig in!" She switched on the TV. "I wanna catch the rest of *Real People!*"

"Ma, that show is so stupid. I don't know why you watch it. Ain't nothin' about none of them people real!"

"You are surely right about that, son," Hope agreed, and they all laughed.

They ate pizza and talked about the finished basement. Esdell couldn't help but brag about the mural that he and Kofi had worked on together. They were having such a good time, Hope was barely paying attention to her show. The program ended and the news came on. The trio just kept on talking until something caught Esdell's attention.

"Hold up, everyone, shh, listen!" All attention was then focused to the newscast.

"The epicenter of the earthquake was approximately twenty-five miles west of Port-au-Prince, Haiti. The death total is yet to be determined."

"What? Did he say twenty-five miles west of Port-au-Prince? An earthquake? That's just a few miles from Kareem's village!" Esdell yelled.

"Oh no!" Hope screamed and ran for her purse. She pulled out her cell phone and called her parents. There was only silence. No beep, dial tone, or busy signal; just silence. "I'm not getting anything! Esdell, you try!"

Esdell was already frantically dialing Kareem's number. Kofi, too, was trying to reach his grandparents and Kareem. He was not getting through either.

"Nothing!" Kofi affirmed. Esdell's house phone rang. He quickly answered it. It was his sister, Christine, who was also watching the news. She wanted to know if Esdell had been able to reach Kareem as she also had tried to call him.

"No, I haven't been able to get through!" Esdell relayed. "I've haven't talked to him in weeks! I keep missing him!" With these words, Esdell remembered that he had missed a call from Kareem only about sixty minutes earlier. "Wait a minute! He called about a hour ago, but the call dropped. He must've been tryna call me to tell me about the earthquake. He's *okay!*" Esdell began to pace back and forth. "He's *okay*, Chris!" Christine worried about how their mother would respond to the news.

They debated on whether or not to call them, knowing that they were probably already sleeping.

"I'll call them early in the morning. Just let them sleep," Esdell directed. "We just all need to pray and pray hard! I gotta believe he's not hurt!"

The pleasant evening had taken a very unpleasant and devastating turn. Esdell continued his efforts to contact Kareem throughout the night without success. His mind raced, imagining just what may have happened to him. He thought of how quickly his life could change. One moment he was enjoying pizza and talking about his budding business, and the next his head was flooded with thoughts of the possible death of his son. Then suddenly, for the first time in a long time, he began to relive the death of his wife, his Kenya. He clinched his fists to his temples.

"Oh, God, no! Not my son! Not Kareem!" He began to breathe heavily, gasping for air. Then he did the only thing he knew to do; he turned to God. He thumbed through his Bible, when he came upon Proverbs 27:1, "Do not boast about tomorrow, for you do not know what a day may bring." He read. He continued on to read Isaiah 26:3 and 4.

"You will keep in perfect peace those whose minds are steadfast, because they trust in you. Trust in the Lord forever, for the Lord, the Lord himself, is the Rock eternal." He closed his Bible and prayed. "Oh, Lord, my God, I believe and have faith in you and you alone. You are my keeper, my strong tower. Every day I prayed for your hedge of protection around my children, and I thank you, Lord, that you have done this, and I have faith that your grace and your mercy continue. My son is safe! Lord, please bless all the people of Haiti. They've been through so much. And, Lord, even if you have called Kareem home to be with you, I praise you, Lord, that he is still in your protective and healing hands. Your will be done, Father God. I claim the victory in the powerful name of Jesus Christ. Amen, amen, amen! Halleluiah to your name! Amen!" Esdell shouted. "But please don't take my son," he begged.

He prayed through the night. He prayed that whatever had happened that he would accept the infallible will of God. He did not try to sleep. He kept trying to call Kareem and watching CNN on TV to see if there would be more breaking news. Hope had called him twice during the night to see if he had been able to get through. Knowing that his mother and stepfather were early risers, he called them at 7:00 a.m. to relay the news. His mother's initial reaction was that of shock and disbelief, but then in her usual way, she became calm, trusting, and believing in God's divine decisions.

"He's a keeper, Esdell. No matter what happens, He'll keep us one way or another!" she said. Her words were especially comforting since Esdell had just read that very scripture.

He called his job to say that he would not be in. When he explained what had happened, his boss told him to take as much time as he needed. He called the Haitian Embassy in Washington, DC to see if they could offer more news than was being broadcasted. He even tried to call the American Embassy in Haiti. He reached them, but they could not give any information about Kareem's town. Esdell recalled the tragic earthquake that had taken place a few years earlier in Haiti. He had discussed this with Kareem who said that the country was still trying to recover from it.

"God, I don't believe you would take my son, not after you've brought me this far!" Esdell's day was filled with prayer along with many phone calls. Everyone was checking with him for updates. Karlena called him immediately after she had seen the story on the news. She was distraught after she had made many unsuccessful attempts to reach Kareem. Esdell did his best to calm her, and as always, he instructed her to pray. He promised to call her as soon as he heard anything. Family, friends, and church members all called for information and to let Esdell know they were in prayer for Kareem and his family. It was the prayer of righteous people that Esdell needed.

Hope left work early, leaving her employee, Mark, to take care of her shop. She rushed to Esdell's house, hoping that he had news. Nothing had changed. She had been in touch with her parent's old church in Chicago to see if they had heard anything. She, too, had called everybody she could think of who might hear from her parents.

Call after call had been made, incoming, outgoing for two days and, no contact had been made with Kareem or the Shahs. Hope and Kofi stayed the night with Esdell, sleeping in the guest rooms. Even though they were drawing strength and comfort from each other, Hope was starting to show signs of despair. Esdell had not slept, and he was showing signs of exhaustion. It was 6:00 a.m. when Hope joined him in the kitchen as he drank a cup of coffee.

"Did you sleep at all, Esdell, or have you been up all night?" she asked, rubbing his head.

"I dozed for a little bit, I think. How 'bout you? Did you sleep?"

"I think I got a couple of hours. I'm trying to decide whether or not to open the shop. Mark could handle it. He just won't be able to make any deliveries."

"Then let him handle it," Esdell advised. He looked at Hope and gave her a half grin.

"What?" she questioned.

"I just thought, this is the first time I woke up with you here. Kinda like it." He stared out of the kitchen window. "Yeah, kinda like it." His head dropped. "I'm tired of this waiting! I called the airport last night. I tried to get a flight to Haiti. Nothin' in or out. Damn it!" He banged his fist on the table, startling Hope.

"Don't do that, babe! Don't lose it on me! I'm depending on you to hold me up!" A look of fear overtook Hope's face. Esdell grabbed her hands.

"Sorry. I'm coo', baby. I just had to get that out. I'm okay. You're okay too." Hope looked away. "What's up?" Esdell asked.

"I'm feeling a little guilty. I know I haven't been really close to my parents over the past few years. And now..."

"And now when you *do* talk to them, you'll have a chance to make up for it! But I know how you feel. I hadn't talked to Kareem in a long time. I was a little worried, but I played it off, blamed it on bad cell phone towers. I shoulda tried harder to reach him. I'll do better this time."

"You believe he's alive?" Hope asked.

"I ain't tryna believe nothin' else!"

Kofi walked into the kitchen, rubbing his eyes.

"Any news?" he asked.

"Not a word," Esdell softly answered. "Coffee's hot, Kofi, or there's juice in the fridge, if you'd want it."

"Juice is good." Kofi got two glasses from the dish drainer and removed the orange juice from the refrigerator. He poured a glass for himself and for Hope. "Here ya go, Ma," he offered.

"Thanks, sweetie."

The trio sat quietly, sipping their beverages, giving no thought to what the others were thinking. The silence was broken by the ringing of a phone. Esdell automatically picked up his cell phone to answer, but it was dead. He had not charged it. He then realized it was his house phone ringing.

"Man, I'm trippin'!" He answered the landline phone and looked at the caller ID. He knew the area code to be Haitian. "It's Haiti, but I don't recognize the number! Hello? Hello?" he yelled again, waiting for someone to speak. He exhaled heavily. "Son!" Hope and Kofi gasped. "Kareem, boy. Praise Jesus! Are you all right?"

"I'm here, Dad. I'm kinda banged up, but I'm here!"

"Where're Mr. and Mrs. Shah?" Esdell asked.

"They're at the mission with the kids."

"How are they? Were they hurt?"

"Dad, our village was spared! It's still standing and taking in the injured from the surrounding areas."

"What's happening?" Hope pleaded for an answer.

"Your parents are fine! They're at the mission. The earthquake missed their village!" Esdell answered. "What happened?" he asked Kareem.

Kareem recounted the last two days, starting with the day of the earthquake. He had, in fact, tried to call Esdell that day, but the call did drop. He was in Port-au-Prince for another meeting regarding his church when the earthquake started. When the news broke, he immediately tried to get back to his village. The roads were all but destroyed, but he plowed through in his four-wheel drive vehicle. He stopped to help with search and rescue efforts; digging, lifting, carrying the injured, and comforting the bereaved. Kareem dug in with his bare hands, suffering cuts and bruises. It took over eighteen hours to make a trip that normally only took thirty to forty-five minutes. He braced himself for what he would find when he arrived home. When he got there, he was astounded; not one house shaken, not one stone overturned. Kareem had worried about the fragile state of the water system where the digging had just begun. It was undamaged.

"Dad, all I saw was the glory of God. That hedge of protection you always pray for was all around our village. By His grace, we were protected! Life is so precious. Things can change in a twinkling of an eye! We can't take one moment for granted, Daddy."

Esdell closed his eyes and held his breath for a second. It had been years since Kareem had called him daddy. He saw the image of his six-year-old son crying after he had fallen off his bicycle. The rest of the years flashed before his eyes, bringing him back to the present where his baby boy was now a grown man; a man of God who recognized the great gift of grace and mercy he had received. This gift had humbled him to the point where he would, again call his father daddy.

"I love you, Dad. Please tell everyone that I'm fine and that I love them all! Hello?" The connection was breaking up. "Dad, I think I'm about to lose you. Tell Miss Hope that her parents weren't hurt at all. They'll call when they can. They stayed with the children. Uh, I gotta go. Hug everybody for me. Cherish every minute, Dad, and remember what I said: don't take anything for granted!"

"Be careful, Kareem. I love you." Esdell turned to Hope. "Everybody's *okay*. He said your parents will call when they can. They didn't want to leave the children alone. Do you believe it? Nothing happened to the mission. It's a miracle, Hope! A answered prayer."

Esdell's body slumped in exhaustion and relief. All that happened over the past few days, the call he had just gotten from his son put everything into perspective. He stood and pulled Hope to her feet. He hugged her with what seemed to be all the strength he had left in his body.

"It's all good, baby! Everything worked out. God is good!"

"He is!" Hope agreed. "He is!"

Kofi came a put his arms around them both. Esdell's worry was dispelled, and a fresh spirit overtook him. He stepped back, breaking the group embrace.

"Hope, I love you. I love you! Marry me! Will you marry me?"

Hope looked at him in hopeful disbelief. "What did you just say to me?"

"He asked you to marry him, Ma!" Kofi answered. "Mr. B, don't be playin' with Mom's head like that!"

"What makes you think I'm playing? I know what I said, and I meant what I said. My son just gave me the best advice. He told me not to take anything for granted," Esdell said, taking Hope by her hand. "I thought I had to take thing slow with you, Hope, but for what? I know I love you. What am I suppose to do with the love, just waste it? Or waste time bein' here in this house by myself, wanting to be with you every day? I know we ain't even talked about us getting married, baby, but I love you! I spent years not even wanting to love nobody. I even pushed back what I was feeling about you. I tried to deny my feelings then but couldn't. I'm not wasting no more time." Esdell turned to Kofi. "Kofi, I'm asking you. Do you have a problem with me bein' her husband and your stepdad? Let me know now." Kofi thought just for a second.

"You like my dad already. No problem here, but it's up to Mom."

Esdell dropped to one knee. Tears began to fill Hope's eyes.

"I don't have a ring for your finger, but I got love for you that outshines any diamond. I'ma ask you again. Miss Hope, will you marry me?"

"Yes, E. Brown! You know I will!" Esdell stood up and Hope through her arms around his neck. He held her tightly around her waist. Kofi looked on, smiling.

"Uh, Mr. B, you should call your family and tell 'em about Kareem, and, uh, some other stuff too!"

Esdell looked at Kofi over Hope's shoulder but didn't let her go.

"You sure right about it, man!"

25

The next morning, Esdell opened his eyes in response to the sun shining through his bedroom window. He sat up. He smiled. He rolled out of his bed onto his knees. He began to sing.

"My God is an awesome God. He reigns from heaven above!" He cleared his throat. "Ahem. Lord God, my God. I thank you! It is *not* enough, but all I can do is praise you! Thank you for protecting my son and his mission. Thank you for blessing me with a peaceful night's sleep and waking up to this beautiful day! And thank you for hope, the hope and joy that you bless me with every day and for my love, Hope. She's a blessing from you. I didn't ask for her, but you lead me to her. Keep us all through this day. I love and praise you, Lord. Amen!"

He took a shower, being warmed by the water and by the thoughts of his many blessings. He had called his family to give them the news about Kareem, but he did not tell them that he had proposed to Hope. He wanted to tell his mother first. He called her to tell her he was coming over, and after he had a light breakfast, he was on his way.

"Mama!" he yelled entering the back door.

"In here!" Grace called back. She met Esdell as he entered the living room. "Hi, baby!" She said as he kissed her cheek.

"How you doin', Mama?"

"I couldn't be doing any better if I tried! I'm still praising God for keepin' Kareem safe."

"I know. Me too! Where's Pops and Junya?"

"Isaiah went down to the church and Sammy's just out. You know how that boy is!"

"Yeah, I do," Esdell answered. "He still acts like he's in high school!" They both giggled. "Sit down, Mama. I need to talk to you about something."

"You didn't keep something from me about Kareem, did you? He's not hurt, is he?" She frowned.

"No, ma'am. I told you everything I know. He's good!"

"Okay! Let's sit and talk." Grace sat on the couch and patted that cushion next to her, gesturing for Esdell to sit.

"Mama, what do you think about Hope?" Esdell asked.

"I think she's nice enough. I think she may have a few issues. She's a little sassy but, honestly, that just kinda reminds me of Christine!"

"I know, right?!" Esdell agreed, laughing.

"Why you ask?"

"Do you think we can stand another Christine in the family?"

"What're you saying, Esdell?" Grace asked suspiciously.

"Well, Mama, I asked Hope to marry me, and she said yes. We're gonna get married. What you think about that?"

"I think it's about time!" Grace answered, slapping Esdell on the thigh. "It's about time! She's good for you! She brought you back to yourself!"

"She did, didn't she? Mama, I never thought I'd be in love again. After Kenya got killed, I dried up inside. I was pining away for her, 'bout loss my mind!" Esdell laid his hand on top of his mother's. "Mama, I'ma tell you somethin' I never told nobody. Kenya came to me in a dream and sorta told me it was okay for me to let her go, to fall in love again. She practically called Hope by name! I never thought I would love anybody that way again. Didn't want to. But here I am!"

"Son, the Bible tells us that God can speak to us in a dream and also says it's not good for man to be alone. I know how you feel though," Grace confessed. "I felt the same way after your dad died. Sammy Senior was my heart, and I loved him dearly. I thought I would never match that love again. And I didn't."

Esdell looked confused.

"What d'ya mean, Ma? You love Pops, right?"

"With all that's left of me! It's true love all right. It's just different. It's meant only for him, just like the love I had for Sammy was only for *him*. Does that make sense?"

"It makes perfect sense! I never thought about it like that." Esdell sighed. "You sure cleared that thang up for me, Mama!"

"Yeah, our stories are pretty similar. When you were in Iraq, I thought, just for a moment, that I had lost you, but I had faith. You thought you'd lost Kareem just yesterday, but you had faith. Just look at God! He brought our loved ones back and gave us new love to boot! Ain't that something?"

"Yes, ma'am, it is! I love you, Mama!"

"I know, but never stop tellin' me that! Now! When's the big day?" Grace asked.

"I don't know. We didn't get that far yet. I don't even have a ring for her. I don't wanna wait too long though. Hope's never been married. I guess she'll want a big wedding. I'd better take care of that ring issue and then talk to her about it."

"Oh, I know it's gonna be glorious! Hope's so talented with weddings and decorations. If she works with Chrissie, it'll be just beautiful!"

Oh no! Chris and another wedding! She was like a drill sergeant when Karlena got married. Lord help!"

"Oh, He will!" Grace guaranteed. "Just look at what he's done already!"

"Yup! He gave me Grace, and now He's giving me Hope!" Esdell chuckled at his double entendre.

"I hope that Hope realizes how blessed she is to have you!"

"I'm the blessed one!"

Esdell later called Karlena to tell her of his engagement. She was excited to receive even more good news; first her brother was safe and now her dad was getting married. She made him promise to keep her updated on all the wedding plans. Karlena asked him about an engagement ring.

"Oh, I'ma get her one, I'm tryin' to decide if I want to pick it out myself or take her ring shopping. What do you think, Karlena?"

"Well, it's not like you'll be surprising her with the proposal. I say take her shopping and let her choose."

"Good advice. I'm gonna go over there now!"

Esdell left home and drove straight to Hope's apartment. He knocked on the door, and she quickly answered. Esdell entered and attempted to kiss her. She turned away and walked toward the couch.

"C'mon in," Hope said casually.

"Hey, babe," Esdell said with concern. "You okay?"

"Yes, I'm fine!" Hope snapped.

"Where's Kofi?"

"He's out!"

"You wanna take a ride or do you have somethin' else to do?"

"No, I have no plans! Why?"

"Okay. Uh, are you sure you're okay?"

"I told you I was fine! What's with all these questions? Did somebody die and make you head of the CIA?"

"What's with the attitude?" Esdell snapped back. "What's the problem? Are you tryin' to start a argument or something?"

"You…I…We…" Hope stammered. "Esdell, I'm sorry, but you don't really want to marry me! I've been thinking all day, and I still think you…You were just overreacting to the good news about Kareem. I've thought about it, and I'm going to give you the chance to back out. I'm going about it the wrong way. I thought if I made you mad enough, you would come clean and break off the engagement. I'm giving you a way out. We can just go back to the way it was. You don't—"

"No! *You* don't! You don't tell me what I wanna do!" Esdell took a deep breath through his nostrils as he bit his bottom lip. He exhaled hard through his puckered lips. "Get your purse and let's go!" he ordered.

"Go where?"

"I came over here to take you ring shoppin'! You might wanna grab a jacket. Let's go! I got a charge card with a zero balance that I was saving for an emergency or a special occasion. This is it. Now get your stuff!"

"You know you need to stop hollering at me, right?" she reminded.

"Oh, don't try to go all Betty Bad Butt either. You ain't as tough as you think you are!"

"Excuse me?" Hope shouted.

"Uh! I'm sorry." Esdell flopped down on the couch. He leaned back, grabbed his chin, and stared at Hope. "Do you want me to beg? 'Cause if you do, I will. Do you want me to bust into tears? I can muster up a few, I guess. You want me to have a temper tantrum? 'Cause if you do, I can kick around on the floor in a circle LIKE A FREAKIN' TWO YEAR OLD! TELL ME WHAT YOU WANT! Just don't tell ME want I want to do!"

"Don't yell!" Hope warned. She had never seen Esdell act like this before and was becoming leery. "You're serious, even after you've had all night to reconsider."

"Woman, you are exhausting. Sometimes you get on my nerves so bad I could eat glass! When you act all insecure, it pisses me off!"

"Oh my!" Hope said with a grin.

"And, AND…You, you're beautiful, you're smart, you're sexy, and blah blah blah! You wanna get married or not? I ain't tryna go back to the way we were. I don't feel like playin', I got better things to do." Esdell stood and looked down at Hope. He shrugged his shoulders and walked toward the door. "Bug this! I'm done! I'ma go home and feed my cat!"

"Do you think they'll get along?" Hope asked.

"What the hell! Who?" Esdell barked, turning around.

"If we get married, I'd probably move in with you. Do you think Woodstock and Solo will get along?"

He smirked.

"Get your stuff. We're goin' to a jewelry store!"

"Esdell, I don't need an engagement ring. Like you said, the love I have for you outshines any diamond ring you could buy me. Sounds corny when I say it!" she said. "Anyway, I just want that gold band that'll tell the world that I'm married!"

"You really don't want an engagement ring?" Esdell asked in amazement.

"Nope, not now! You can make that my twenty-fifth anniversary present."

"So, when we gonna do this thang? Set a date! Karlena told me that women start plannin' their weddings when they're little girls. What's yours?"

"I used to dream about getting married all the time before Kofi was born, but after that, and a lot of worthless relationships, I stopped thinking about it. My mind was on just surviving and keeping a roof over our heads. I was settling for whoever would have me. Then you came along," Hope softly said. "We can get married downtown at the city county courthouse. At this point in my life, it's not about the wedding, it's about the marriage. I don't need to put a lot of time into being your bride. I'll be focusing all my energy on being your wife! Your wife for life! I know Kenya's a tough act to follow, but I promise I'll be the best wife Hope can be!"

"I don't compare you to Kenya—ever! A wise woman told me that the love I have for you is for you and nobody but you." Esdell recalled his mother's words. "So are you saying you don't want a wedding either?"

"Well"—Hope giggled—"not a real big wedding!"

Esdell and Hope then started a discussion they had never had: the subject of them getting married. They first decided that Hope, Kofi, *and* Woodstock would move in with him after the wedding. Separately, financially, they were both doing fine. They would continue to work as usual, including working hard to get Esdell and Kofi's business up and running. Esdell said that he would eventually go back to school to get his bachelor's, but that was probably awhile away. They even discussed the possibility of having a child together, but they were both well into their forties. They both agreed that though a new baby was feasible, it was not practical. They finally began to discuss their wedding. They, of course, discussed getting married at their church, but Hope decided that since she only wanted a small wedding, she wanted to get married where she would probably live the rest of her life; at Esdell's house.

"If we get married in late spring, the yard will be in bloom. Reverend Edwards, you, and I can stand in the gazebo. Wow, I never imagined my wedding in that gazebo in your backyard when you bought it, and when I did all that planting back then. Hmm! And the guest will be seated in the yard. We can serve food from the deck." Hope's ideas started rushing in. "It'll be perfect! Your yard is where we had our first argument!" They both laughed.

"Women, you silly!" Esdell's smiling face turned to one of complete sincerity. "God! I love you! Set a date! What's the date?"

Hope looked at a calendar.

"How about the first Saturday in June?"

"Perfect!" Esdell quickly agreed.

Their plans continued. Hope said she would have Kofi, if he was willing, give her away. Other than her cousin, Dameon, she had no other family in Indianapolis and no really close friends, so she thought she would ask Christine to stand with her. Sammy would be Esdell's best man, and Pastor Edwards would officiate. Hope decided her colors would be off-white and magenta. When she stated that, Esdell's face turned wistful and Hope noticed.

"What's the matter?"

Esdell thought for a moment. Should he tell her about his dream and the magenta flower Kenya tossed from her hair into a river? Should he tell her that was the inspiration for the flower he had painted and was now hanging in her shop? He thought not; at least not all of it.

"It's time to tell you about that painting that's in your shop."

"Oh yeah!" Hope recalled he said he would tell her what it represented. "What about it?"

Esdell smiled silently, deciding just what to tell her.

"That color has come to represent something to me," he began. "That day you came to my parent's anniversary, you were wearing a hot pink or magenta sundress."

"It was fuchsia," Hope corrected.

"Okay, my mistake! Anyway!" he continued. "Then when I picked you up for our first date, you wore a pin on your sweater that was the same color. I had a dream one night that a flower was floating down a clear stream. It was beautiful. The color of that flower came to mean freedom to love to me. I had to paint it, and when I finished it, I had to give it to you. Loving you set me free. Now you choose that color, without even knowin' what it meant to me. That just proved to me this thang is sooo right!"

Hope smiled. She was touched by Esdell's story, especially the part about his loving her set him free. The story freed her as well. Whatever bit of doubt she had held was now gone. She continued making plans.

"I hope Mom, Dad, and Kareem can fly in," Hope said.

"Me too. We can't say now, so soon after the earthquake. We know how dedicated they all are. They won't leave if there's still work to be done."

There was then the sound of the front door being unlocked. It was Kofi coming in.

"Hey, Mr. B. Hi, Ma. What y'all up too? Planning the wedding?" Kofi asked.

"As a matter of fact, we are, son. Sit and let me tell you what we got so far!" Hope responded.

She repeated all that had been discussed. Kofi was happy with all but one thing.

"That all sounds real good, except for one thing," he started. "I'm not gonna move in with y'all!"

"But why not? Sure you will!" Hope protested.

"Listen, Mom, I'm a grown man. I should have my own place."

"Can you afford your own place?" Esdell asked.

"I've got a few grand left in the bank. Ma's paying me back, a little at a time for the shop. Even though she doesn't have to," he interjected. "And like you say, I've learned to depend on God. I'm claiming that our business is gonna take off, and I continue to sell my work."

"Kofi, it's too soon to be depending on income from your business. Esdell is gonna keep working his regular job! Right, honey?" Hope looked to Esdell to back her up.

"It's his decision. He's over eighteen. You gotta let him try!" Esdell differed.

Hope's face clearly showed that she was not happy with him disagreeing with her. Kofi spoke again.

"Listen to him, Ma. I've been around Mr. B for a few years now. I've been watching him, and I learned a lot. He offered to give you money to help you buy the shop and pay my college fees. I see how he dealt with both his kids moving away, and just yesterday, I saw how he kept faith that God had protected Kareem and my grandparents. And his son is just like him. I watched them both, and I know what a man's supposed to be!"

"Okay then," Hope said reluctantly.

"Thanks, Kofi. I appreciate the kind words. But know this, you can come live with us at any time. You got a room reserved for you."

"Thanks, Mr. B." Kofi paused. "Do I have to call you dad now?" he asked.

"No," Esdell replied. "Mr. B is fine."

"What if I wanna call you dad? You're closest thing I got to a dad."

"That's fine too! I'd be honored, Kofi!"

"Well, I know one thing though!" Kofi said.

"What's that?" his mother asked.

"I'ma be one fine brutha at the wedding!"

"Whatever, boy!" Hope said, gently pushing Kofi's head with her fingertips.

They decided that Kofi would stay in the apartment where he and Hope lived, taking over the lease.

Within the week, Hope had completed her wedding plans. With her now being a wedding coordinator, it was easy. Once she called Christine to tell her about the engagement, she immediately offered Hope her help. Though Hope really did not need Christine's help, there was no way she would leave her out in bringing all the plans to fruition. Christine was surprised to be asked to be Hope's matron of honor and was honored to accept and to become a special part of her day.

The wedding was three months away; plenty of time since it was going to be so small. Esdell started to prepare his house for the ceremony and his bride-to-be. He started in his bedroom, making room for Hope's things. She would start moving in her nonessential belongings about six weeks before she would completely move in. Esdell purchased a new dresser exclusively for her. Solo watched him curiously.

"You wonderin' what's goin' on, don't you, fella?" Esdell lifted his cat and sat on the bed. "You about to get a new big brother and a new mommy! Ain't that something? I'm real happy 'bout it! Uh-oh, phone! Hello? Kareem! Wussup, son?"

"You're what's up. How you feelin', Dad?" Kareem asked. About a week after the earthquake, Kareem called to give Esdell an update. Haiti was rebuilding. Refugees from nearby stricken areas were finding their way to Kareem's village, knowing that it had been unaffected. The fact that the village was building a new water system and that there would be fresh water made the small town even more appealing. The mission congregation had grown along with the town's population. Kareem and the Shahs' work had become essential. After Kareem got his dad caught up on what was going on in Haiti, he was eager to hear about the wedding. "So how're the plans coming?" Kareem asked.

"Plans are done. We just need to shop and do," he stated.

"Did you get your guest lists done?"

"It's short and sweet. We're expecting about seventy-five people."

"Can you handle three more?" Kareem asked in an excited voice. "Because the Shahs and me are coming!"

"Are you serious?" Esdell's excitement clearly topped Kareem's.

"Yes, sir! We're gonna take a two-week vacation, and we're coming to the wedding!" Esdell was almost in shock.

"This is just the best news! Does Hope know?"

"She will soon. Mr. Shah is probably talking to her now. We just worked out all the details. God just blessed us with a new associate minister. The church where he lived was destroyed by the earthquake. He came with his wife and children. His wife is a school teacher and so is their oldest daughter. Even though they came under bad circumstances, they really are a blessing to us. They can totally run the mission while we're gone!"

"Won't God take a bad thing and make it good?" Esdell knowingly asked.

"Yes, sir, he will!"

With the phone call from Kareem and the Shahs, some of the wedding arrangements changed. Now Hope would be given away by her son and her father, and Kareem would perform the ceremony; the most exciting change of all!

The news that Kareem and her parents were coming threw Hope into overdrive. She and Esdell started working together to get Esdell's yard into shape. They started trimming, pruning, and raking. As the months passed and the yard started to turn green, it began looking like something from a home and garden magazine. Hope visited several bridal and tuxedo shops looking for just the right apparel for the wedding party. She ordered all the flowers she would need for bouquets, corsages, and boutonnieres. At home, she began throwing away and donating items she was no longer using and helping Kofi move into the master bedroom. From time to time, she took her cat, Woodstock, to visit Solo so they could get acquainted. It was rough going the first couple of visits. There was a lot of angry hissing, but eventually, they started to adapt to each other.

Esdell finally got Hope to go ring shopping. They picked out matching yellow-gold braided bands. They were simple rings, but elegant. They returned to Esdell's house, pleased with the selection they had made. They sat in the living room drinking pop. Hope had her Coke and Esdell drank his Pepsi.

"So, what about our honeymoon?" he asked.

"You know, I had thought about that. I'm gonna be taking off a week before and the week of our wedding. I'm gonna get a temp to come in and help Mark while I'm off. I don't want to be away from the shop too much more than that," she replied. "Maybe we can go somewhere later in the year."

"You're turnin' out to be real low maintenance. First you didn't want an engagement ring, then only a small wedding, and now you don't want a honeymoon!"

"I don't need that. You're all I need," she said, squeezing Esdell's knee.

"You deserve everything I can give you, Hope! But I understand you gotta business to run."

"You do too! Don't forget we'll be in the middle of wedding season! Both of us will have work to do."

"You're right. But we *are* going to have a honeymoon!" he insisted.

"Maybe September, or the end of December. We could go somewhere warm! We're having our wedding and our reception here, and I'd be satisfied with spending our wedding night here too."

"Okay then. Babe, I want to ask you something else," he said.

"Yes, sir."

"I been thinkin' about the wedding vows, and I kinda think I wanna write my own. Would you wanna do that?"

"I sure would! I thought about that too, but I didn't want to put anything else on you, trying to get this wedding together."

"I got some things I wanna say about us getting together."

"Me too," she agreed. "Do you think we can write our vows together?"

"Well, let's see!" He got a pen and pad, and they began writing.

26

The week of the wedding, family members were flying in. Kareem and Hope's parents had arrived safely from Haiti. Knowing that the newlyweds would be spending their wedding night at the house, Kareem was staying with his grandmother. Mr. and Mrs. Shah were at Hope's. When Karlena, Joseph, and Micah arrived, they went directly to Joseph's parents' home.

The day before the wedding, the family had come together, along with some church members, to decorate and put the finishing touches on the yard. The tables and chairs were arranged for the wedding guest. They were both covered with off-white fabric, and the chairs had magenta sashes tied around them. The flowers were in bloom, and the gazebo was prettier than anyone even imagined. They had finished, and everyone had gone home except Kareem, Karlena, and Micah.

"Everything is beautiful!" Karlena remarked. "It's amazing how all these flowers, planted so long ago fell right in place with the wedding colors! Isn't it pretty, Mick Mick?"

"Pretty, Mommy!" Micah agreed.

"It's like God himself decorated," Kareem added.

"It's all by His plan and design, son," Esdell said. "Well, His and Hope's!"

"Are you ready, Daddy?" Karlena asked?

"Yes, I am. It's been rough goin' here that past couple of days though. Hope's been like crazy woman!"

"I know!" Kareem yelled. "We almost needed a court order to get her outta here today! I'm glad we had some church members come over to help us or she woulda worked herself to death. She'd be getting buried in the backyard instead of getting married in it!" They all laughed and then there was silence.

"Look at us!" Esdell began. "When I bought this house from Pops, I never saw it being like this. I thought we'd all still be livin' here together. But look at us! Karlena's married and livin' in Louisiana, and Kareem is pastoring a church in Haiti. And li'l buddy's is a little man!" He softly pinched Micah's cheek. "Wow! I'm getting married! Yup, everything's changed!"

"Hey, Dad, you said it. It's by God's plan and design for our lives."

For the next hour, the Brown reminisced about the journey over the past years. They laughed and laughed. It felt good to share their memories, both good and bad.

Kareem decided to stay the night with Esdell to be there the next day to help his dad. The wedding wasn't until 6:00 p.m., so they had plenty of time. They began the day by meeting Karlena and her family for breakfast. His wedding day was close to Micah's birthday, so Esdell, despite Karlena's objection, ordered chocolate chip pancakes for him. After that, Esdell and Kareem went to the barbershop for a little male grooming. And in spite of *his* objection, Kareem paid for Esdell to get a manicure. They both got haircuts and shaves. They speculated what Hope was doing to get ready, and then laughed about it. They went to pick up everyone's tuxedos. Esdell's tux was cream white and so was his tie and shoes. The rest of the men were wearing black tuxes with magenta ties, except for Kareem who would be wearing his black pastoral robe.

By three o'clock, they had returned home. They were greeted at the front door by Solo and Woodstock. Woodstock had been living with Esdell for the past week. Esdell took his tux into his room, and Kareem hug all the others up in his old room. He looked down at the cats who were rubbing against his legs.

"You guys gonna be in real trouble if you get your hair on these tuxes! Dad, you need to put these cats away until after the wedding!" he yelled.

"They'll be all right. I'll close 'em up in my room before the ceremony starts." Then they heard Christine calling from downstairs.

"Coming in!" she shouted. "You and Kareem up there, Esdell?"

"Yeah, sis, we are!" he answered.

"You stay up there and send Kareem down to help me and Hope with our stuff!"

"Hey, babe!" Esdell called to Hope.

"Hi, honey! Don't you dare come down here!" Hope commanded. "You're not supposed to see me before the ceremony! I'm going to the downstairs office!" Woodstock darted down the stairs in response to Hope's voice.

"You can take your little kitty with you, Miss Hope!" Kareem said, coming down the stairs. "You ladies look nice," he noticed.

"We just left the beauty salon. We got the full treatment!" Christine stated. She handed Kareem a suitcase. "Take this downstairs."

Kareem took the suitcase. Hoped picked up her cat, and they all went into the basement. Christine went upstairs to talk to her brother.

"You decent, Esdell?" she asked, tapping on his door.

"Yeah, come in," he answered. She entered the room. "Lookin' good, Chris!"

"Thanks, big bro. You look pretty okay yourself. You wait 'til you see Hope. She's gorgeous!"

"Oh, I already know. My baby's fine!"

"Hope told me to bring this gift bag up here." She sat the bag on the dresser.

"Did she buy me a gift?" Esdell asked.

"It's a gift for you, all right! Not for now, but for later! Don't you look in that bag!"

"Ooo! I gotcha!" Esdell smirked.

"Well, I'm going in the basement and rest a minute before we start getting ready. I'm so happy for you, E. I pray God blesses you with a full lifetime of happiness this time. Nobody deserves it more than you." Christine turned her head.

"Are you cryin', Chris?"

"No! Ain't nobody shedding tears over your dumb butt!" she denied.

Esdell wrapped his arms around her. "Thanks, Chris. I love you too!"

"Let go of me before you mess up my hair." She sniffed. "Sammy and Kofi should be here soon. They're picking up the bouquets and boutonnieres from the shop." As she left the room, she paused in the doorway and said, "And I do love you! I was so worried about you, you used to be so sad. I'm happy for you!"

Esdell watched Christine as she exited his room.

"That girl ain't as hard as she think she is!" he said. He sat in his lounge chair, and before he knew it, he had dozed off. He began to dream. He again saw Kenya crossing that bridge and tossing that flower into the stream. She blew him a kiss and waved. He woke with a start when he felt someone shaking him.

"Wake up, Dad. It's time to get ready," Kareem was saying. "Everyone's here. All the guys are in my room getting dressed. You need to start getting dressed."

"What time is it?" Esdell asked.

"It's five o'clock."

"Yeah, I need to get rollin'!" He stood up and went into the bathroom to wash his face. As he got ready, he thought it odd that he was not the least bit nervous. He knew this union was ordained by God before the beginning of time. He was comforted by knowing he was basking in the will of God.

Esdell went into Kareem's old room to find Kareem and Sammy.

"Hey, y'all lookin' good! And check out my son, Pastor Brown, in his preacher's robe. Sharp as he wanna be! Where's Mr. Shah and Kofi?" he inquired.

"They're downstairs with Miss Hope and Mrs. Shah. They're having a family moment," Kareem answered.

"Check you out, Mack Daddy!" Sammy said. "You lookin' good too, bruh! That off-white tux is tight!"

"Thanks, man!"

"Here, let me pin on your flower," Sammy offered.

"Please don't stick me!" Esdell pleaded.

"Christine showed me how to do this. I pinned them pink rosebuds on all the dudes!" Sammy assured. "Yours is a lot different though. Just relax!" Esdell's boutonniere was made of a small magenta and white star lily, a magenta rose, and baby's breath accent; tied together with an off-white satin ribbon. Sammy carefully pinned it to Esdell's lapel. "There you go. See, I told you. I'm an expert!" Then they heard music playing from the backyard.

"Oh, the prelude's starting. I guess we should get downstairs!" Kareem put his hands on Esdell's and Sammy's shoulder. "Be with us now, Lord. We claim victory over this ceremony and this marriage in the name of Jesus! Amen!"

"Amen!" Esdell and Sammy repeated.

"I'm going down. See you guys in the kitchen." Kareem left the room.

"Oh, here, Junya!" Esdell gave him a ring box. Sammy opened it and looked at the ring.

"This is it, huh? Wow, okay." Sammy put the box in his pocket. "Big E, I have to admit I'm a little jealous. I know everybody thinks all I wanna do is party, but I do wanna settle down someday."

"Your days comin'. You and Danielle been hangin' pretty tough!"

"Yeah, maybe." Sammy nodded his head. "But your day is today, dog! I'm happy for you, man. You was messed up! You were so, so sad."

"I must've really been messed up. That's the same thing Chris said to me!"

"Man, you mourned Kenya way too long. But it's all good now!" Sammy hugged Esdell, slapping him on his back.

"Yeah, it is! Let's head downstairs."

Christine met them at the foot of the stairs and herded Esdell and Sammy into the kitchen. She yelled down to Hope, warning her not to come up. Esdell looked out the back kitchen window and saw that the yard was full of guests. The deck bannisters were covered with off-white tulle affixed with magenta satin ribbon. On the far left of the deck were the cake and gift tables. On right, tables were set for the wedding party and their parents. An aisle runner went straight down the middle of the deck and through the yard, leading to the gazebo. The mothers had already been seated, and it was time for Kareem, Sammy, and Esdell to enter. Kareem led the way, carrying his Bible. Esdell and Sammy followed. They walked down the covered aisle stepping up into the gazebo. His family watched with smiling faces. Hope's cousin, Dameon, was back on the job, acting as DJ, playing soft music. Kareem looked at the back door as Christine was walking out. She wore a sleeveless, cowl-necked magenta gown with a belt with a rhinestone buckle. She wore bronze shoe, diamond teardrop pendant necklace and earrings, and carried a bouquet of cream-colored roses. The music changed, and Kareem motioned for everyone to stand. Kofi opened the back door; Mr. Shah stood to one side of the door to help Hope as she came out. She then locked arms with both of them, and they escorted her down the aisle. Esdell was in awe of her beauty. Her cream white, spaghetti strap gown had a bodice with crystal and pearl beaded floral appliques. The long chiffon skirt flowed as she walked. The back was fastened with five pearl buttons. Her bouquet, like Esdell's boutonniere, was magenta and white star lilies, cream roses and baby's breath, and the stems were wrapped with knotted cream satin ribbon. Hope's hair was a mass of dark curls held back with a pearl and crystal tiara; her necklace and earrings matched. As she approached Esdell, she fought back her tears of joy. They reached the steps of the gazebo and stopped. Kareem instructed the guest to be seated. He opened his Bible and began to read.

"Genesis 2:18 says, 'And the LORD God said, It is not good that the man should be alone; I will make him an help meet.' He caused a deep sleep to fall upon Adam and taking a rib from his side, he formed a woman and brought him before the man. The Bible then says, 'Therefore shall a man leave his father and his mother, and shall cleave unto his wife: and they shall be one flesh.'" He closed his Bible and continued, "With these words, God ordained the first human relationship: marriage. It is by His design, His divine plan, that we are here today, my brothers and sisters, to join together this man and this woman in holy, I say again, *holy* matrimony! Praise God! Who gives this woman to be married to this man?"

"I, her father, do!" Mr. Shah said.

"I, her son, do also!" Kofi said. They both kissed Hope on the cheek. Esdell extended his hand to help her up the steps.

"Thank you, gentlemen, please be seated," Kareem instructed and then proceeded. "Marriage is the joining of husband and wife in heart, body, and spirit. It is meant for the mutual joy and pleasure of the couple. It is done before the sight of God and you, as witnesses. As witnesses who are also in the sight of God, I must ask if anyone knows of any reason that these two should not wed, I compel you to speak now." Kareem paused for a response; there was none. "This couple desires to express their love for each other. They have written their own vows. They will speak them now."

Esdell took Hope by the hands and faced her. He was the first to speak.

"My heart was like the beam from a lighthouse circling aimlessly in the darkness, circling around and around looking for and expecting nothing."

"My heart was like a ship drifting aimlessly, hopelessly in the darkness. Accepting the darkness, expecting nothing better," Hope answered.

"Then my heart's light found you: giving it purpose and hope."

"I saw the light from your heart. It gave me hope, teaching me to expect greatness."

"Hope, my love, I found you though I was not looking. God knew that I needed you. I promise you, this day, to always give you my best. I promise to love, honor, and respect you. I promise to protect and comfort you. I will do these things in good and bad times, in times of feast or famine, in sickness and in health. I pledge my devotion and all that I have and all that I am to you for the rest of my life. I am yours alone as God is my witness!" Esdell vowed.

"Esdell, my love, you are a man that I saw only in my dreams. God saw into my dreams, and when I awoke, He had sent you. I promise you, this day, to always give you my best. I promise to love, honor, and respect you. I promise to protect and comfort you. I will do these things in good and bad times, in times of feast or famine, in sickness and in health. I pledge my devotion and all that I have and all that I am to you for the rest of my life. I am yours alone as God is my witness!" Hope vowed.

"May God bless these vows. Are there rings?" Kareem asked.

Christine gave him Esdell's wedding band, and he handed it to Hope. "Hope, place the ring on Esdell's finger and repeat after me. This ring is a symbol of my endless love for you. May God forever bind us." Hope put the ring on Esdell's finger and repeated after Kareem, just as instructed. Kareem then turned to Sammy, nodding for the ring. Sammy took the ring from the box gave it to Kareem who passed it to Esdell to put on Hope's finger. She looked down at the ring.

"What?" She gasped.

It was the ring that they had picked out, but it was so much more. Soldered to the braided gold band was another ring; a diamond engagement ring. In the center, there was a large square diamond, and on each side of the band, there was a double row of smaller diamonds. When the sun hit it, prisms reflected in her face.

"Shhh!" Esdell said. "No need to wait twenty-five years on what I can do for you now." He then repeated after Kareem.

"As a child, I would have never imagined that I would stand as minister over my own father's wedding. But this, too, was ordained for me by God, as is this marriage. It is my honor and my joy to join this woman and this man that I love and respect so much together. Dad, you are the man I aspire to be and I love you." Kareem smile and sighed. "So, now, by the authority granted to me by Almighty God and by the state of Indiana, it is with great pleasure that I now pronounced that you are husband and wife. Dad, you may kiss your bride, your *wife!*"

"All right, now!" Esdell said. He cupped Hope's face in his hands and gave her a gentle kiss.

"Lock them lips, boy!" Sammy screamed.

"Ladies and gentlemen," Kareem announced, "I present to you Mr. and Mrs. Esdell Brown!" The backyard exploded with applauds and cheers. Esdell and Hope walked from the gazebo on to the yard into the waiting arms of their family and friends.

* * *

After the ceremony was over, the reception immediately started. The caterers were in place and brought out the food. Hope was still excited about her ring and eagerly and proudly showed it off to everyone. After they mingled for a while with their guests, the newlyweds and the wedding party took their seats on the deck to enjoy their meal. After that, Esdell and Hope cut and fed each other wedding cake. Esdell removed a blue garter from Hope's thigh and threw toward a group of unreceptive bachelors. Hope tossed her bouquet to crowd jockeying bachelorettes. Dameon kept the music playing, and as soon as most everyone was finished eating, they began to dance. The couple danced together and then with their parents. Their guest later joined in, and they all danced into the night.

Esdell and Hope were embraced in a slow dance in the moonlight. They gazed lovingly into each other's eyes and shared a gentle kiss. Sammy looked at the newlyweds and could tell they were well past wanting everyone to leave. He gave Esdell a knowing winked.

"I got this bro! Okay, everybody," Sammy yelled. "It's time for all of us to leave! You ain't gotta go home, but you gotta get up outta here!" With Sammy's rude announcement, everyone pitched in to clean up and put away. The yard emptied quickly.

Esdell took Hope's hand and led her into the house and then upstairs to the bedroom. She glanced at Esdell as she grabbed the gift bag off the dresser that Christine had dropped off earlier.

"I'll be right back," she whispered as she went into the bathroom. Esdell changed into a pair of black satin pajama bottoms. He rubbed a little cologne on his bare chest. He looked at the bed to see Solo and Woodstock sleeping on it.

"Sorry, dudes, but y'all gotta be up outta here!" He picked them up, gently placed then on the hallway floor, and closed the door behind them. After a few minutes, Hope appeared in the bathroom doorway wearing a shear red robe that was flattering against her skin. It was tied shut with a black sash. Esdell smiled broadly as she approached him. He slowly untied the sash and the robe opened. He put his hands around her waist and pulled her toward him. Then he kissed her. It was a kiss with no boundaries; an undefiled kiss, deep and passionate.

"Dang, Miss Hope!" Esdell breathe. Hope continued to kiss him as she stepped back toward the bed.

"Uh-huh, baby." She sighed. "That's Mrs. E. Brown!"

"All right then!" he said, laying her down.

The next morning, Esdell awoke to find himself spooning with his new wife. He smelled her hair. He rubbed her hip. Hope squirmed, shifting her position just a little. Esdell smiled.

Oh, grace. Oh, mercy! Thank you, Lord, for letting me find this woman, he prayed silently. *She is my gift from you. I've tried to live a good life before you and you have blessed me with her to be my wife. I'm so grateful that I've found favor in your eyes.* He kissed Hope on the side of her forehead. She hummed and nuzzled closer to him. "Amen," he whispered. He smiled again, hugging her just a little closer and drifted back to sleep.

CPSIA information can be obtained at www.ICGtesting.com
Printed in the USA
BVOW06s2107110716

454836BV00020B/116/P